CHASING GHOSTS IN THE NIGHT

SHIFTER'S DAWN

2

CHASING GHOSTS IN THE NIGHT

SHIFTER'S DAWN, BOOK TWO

Copyright © 2023 Brantwijn Serrah
2ND EDITION
ISBN: 9781954031159

Written by Brantwijn Serrah
Edited by Jo Huysamen
Cover design by Brantwijn Serrah

BRANTWIJN
SERRAH
FANTASY ROMANCE

ALSO BY BRANTWIJN SERRAH

Join Brantwijn's newsletter for a free book!
Get updates and special offers from Brantwijn and other indie authors.
https://www.brantwijn.com/newsletter

AUTHOR'S NOTES

Dear Readers,

When I wrote *Leaving Tracks in the Snow*, I didn't know I would end up getting so attached to these characters and become so engrossed in their stories. I hadn't really dipped my toes into the world of shifters as supernaturals and I'd never really been swept away by them. I've always been a vampire and werewolf girl, a dark magic and demons girl. Shifters, at least as they appear in stories like *Shifter's Dawn*, are a bit of a neutral supernatural force, and as such, I was always lured away by the Eric Northmans and Lestats and Willows and Wynonas, rather than the Sam Merlottes or the Micahs or the Damon Salvatorres.

The characters of *Shifter's Dawn* have stolen my heart. This book in particular presented a complicated and very time-consuming first draft phase, but unlike most other projects, I never felt bored or frustrated or tired of this world. Every day I'd check in with my writing group lamenting that I kept falling farther and farther behind on this project, and yet every day the words kept coming and they kept feeling right. I loved writing this book. I was almost sorry when it finally came time to wrap up the final chapters. Thank the spirit mother there's still one more book to go!

Once again, I beg your indulgence, as I've taken significant artistic license in the history and setting of the Stolby Nature Preserve in Krasnoyarsk, Russia. As far as I am aware, there are no resident colonies of mystic indigenous shapeshifters living on the preserve. It is true, however, that the preserve is home to many beautiful rock formations enjoyed by climbing enthusiasts around the world. This detail is what first drew me to the setting, and why I selected Stolby as the home of my shifters. While researching these tales, I had the opportunity to view several videos online shared by rock climbers and outdoor enthusiasts sharing their experiences at the preserve. If you find yourself with a little free time on your hands, I highly recommend watching a few. A simple search for "climbing the rock formations at Stolby" will lead you to plenty. You can enjoy the breathtaking scenery of the preserve as well as the skill of local free-solo climbers ascending the rocks with their bare hands!

While writing this particular book, I also had occasion to do some research into traditional methods of bone carving and several cultural practices from indigenous cultures around the world. The fictional indigenous tribe I have created for the *Shifter's Dawn* series does not correspond to any specific real-life culture, though where I've drawn from real-life examples, I've mostly based them upon indigenous cultures, with some influence from Inuit and aboriginal peoples. That being said, I hope I've not inadvertently misrepresented anyone, and in any place where I may have gone wrong, I take full responsibility.

All that being said, I hope you are ready to return to the Stolby sanctuary of my imagination, and the tribe of shapeshifters running wild beneath the Northern Lights.

Come run with me, Wayfarers,

Brantwijn

DEDICATION

This book is dedicated to Jo, a multi-talented editor, assistant, friend, and international feline fairy godmother. Jo's assistance has seen the Shifter's Dawn trilogy through its paces, and she's provided an enormous amount of support, suggestion, and inspiration throughout the process. As an author, it's always an amazing feeling to know you have at least one person out there who gets as excited for the next part of the story as you do. Thank you, Jo, for everything.

CHASING GHOSTS IN THE NIGHT

SHIFTER'S DAWN, BOOK TWO

By Brantwijn Serrah

CHAPTER ONE

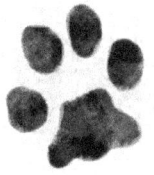

"NIKITA!"

Elaina Jacob pounded a fist on the door of the neat wooden dacha house. "We've got business, Nikita!"

The house stood alone, just on the edge of a field in the Stolby woods. The land was restricted, far out in the quietest reaches of the nature preserve, where park visitors were not typically allowed. From the road—really no more than a rough dirt path—Elaina's mate Grisha sat astride his motorcycle, watching her with his customary cool, inscrutable gaze. He'd brought her to the home of the *oboroten* leader over the protests of her other mates Gavri and Kolya, but he had no intention of confronting the alpha wolf alongside her. Grisha understood Elaina had to handle this herself.

Only a few days ago, she'd met with Nikita in public, before all the wolves of the Stolby pack. She'd only meant to plead with him for a pardon of Gavri and Kolya, whom he'd exiled from the pack and from their lands. Instead, she'd lost her temper, and wound up challenging Nikita for the mantle of alpha wolf.

Now she had until the summer solstice—just a little over three weeks—to learn the ways of the *oboroten,* claim the power to change her shape, and fight Nikita for his title.

Not exactly the best way to make friends, Elaina.

She delivered another series of furious knocks to Nikita's door. "Come on, you know why I'm here!"

The door opened abruptly, and her next blow fell not on handsome teak but on the tall, striking man who filled the doorway. Her hand hit his chest with a dull smack and, startled, Elaina snatched it back.

"Oh!" She brought her fingers to lips in surprise. "Sorry, I didn't mean—"

Nikita cocked an eyebrow at her. He stood more than a foot taller than she, and regarded her with a lazy, disinterested expression. He hardly seemed to have noticed she'd hit him at all. Crossing arms over his chest, he leaned against the doorjamb, and his fair blonde hair fell carelessly in his eyes. His impeccable white polo shirt bore a small logo on the left side, and for a moment she thought it was the tiny, familiar Lacoste alligator. As she looked closer, though, she discovered it to be—what else?—a small wolf in silver thread, embroidered in mid-run. The logo, she imagined, of the Stolby tribe's trade enterprise.

"Did you need something?" Nikita asked.

"I want to know who attacked Kolya," she demanded. "Three mysterious assailants, Nikita. Day before yesterday. Ring a bell?"

He shrugged. "I know nothing about it."

"I think you do." She squared off with him. "They put him in the *hospital.* You gave me your word you'd call off the blood hunt until our duel. He's one of your pack, Nikita!"

The alpha wolf tilted his head to the side, frowning. "Human," he said, with a hint of growl in

2

his voice. "I *keep* my word. I didn't send anyone to hurt your dog."

"*Don't* call him a dog," she hissed.

Nikita straightened. Looking past her, he spied Grisha by the road. He tipped a wave at the other man, and asked her, "Is he your chaperone? Did you bring him along to protect you from the big, bad wolf? Or can I invite you in to discuss this like two normal, rational adults?"

Elaina glanced over her shoulder at her mate. Grisha looked aloof as ever, but his bright green eyes were locked on her. He was more focused on their exchange than he appeared.

"I'm not afraid to come in," she told Nikita. She gave a nod to Grisha, and he returned it without getting off the bike, indicating he'd wait for her.

Nikita stepped aside and gestured for her to enter.

Inside, the dacha was bright and tidy, surprising her. She didn't know what she expected from Nikita—maybe an overtly masculine den full of mounted animal heads, antlers and bearskin rugs and pewter beer steins on a rough wooden table. To the contrary, the house looked quite modest. Downright warm. The living room opened up on her left, lowered a step, filled with soft, mid-morning light from a wide bay window. A small fire burned in the hearth before an arrangement of a loveseat and two easy chairs. Stretched out on the loveseat, nose in a book, sat Nikita's sister, Sofie. She paused in her reading, marking her place with her finger, and peered up at Elaina with distrustful eyes.

That's right. I forgot he had a sister. Does she live here with him?

3

Nikita said something to Sofie in Russian, and the girl nodded, rolling up from her spot on the couch and slinking off down the hall. Gavri had told Elaina Sofie was a wildcat shifter, unlike the rest of her family, who were all wolves and part of the Stolby pack.

Oboroten—a tribe of shapeshifters following the ways of Diezana, spirit-mother of these lands—didn't choose the bestial forms they took when they shifted. The wolves of the Stolby tribe, like Nikita, Gavri, and Kolya, formed a pack, and the pack doubled as the tribal leadership. But not all the *oboroten* became wolves. Some, like Grisha and Sofie, became large hunting cats. Rini, the sweet and smiling housekeeper employed by Gavri's family, turned into a snowshoe hare.

How involved are they in making decisions? Elaina wondered as Sofie disappeared. *Does she resent not being a part of the pack, like the rest of her family?*

Hard to tell. Sofie wasn't just a cat; she was a teenager. Sulk factor doubled.

Elaina switched her attention back to Nikita and gave a start when she found him closer than she'd expected. Nikita leaned toward her, and his nostrils flared, pupils dilating. She stepped back, refusing to cringe, but she recognized the expression on his face. She didn't like it on him. Not Nikita.

"The outsider too, hm?" His lips curled into a hint of sardonic grin. "You're collecting boy toys just like keychains and tourist tchotchkes, aren't you?"

Heat flashed at the back of her neck. "Ex*cuse* me?"

He strode past her, into the airy, open kitchen. "You have Grisha's smell on you. Him, Gavri, and Kolya. You're a salacious woman, aren't you?"

"I thought your tribe acknowledged such arrangements. A marriage of many hearts, didn't you call it?"

"We do. Among alphas. You're not one of us *nor* are you a leader, so in your case, it's just kinky group sex." Nikita gestured to the kitchen table, inviting her to sit. "I was preparing lunch. Would you like any?"

Elaina gritted her teeth but settled into a chair. The makings of what appeared to be a beef and barley stew lay out on the counter, and Nikita returned to them, picking up a knife and beginning to dice some carrots.

"No lunch, thank you." Elaina tucked a loose curl behind her ear. "I'm not here for a social visit."

"How tragic," the alpha wolf muttered.

"I want to know what happened to my mate," she demanded. "Did you send your enforcer after him again? With his two cronies?"

"I most certainly did not." Nikita scooped up a handful of carrot chunks and dropped them in a big cast-iron pot. "I told you. I keep my word. As distasteful as it is to me to have that dog still within our lands."

"I told you not to call him a dog," Elaina shot back, slapping her hand flat on the table. "Just because you have a problem with his sexuality—"

Nikita brought the knife down hard on the cutting board with a loud *thwack.*

"And I told *you* it is not your place to judge our ways. I have *explained* to you why we cannot tolerate his deviancy. Do you know you could be arrested for talking about this with Sofie nearby? Perhaps in your home country you can say whatever you like without consequence, but here it is a crime to spread such propaganda around children."

"Stop!" Elaina demanded. "*God,* you're disgusting. He's not perverted or immoral or anything of the sort. And he's *my* mate! Me, a woman. Surely you can't have a problem with that?"

"I have a problem with the fact he is the son of a skinwalker," Nikita sneered. She knew he didn't mean the nightmare creature of the Navajo people in the States, but a different kind of monster, savage beasts twisted by a dark spirit. The ones that her mates had told her about. The *vukodlak.*

"His very blood, the blood of his sire, taints him and has led him to indecency. And I have a problem with his predilections inviting more corrupted kin into our midst. If Kolya indulges one unnatural fetish, he will soon pursue others as well. Gavri did explain to you how his mother—our last alpha—was betrayed by her mate, when the stain of the *vukodlak* swallowed him, *da?*"

"That won't happen to Kolya—"

"And just how do you know?" He stabbed the knife into a large root vegetable and left it there, sticking up like an absurd exclamation point. He spun to face her, blue eyes blazing. "But you come here thinking you can change his luck by fighting me for leadership. The safety of the tribe means nothing to you. You have never lost anyone to the *vukodlak.* You don't know the ancient battle between our two peoples, or between our goddess and their twisted god. You know *nothing* of any of it! You come here to defend a simple dog, the least among us, and put his life above the rest, and why? Is it so thrilling to fuck a *dog?* A cringing, submissive, sissy dog?"

Elaina shot to her feet so fast she knocked over the chair she'd been sitting in. "Whatever you think of him, you promised you would call off the blood hunt until I have the chance to knock you off your paper throne. So why did three shapeshifters attack him?"

"As I said, I had nothing to do with whatever fight Kolya got into."

"Are you sure you made it clear enough to the rest of the pack?" she demanded. "Are you sure they'd listen to you? Maybe some of the tribe don't take you seriously enough as their leader."

Nikita leaned forward, planting his palms flat on the table, fixing her with a look of fury.

"It was not any of the Stolby tribe. I gave you my word. And for the last time, I *keep* my word."

Elaina met him eye-to-eye. "What about Pasha? Would he take his two idiot friends and go stir up trouble despite your decision?"

"Pasha is honorable. He respects our agreement."

"How about the other two? His scouts?"

"They wouldn't do anything without his instruction."

Elaina threw her hands in the air. "Then who, Nikita? Who would want to hurt Kolya besides you?"

His gaze never wavered. "The skinwalkers. Obviously."

That made her pause. Elaina frowned, considering Nikita's expression. She hadn't even noticed during the argument he'd started to change: his shapeshifter's magic seeped through on the surface, casting his features in a decidedly lupine slant. His ears had elongated into points, his hair standing up like a white mane. His eyes had fallen dark, like black marbles full of anger.

Elaina took a deep breath. "I thought they hadn't crossed into your lands in years."

"Adelaida's betrayal at the hands of her mate wasn't very long ago, human."

Nikita straightened. He sighed, shaking his head, and returned his attention to making the stew.

"Go home to your lovers. Don't bother me again. I will not be responsible for every bump and scrape Kolya gets."

Elaina brought a hand to her temple, kneading at the angry headache forming there. "Nikita... I'm sorry. Look, before my mate was attacked, I... I meant to come to you for a truce. I know I didn't really go about this the right way—"

"No," he cut in. "You didn't."

"Could you try not to interrupt me when I'm apologizing?" she grated. "I didn't come to the pack as I should have. But I *do* believe Diezana is calling me to be here. Is there any other way for us to resolve this?"

Nikita scooped up the last of his vegetables and dropped them into his stewpot without answering. He clicked on the stove burner, then turned his back on her to wash his hands in the sink.

"No."

She'd expected as much, but Elaina's shoulders slumped, nonetheless. Nikita turned back to her, his lupine features now receded, replaced by cool, stony pride.

"Had you come to me today in peace, perhaps we could have discussed another way. You and your disobliging mates could have petitioned me with at least some modicum of regard, as I *am* the one Adelaida chose to lead her pack until Diezana's will is made known. Now, though, for a second time, you come to me full of obstinate anger, accusation, and demand. So no, girl. There will be no other way. You will either do as you claimed you would and face me at the solstice with the power of the *oboroten* in your grasp, or you and the *dog* leave our lands. I don't care where you go, but as long as I am the alpha of this pack, the tainted son of a skinwalker will not bring his corruption among this tribe."

Elaina scowled at him, fighting back tears of violent anger. "You... you're just *cruel,* Nikita!"

His lip curled. "You don't know what *cruel* is, girl. Remember, you have not yet met the *vukodlak.*"

An odd shiver seemed to go through the whole house, an icy frisson incongruous with the warm, midmorning sunlight shining in through the windows. A very low, very quiet growl drew Elaina's attention; two shining, unfriendly feline eyes glowed in the shadows of the dim hallway. Sofie, eavesdropping.

If Nikita noticed his sister crouching there, he gave no sign. He extended his hand toward the door to the dacha.

"I have nothing else to say to you, human. You can see yourself out."

CHAPTER TWO

ELAINA SAID NOTHING TO GRISHA most of the way home. Her look of chagrin must have been enough to tell him all he needed, because he didn't ask her any questions, either. As she settled in behind him on the motorcycle, he gave one thoughtful glance back at the dacha before gunning the bike. He wheeled them back onto the road, and they were on their way home.

Elaina clung to her mate, comforted by his presence. She was glad it had been Grisha to bring her on this errand. Gavri and Kolya would have been full of advice or reflection or concern. She didn't want their concern now. Anger simmered in her, but Nikita had been right: she'd come to him full of accusation and anger, bullying him right from the start.

Posturing. What young wolves did when searching out their place in the pack. Only, when you played games like that with the alpha wolf, you were asking for the teeth.

She sighed, leaning her head on Grisha's back. *I was so, so sure he sent his people after Kolya. Part of me is still sure.*

She brightened when they crested a rise, and ahead of them she caught sight of Gavri's lodge. In just a few short minutes she could put this errand behind her, slip into a warm bath and wash away the nasty, ugly attitude she'd shown the alpha wolf.

Why is it every time I come face-to-face with him, I turn into a time bomb? I'll never be able to take him in a fight like this. What is it about him that makes me so mad?

The way he talks about Kolya, she answered herself. *Calls him* immoral *and* deviant.

While true, Elaina suspected there might be more to it.

Grisha pulled into the covered section of the driveway where Gavri and Kolya's bikes were usually parked. Elaina frowned. Gavri's truck had been pulled out to the road, and in its usual driveway spot stood a sleek, steely-blue sedan.

Grisha killed the bike's engine and got off, examining the new car with his usual indifference.

"Do you know whose it is?" Elaina asked him.

The snow leopard pulled a pack of cigarettes from his jacket pocket and tapped one out, shaking his head. "Guess you'll find out when you go inside."

Elaina punched him in the arm. "While you hide safely out here? You *do* know, don't you?"

Grisha lit his cigarette. "I promise you, little girl, I have no idea whose car it is, nor do I know who Gavri or Kolya expected today. However, I *do* know Gavri has a strict no-smoking policy inside the house, so I'll just hang tight right here for a bit."

She wrinkled her nose. "Coward."

Grisha leaned against the post holding up the house's second-level deck. He took a long drag on his cigarette and exhaled with an almost inaudible purr of pleasure.

Scowling at him, Elaina turned on her heel and climbed the steps to the front entrance.

Almost all the rooms in Gavri's house had wide, bright picture windows letting the sunlight stream in during the day and offering glorious views of the Stolby Nature Preserve all around them. As she approached the front door, Elaina hoped to catch a glimpse of one of her mates, or maybe a stranger in a black suit and mirrored shades—*something*. But, perhaps for the first time ever, the voile curtains on the living room's windows had been drawn, and all Elaina could see behind the thin white sheers were several vague shapes spaced around the living room. A quiet dread crawled up her spine.

"Hello?" she called as she opened the door. "Gavri? Kol—"

Before she finished, Rini hurried into the entry and began helping her out of her jacket. The sweet housekeeper looked more nervous than Elaina had ever seen her, bustling to make Elaina presentable, swatting dust from her jeans and tidying her hair.

"Whoa, Rini!" Elaina put up her hands. "What gives?"

"I'm sorry," Rini whispered, plucking at a wrinkle in Elaina's shirt and smoothing it down. "It's my fault. I didn't think she'd come all the way back for this, but—"

"What are you talking about?"

Rini grimaced, but before she could explain, Gavri joined them in the foyer.

"Elaina," he said, voice low. He extended a hand to her. "We have guests. Come and meet them."

An uncomfortable hollow feeling filled her gut, but Elaina took her mate's hand as he led her into the living room.

Sitting in one of the easy chairs was a woman with impeccable style and elegant poise, severe in a crisp white shirt and tailored black trousers. In an oddly domestic twist, she'd removed her shoes and tucked them to the side of her chair—expensive designer heels, Elaina noted. The woman leaned on one arm, legs crossed, and her gaze locked on Elaina as soon as Gavri brought her in. Elaina recognized her immediately: with Gavri's same dark, glossy hair, sharp lupine features, and bright, almost electric-blue eyes, she could only be Adelaida. His dam, and former alpha female of the Stolby pack.

Elaina straightened. Part of her thought she ought to drop into a bow, genuflect before this famed leader. She held herself back, though; she had the sense Adelaida might consider it mockery.

A man stood beside Adelaida's chair: paunchy and pleasant looking, in a comfortable shirt and slacks. He didn't smile now, but from the lines on his face Elaina thought he must do it often enough. In contrast to Adelaida, his features were softer and more rounded. He must be one of her two remaining mates, Bernard or—

"My sire, Timofei," Gavri said, presenting Elaina to the man. On reflex, Elaina held out her hand, and Timofei took it—yes, there was the smile, and a warm one, well-practiced and easy—giving it a hearty shake.

"My dam, Adelaida," Gavri added, gesturing toward his mother. Nobody offered a handshake this time. Adelaida eyed Elaina with shrewd, sharp scrutiny. Elaina held herself steady, giving the woman her moment but resisting the urge to shrink under the hard gaze.

"So you are the human causing us so much trouble," Adelaida finally said. She spoke flawless English, but with a pronounced Russian accent, reminding Elaina of old spy movies and sleek femme fatales. Adelaida must be in her mid-fifties, and the first streaks of silver had appeared in her black hair, but she retained the lean, dangerous edge of a wolf in her prime.

Elaina recalled the photo upstairs of this woman—Gavri's mother—seated in tall, green grass, holding a stylized shamanic drum in her lap. She tried to imagine her leading spiritual rituals the way Baba Yasmin, the Stolby pack's wise woman, did; petitioning the spirits for visions and going walkabout in the woods for their wisdom and guidance. Attaching a spiritual side to this fashionable corporate chief did little to comfort her.

"Yes, I guess I am," she replied.

"I'm disappointed I had to hear about your rather unfortunate exploits from Rini." Adelaida leveled a stern glare at Gavri and Kolya. "When I'd have much preferred to be told by my sons."

Standing far back from the discussion, Rini flushed, twisting her hands in the skirt of her apron. The poor girl stared down at her feet, and Elaina thought she understood. Rini worked for the Dvorak family, which really meant she worked for Adelaida. She must have mentioned Gavri's new flame in their last conversation, never intending for Adelaida to take the news quite this way.

But did she tell Adelaida about my challenge to Nikita?

Rini worried over the danger Gavri and Kolya faced, defying Nikita's order of exile and living under the threat of his blood hunt. The two wolves had made it clear, though, they didn't mean to entangle Adelaida in the conflict, regardless how much sway she might still wield over the pack.

She was bound to find out at some point, though, Elaina admitted with a sinking feeling in her gut. She hadn't even considered how the former alpha female would respond to a human making a play for leadership of the *oboroten.* Much less what she'd think of a human trying to *become* one of them. Most importantly, though... she hadn't considered what Gavri's mother would think of his new mate.

"It's my fault," Gavri said to Adelaida. "I told Rini and Kolya not to tell you about the blood hunt. I didn't want you involved."

Adelaida narrowed her eyes at him in an expression of grim disappointment. "And why in the world not?"

Gavri seethed. "I won't go crying to my mother just because Nikita is being an ignorant asshole."

Adelaida shot to her feet. "Just because? *Just because,* Gavri? I've barely been in Omsk a year and you've managed to get yourselves exiled from our ancestral lands, put under a blood hunt, *and* brought a human into our circle, one who has issued a challenge to the alpha wolf *I* appointed!"

"Rini didn't tell you all of that," Gavri muttered. "So you must have called Nikita yourself."

"Damn right I did." She crossed her arms over her chest. "He is the leader of this pack now, Gavri. If you'll recall, he was my second choice, but *you* had no interest in taking over."

"And still don't," he affirmed, jutting out his chin. They faced off, and there was no mistaking which parent Gavri had taken after. Elaina snuck a glance at

Timofei, who watched and waited, but said nothing. A painful sting of regret filled her chest—her father had always done the same, when her mother was on a tirade. He just kept silent.

"Adelaida," Kolya spoke up, voice meek. "Please. This is all because of me. If I go, Gavri will be allowed to stay. I'm the one Nikita has exiled."

Adelaida whirled on him. "You'll do no such thing, Kolya. You belong to this family."

"How can you stay silent then?" Elaina burst out before she could stop herself. "Why not go to Nikita and tell him to call off his order of exile?"

Adelaida studied her, glaring down her nose at Elaina as if considering what to do with a troublesome stray animal. If Timofei had reminded Elaina of her father, Adelaida most certainly looked like her mother, about to unleash some toxic verbal assault.

She didn't, though. Without saying a word, the former alpha took a step toward Elaina, gaze traveling up and down, taking in the whole sight of her. She let out a tired huff.

"You actually let her challenge Nikita?" she asked Gavri.

"She didn't give me an opportunity to object," Gavri said with a shrug.

Elaina bristled. "I can speak for myself, you know."

"And when I'm interested in what you have to say, I'll let you." Adelaida replied.

"Now just a goddamn minute—"

"Elaina," Gavri commanded. "You said you would respect our ways. Sit down, be quiet, and let my mother process this."

She nearly turned on him, anger boiling inside her. She managed to catch herself, though, when she remembered her confrontation with Nikita earlier.

Posturing. But when you play games like that with the alpha, you're asking for the teeth.

She took a deep breath, taking a slow count to five. Then she inclined her head toward Adelaida.

"I'm sorry, Mrs. Dvorak. I've had a very upsetting couple of days, but that's no reason for me to be rude."

Adelaida gave no reply. Elaina shuffled back toward the couch and took a seat beside Kolya. He slid an arm around her, and she slipped her hand into his.

"All right," Adelaida sighed after a moment of silence. She returned to her chair, descending into it like a queen on her throne, and gestured to Gavri. "Tell me *all* of it."

Gavri scowled at her—*Fine enough for* him *to scowl,* Elaina thought—but with a sniff of disdain, he recounted the story.

"After Viktor betrayed us," he began, "and you stepped down, Nikita took a hard line against the *vukodlak*. Once the wounds were healed and our mourning done, he urged us to be watchful against any new incursion, any vulnerability the skinwalkers might exploit. It was to be expected, I suppose. He wasn't entirely wrong, either: the *vukodlak* have been skulking about, certainly, hunting on our lands and leaving their marks in our territory. So he had reason to be vigilant."

Adelaida gave a measured nod. Elaina noticed Timofei take her hand at the mention of their former lover, Viktor, and give it a gentle squeeze.

"Eventually, though," Gavri continued, "He let his concerns overshadow his sense. He came to me to say Kolya must be driven out, or else we left the pack open to attack. Because of Kolya's father... and because of his sexuality."

Adelaida drew in a deep breath, stroking her chin. "And, of course, being the little spitfire you are, you took offense and told Nikita to go fuck himself. Didn't you?"

Gavri cast his gaze down to his feet. "Yes."

"Typical." The former alpha rolled her eyes. "Rini, darling, would you mind pouring us all some tea, and perhaps setting out something to eat? Sandwiches I think."

"Yes, Adelaida." Rini dipped into a curtsey and slipped out of the room. Adelaida leaned forward in her seat, resting her elbows on her knees, and let out a low, husky sigh.

Elaina bit her tongue before she could say something sharp again. She wanted to demand the matriarch of the family *do* something, or at least apologize for behaving like such a bitch when her son—and her surrogate son—were in such danger. Evidently, Elaina's bristling displeasure was palpable, because Kolya gave her a tiny nudge with his elbow.

"Well," Adelaida said. "And what about you, human girl?"

Elaina stood, as though presenting herself for inspection. "My name's Elaina Jacob. Gavri and Kolya found me lost in the woods. There was a blizzard, a freak snowstorm. Nobody could have expected it to be so bad, not in the middle of May. And... they saved me."

"And because of this, you feel you owe them?" Sharp eyes glittered with a shrewd calculation Elaina didn't like. "So you've jumped into a dog fight without any lick of sense."

"Please excuse me. But it's not just for them." Elaina stepped closer, spreading her hands before her. "I... well, ever since the night in the blizzard, I've heard this music in my head. Baba Yasmin says it's the song of Diezana. There's a magnetism here, something pulling on me. Not just Gavri and Kolya, though they *are* part of it. Your people. Your magic. Your goddess. Everything."

"What can you possibly know about any of those things?" Adelaida challenged. She wasn't the first person to ask, though, and Elaina cut a hand through the air.

"I've said to these two, and to Nikita, and to Baba Yasmin. I mean to learn. Like your husband." She tilted a nod at Timofei. "He's converted to your ways, hasn't he?"

"*Da,* but he never challenged the alpha of our pack to a duel." Adelaida's sharp eyes grew cool. "Nor would he. It is not your place as humans to challenge *our* leaders."

"I don't mean to remain human."

The older woman regarded her for long moments. Rini returned, with glasses of iced tea on a tray, and in the silence, she passed them around. The red blush still rose high on her cheeks, and when she offered the tray to Elaina, Elaina declined a glass, but touched the sweet housekeeper's hand.

"It's okay," she told Rini softly. "I know you meant well."

Rini gave the tiniest squeak of relief, and she touched Elaina's arm with a nervous smile. Quickly, though, she scurried out of the room again, and from the kitchen the sounds of flatware and food containers rattled.

"Mrs. Dvorak—" Elaina began.

"Please call me Adelaida," Gavri's mother told her, kneading at one brow. "This is a family visit, not business, and besides, Dvorak is my maiden name."

When she met Elaina's gaze this time, her gaze had softened somewhat. "An alpha female who takes many husbands does not take their names. For obvious reasons. If you really intend to step into the role, and take both my boys as your mates, it is something you should know."

So she's not opposed? Elaina relaxed slightly and inclined her head. "Thank you... for the information."

"Mother, I am sorry you have come all this way for bad news," Gavri spoke up. "But we have the matter under control, and—"

"Do you really?" Adelaida took a sip of the iced tea. "Then tell me, where did your mate go this morning?"

Gavri clammed up with a frown, but Elaina provided the answer. "I went to see Nikita."

Adelaida raised her eyebrows in an almost coy expression. "Yes, you did. Had a pleasant, polite social call, did you?"

"No." Elaina frowned. "How do you know, though?"

"I smell him on you." She sat back in the chair again, appraising Elaina. "And stress. And anger."

Elaina marveled. "Really?"

"No." Adelaida produced a cell phone from the pocket of her slacks. "Nikita and I were on the phone just before you arrived there. We hung up when he said a yapping, irritating pup had shown up on his doorstep."

"Oh." Heat rushed to her face.

"You must know this is not how an alpha female behaves," Adelaida said. "Leaders do not *yap* and *bark* like angry puppies. They maintain control of themselves and their subordinates with a firm hand."

Elaina had no answer. She nodded in understanding.

"Please," she begged in a low, humble tone. "Can't you ask Nikita to call off the blood hunt? If you see Kolya as your son, can't you protect him?"

Adelaida ran a hand through her dark hair, regal, yet resigned. "No. I will not intervene, as these two have made it clear they do not want my help. Furthermore, Nikita *is* the alpha of this tribe, at least until the solstice. I abdicated my place. I will not simply storm back in and undermine him in front of his people, to shield a disobedient dog."

"Don't call him that!" Elaina burst out. Immediately her hand flew back to find Kolya's again, and she pulled him from the couch, holding him to her. "Everyone needs to stop calling Kolya a *dog!*"

"She didn't mean Kolya," Gavri grumbled, miserable. "She means me."

"Well, you're not, either!" She crossed to him, taking Kolya with her, and completed their chain by taking Gavri's hand as well. Turning a ferocious expression on Adelaida, she declared, "These two are mine. I won't hear them insulted."

Adelaida, surprisingly, quirked a smile. "Oh, hush. Have you never told a man he's in the doghouse, when he's done something stupid?"

No. More often, with her last lover Dominic at least, it had been the other way around. Still, she caught the alpha mother's meaning.

Adelaida shook her head. "Gavri should have come to me before. You've always had a proud streak in you, Gavri, and there are times it does you no favors. This is one of them. I won't undercut Nikita's declaration. And I won't petition him for you. That was for you to do, and you let your pride overwhelm your common sense. And while I can't condone such pig-headed chauvinism over Kolya's personal business, this is not my pack to lead anymore."

Switching her gaze to Elaina, she added, "But *you* have managed to tangle yourself in a problematic knot, human girl, and gotten my boys in it with you. You truly believe you can do the impossible? Manifest the gifts of Diezana when none of your kind has done so since time long forgotten?"

"Baba Yasmin said there might be a way," Elaina replied. "And I walked with spirits. Three of them. They told me of seven tasks I would have to complete, to become like you. *Oboroten.*"

"And this is what you want?" Adelaida asked.

"Yes." Elaina squeezed both her mates' hands. "I think it's why I'm still here. Why I survived. Yasmin and Grisha said the music I hear—the singing?—they said it's how Diezana calls out to her chosen. A song to guide them. Why would she guide me here, if she didn't mean for me to do this?"

"Still," Adelaida reminded her. "You have been very clumsy about it so far. You act like a wild pup who still needs its mother's correction. Picking fights with the bigger dog? With the recognized *leader,* and in front of his pack? You realize how hard it will be for them to welcome you now, don't you?"

"I admit, I hadn't thought of it."

"Exactly my point."

Adelaida stood. She turned to Timofei, taking his hand and giving it an affectionate kiss. A look of tenderness passed between them, something Elaina had never seen happen between her own parents. Then Adelaida returned her attention to Gavri, Kolya, and Elaina, and raised a hand in gesture to the dining room. Rini stood quietly in the doorway.

"I believe Rini has those sandwiches ready. Let us sit down, eat, and then we can discuss more of this plan the three of you have hatched."

"Oh, wait," Elaina said, as Kolya and Gavri moved to follow Adelaida's instruction. "Grisha is still outside."

"Let him stay out there." Gavri crossed his arms over his chest, but his eyes glittered with mirth. "He didn't want to deal with the dressing down, so why should he get to enjoy the aftermath?"

"Because *he* didn't need a dressing down," Elaina pointed out. She let them go ahead of her, into the dining room, while she returned to the front door to call for her third mate.

Adelaida remained in the living room as the men disappeared. As Elaina called Grisha, the silvery matriarch put a thoughtful finger to her lips. The prickling sense of her attention made Elaina's stomach flutter.

"You've taken Yasmin's student as your mate as well?" Adelaida asked. The note of interest in her voice carried a hint of danger, and Elaina didn't know why.

"Y-yes," she stammered. "I, uh... Gavri and Kolya said alpha wolves bond this way sometimes. They both knew I meant to bring Grisha into our circle. It wasn't... I didn't do anything sneaky."

"No," Adelaida held up a hand, deflecting Elaina's protests. "But you *aren't* an alpha yet, human girl."

"I'm *their* alpha," Elaina asserted in a quiet voice. "Whatever else happens, I'm theirs."

Grisha appeared in the doorway, wearing his usual cocksure grin. He looked from Elaina to Adelaida, gave the latter a reverent nod, and then headed into the dining room where the sounds of the others passing around sandwiches drew him.

Adelaida remained staring at Elaina. Trying not to be rude, Elaina gazed back.

It looked as though—like it or not—she had another new hurdle in her way.

CHAPTER THREE

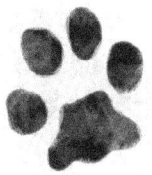

ADELAIDA AND TIMOFEI EXCUSED THEMSELVES after lunch, assuring Gavri and Kolya they'd remain close, in Stolby, until the solstice. The idea obviously rankled Gavri, but Kolya seemed pleased. When the former matriarch and her human husband finally left, Kolya—who no longer needed his crutches but still moved stiffly and limped when he walked—saw them to the door and kissed them both fondly on the cheeks. Gavri also accompanied them, but only offered his mother a polite nod of the head and shook his father's hand.

Keeping a sly eye on them from her place at the dining room table, Elaina nibbled on the last of her sandwich, pondering. Rini, more comfortable now the arguing had tapered off and tempers had cooled over a nice midday meal, studied Elaina in turn.

"I'd like to tell you she's not always so harsh." Standing, the housekeeper gathered plates and glasses from around the table. "But she *is* protective. Of both her children, and of her pack. It's nothing to do with you, Elaina."

"But it is, though." Elaina stabbed a salad leaf with her fork, not taking her gaze away from the group huddled in the entryway. "She doesn't want me to become the alpha any more than anyone else does."

"I don't think that's true."

Elaina switched her gaze to Rini. "Why not?"

"Because when alpha wolves take a disliking to another wolf in their territory, they drive them out." Rini reached for the plate in front of Elaina, and Elaina let her take it. She'd managed to eat the cold cuts on sourdough Rini prepared for them, but the rest of the meal seemed wholly unappetizing. Not because Rini had failed to prepare it well—Elaina didn't think Kolya or Rini could flub a meal if they tried. The frustration of the afternoon's fight had simply robbed Elaina of her appetite.

"Nikita can't very well turn you away when you've challenged him," Grisha put in. He sat across from her, snacking on a cut of deli meat. "I mean, he could have, but he chose to accept your challenge. Driving you out now would be a sign of fear or weakness on his part. Adelaida, however, could very easily bring her resources to bear against you, and have you driven out before you even start making headway on your seven tasks."

"Why didn't anyone tell me that?" Elaina grumbled. She snuck a slice of meat off Grisha's plate and nibbled at it.

"Well..." Rini avoided her eyes. "Mostly because we didn't expect to see Adelaida until the solstice. And by then, maybe you'd have won Diezana's blessing and be able to shapeshift. Nobody could have any serious problem with you challenging Nikita then."

"Yes, so we'd planned." Gavri returned from the foyer. Crossing his arms over his chest, he gave Rini a dark look. "Until someone squeaked."

Rini flushed, her face falling into misery, and hustled to the sink to wash the dishes she'd collected.

"Don't be mad at her, Gav," Elaina beseeched him. "She didn't mean to."

"I didn't!" Rini said. Her voice cracked, and Elaina got up to join her at the sink, putting her arms around Rini's shoulders.

"I understand," she assured the poor, sniffling girl. "It was an accident."

"Maybe," Gavri rumbled. "But let's try to avoid bringing Adelaida into any more of this business, shall we?"

"Why?" Grisha rolled up his last slice of ham and gestured with it at Gavri. "She didn't cast Elaina out, did she? We could use her help teaching this one how to be like us."

"I don't want her help," Gavri growled.

Elaina frowned at him. Giving Rini one last encouraging squeeze, she whispered, "Really, it's all right. Nobody's mad at you," and kissed the girl's cheek. Then she returned to the table, just as Kolya appeared. Looking exhausted even from a short trip between the front door and the kitchen, he collapsed into a chair.

"Gav," the russet wolf said. "Come off it. Adelaida is as much a part of this tribe as you or Nikita. She is going to take a side somewhere, so it might as well be ours."

"You think she would?" Elaina asked. "She didn't seem to like me at *all*."

"She didn't like being cut out of the situation," Kolya explained. "Or—sorry, *krasavitsa,* but you did speak back to her rather disrespectfully."

Elaina sank into her chair and rested her elbows on the table. "I know. I'm doing it a lot today." Rubbing at her temple, she added, "I'm still so *angry* someone put you in the hospital, Kol. It's hard to keep my head on straight, when we still don't know who."

"Nikita didn't admit anything, I take it?" Gavri leaned against the massive refrigerator.

Elaina shook her head. "He swears he'd never break his word, nor would Pasha. And Pasha's goons wouldn't act without his permission."

"I know you don't like to hear it, *krasavitsa,* but I believe him." Kolya picked up his glass of tea and topped it off from the pitcher on the sideboard. "I don't think Pasha attacked me, and I'm certain Nikita would not break his word."

Elaina groaned. "Kolya, *he's* the one who wants you out!"

"*Da.*" He took a sip of tea. "But he is not a liar."

No one added anything for several minutes. Gavri shot a glance at Rini, still sniffling as she washed the dishes, and a look of chagrin crossed his face. He crossed to her, touching her gently on the shoulder as he took a plate from her hands. Without a word he took over—his way of apologizing—and Rini returned to the table, dabbing her eyes.

Kolya set down his glass, and Grisha helped himself to it, draining the last of the tea without asking. Elaina kicked him under the table.

"Go get him another drink," she snapped. Grisha cocked an eyebrow at her. She narrowed her eyes and jabbed a finger at the pitcher of tea.

"You're closer," he taunted.

"*You* drank it," she snapped. "Because you're an asshole."

Grisha cracked a smile, as though he'd somehow won. He got up, though, and came around the table to pour Kolya a fresh glass, as she'd instructed.

"So what do we do now?" Elaina asked. "I mean, who's next on the list of suspects who might have tried to hurt you, Kol?"

Kolya shook his head. "Next, we do not concern ourselves with my attack. I'm an omega wolf, *krasavitsa*. Omegas get picked on regularly."

"But you ended up in the hospital!"

"You have bigger concerns," he reminded her. "*You* have only twenty-two days until the solstice. You must focus on Diezana's seven tasks, not on a few *oboroten* bullies."

Elaina pursed her lips. She didn't mention the other possibility Nikita had brought up. The *vukodlak*. The skinwalkers.

"What's the next task?" Rini asked. Most of her tears had dried, and her eyes sparkled with keen interest.

"A hunt," Elaina said. Folding her hands before her, she stared at them, thoughts racing. "A ritual hunt, I guess. With the pack."

"Probably not the pack." Gavri turned toward them again, drying a glass. "It is... too early, I think, to hope to have them along for support."

"You think they'll accept her later?" Grisha asked. "Once she wins enough points?"

"I think eventually Elaina must run with them," Gavri said. He put down the glass and started on the flatware. "But perhaps *after* she's learned a bit more from us."

Grisha nodded. "Agreed. We three can teach her about hunting, easily enough."

THEY STARTED EARLY THE NEXT morning. While Elaina, Gavri, and Kolya waited at the lodge, reviewing her strategy, Grisha slipped into the wilderness in his feline form, leaving a path for her to follow in a game of modified hide-and-seek. At first, they focused only on tracking: Elaina led the way with Gavri following, until she discovered Grisha's hiding place. Then, Grisha and Gavri would trade places and the game began again.

Over the course of the morning they ranged farther and farther from the lodge. As the hours went by the men led Elaina over more and more challenging terrain, their routes growing more and more complex, pulling tricks as they went in a bid to throw her off.

"Thank the goddess I've done so much hiking and tracking already," she confided to Grisha on one circuit, as they followed Gavri's trail. "Even if only to hunt for great photo opportunities."

The sun climbed high, gleefully approaching the apex of its daily journey, and the fresh green scent of the woods had swallowed up all memory of civilizations in cities, or of vehicles dumping carbon and smoke, of dry grocery goods or stale offices. She couldn't remember if this was their fifth or sixth round of the game—she'd lost track at about round three. She pointed out a tuft of black fur snagged on a log ahead, and grinned with satisfaction to find a scuffed set of prints on the path just beyond it.

Grisha, in his snow leopard form, gave a quiet chuff of agreement. They moved on stealthily together until the path came to a fork, and she led the way north, past a wild raspberry bush with a broken branch low on the right side.

It took forty more minutes of careful search before she spied Gavri, perched on a fallen pine. He gave a happy bark as she emerged from the trees, and jumped down to greet her.

"Back home for lunch now?" she asked, pushing back a damp sheaf of her curly hair. The afternoon would likely bring more heat. She hadn't checked the weather before they left that morning but June in Krasnoyarsk could climb into the high seventies or even the low eighties. Her wolf and snow leopard nodded, and together the three of them turned back in the direction of the lodge.

The men returned to their human forms as soon as they reached the back patio. With a groan, Gavri pointed out Adelaida's car, back in the driveway.

"Damnit!" he snarled. "Why is she here again?"

Elaina frowned at him. "Why does it make you so angry? I mean, I'm not happy to see her either, but I don't think she likes me. *You're* her son."

Gavri didn't answer. He stormed toward the house, heading for the entrance to the sunroom rather than the door leading into the kitchen.

Grisha lifted one shoulder in a half-shrug. "Gavri is the son of an alpha. He does not wish to appear weak or incapable in front of her."

"Makes sense, I suppose." Elaina ran both hands through her hair, brushing out pine needles and stray leaves she'd accumulated from the long hours of hiking. "But she's here now, and these things all affect her pack. I don't think we can ask her to turn away."

Her snow leopard regarded her with a curious glimmer in his eye. "Well, well. That *almost* sounds like something a leader would say. Now, you just have to say it to *him*."

"What do you mean?"

He gestured after Gavri. "He is your beta wolf, Elaina. Which means he listens to you. If he misbehaves, it is for *you* to put him in his place."

She furrowed her brow and nodded.

Grisha followed her into the kitchen, where Adelaida, Timofei, Kolya, and Rini all gathered, sharing another round of iced tea and a tray of something Elaina didn't recognize.

"*Golubtsy,*" Rini announced, noticing Elaina's look of curiosity. She held out a platter of steaming cabbage rolls, each topped with a spoonful of sour cream.

"Stuffed with beef and rice," Adelaida clarified. "It is one of Gavri's favorite meals. I thought it might mollify him a little, after my unexpected arrival yesterday."

The golubtsy smelled amazing, and Elaina was just about to have a seat and dig into a piece when she remembered how dirty she must look. Grisha strode past her, excusing himself to the rooms upstairs to gather some clothes, and she gestured after him.

"I'm filthy from hiking. I'll pop into a quick shower to rinse off and be right back." She glanced at

Adelaida to see if the older woman had any reaction. "If it's all right?"

"Perfectly all right," Adelaida replied. Her tone had softened considerably from yesterday, carrying a much gentler, more maternal tone. "And would you please let my son know?"

Elaina tilted her head to the side. Grisha's words reoccurred to her: if she meant to be the alpha, it fell to her to ensure her beta wolf conducted himself with respect toward Adelaida.

"Yes, of course I will."

Instead of following Grisha up the stairs, she made her way down the back hallway toward Gavri's office. She poked her head in to find him working on his latest metal model, a series of snapping and sliding panes of aluminum, which, when constructed, would form a scale model rendition of the Notre Dame cathedral. Gavri had slotted one thin segment between the prongs of a pin vise and studied it under the curved glass of his magnifier as he delicately applied a dab of glue to one edge.

She waited for him to settle the second piece in place, holding it fast as the glue bonded, before she spoke up.

"What exactly are you doing?" she asked when he looked up from his work. "You can't just freeze out your mother at a time like this, Gav. It's childish and it doesn't help our situation."

"I think I've made myself clear." He rubbed at his eyes, a thing she'd seen him do before when he worked with these miniscule model pieces. "I did not want Adelaida *involved* in these matters."

"Maybe not. But she's involved now, regardless of how you feel. Giving her the cold shoulder won't change things. It will only make them harder."

With a growl, he stood, adjusting a work light to shine directly on the freshly glued segments. "You will excuse me for saying so, Elaina, but this is between me and her."

"*No.*" She squared her shoulders, taking a step closer to block his movement as he tried to step out from behind his desk. Gavri's glacial blue eyes widened in surprise, and his lip curled in reflexive anger.

"We are a pack, Gavri. You and Kolya have said it yourselves. We are a pack and at least for now, you've made me the alpha. And she is your former alpha. You owe both of us more than this petulant pouting fit."

He snarled. "Kolya's exile, and mine—"

"Are problems the whole pack will address together. As a unit."

She reached up to cup his chin in her hand. His sharp, fine features endeared him to her. She wished she could soothe his ache and frustration in another manner, with soft kisses and sensuous stroking—but for now, she must be clear with him.

"Go shower. Then join us in the dining room. Your mother brought golubtsy."

He lifted one dark eyebrow. "She did?"

"Yes. So don't spend a lot of time making excuses."

His anger softened. He glanced away from her and bowed his head. "Very well. If this is the way you must have it."

In one quick motion, he snatched her wrist. "But *you* must join me in the shower."

Elaina broke into a smile, unable to help herself. She slapped him playfully. "Gavri Dvorak! With your *mother* in the house?"

"She'll never know." He winked at her. "The shower in the exercise room is far enough from the kitchen, she will hear nothing."

Adelaida most certainly *would* know, though, and Elaina was sure Gavri knew it, too. Even if they weren't heard and even if they rinsed off clean as could be, she'd know it from their faces and the guilty grins they wouldn't be able to hide, like naughty teenagers.

But when Gavri pulled her down the hallway and toward the stairs leading to the home gym, Elaina didn't stop him.

They made quick love in the shower, Gavri holding her up against the smooth, aqua-blue tiles, his big, hot hands under her thighs. Elaina wrapped her arms around his neck and moaned, the sound of her pleasure close and intimate in the thick steam. She'd had a few experiences with quickie sex before, always furtive and uncoordinated, full of giggles but rarely, if ever, ideal for climax. At least, not hers. Men were easy—a few hard, rude thrusts and they gritted their teeth with a hissing *Yes!* or *Oh, yeah, I'm there!* or some other arrogant declaration of prowess, but for her the experience only really made for blushing self-satisfaction. A secret delight. Not with Gavri, though: his rush came in an artful sort of attack; his hips rolling to hers, sending him deeper, stirring her with teasing, fluttering arousal; he lifted her with his body so they rocked together in magnificent rhythm. His mouth found her breasts and he tormented her with fleeting kisses and playful nips of the teeth, making her yip and gasp and sigh.

Before she realized it, her body raced toward completion. The mounting, galloping pleasure, rising and rising with each thrust, cresting toward that beautiful peak and tipping her over the edge. And then she was there, thrusting her hips to receive him, demanding him, hungry and fulfilled all at once. Gavri slowed his strokes but only to draw out her orgasm, whispering hot, steamy words of encouragement into her ear.

He hadn't even come himself. It occurred to her with a curious spark of certainty. "But—"

Gavri didn't answer. He withdrew from her and let her find her feet, but the instant she was steady he closed one hand on her shoulder and pressed her to her knees. Before she could react, fierce bursts of his seed jetted across her face, the bridge of her nose, and over her breasts. The last of it she swallowed, taking his cock into her mouth.

When they returned to the dining room and the others, freshly cleaned off and well-scrubbed of any lasting evidence of their frantic sex, Elaina couldn't wipe the smile from her face. She caught Kolya looking at her with a knowing lilt of grin, and Grisha, who had returned before them, recognized their flush with a quick blaze of his green eyes. But as Gavri took his seat beside his mother, accepting the plate of stuffed cabbage leaves, his temper had taken a sharp upturn. He leaned over to kiss Adelaida on the cheek, thanking her for preparing his favorite meal.

"And *mors!*" He picked up the pitcher of what Elaina had assumed to be iced tea, pouring himself a glass with a look of relish.

"Fresh made this morning," Adelaida told him. "I added some lingonberries to the recipe this time. You will have to let me know how you like it."

Elaina reached for the pitcher next. "What is... mors?"

"A berry drink." Gavri dipped a spoon in a small tureen on the table before him, spooning out a dollop of honey to stir into the drink.

"I use mostly cranberries and raspberries in mine," Adelaida told her. "For some, it is too tart or sweet. But you can dilute it with water, or seltzer water, as you like."

Elaina wrinkled her nose at the first taste. It *was* very, very tart, and her own spoonful of honey did nothing to cut the taste. She settled for scooping up a good deal of ice, and a sprig of mint Rini offered her.

"So, Elaina..."

Adelaida's easy tone put Elaina instantly on her guard, chasing away her cheerful mood. She recognized it: the tone of a mother ready to interrogate the new woman in her son's life.

"Tell me a little more about yourself."

Ugh. It seemed like a heavy stone had just dropped into Elaina's stomach. She'd been about to try her first bite of the cabbage rolls, excited by the savory smells and the cool, crisp white daub of sour cream on top, but the awful question chased away her appetite in a flash.

Setting the cabbage roll back on her plate, she studied it, if only to avoid looking anywhere else. She picked it up again, considering it, and finally took a bite. The sharp, flavorful taste took her by surprise, but filled her with renewed delight. Juicy, seasoned beef and soft, faintly buttery rice; a hint of fresh, light green onion. The sour cream gave it a sweet, clean finish. She wished she could have enjoyed it more, but the weight of Adelaida's question—and her distinctly sharp, lupine stare—pressed on her.

"Well..." she hedged. She hated this part. Why not just submit a resume, citing all her accomplishments and certifications as a domestic partner? *Please submit personal and relationship history for the last ten years.* Worse yet, Adelaida would no doubt interrogate her with the same questions Elaina had already received from everybody in the Stolby pack. Who was she to insert herself in their business? Why should she have any right to weigh in on the exile of Gavri and Kolya? Did she *really* think she could become one of them? Would she lose interest in the tribe as soon as this challenge was over?

Moms ask these questions, she tried to reassure herself. *It's just how they are when their sons bring home a new girlfriend. Or, in this case, hide a new girlfriend and her blatant, clumsy intrusion into their ways.*

"Elaina?" Kolya nudged her.

She steeled her nerves.

"I'm a travel writer, originally from Chicago. Earned my degree in photojournalism and took off to find adventure. I've been to almost every major continent, but this is my first time visiting Russia."

Adelaida tipped her a nod. "And your family?"

Elaina paused for a long sip of her mors, swallowing back the dread clawing at her throat. "Just me and my parents. No siblings. But my mother and father aren't travelers, at least, not like me. They're perfectly cozy at home."

"Mm-hm." The former alpha's gaze was sharp. "What do they do?"

"Mother's a... well, mostly a social butterfly these days. She serves on community boards and organizations, raising money for Historical Society projects, museum funds, political campaigns and the like. My father used to be in aerospace research, but he's retired."

What else was she supposed to say? *Dad hardly seems interested in what I do or where I go. Happy to spend an hour or two catching up when I drop by but then, out of sight, out of mind. Mother always tells me my smile is too crooked or my visit has been nice, but also very inconvenient for her and I should have come at a different time. She's never approved of a single man I dated besides the last self-absorbed asshole, and I think she only liked him because she recognized some kind of kindred spirit in the battle to browbeat me into submission. And it almost worked. Except I decided to run away to Siberia and it's going to be hard for either of them to poke and pick on me and put me down now.*

Bitterness hit her like curls of rotten lemon rind in her stomach. She managed to get down another bite of golubtsy but then set what remained of the cabbage roll down, no longer hungry at all.

Adelaida's sharp blue gaze held her pinned to her seat. "What puts such a sour expression on your face, girl? Is the food too strong for you?"

"No, it's quite delicious." Elaina took another drink of mors. "I just don't want to spend lunchtime talking about me."

"But my sons have taken you as their mate." Adelaida's voice turned soft. She leaned forward, putting her elbows on the table and resting her chin on her folded hands. "I should like to know more about the woman they have taken into their den."

"I know. But ever since I met the other *oboroten*, all anyone wants to find out is how foolish I am, or how audacious, and how unsuited to leadership. I've had this conversation enough already. I just want to train for my next task and get to it."

"Ah, yes, the seven tasks." With an abrupt change in manner, Adelaida straightened again, folding her hands on the table before her. Timofei took it upon himself to refresh her drink, and Gavri leaned a little closer to his mother, extending a hand to touch hers.

"Mother, we have good reason to believe this will work. We just need to prepare her—"

"I know it can work," Adelaida assured him. Her conviction startled everyone at the table. Even Grisha gave a twitch of surprise at the dramatic reversal. Yesterday Adelaida had been furious at the very thought of a human intruding on their tribe, but now—

Elaina furrowed her brow. *Had* Adelaida been furious at Elaina's bid to become *oboroten*? Or had she been angry for a vast myriad of reasons like her son's reticence? She hadn't been kind about the challenge, but she hadn't given any indication she'd interfere, either.

"Diezana plays a long game," Adelaida mused. "If she truly has communicated with you, Elaina, she didn't do it out of idle boredom or capriciousness."

Elaina didn't reply. She didn't want to have to point out Diezana *hadn't* exactly spoken with her; three other spirits had manifested during her mystic walkabout, but the spirit mother of the *oboroten* had remained conspicuously absent.

But then... the song.

Yes, Diezana's song. As far as anyone knew, no other human besides Elaina had ever heard the rolling, weaving music like flute-song and a breeze dancing through wind chimes. Diezana's voice. Her cry to her most favored, those she had led away from the brink of death.

Timofei checked his watch. "Dear, it's time to go. We should have been at Nikita's ten minutes ago."

Elaina straightened. "You're meeting with *Nikita?*"

Adelaida folded up her napkin and set it aside. "Of course I am. He is the alpha of this pack, and I, his mentor. There are leadership matters which we must discuss."

"Shouldn't I come? Since it's possible *I* might be the next leader, after the solstice?"

Adelaida cut a gaze at her sharp enough to make her flinch. *I did it again,* Elaina realized. *Stepped up to the big dogs for a game of chicken. I've got to stop doing that!*

"I think it best you concentrate on your tasks for now," Adelaida told her in a distinctly withering voice. "You're still a long way from the issues an alpha must tackle."

With a soft, weary exhalation, Elaina relaxed in her seat. "You're right. First thing's first. We figure out what to do about this ritual hunt. Then—if I survive it—we'll move on to what's next."

"We shall see."

Adelaida bent to kiss Gavri on the brow—she didn't have to bend far—and then gave the same to Kolya. Taking Rini's hands in hers, she thanked the delicate housekeeper with genuine verve. Then, in an odd and almost disconcerting gesture, she came to Elaina and took her face in her hands. Adelaida stared into Elaina's eyes, but the flash of authority and reproof had faded. Now, she gazed at Elaina with a gentle, thoughtful interest.

"Let me know how your training fares." She caressed Elaina's cheek with one thumb, then stepped away again, joining Timofei at the doorway. "Perhaps I will tag along on your hunt and see for myself what sort of wolf you are."

CHAPTER FOUR

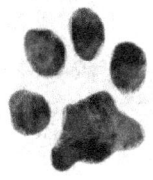

AFTER LUNCH, THEY DOVE RIGHT back into training. Grisha took off ahead of Gavri and Elaina, slipping into the trees and disappearing for them to follow. While they waited, giving the snow leopard a healthy head start, Gavri kneaded Elaina's shoulders, and kissed the top of her head. She leaned into his support, but more than ever her mind hung on the hunt, and how she would manage it, and whether she had any hope of pulling off even a single task. Let alone Diezana's full challenge.

Kolya, her sweet, sensitive one, joined them on the patio and gave her hand a squeeze. His sympathetic smile warmed her. Gavri slowed his massage to a stop and rested his arms around her, leaning his head on the shoulder to kiss his earlobe.

"Ease your worries, *krasavitsa*." He offered a firm, lingering hug. "You can do this. You *will* do this."

When they set off after Grisha this time, Elaina surged ahead to take a fast lead, keeping her strides low and smooth, searching the shadows and the underbrush almost in a sense of panic.

He usually lets the pricker bushes catch a bit of his fur. Or drops a print or two down close to the base of the trees.

43

Real prey won't be so easy, came Dominic's caustic voice. *You're chasing a big, fuzzy pet who wants to be found. This isn't hunting. It's just a game.*

"It's a game I'm going to win," she vowed under her breath. The sound of padding footsteps caught up to her on her left; she'd been moving ahead so quickly Gavri had taken his wolf shape to match her pace.

Twenty minutes later, Grisha's trail led them down a short embankment into a mossy green glade. A wide, flat, sweet-smelling river rushed through the vivid ferns and dark, shaded soil, and long, low-hanging trees stretched nearly horizontal over the water.

Grisha, in his snow leopard form, lounged on one of the trunks, tail twitching lazily, broad furry head resting on his paws. As Elaina and Gavri broke through the underbrush, the big cat perked up, flicking his ears at them. Elaina planted her hands on her hips and let out a triumphant, "Ha! Found you in record time. Switch it up, and let's see if Gav gives me more of a challenge."

Grisha's lambent green eyes flashed. He gave a low, rumbling sort of huff as he came to his feet. Instead of crossing to their side of the river, though, he turned pointedly away, tail lashing, and bounded down the tree trunk to the opposite bank.

"Grisha!" Elaina stamped her foot. "I don't have time for you to screw around!"

He shot her a cool, very *catlike* gaze, and sat down on one of the flat, mossy rocks. Lifting a paw, he casually began to groom himself.

"*Grisha!*"

Beside Elaina, Gavri uttered a funny half-yipping, half-coughing sound. She peered at him with a cold, humorless expression. "What are *you* laughing at?"

The odd coughing sound grew into a short series of high-pitched, chuckling barks. Gav swept his tail back and forth and lunged to jump up on one of the big tree trunks, then trotted across after Grisha. Elaina let out a groan.

"This isn't funny for me!" she warned. They probably couldn't even hear her over the rush of water. Grumbling, she climbed up after her companions, sneakers skidding in the wet moss atop the river stones.

The damp, soft feel of the tree bark gave her pause, but as she worked her way atop the trunk, her grip held. She swung one leg up and over a jutting branch and pulled herself the rest of the way without a slip. The fresh, invigorating scent of pine threatened to ease her annoyance, but she'd built up a good head of steam and she wanted to be good and angry when she reached her mocking mates.

Crossing the natural bridge formed by the trunk required careful attention. A clutch of rotted bark gave way under her foot and disappeared into the water, carried over a short, broad waterfall. She wouldn't necessarily hurt herself if she slipped and fell—she'd take a good tumble over some broad stones, but they were smooth and the drop would be negligible. The real damage would be the humiliation she'd suffer in front of her two mates.

As soon as she made it across and planted both feet firmly on the ground again, Grisha lunged at her.

"Shit!"

Taken by surprise, she stumbled back. The snow leopard collided with her and took her to the ground. They landed in a soft bed of ferns, and all at once Grisha returned to his human form, straddling her.

"*Ha!*" he pronounced. "Caught *you.*"

With a snarl, she beat at his chest. "Get off. I said we didn't have time for this."

"But it is part of your training, little girl." He grabbed her wrists and pinned them to either side, grinning an evil grin. "What will you do when your prey fights back?"

"*Grisha!*"

Elaina threw a look at Gavri. "Aren't you going to help me? Get him off!"

Gavri, returning to his human form, rubbed his chin with an impish smile of his own. "I don't know. He has a point, *krasavitsa.* I think *you* should, eh..." He chuckled. "*...get him off.*"

She thrashed against Grisha's hold, and glared daggers at her beta wolf. "Whose side are you on?"

Grisha dipped in, and his mouth covered hers in a wicked, rough, tantalizing kiss. Elaina gave a cry of surprise, muffled by his lips, but after an instant she relaxed. Her struggles ceased, at least for the moment.

When they parted, she got one hand loose of his grip and slapped his cheek. "Okay, you've had your fun—"

"Oh, no I haven't," he growled. He closed his free hand around her neck—firm, but gentle enough to be thrust away, if she'd wanted to do so—and slid off her. Releasing her other wrist, he snatched the band of her light jogging shorts and yanked them down her legs.

Elaina grabbed his wrist with both hands, but she didn't fight his hold. In a whisper, she demanded, "You quit it right now, mister!"

"Make me," he rumbled, and kissed her again, stroking her bare, smooth legs with tender appreciation. Soon his fingers brushed her panties, and he ran his thumb lightly down the warm cleft beneath them.

"Don't make me tell you twice," Elaina threatened. A smile betrayed her, though; a brief shiver of anticipation traveled down her legs.

Grisha purred, an amazing talent provided by his connection to Diezana and the big cats. It filled Elaina's heart with warm, wonderful feelings, while his wandering hand gave her sex a tight, hot squeeze. She gasped, body going taut, and her grip on his wrist loosened.

"You're too stressed. I'm going to fuck all the tension right out of you, little girl," he promised, and this time when he kissed her his tongue stormed her mouth, finding hers and waging battle, tasting and tormenting her. As they parted she gave out a breathless gasp, the first dizzy stirrings of arousal tugging her careful, driven determination from her mind.

She shot a glance at Gavri again. "What about you?"

"He can watch," Grisha answered for the wolf. "Or he can join us. Except he already had his turn with you in the shower so he's going to have to settle for whatever I leave him."

His ferocious tone thrilled her. He slid his hand beneath her shorties and ran two fingers down the length of her sex. Elaina closed her eyes with a groan, lifting her hips to him.

"Oh, no," he growled. "This won't do at all. I'm going to need you much, *much* wetter. Gav, come hold her down for me."

"Don't you dare!" she told Gavri, but laughter bubbled up and stole away her authoritative tone. Gav bounded up the bank to join them, and his erection jutted up, prominent and eager. He knelt by her and stripped her hands from Grisha's wrist, pinning them above her head.

He smelled of wild pheromones and heated desire. Elaina couldn't help herself: straining up from the ground, she lifted her face to nuzzle at his cock, basking in the welcome, thrilling hardness.

Grisha moved lower on her body, seizing her underwear and tearing it from her.

"Hey!" she shouted, but in the next second he'd buried his face between her thighs, devouring her like a starving man. A rush of wet desire poured through her. She arched, crying out in pleasure, pressing herself to him.

Grisha feasted on her, sliding his tongue along her folds, curling it over her clitoris. Looping his arms under her thighs, he opened her to him and plunged himself into her, lapping up the hot, bittersweet taste. Nuzzling, kissing, licking, he ate her up like a juicy treat and when he peered up at her, meeting her eyes, the glistening sheen of her arousal lingered on his lips.

A rumble escaped Gavri's throat, a rough, animal sound. Elaina glanced up to find him staring intently at her, eyes and ears gone wolfish in his hungry interest. His cock, adamantly hard, hung so close to her face. Closing her eyes again, she lifted herself just enough to kiss it, making an eager sound of her own.

Grisha uttered a husky laugh. He rose over her, planting his hands on either side of her hips, and shot some quick direction to Gav in their native tongue. Together they seized her, greedy hands hot upon her skin, and turned her, putting her on her knees between them, her back to Grisha.

"Hey!" she protested. Gavri folded her arms behind her back and Grisha took hold of them in a hard grip. At the same time, he bobbed his hips against hers, and the fierce weight of his studded cock pressed between her cheeks.

Gavri, kneeling in front of her, had taken his own cock in one hand and begun pumping it, his dark eyes—full black with bestial magic—gleaming in hungry, savage desire. Elaina peered up at him, unable to keep up her objections, now flush and brimming with excitement. The cool, soft soil under her knees and the light breeze over the river brought a furtive tingle to her skin, a rush of excitement over the openness and exposure.

Is this one of the restricted areas of the park? She couldn't remember. What if hikers came by, or rangers from the reserve? It made her heart race.

Another moan escaped her as Grisha pressed himself to her again, his cock rubbing against her sex, the metal stud of his piercing cool against her clit. He held her wrists with one big hand, and with the other, he guided himself to her entrance, teasing, flirting.

"Go on," Gavri urged the other man. "You said it yourself: she's much too tense. Work some of that anxiety out of her, brother."

"Please, wolf..." Grisha chuckled. Without warning, then, he entered her, plunging deep into her tight, resisting flesh. Elaina cried out, wriggling in his grasp, a ticklish thrill racing up her body.

"I *know* how to *fuck* a woman." He emphasized this with a series of firm, fierce thrusts. Elaina gasped and moved in response, undulating with his body. Grisha slapped her ass with his free hand, getting a startled shriek out of her, and before the hot red sting of his strike could fade, he gave her a hard squeeze.

His leaned over her, thrusts deepening, and his husky voice grated in her ear. "What were you saying about me not giving you a challenge? How's this for a challenge: let's see how much you can take before you're all wrung out and begging me to stop?"

"Please," she beseeched him, though by now they both knew she was only playing along. "Grisha, we need to think of my seven tasks..."

"Right now the only task before you is to shut up and fuck your pack." He squeezed again, renewing the raw, lovely tenderness under his palm. "Maybe your beta wolf can help you out with the first part."

As if he'd been waiting for a cue, Gavri inched closer, still tugging at his cock, which glistened at the head with his readiness. Elaina cried out as he seized her by the hair and guided her to him, filling her mouth with his rigid, heady flesh. She moaned around him. A tingling satisfaction rose in her breasts, nipples growing taut against her clinging sports bra.

Grisha rode her with ferocious pleasure; each hard, mean thrust rocked her forward and she had to manage Gavri's choking cock. Her brain whirled with drunken delight, a primal, gluttonous part of her reveling in the vicious, violent motions. Both of them felt too large, their need too much, but she embraced the sensation. The way Grisha had snarled at her, the way he told her *fuck your pack,* infected her with a greedy, self-effacing desire. *Yes,* this devilish hunger insisted. *Yes, these are my pack. Yes, I will be their pleasure, their wet, well-loved toy. They love me and in return I give them my body to satisfy their every animal need.*

Gavri's grip on her hair tightened. He groaned, free hand joining the first, tangling in her wild brown curls to hold her there, trap her, as his first orgasm approached. His cock swelled, and he threw his head back with a shout, as the first coursing jet of his semen filled her mouth. He came hard, again and again, forcing her to swallow down every bit. And Elaina did, gladly: she accepted his offering, eager for more.

Gavri withdrew, but she knew he wouldn't have to wait long before his erection renewed. She uttered a soft moan, pleasant shivers making her quake in Grisha's grasp. Grisha hunched over her, driving himself into her, growling filthy language in her ear. She murmured and whispered to him, "*Yes,* yes more... oh, *yes...*"

With a mad roar he came, each throb of his cock driving her, filling her, and she felt like she couldn't get enough. She begged for more, and murmured with wordless, senseless gratitude. He'd barely withdrawn from her—leaving a small gush of their mingled wetness running down her thighs—when he wanted to flip her again. This time, though, once he'd rolled her on her back, he lunged and pushed her backward into Gavri. Elaina scrambled, giggling and thrilled, until she was sandwiched between them. Grisha backed her onto Gavri's lap, and Gavri slid his hands under her to part her thighs. Before she knew it, his cock pressed eagerly against her rear.

"Oh, oh, wait—"

Gavri's hand moved between their bodies, his wandering fingers teasing her folds, soon becoming slick. Gently he eased first one finger, then two into her rear, his ministrations ensuring that she was ready for him.

"*Oh…*" Elaina moaned, overwhelmed.

Grisha climbed on top of her and plunged into her a second time. She arched, giving up a breathless moan, and an instant later Gavri thrust into her as well. The sharp, sweet sting of his invasion wrung another long, dizzy sound of bliss from her, and together her two mates worked her body, thrusting in alternating rhythm, grunting, *growling,* until she surrendered completely to them. Their hard, hot, unyielding motions electrified her every muscle—her legs trembled and her toes curled, her nipples blazing with tantalizing sweet arousal, heightened more and more under the brush and rasp of her sports bra. Her muscles and limbs turned to shivering water, but deep in her core, every harsh thrust strummed an elusive desire.

Gavri's urgent, wolfish sounds of pleasure intensified. As he held her on his lap, his hands wandered up under her shirt, and he found her nipples, rigid pebbles under her bra. He shoved the elastic sports material up, freeing her breasts, and seized each pink tip between thumb and forefinger.

"*Ah!*" Elaina flinched as he squeezed and tugged them, rolling them between his fingertips. He pulled and pinched until she yelped, and then she moaned, writhing on his lap.

"Oh, Grisha—" She locked eyes with her beautiful big cat. "Yes, I'm... I'm going to—"

She didn't need to finish the sentence. Her orgasm swelled to a peak and crashed over her, a rush of bliss like an enormous wave. She cried out, invoking their names, her body seized by wild contractions. Her nails dug into Grisha's back, and a second later he joined her in climax, coming inside her in hot, coursing throbs. With a heavy snarl, Gavri bit down on her shoulder, the intensity of the sensation heightening the force of her pleasure, building it to new peaks. At last he came, hard, each swelling beat of ejaculation sending a twinge of aching satisfaction through her where their bodies connected.

"Oh," Elaina murmured, clinging to Grisha, leaning her head back onto Gavri's, as she heaved with wonderful exertion. As her mates withdrew from her, their mingled seed ran down her thighs, and she shivered with raw, sweet, scandalous delight.

"Feel better?" Grisha purred. He took her chin in his hand and planted a rough kiss on her mouth. "Did we manage to ease some of that worry you're carrying?"

"If I say no, can we do it again?" She gave him a crooked, drunken smile.

They had a quick rinse in the stream, and a long rest in the shade under the trees, lying together in cool, fresh grass. Gavri shook Elaina out of a doze just as the afternoon shadows started growing long, and at last they returned to their hunting games. One more round each of tracking down her men before they called it quits for the night. Hunger called them home.

Tomorrow came the hunt.

CHAPTER FIVE

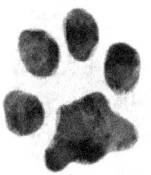

"*EDO DOM. EDO. DOM.*"

Elaina frowned, studying the Slavic letters on the tablet screen. She leaned on Kolya, who lounged in the spacious bay window of the sunroom, watching her work and giving her a helpful nudge here and there, as she embarked on a task which had nothing to do with becoming *oboroten.*

"*Edo dom,*" she repeated after the monotone computer voice. "This is a house."

Kolya nodded, combing his fingers through her hair. Elaina typed the English translation into the app, and the program dinged happily. She swiped to the next phrase.

"*Dima medik.* Dima is a medic. That one's easy."

As she took a moment to review the foreign letters making up the words, she gave her mate an affectionate caress. Kolya's chin was rough with stubble; she ran her fingertips over it, smiling, pleased by the rasping sensation under her hand.

"End of the lesson," he pronounced as the app played a short fanfare and congratulated her. "Good job."

"Well, it *is* the beginner's course. I'd be ashamed if I couldn't at least identify *Dima is a medic.*"

"Perhaps, but it's the alphabet you need to learn, as much as the vocabulary."

"Come on," Elaina coaxed him. "Gavri's probably got breakfast ready."

"And what about Grisha?" Kolya asked. Though he was as much Elaina's mate as either Gavri or Kolya, Grisha—just like a cat—valued his independence and didn't often stay the night at the lodge.

"He'll be back for the hunt." She tapped the tablet to clear the screen and switched it off. Gavri had loaned it to her so she could begin her study of Russian, and she slipped it into the built-in drawer under the bay window. She'd run through another lesson or two after the day's *real* work.

Kolya tilted her face to him and kissed her. "I think you will enjoy this, *krasavitsa*. You have the spirit of a hunter."

Elaina laughed. "Kolya, I've never hunted anything in my life, unless you count the last few days with you three and our hide-and-seek games."

"I say *hunter,* my love. Not *killer.*"

She stood and allowed him to unfold himself from his position as her backrest. Kolya rose and stretched.

"I know you've never felt the rush in your blood or the hunger in your belly when stalking prey, like wolves do. When you are one of us, you will come to know such things. But even now, you track with a thrill in your heart. You like the game, the competition, and in the beginning, that is the way all wolf pups start out. You will grow into a keen hunter, I know."

He slid an arm around her waist as they left the bright sunroom, heading for the kitchen with their stomachs growling.

"Mind you," Kolya went on. "We don't hunt for trophies. These are sacred rituals and our prey very integral to the continued health and resources of the tribe."

Elaina agreed absent-mindedly. As they emerged into the kitchen, though, everything was still off, even the lights. Gavri's voice drifted to them from the living room. His dark tone—low and troubled—made them pause, and they exchanged glances, brows knit.

Gavri stood before the fireplace in the living room, resting his brow against one arm propped on the mantle. In his other hand he held his phone. He spoke in a blend of Russian and the *oboroten* native tongue, leaving Elaina for the most part shut out of the conversation. As Kolya listened, his expression grew troubled, and when Elaina tugged at his sleeve for an explanation, he shook his head.

"Let us go start breakfast. Gavri will explain when he is finished."

"But who is he on the phone with, Kol?"

He put a hand on her shoulder and led her toward the kitchen. "Adelaida. It is pack business."

Then I should know, she wanted to protest. She kept her mouth shut though, as she opened up a cupboard to search for a mixing bowl.

"I feel like waffles," she told her mate. "What do you think?"

"Waffles sound wonderful. And I will make you some eggs as well."

They each started on their half of the breakfast menu, Elaina selecting a box of multigrain waffle mix,

Kolya pulling a carton of eggs from the refrigerator along with diced ham and green onions. Neither one spoke as they worked, and Elaina noticed with mild irritation how Kolya paused now and again to pick up part of Gavri's conversation, or to react to something their mate had said.

"Eyes front, Kol." She whapped him in the butt with the plastic spatula. Kolya gave her a sheepish grin but returned his attention to chopping his onions.

Elaina had just finished mixing the waffle batter when Gavri at last came into the dining room, running a hand through his hair as he pocketed his cell phone.

She practically jumped on him. "What's wrong?"

"One of the tribe," he replied. Shooting a glance through the sliding back door, he added, "Let me bring Rini over first. I'd rather not tell the story twice."

He slipped out onto the patio and crossed toward Rini's small domicile in quick strides. Elaina huffed, blowing a loose lock of hair out of her face, and started ladling batter over the waffle iron.

Moments later, Gavri returned, with a bright-eyed and nervous Rini in tow. Elaina stepped forward to give the sweet hare a good morning hug and kiss on the cheek before resuming her watch over the waffles.

"Okay, Gavri," Rini said, taking a seat in one of the barstools pulled up to the kitchen island. "What's wrong? Are your mother and Timofei all right?"

"Yes, and Bernard." He slumped onto the stool beside her. "But one of the tribe was attacked last night. Polina. She... did not survive."

Kolya set down the mixing bowl he'd been stirring, his expression darkening. Rini let out a pained gasp, clasping her hands over her heart. "No.... not Polina!"

Gavri turned to Elaina. "Polina is—*was*—one of our wolves. You saw her at the meeting place when I took you there to meet Nikita. Yellow coat, like saffron. She had a mate, but he got sick some years back. Pancreatic cancer. They had two boys."

Elaina swallowed back a hard lump in her throat. "How old?"

"Oldest boy's eight. Old enough to understand. Younger's only five... he might not... might not—"

He broke off in a strange, rumbling growl.

"Did they say how she died?" Kolya asked, though Elaina imagined she already knew.

"*Vukodlak,*" Gavri snarled.

"How could they?" Rini's big brown eyes glistened with tears. "Just... just how *could* they?"

Elaina took a step back, feeling faintly wobbly. She rested a hand on the counter to steady herself.

"The *vukodlak* have no sense of honor or mercy, Rini," Kolya said softly. "You know that."

"But she was a mother! Her two boys... they'll..."

"They will be taken care of," Gavri assured her. "The pack would never let her pups come to harm."

"How did it happen?" Elaina asked. "Did she get lost somehow? End up somewhere they hunt?"

Gavri's ice-blue eyes flashed with anger. "No. They came onto our lands. They attacked her in her *home.*"

He paused, shooting a cautious glance at Rini, then continued in a miserable voice. "The boys were there when it happened."

Rini uttered a short cry and buried her face in her hands. With a heavy sigh, Gavri extended an arm around her to hug her close.

"They've killed one of the tribe?" Elaina's head hurt. Her mouth tasted sour, and it seemed as if a foul smell had all at once invaded their little circle. "What does it mean?"

"It means they grow bolder." Gavri shook his head. "They have always wished to drive us out of our lands, *krasavitsa*. Sometimes, they lash out to remind us."

"*Sometimes*," Kolya corrected. "*This* makes two provocations within a week. One of them fatal."

"And yours could have *been* fatal," Elaina whispered. She still worried it had been his own tribal brothers who had attacked Kolya, however. Out to make a point, or to drive away the man they blamed for the incursion.

"There is nothing we can do." Gavri looked down at his own hands, as though they'd been the ones to murder the mother wolf in front of her two cubs. He clenched his fists, and Elaina thought she could read his mind in that moment—*If I had agreed to become alpha,* he might have been thinking, *could I have stopped this? Would those boys still have their mother, if it had been me instead of Nikita leading us?*

Too late to decide that now.

The four of them stood in silence. No one seemed to know what to say next. All at once Rini looked up from her contemplation and swore in Russian.

"Elaina!" Slipping down from the barstool, she bustled behind the counter to join Elaina and snatch the ladle from her hand. Elaina stared wide-eyed at the girl, startled.

"The waffles, silly thing." Rini shooed Elaina from the counter, wiping her eyes as she took over. "You're letting them burn."

THE NEWS OF POLINA'S MURDER hung like a wraith over the morning. After breakfast, Gavri retired to his office, no doubt to bury himself in some detailed and difficult work on one of his metal pieces. Rini, looking wilted and battling a persistent spill of quiet tears, decided to get a head start on the washing—a task which would conveniently allow her to be alone in the laundry room. That left Elaina and Kolya to work through awkward grief together. Elaina hadn't really ever met Polina, so Kolya told her about the woman, who had apparently been stalwart and athletic, and one hell of a mother.

"The way she protected her boys, you'd think she was a bear, not a wolf." Kolya gazed, distracted, at some vague spot on the ceiling as he spoke. They sat together on the sectional sofa in the living room, warm morning light pouring in on them. "We grew up with her, Gavri and I. Though she was probably six or seven years older than us."

Neither one of them spoke about the *vukodlak*, although Elaina wanted to. *Another time,* she told herself, and patiently listened to Kolya's old stories of Polina, and the pack when he'd been young, and the bonds they'd all shared... before his exile.

"You and Nikita weren't always enemies, I take it," Elaina said.

"We're not really enemies now." Kolya shifted, putting his arm around her and pulling her close. "He's made his decision because he believes it necessary, not because he bears any personal grudge against me."

It's ignorant and stupid bigotry. Elaina pressed her lips into a fine line but held back her contempt. She twined her fingers with Kolya's and relaxed against him.

Shortly after eleven, Rini peeked out from her hideaway and announced she'd be starting lunch soon. "Gavri asked for borscht. Beef and beet. Would you two like the same?"

"Yes," Kolya answered for them both. As Rini disappeared into the kitchen, he told Elaina, "It will be a good meal for you, before the hunt. Protein and energy."

"Sounds just fine to me."

Gavri emerged from his study when Rini called them to the table, and they ate together. Rini had opted for a version of the soup with beets only, ladling it up from a smaller pot beside the first before joining them at the table. As usual, Gavri gave her meatless option an exaggerated look of befuddlement and shook his head. She gave him a playful slap on the arm, and though it was half-hearted, it seemed a sign the worst of the shock and grief had started to ease.

"Shower," Gavri commanded, pointing a finger at Elaina as soon as she finished her borscht. "We're going to hike to the hunting grounds and it's a good ways from here. A long walk through thick woods. You'll want to wash off very thoroughly with a neutral soap, no shampoo, and then put on unscented deodorant."

Elaina gave an obedient nod. All thoughts of Polina and the awful attack fled; the time had come, at last, for her to put herself to the test. Gavri got up from the table and walked out the back door, heading in the direction of the lawn equipment shed, while she stood and carried her bowl to the sink.

Kolya followed her upstairs. As Elaina undressed and climbed into the shower, he crossed his arms over his chest and leaned against the counter. "How do you feel?"

"Anxious," she replied. The low drone of the lawnmower began outside. "But... in a sort of good way, I suppose. Intimidated, but eager to get out there. Excited."

"Anything I can go over with you before we set out?"

Elaina laughed, the sound soft and close in the steam. "I guess everything!"

Kolya snorted, but when she peered out from behind the glass shower door, he smiled at her. She held out her hand for a bar of unscented soap, and he retrieved one from the cabinet to pass to her.

After her shower, she and Kolya met Gavri on the patio, and the three of them awaited Grisha's return. If her mates hadn't warned her head of time, she'd have been baffled when Gavri pointed out the heap of freshly mown grass clippings he'd collected and told her, "Go roll around in that, and get the smell on you. Even your clothes. Get some in your hair, if you can."

She blinked at him. She'd known she'd have to do something like this, but the utter seriousness with which he pronounced it made her feel silly. Elaina tried to maintain a somber expression and simply nod her understanding, but then, like bubbles rising to the surface, she couldn't contain her grin. She tried to suppress the giggles and ended up giving an indelicate snort—and then she lost it. She doubled over, choking on laughter, and tried not to look him in the face.

When she finally did look up, his dark, unamused expression threw her into snickers all over again. Behind her, Kolya tried to cover a chuckle by clearing his throat. Gavri cocked an eyebrow at the other wolf before switching his attention back to Elaina.

"All right, *krasavitsa*..."

In one smooth lunge he swept her into his arms. Elaina struggled and kicked, but her laughter had grown out of control, and she couldn't stop, even as she beat against his chest with her fists.

He carried her toward the pile of clippings. "If this is how you want it!"

"Gavri, stop!"

He dropped her unceremoniously onto the pile of grass, and Elaina wriggled and rolled to get back on her feet. All at once her dark black wolf jumped in with her, barking and pouncing at her, and with a shriek she tried to twist away. Seconds later, Kolya bounded over to join them, and the two big canines rolled her over and over in the sweet-smelling clippings.

"You jerks!" She laughed so hard tears had sprung to the corners of her eyes. "Do you have any idea how *itchy* this is going to be?"

They wrestled for several minutes before a third body toppled in with them: Grisha, rumbling and growling in his flat feline tone. His long, white tail whipped cuttings into the air, and in a renewed gale of laughter Elaina inhaled a mouthful and fell into a coughing fit.

"*Grisha!*"

He butted her with his head, nuzzling and *miaowing*. His whole body vibrated with a thunderous purr.

"All right, all right!" Elaina scrambled to her feet again. "Sure, it's all fun and games to you boys, isn't it?"

"They have the right idea," said a cool, husky voice behind her. Elaina spun. Adelaida had arrived, along with Timofei and a darker, stockier man who must be Adelaida's other remaining mate, Bernard.

Elaina ran her hands through her hair, struggling to tidy it and pull it back into a ponytail. "Hello! I didn't think you'd come."

I thought you'd be with Nikita and the rest of the pack. Mourning Polina without giving a thought to my *mates and their grief.*

She bit the insides of her cheeks to keep from spilling such uncharitable words. Adelaida, still strikingly poised and beautiful, nevertheless wore her own sorrow on her face. She'd made no attempt to hide it: her eyes still bore a faint redness and a gleam of unshed tears; her proud shoulders seemed every-so-slightly stooped, as though the collar of her coat hid an actual wooden yoke of some kind, bearing her slowly but surely down.

Despite these things, Gavri's mother stepped up to Elaina and pulled her into a polite, obligatory hug, planting a kiss on both her cheeks. Gavri and Kolya stood and shook themselves off, sending little bits of grass flying, and trotted up to greet Adelaida. Grisha, meanwhile, remained lounging in the grass, staring with an expression of cool, feline aloofness, and idly licked one paw.

"Now that you have masked her scent," Adelaida asked Gavri, "are we ready to begin?"

The large black wolf dipped his head in a nod. Adelaida took a step back, extending a hand toward Timofei, and Gavri's father came forward to join them. On Adelaida's other side, Bernard silently began unbuttoning his shirt.

"I brought something for you, little one." With her free hand, Adelaida beckoned Elaina closer. Wariness made Elaina hesitate for just a second, but she sensed no duplicity in the alpha female's words. She obliged Adelaida, and as she did Timofei produced a long, rough-hewn object from a duffel bag at his side.

"A spear." Adelaida took it ceremoniously from her mate and handed it to Elaina. "Since, as of now, the mother has asked you to accomplish this task without the benefit of claws and teeth."

Wide-eyed, Elaina took the weapon. The shaft had been made of a rich, hand-carved and polished wood, glossy and beautiful. The blade, fashioned of carved bone, bore a familiar symbol etched into its rough surface: a more stylized version of the pack's icon, the running wolf she'd seen embroidered on Nikita's shirt. A set of leather cords dangled from the neck of the spear, adorned with beads and two sharp canine teeth at the ends.

"Mine," Adelaida explained. "Crafted when I still led our pack. If you seek to please our spirit mother and prove yourself worthy as an alpha female, I think it suitable you should bear the weapon of an alpha in your first hunt."

Elaina met the woman's gaze, a rush of heat rising at the back of her neck. "Are you... are you sure?"

Adelaida wrinkled her nose as though the question had confused her. She fiddled with the clasp of her luxurious coat and Timofei helped her remove it. "Of course I'm sure, girl. Do I strike you as an indecisive person?"

Despite her nervousness, Elaina chuckled. "No. No, you really don't."

Bernard had shucked his clothing and taken on his animal form, which Elaina was surprised to see was *not* a wolf. Rather, the dark-haired German man had traded his shape for that of a short, shaggy creature somewhere between a badger and a bear. A wolverine. Padding over to join them, he gave Adelaida a quick, gentle bump, as if to say *let's go, then*. If Adelaida felt hurried, she didn't show it: she took her time with the buttons of her crisp, stylish blouse—a rosy cream color, today—and Elaina found an excuse to turn away from the woman before she could remove any more. She'd gotten used to the nakedness of the *oboroten* when they changed their forms, but watching Gavri's mother disrobe? *Too* weird.

In a moment, a female wolf with a thick coat of black and silver joined Gavri and Kolya, with Bernard the wolverine trotting close behind. Elaina took a deep, quiet breath, watching the shapeshifters assemble, readying herself to go.

"Good luck, little one." Timofei patted her on the shoulder and offered her a warm smile. His thick Russian accent warmed her, completing the strange gesture of approval Adelaida had started with the spear. Elaina had not expected Gavri's parents to take any sort of interest in her success—in fact, she'd expected the exact opposite.

"Thank you," she told Timofei. Then, addressing the small pack of hunters assembled before her, she said, "All right. I think we're all ready. Let's go!"

Gavri led the way, with Grisha following jauntily on his heels. Though Gavri had said Grisha knew how to hunt with the wolves, Elaina had the distinct sense the big cat didn't belong in the lead and, as usual, wanted to cause some trouble being an asshole and taunting her beta wolf. Now and again he got too close and Gavri gave a snap at his big white paws, driving Grisha aside. Her big cat only moved right along, flicking his tail.

After Gavri—and misbehaving Grisha—Adelaida trotted, small and lithe. Bernard and Kolya flanked Elaina, loping at a slower pace while the other three ranged ahead. The group moved in near silence; even Elaina had donned an old and soft pair of lightweight trail runners, and took care where she stepped to avoid rustling any leaves or scraping any rocky patches of dirt. Still, to her it seemed she must be the loudest thing in the woods. None of the *oboroten* gave any indication they noticed, however, so she pushed on, hoping only she heard the blundering cacophony of her clumsy human gait.

They hiked northwest, in search of musk deer. They'd decided to avoid reindeer or antelope, saving Elaina the risk of being gored by horns; even male musk deer lacked antlers, and instead had a bizarre, vampire-like pair of small tusks. After almost an hour of walking, Gavri lowered his head to the ground and began sniffing, searching for a trail. Elaina studied the trees and bushes, looking for the signs she'd grown so used to picking out over the last couple of days: nibbled leaves; cropped patches of grass; tufts of short, dark hair. Gavri and Grisha ranged ahead until she lost sight of them, and Adelaida loped slyly in and out of the trees on either side. Even Bernard had begun to pull ahead, leaving Elaina and Kolya to take up the rear.

But when we find the deer, it will be my job to select the one we take down.

A warm rush of hungry pride filled her chest. With the spear in her hand and her big russet wolf at her side, she slid into a primal, predatory place in her mind. The sharp scent of the berry bushes and deep, earthy soil pleased her; the rustle and call of birds overhead pricked her excitement. They moved with focus, keen on their goal, and yet it reminded her of her race with the spirit Inferi through the moonlit fields. A game of tag—of Bobcats and Rabbits, which she had played in her childhood summer camp days. Though they hunted prey, a kill they would use for sustenance and resources, a living heart they would stop with their claws and teeth, still her heart raced with the pleasure of it. And something else. A unity. Camaraderie. Her first task—the spirit walk—had been a lonely task. A solitary journey, and she'd been afraid, so afraid of being lost again. Today, she ran with the pack, *her* pack. Like the night under the stars when Inferi had led her in a merry chase, whisking away doubt and fear to replace it with the thrill of *running* together—

Run with me. Always run with me.

A bright patch of raw bark caught her eye, and she slowed. Kolya altered his gait, heeling close to her side as she approached a pale, soaring aspen tree and inspected the spot where the dry outer bark had been scuffed and worn away.

"Musk deer, you think?" She knelt to touch the tree. "Maybe a different kind of deer, though. Or maybe a mountain sheep, with its horns."

The big russet wolf scented the air, tail sweeping low against the woodland floor. He threw a glance back and forth, as though searching for the others.

"Go ahead and call them back." She'd noticed a low, broken patch of raspberry brambles, and she thought she spied hoof prints amid the fallen woodland twigs and leaves just past it. A triumphant thrill surged through her.

Kolya gave a hesitant sniff and a low *huff,* then bounded off to fetch the others. Elaina, in a crouch, followed the direction the prints seemed to lead. Yes, they hunted as a pack, and yes, Gavri and Grisha probably had a lead on the deer herds already... but *she'd* spied this trail, and a sparkling bright excitement trickled through her veins as she crept along.

Past the raspberry bushes she found a sharper set of prints. They pointed east, and she knew from her hide-and-seek games with Gavri and Kolya a tributary of the river ran through the area nearby.

So our friend the deer had himself a good scratch against a tree, some raspberry leaves, and then off this way for a fresh drink of water. Her grip around the spear tightened and she sped up, taking long, careful strides. How proud Gavri would be, if she managed to track and kill the creature all on her own and bring back a lovely set of tusks or elegant bones for carving into art like dreamcatchers or tiny wolfish figurines. Her imagination turned to a whole wolf-inspired chess set she could make for him, and a sharp, predatory smile spread across her face. *It'd blow him away!*

She pondered over what sort of gifts she could also make for Grisha and Kolya, and practically stumbled right into the stream. Elaina backpedaled gracelessly as her foot skidded on a slippery clutch of river rocks, and lost her balance, tumbling to the dirt.

"*Ow.*" She winced and rubbed her hip. The bright flash of three deer disappeared into the undergrowth across the water.

"Damnit!"

Elaina stood, dusting damp soil and leaves from her jeans. At least none of the others had witnessed her falling on her ass while sending her prey racing off and out of sight. *Nice job, little girl,* she scolded herself, mentally affecting her best Grisha impersonation.

A snort drew her attention. A flash of certainty— her asshole snow leopard *had* witnessed her fall, somehow snuck up on her just in time to see her awkward, stupid fumble—lit up her mind like startled bird taking flight. Then, she saw the creature at the water's edge, with its dark, shining eyes fixed on her.

The boar—a massive male specimen with yellowed, fearsome tusks—pivoted from its peaceful, quiet drinking place, and stamped the ground with an agitated whine. Its coarse, thick black bristles stood up like the raised hackles of an angry dog. It chomped its teeth at her, letting out an ugly wet sound somewhere between a squeal and a naked, human cry.

Elaina's chest flooded with cold panic as she scrambled backward in the dirt. The pig lumbered after her. With another snort and a violent gnashing of its teeth, it squared its shoulders and stiffened its front legs.

Oh... Oh, spirit mother... is it going to charge?

Her back hit a tree. She pushed herself up against it, gripping Adelaida's spear in both shaking hands. A howl filled her ears, not the familiar howl of her beautiful wolves, or the howl of *any* earthly wolf, but a distant, ghostly, echoing cry. The voice of Inferi, the spirit who had run with Elaina through the night. A hectic, delirious strength flooded her limbs and a part of her brain rose giddily to the challenge—*I have a spear, don't I? I'm here for a hunt, aren't I?*—but at the same time, she couldn't push aside the very real knowledge of the danger. She stood alone, without her pack. And those *tusks...*

The pig gnashed again, froth bubbling up along its mouth and the violent curl of its muzzle over massive ivories. It feinted a lunge in her direction, uttering an angry series of grunts and squeals.

Her grip on the spear tightened. A dozen conflicting directions raced through her brain. *I need to run. I* can't *run, running will make it chase me. It is my prey. I am here to kill it! But this wasn't the prey we expected, and I know almost nothing about boars except they bite, and those teeth—*

Another howl rose up in her mind, and on the heels of it, the song of Diezana lilted faintly. Diezana's voice led her children away from danger; but here *was* danger, a great wild hog Elaina hadn't been prepared for. Why had none of her mates *smelled* the damn thing? The foul, unabashed odor of musk and swampy mud rose from its hide, and its hot breath reeked like sour mash.

The pig's dark eyes glinted. With a final hungry snort, it broke their stand-off, rushing at her.

Elaina whirled away from the tree she'd braced against, and a half-second later the boar crashed into it with a loud, thick crack and a jumbled mix of squeals. Elaina spun, lifting the spear and jabbing for the creature's side, but hit it at a bad angle: the weapon skated, nearly harmless, across one broad, tough shoulder.

The boar shrieked and wheeled for her, charging again and forcing Elaina to duck into a roll. Grisha had playfully pounced her enough times during their practice to give her some feel for the movement, and she came up on her knees with the spear still in her hands. When the pig lunged a third time, foam spraying from its muzzle as it squealed, Elaina dropped back, bracing herself with the spear jutting up and out.

This time the pig hit the weapon straight-on, and bellowed with outrage. The spear jabbed into its muscular foreleg, and when the boar jerked back it nearly yanked the spear from Elaina's grip. She pulled her weapon free, though, and stood, thinking she must strike it again *now* while it retreated. The pig surprised her, though, advancing and butting her hard in the stomach, sending her into the stream.

The water in this spot ran shallow, luckily for Elaina, but she hit the smooth, rounded rocks with a shout of pain. Those would leave plenty of bruises in the morning. She'd managed to keep hold of the spear though, thankfully, and as the boar raced at her—*Is it still coming? Even wounded?*—she sat up and raised the weapon in front of her.

A series of excited, agitated growls filled her ears as a pair of wolves and a dark, shaggy wolverine come bounding toward her attacker. Behind Gavri, Kolya, and Bernard, sleek Adelaida and slinking Grisha followed, ranging wide to close off escape. But before any of her pack could leap for the pig, it crashed into her at frightening speed, and the spear sank deep into its barrel of a chest.

Elaina fell back, crying out. Ice-cold water soaked through her simple white shirt and splashed her face; she lay half-submerged with the pig hanging over her, blood gushing from its wound in a hot spray. It gave a few weak, dying squeals, foam and saliva dripping from its muzzle.

The weight of it shook the spear in hand and it started to slip. Elaina released the weapon and rolled to the side with a short yelp; the pig crashed down into the stream behind her, blood and gore washing away.

She breathed a sigh of relief. *Rini will probably have a heart attack when I bring her these blood-soaked clothes, though...*

"A *boar?*"

Gavri knelt over her, human and naked again. "Elaina, what possessed you to attack a boar? With none of us here to help?"

"She wasn't after the boar." Kolya splashed into the stream and reached out a hand to help her up. "She found a musk deer trail. I know. I scented it. The boar must have been downwind."

As her big russet boy pulled her up, Grisha and Bernard hauled the pig off the spear and laid it out along the shore. Adelaida remained in her wolf form, ears alert, watching the clearing.

"Right." Elaina came to her feet and pulled her wet mop of curls away from her face. Pointing in the direction the deer had gone, she said, "I saw three of them across the water. The pig surprised me, though."

"Surprise or not," Grisha put in, "you killed it. Diezana's second task is met."

She tried to hide her obvious pleasure, but a smile crept across her face anyway. "Well, only by accident."

Grisha smirked. "Maybe she won't hold it against you."

Bernard offered her the spear and she took it back with a word of thanks. Adelaida, seated patiently on one of the large stones, favored Elaina with a secretive lupine grin.

CHAPTER SIX

ELAINA WOKE UP THE NEXT morning *starving*.

Not for food. Grisha had promised to prepare some boar bacon but as mouthwatering as it sounded, breakfast was the farthest thing from her mind. She surfaced from her dreams—wild dreams full of lithe, silvery bodies running under the gorgeous spread of northern lights—to an immediate arousal tingling over her skin. The satin sheets of Gavri and Kolya's bed slithered deliciously under her; she'd slept naked and hadn't bothered with the luxurious warm furs usually piled atop the sheets. Feverish joy had suffused her from head to toe, and she had no need to cover herself.

Gavri and Kolya sprawled to either side of her. Both still slept, their easy breathing deep and untroubled. She couldn't stand the wild desire running electric through her body, and she vowed they wouldn't sleep long.

Sliding from the bed, Elaina indulged in a long stretch. Dawn hadn't even broken yet: through the wide window overlooking gorgeous Stolby wilds, the thin, tremulous light of sunrise still hovered just behind the line of the mountains. A quiet, golden time, like a gentle prelude.

It would be hours before anyone came to the house for business. Even Rini wouldn't arrive until at least eight in the morning. Elaina and all three of her mates were blessedly alone.

She tiptoed out of the master bedroom. Grisha had stayed the night for once, falling asleep on the couch in the living room, succumbing to the lazy warmth of the cozy fire. Elaina had even tried to wake him when she, Gavri, and Kolya retired for the evening, meaning to offer him one of the guest rooms for the night. Grisha and her two wolves got along just fine as far being part of Elaina's stable of studs and sharing her affection, but so far, the snow leopard had not seemed comfortable sleeping in the wolves' bed.

Making love in that bed, however, had not posed a problem.

Elaina slipped downstairs on silent feet and found her beautiful feline shifter stretched shirtless on the couch. She tickled his belly with a soft grin, and Grisha stirred, rolling into his own satisfying stretch. Those wonderful, vivid green eyes opened, lazy and still dreamy with sleep, and his usual smarmy expression crossed his face.

"Morning," Elaina whispered. Taking his hand, she tugged at him. "Come with me. I need you."

"Oh, do you?" Grisha sat up, twining his arms around her and pulling her into an embrace. "I can oblige you right here, little girl. Bend you over the arm of this couch..."

Elaina returned his wicked smile but shook her head. "Upstairs. I need *them,* too."

Grisha raised both eyebrows in a suggestive expression but followed as she asked. She led him back to the master bedroom and her two still-sleeping wolves. As Grisha slid off the jeans he'd slept in, Elaina leaned over Gavri and planted a kiss on his mouth. Her hand strayed down between his legs and stroked him to a quick morning erection.

Gavri murmured with curious joy, nuzzling her. His fingers closed over hers and guided her strokes. At the same time Grisha closed in behind her, kissing the back of her neck and rubbing his hardened cock against her.

"Wake up," she whispered in Gavri's ear. As he stirred and rose up on his elbows, blinking sleep from his eyes, she crawled up onto the bed and across him, prowling over Kolya and kissing him as well.

"Come, my darlings... *oh,* I want you all so much..."

"Look at you," Grisha whispered. As Elaina shifted to straddle Kolya, the snow leopard circled the bed and climbed up to join them, leaning over her and wrapping one arm around her stomach. "The hunt has put you in heat."

In heat? Is that what this is?

Kolya opened his eyes, smiling as he gazed up at her. Elaina gently ground herself against his groin, and—as quickly as Gavri had—he grew hard at her touch.

"Make love to me," she crooned to him, stroking his cheek with the back of one hand. Glancing at Gavri again, she beckoned him over. "You too. All of you. I want all of you."

Gavri rolled onto his hands and knees and crawled to her. Cradling her head in one palm, he kissed her, tongue invading her mouth to dance with hers.

Grisha rocked against her. A purr rumbled to life in his throat, and he guided the head of his cock to her tight rear entrance.

"Wait!" She shrunk away from him and leaned over to reach into the drawer of the bedside table. She produced a bottle of slick personal lubricant she knew her wolves kept there, and passed it to him.

As Grisha prepared them both, Elaina slid slowly back and forth atop Kolya's rigid member. Her omega wolf groaned, and reached for her breasts, caressing them and squeezing them with tender, but greedy affection. At last, Elaina reached down between them and guided his cock home, sighing with delight as he filled her, thrilling her, a hot, gratifying stud.

"I'm so hungry for you," she whispered between kisses. "Please... please, until I can't take anymore. I want it so, *so* much."

"Spoken like a true alpha female." Gavri rose to his knees, stroking his lovely flesh, reaching out with his free hand to tangle his fingers in her hair.

Elaina uttered a short, startled sound of delight as Grisha—now wet and slick and smooth—slid into her, triggering her body to tighten around him. Elaina moaned, tipsy with the brazen pleasure, thrilled almost straight to orgasm with the dual invasion of two men at once.

And Gavri made three. He came nearer, straightening on his knees, and Elaina happily took him into her mouth. Kolya and Grisha found a rhythm, Grisha's thrusts rocking her on Kolya's cock, satisfying her so deeply her nipples tingled, and her entire sex trembled right on the edge of climax. Gavri rolled his head back with a groan as she ran her tongue over his crown, savoring the heady, intoxicating taste of his flesh. She'd never felt so full before, so gloriously satisfied, and yet the primal part of her hungered for even more. She never wanted to leave them or this bed; she wanted their hands, their tongues, their rigid and demanding cocks, pleasuring her until she slipped right out of her mind, overdosed on bliss.

Her first orgasm came almost too soon, the overwhelming pleasure of Grisha and Kolya too much to control. Her arousal climbed too high at last and before she knew it, she was shuddering and crying out with joy, reveling in the sweet tremors as both men refused to stop, driving harder, deeper into her, dragging out the climax until they fucked a second from her.

She'd pulled away from Gavri in her sudden, urgent swell of excitement, and her beta wolf gave an urgent sound, guiding her back to him. She welcomed him again and in seconds he came, hot seed filling her mouth, and she swallowed hungrily, drunkenly, dizzy with delight.

Grisha came next, driving himself deep enough to border on the verge of pain, and Elaina wanted to shriek his name as he throbbed within her, spilling himself into her, growling in her ear and clutching her tight against him. He withdrew before it was over, marking her round, sweet bottom with wicked jets of his seed.

"Yes, *yes,*" she begged, rocking herself harder against Kolya, desperate for another uncontrollable rise. Kolya closed his hands around her hips and guided her, no, *held* her down on him, driving up into her deepest, most intimate reaches until he threw back his head and howled. His cock swelled and pulsed within her, pumping into her, filling her. When it was over, he didn't withdraw right away. Instead, Kolya covered her face in starving kisses and gave each pebbled pink nipples a lavish suck. Elaina trembled, full of bliss, on top of him.

"More?" she begged. "I still want you... I want all of you, forever. Never stop, please..."

Kolya buried his face against her, murmuring in Russian, as Gavri stroked her hair and kissed her naked shoulder, neck, and temple.

Grisha crawled up on her other side to stroke her face and turn her toward him for a deep kiss.

"I'm sure we can oblige you," he purred. Gavri tugged her toward him next, claiming her mouth with a long, sweet kiss of his own.

"*Da, krasavitsa...* give you every pleasure you desire."

"You," she repeated. "All of you. Goddess, how I love you..."

They played for hours as the sun rose outside, bathing the room in rosy, warm light. Their frantic, needful mating gave way to slow, tender lovemaking, and long stretches of lazy kissing and caressing, even a sensual massage delivered by Grisha. Gavri and Kolya lay on either side of her, lavishing attention on her breasts until she writhed and wriggled against the satin sheets.

At long last, they were interrupted by a polite rap on the door. "Sorry to break up the bacchanalia," came Rini's voice from the other side. She must have arrived for work some time ago and busied herself with downstairs chores to give them their privacy. "But Baba Yasmin is here, to chat with you about your progress."

Elaina sat up. "Oh, wow... what time is it?"

"Nearly noon." Gavri got up and stretched, displaying his gorgeous lean body. "Think you can break from this rampant sex orgy long enough to see the shamaness?"

"I'll need a shower first." Elaina assessed the state of their disheveled little love nest. "And we should probably tidy up."

"Isn't that what your housekeeper is for?" Grisha gave a wide yawn.

"We don't make Rini clean up after our... amorous pursuits," Gavri said.

Elaina curled herself against Kolya, a rush of adoration filling her as he squeezed her close and kissed her brow. "Will you come wash my hair?"

"Of course, *krasavitsa*. But let's hurry. It's bad form to keep the wise woman waiting."

Grisha donned his pants again and tipped them a careless wave. "I'll just have a quick rinse in the guest bathroom and head down to meet her. You three, don't take long."

Despite the interruption, Elaina found herself still yearning. While Gavri stripped the bed of their messy sheets, she nearly dragged Kolya after her into the shower. She pulled him to her, claiming him with ravenous kisses. Even after hours of libidinous indulgence, she craved him like breath, drank him in like fresh, clean, cold water after years of drought.

Gavri joined them, sliding in behind Kolya and pressing his own mouth to the larger man's muscular shoulder. He kissed Kolya's throat, his jaw, and finally his ear, growling playfully as he nibbled his lover's earlobe.

Elaina, standing on tiptoe, pulled Gavri into a kiss with her.

"You two..." In the growing steam, her voice sounded hushed and rough and close. "I love you. I love you both so much..."

"*Krasavitsa.*" Kolya slid his hands around her waist, holding her close to him, letting her feel the weight of his renewed erection. Wolves could mate continuously for hours, her mates once told her, and have very little need for rest. "Are you already hungry for more?"

"I feel like I could stay here all day with you, making love." She stroked both hands along the wet, rigid shape of his cock. "But right now, I think someone else wants his turn."

"Too right." Gavri nipped Kolya's earlobe again and rocked his hips against his pack-brother's body. "I've been watching you fuck our female for days, Kol. Much as I love it, I've needed a go at *you* for a while."

Probably since before Kolya ended up in the hospital. Still stroking her lovely russet wolf in one hand, Elaina reached the other one up to run her fingers through Gavri's dark hair. She knew they'd never stopped being mates themselves, just because she'd come along to join them. Gavri's ears and eyes and teeth bore a distinctly lupine cast now, as he rubbed himself suggestively at Kolya's backside.

"My beautiful men," she crooned, kissing one, then the other. "I've been so selfish."

"Never think it, *krasavitsa.*" Gavri growled hungrily as he slid his hands to Kolya's waist. "But I am your beta male, and I've a deep urge to remind our omega of his place."

Kolya grinned, a sweet and hopeful expression. Elaina ran her tongue over her lips, thrumming with anticipation, as Gavri kissed Kol again and slid one big hand between them, guiding himself into Kolya's tight entrance.

With a short gasp of surprise and excitement, Kolya leaned into Elaina, planting his hands on the shower tiles to either side of her as Gavri thrust into him. Elaina gave out a breathy, cheerful laugh and met him with a kiss. In her hand, his cock swelled and stiffened even more—Elaina quickened her strokes, murmuring heated encouragement.

The spray of the shower went everywhere, as Gavri—gripping Kolya hard by the hips—worked himself in a slow but forceful rhythm. He whispered in hot, hoarse Russian, between nips and nibbles at Kolya's neck and ear, and though she didn't understand the language Elaina knew he must be pouring filthy, wicked promises on their sweet Kolya. The omega wolf grunted and panted, whispering back feverish please of "Yes, please... *yes*..."

As Gavri's heated rhythm increased, Kolya tossed back his head with a moan. Water pattered and ran down his chest, enticing Elaina to lean forward and run her tongue over his warm, tanned skin, planting kisses along his collarbone.

"Can you take him inside you, *krasavitsa?*" Gavri's eyes blazed. "Try. I want to fuck him until he comes inside of you, as I come inside him."

Kolya moaned before she could answer. "I can't—Gavri, love, I'm—already—"

His cock twitched in her hand. With a groan of pleasure he came, cock throbbing, sending jet after jet of slick semen across Elaina's naked belly. She laughed in surprise, tingling with pleasure, kissing him and petting him and whispering his name.

Gavri cursed in Russian, but he had a smile on his face. Murmuring in Kolya's ear in a harsh, scolding tone, he renewed his thrusts, tugging his omega lover against him. Moments later, his words broke down into urgent, voiceless growls, and he gave several hard, stiff, deep thrusts, reaching his own climax with a low and lustful growl.

By the time they finally made their way downstairs, Elaina, Gavri, and Kolya had left Baba Yasmin waiting more than half an hour. Trying not to grin like a silly teenager caught behind the bleachers, Elaina greeted the wise woman, who sat in the same leather chair Adelaida favored. In it, willowy Yasmin looked almost like a delicate porcelain doll. Although dolls rarely had the rich, fine lines of aged wisdom, or the prim, lean features of a sharp Hollywood starlet in her venerable, fabulous golden years. She held a glass of iced green tea in one hand, and a plate of lightly nibbled toast rested on the arm of her chair. Rini sat with her, mending one of Kolya's shirts and chatting pleasantly on in their shared language of Russian and native *oboroten*.

Glancing up at Elaina and her mates as they entered the room, Rini *tsk'd* at them. "And they say *rabbits* mate uncontrollably."

"Hush," Gavri warned her with a playful flick at her ear.

Blushing furiously, Elaina took a seat on the sofa. "It's the pheromone thing again, I think. The... Wilden Effect?"

"Whitten Effect," Rini corrected, and cleanly tied off her thread, cutting it with a snip of tiny sewing scissors.

"Where did Grisha go?" Elaina didn't want to discuss their hedonistic sex play any more in front of Yasmin, and desperately changed the subject.

"Stepped out for a cigarette." Yasmin had a small bite of toast. "You should break him of the habit. Very bad for his health."

Elaina frowned. "But Baba Yasmin, you—"

"*I* am an old woman." Yasmin brushed aside the concern. "Grisha is a young buck, and one I assume you wish to *keep* bucking for some time."

When Elaina couldn't find a suitable answer, Baba Yasmin smiled with sharp glee. "I mean your rock climbing adventures, of course. I know how much you enjoy them."

Wicked woman! Elaina bit back an unruly burst of laughter and composed herself. Letting down her wet hair from the quick, sloppy ponytail she'd tied it in after their shower, she began combing her fingers through it. "What's brought you by, Baba Yasmin?"

"I've come to discuss your tasks. Grisha told me you managed to slay a boar on your hunt yesterday. Not at all the sort of game I expected for you on your first try, but very impressive."

Elaina tried not to preen, but imagined her pleasure must be clear on her face. "Thank you."

"If Grisha is correct in his interpretation, your third task begins immediately. While the blood and flesh of your kill are still fresh and worthy. Tonight, I would suggest."

"That's the consecration of a shrine to Diezana," Elaina recalled. As she spoke, Gavri excused himself to begin their laundry, and Kolya ducked into the kitchen to return with a glass of tea for himself and Elaina. As she accepted hers, he sat beside her and produced a hairbrush, taking over the task of managing her curls.

"The building of a shrine is a complex matter." Yasmin circled a finger around the rim of her own glass. "A very *personal* matter. Were you building a family shrine, or a shrine of the home, you could rely on your mates to aid you, but given the feat you are attempting, I expect you know this one must be done alone."

"Well, not *entirely* alone."

The front door clicked shut as Grisha returned, the faint whiff of cigarette smoke lingering about him. Elaina contemplated Baba Yasmin's suggestion and decided to discuss it with him later. She reached out for Grisha, hoping he'd take a seat on her other side, but he only let his fingers trail across hers as he passed, dropping her a kiss before he found a spot suitably separate from them all, and dropped casually into it.

"Elaina has already taken up a role of alpha here, among us," he said. "Whether or not she ultimately wins her challenge with Nikita, for now she's leader of *this* circle. Her pack will be part of any totem she builds. At least, if she builds it right."

His expression troubled Elaina. Cool and dispassionate, barely a hint of emotion as he added the last part. Grisha was a pessimist, naturally. It did sting, though, to have him purr and kiss her eyelids and caress her cheeks in a luxurious morning of passion, only to watch him take on this look of doubt in her now.

"The ritual itself—and finding the place of your offering—is on you." He cocked a finger at Elaina. "But I may have a little something up my sleeve to help out."

"Oh?" She sipped her tea, arching an eyebrow at him.

"Yeah. We all might. First, though, you'll need to know what it *means* to create a shrine." The glint in his eyes reminded her of how he'd looked at her in the beginning, with a generous helping of arrogance and disdain for the human outsider stepping into his world. The disdain might be gone now, but the sly feline superiority remained. Yasmin had assigned him to teach Elaina, though; that hadn't changed, regardless he now shared her bed. Still, nodding politely, she mentally resolved to knock the *smug* right out of him.

"So where do we start?" she asked.

"*Learning* of the goddess, and our ways, I should think," Yasmin said. "There is a very good deal you need to know about us, if you really believe you can lead us."

Elaina held her drinking glass in both hands, tapping her fingers lightly along the surface as she nodded. She didn't mention her second thoughts about the challenge to Nikita, or her growing sense of chagrin at having walked into these lands a stranger and immediately asserting she could be a leader. Yes, she exhibited traits many alpha females did, and yes, she felt compelled to join the tribe and learn their ways. She only doubted more and more that the fight for the role of alpha would be necessary, or helpful.

I should have approached Nikita differently. I should have done it all *differently.*

"And once you've taught me your lore and your ways?"

She smiled when she said it, a lopsided grin which made them both shake their heads. Learning the deep-rooted ways of the Siberian shapeshifters wouldn't be an endeavor for a single afternoon, and all of them knew it. No reason to say it out loud. At the same time, though, Yasmin and Grisha both understood what she meant, and what needed to be done.

"Then, you go out." Grisha waved a hand in a vague, *off you go* gesture. "Go where the goddess leads you. Listen to her voice. Discover the tribute you wish to make, within yourself."

"It's so typical you wouldn't actually answer me," Elaina grumbled at him. "What does any of that *mean?*"

Grisha shrugged. When she turned to Baba Yasmin for help, the wise woman gave her a serene gaze.

"Diezana is the mother of shapeshifters and the mother of these lands." She paused for another nibble of her toast. "Grisha is right. Listen to our story. Listen for her voice."

Elaina sighed and pinched the bridge of her nose. Kolya paused in brushing her hair long enough to lean forward and give her a consoling kiss on the top of her head.

CHAPTER SEVEN

IN THE BEGINNING, YASMIN TOLD her, there came the first tribe.

Thousands of years ago, before the continents shifted and before Siberia or Russia or even Asia existed, the first tribe of the *oboroten* lived on the ice, hunting caribou and fishing the frozen ocean for food. They were alone in the great, snow-covered north, cut off from other humans by thousands of miles of glacial tundra. They spoke a language even today's *oboroten* had forgotten. They tamed polecats and ravens to run and scout for them, and warn them when great predators ranged near, monstrous megafauna like saber-toothed tigers and short-faced bears.

Diezana belonged to these first people: the first shamaness born to them.

"Or," Grisha amended, "the first spiritual leader and teacher. What would become the role of each shamaness in the future."

In Diezana's time, though, the realms of the spirits were not known to the minds of human beings, and the people scraped for survival with bodies and souls which were like driftwood on the stormy ocean:

small in the face of nature; hard, but vulnerable; ultimately at the mercy of the elements.

"Famine drove our ancestors almost to extinction." Baba Yasmin spread her hands before her as though gazing over a great expanse. "An evil spirit set his face against them, and drove away the polecats and the ravens, the hunting dogs and their horses, and all the game they relied on to survive. The creatures of wing and hoof fled south over great glacial rifts, but the evil spirit sent down tempests of snow and ice, barring the way after them. Our people could not follow. Blizzards lasting weeks at a time devastated their shelters and killed many outright. The land's massive predators hunted down those who remained."

"Diezana left her people to search for passage to safer hunting grounds," Grisha took over. "She wandered far, and the spirits walked with her. She'd met a pack of dire wolves, and the spirits gave her the gift of their language. She ran with the wolves, and soon learned to hunt with them and sing their ancient songs. But then the wolves ran south and crossed the great glaciers, just as the caribou and tun and great horses had done, leaving Diezana alone, because she could not make the journey as a human."

Yasmin continued. "She cried out for her wolves. By then, she'd forgotten the language of humans and knew only how to yip and howl and sing in worship to the moon. She tried to follow the pack but became lost, and wandered alone and miserable, hungry and ill, for days."

Elaina hardly realized her mouth had fallen open as she listened, or that she'd taken Kolya's hand in hers and squeezed his fingers in anxious dread. *Lost alone in the snow.* Diezana had once been like her, crying out into the snowstorm, begging the wolves to save her.

"At last, the alpha female of the pack returned for her," Yasmin said. "The blizzards across the steppes—the works of the great adversary—blew down with terrible power, driving to keep them apart, but the wolf-mother persisted. She found her human pup, curled up and dying in the ice. When she bowed her head and touched her nose to Diezana's frozen lips, the breath of the wolf spirit entered Diezana's body. She became like them, trading flesh for four paws and a thick, silver coat. Her nose, ears and teeth became those of a hunter. The spirits blessed her with lithe speed to race against the wild gales and tempests of the enemy."

"You said she calls out to those near death." Elaina swept a wisp of curls away from her face. "The song. You said she sings to lead us *away* from death. It's because she died in that storm, isn't it?"

A rare smile of approval crossed Yasmin's face. "Diezana is no Euro-American ghost story, Elaina. Not your *lady in white* or *phantom hitchhiker*. We do not say she died... but *transformed*."

"Though you could look at it your way, too," Grisha added, and Elaina had the impression she'd hit on an important piece of the legend. Whether or not Diezana's heart stopped beating, or whether the woman—the *wolf*—who rose up from the snow was a spirit or a ghost, or the first human to learn the magic of shapechange, all those things largely came to the same thing. Diezana was *reborn*. The magic of the *oboroten*, of *shapeshifters,* was a magic of rebirth.

"So then she returned to the tribe?" she asked Yasmin.

"First, she ran with the wolves and crossed the impassable glaciers. She found the new grazing lands where the caribou and horses had gone. She ran with the wolf pack for many years, and almost forgot about humans entirely. Then one night, as she and the wolves sang the ancient songs, she remembered a time when she hadn't sung with them, but watched from a distance, hearing them with human ears and a human heart. When she remembered this, she became a human again, and then she remembered her people, and her promise to them to find new hunting grounds and shelter from the evil that persecuted them."

"*Then,* she returned," Grisha said. "Crossing back into the northern lands past the glaciers, and tracking down her people. When she found them again, three generations had passed, and only two of the tribe's elders remembered who she was. They had been children when she left; now, she could have been their grandchild. One of them denounced her and called her a witch. An agent of the adversary come to lead the last of them to their doom. The other called her blessed and asked her to teach them the secret of changing shape."

"I think I see where this is going." Elaina glanced from Grisha to Yasmin. "The tribe split down the middle, didn't they?"

"You're getting ahead of the story," Yasmin warned, her eyes sparkling like a child with a secret.

"Diezana convinced her people to follow her across the glaciers," Grisha explained. "She would teach them to become wolves, and together they could outrun the enemy's great storms. She led them to the edge of the glacier bridge and showed them how to change their forms."

"They didn't *exactly* split down the middle," Yasmin said. "Those who believed in Diezana and showed faith in her when she led them across the ice—those who embraced her and her ways—found the magic as she promised. They ran together to escape. But those who feared her and suspected her in their hearts were subverted by the evil spirit."

Elaina could picture it: two groups, equally desperate, beaten down and ravaged by the storms. "They changed... but they didn't become wolves."

Grisha gave a slow, solemn nod. "They became *vukodlak*. Wendigos. Skinwalkers."

"The broken ones." Kolya, who had remained silent through the retelling, rubbed one palm in circles over Elaina's back. Gavri had come back sometime during the story, and Elaina had been so engrossed she hadn't even noticed him take a seat on the floor by her knee. He leaned his head against her, as though listening to a campfire story, though he'd surely heard the legend of Diezana hundreds of times over the years.

"The first *vukodlak* attacked Diezana and her people on the glacier bridge." Yasmin paused to take a long sip of her tea, before coming to the end of the story. "Creatures from both groups were killed: some murdered, some lost in the storm and driven over the edge of the icy paths. Diezana and the first true shapeshifters found their way across... and the *vukodlak* followed."

"That's when your people came to this land?" Elaina asked. Yasmin nodded.

"Our people, and theirs," Grisha concluded darkly.

He hadn't meant to single out Kolya by saying it. Even so, Elaina sensed a tremble pass through her sweet russet wolf, and his hand dropped from her back. Turning in her seat, she embraced him.

"Don't pull away," she whispered at him. "I don't care what Nikita or the rest of them think. You don't belong to the enemy, Kol. You're not *theirs*. You're mine."

Kolya smiled at her, though it looked very sad. Stretching an arm around her, he pulled her in for a kiss. "*Spasibo, krasavitsa.* Thank you."

She sensed his pain. Taking both his hands in hers, she gazed into his eyes. "Come with me, Kol. To find a place for the shrine, I mean. He can come, right, Baba Yasmin?"

When she glanced at the wise woman, Yasmin gave a sage nod. "If you wish it. But the shrine must be yours alone."

"Do you want us to come too, Elaina?" Gavri asked, gesturing at himself and Grisha.

"Not this time, Gav." She patted his shoulder and gave him a peck on the brow. "I think this hike's going to be just me and Kolya. As long as you don't mind?"

She asked as a courtesy, but the look in his eyes told her Gavri understood the matter had been decided. Even if he had wanted to argue, she'd have gotten her way in the end. She'd spent a great deal of time running through the wilderness with Gavri and Grisha lately, anyway.

Today would be Kolya's day to spend with her.

WHEN SHE STOPPED TO THINK about it, Elaina was astonished by how quickly Kolya had recovered from the attack which hospitalized him only a week ago. He and Gavri assured her the *oboroten* could heal their injuries at a significantly accelerated rate, but now she'd watched it for herself. Of course, in the beginning his progress had been slow. He'd needed crutches to walk, just like a mortal man might have, and the cuts and bruises lingered like stubborn, heartbreaking blemishes. For the first two days after his return, Elaina doubted his promises of speedy reversal; he seemed almost to be suffering *more* than a human would, not less. Then, though, the process had gained momentum, and soon enough she'd forgotten how terrible he'd looked in his hospital room, and how stiffly and awkwardly he'd moved on those crutches. Certainly weeks had passed as poor Kolya worked off his marks and scars! When she consulted the calendar, however, she came over dizzy: it had only been *six* days.

As they set out together for their hike, she took his hand in hers and slid in close at his side. Fond feelings—chiefly pride—welled up in her chest, as Kolya beamed down at her.

"I can't believe how fast you've healed." She traced her fingers along part of his forearm, where his attacker had left a hideous, deep bite, which now seemed entirely forgotten. She'd imagined he would need stitches or even minor surgery, and yet he barely had a scar.

"Must be all the clean living. Though I have to wonder, *krasavitsa...* does it not frighten you to venture with me alone into the wilderness, when clearly there are mysterious thugs skulking about who might attack again?"

"I'd rather be with you, if they do." Elaina picked her way up the path, jaw set. "Grisha gave me a hunting knife, just in case."

Always the most upbeat of her mates, even Kolya couldn't suppress a guilty, disdainful tone in his voice. "If we run into the *vukodlak*, a hunting knife may not be enough."

"You know," Elaina said softly. "You've all told me how the *vukodlak* are the enemies of Diezana's children. How they're bred from corruption, and how Viktor betrayed the tribe to them. But... I don't know exactly *what* they are. How would I know one if I saw one?'

Kolya's voice dropped an octave. After a heavy pause, he said, "Are you asking me because I am the son of a *vukodlak*?"

"No." Elaina brushed a broad, light spray of leaves out of their way. Then, on second thought, admitted "Maybe a little. Did you know him?"

"Yes. He was..." He ran his fingers through his hair. "Sometimes, I think he wished he could be different. It is like a madness, like rabies, driving their kind to ravage and devour and destroy. But sometimes, there were moments of clarity in him. Glimpses of a man, behind the beast."

He stopped walking and spread his hands before him.

"My mother was a young woman, and headstrong, you could say. I imagine she was much like you." He gave her a sheepish grin. "Breeding with a *vukodlak* was perhaps very thrilling for her, and certainly shocked the rest of the tribe. Of course, then she bore the burden of a skinwalker imprinting on her. He stalked her, sometimes in the guise of a human, sometimes in his broken, mutated form. It terrified her, though she tried to hide her fear from me. When she and I played in the fields, sometimes he would howl to her and call her to him. The *vukodlak* can imitate voices they have heard, and so he'd mimic her pack mates or my grandparents, and try to lure her away from me."

Elaina sucked in a breath. "It sounds awful, Kol."

"It was always very mysterious to me." He twined his fingers with hers, and they resumed their hike. "He must have been sane enough at some point to mate with her and not murder her. But the creature I saw—when I did see him—knew only violence and hate. And though he frightened her, too, and though she warned me never, ever to follow him, I suspected some nights—some very few nights, when the moon was in her blood and she felt very *wild*—she went out to him. Perhaps, in a way, she had imprinted on him as well. I remember bruises on her arms and neck, sometimes bite marks... the kind we leave on you."

His eyes glimmered with mischief, and Elaina couldn't help a soft smile.

"I only ever remember happiness in her, though." Kolya's tone brimmed with wistful love. "She was beautiful and young, and full of fire. A troublemaker, sure, and the pack always found things in her to disapprove of. She wore sundresses and ran about in her bare feet, with red hair like cognac, always loose in the wind."

"You loved her very much," Elaina observed. Kolya nodded.

"I think you would have loved her as well," he said softly. "And she, you."

"Will you tell me what happened to her?"

She thought she already knew the answer. Kolya's mother, wild and carefree, bright with light and laughter, but with an unfortunate attraction to the *wrong* man. Elaina's imagination treated her to a few very abrupt, very tragic conclusions, but Kolya surprised her.

"We don't know."

Elaina blinked. "You... you don't know?"

He paused, squatting down to pluck a few berries from a low bush. A rush of delight filled Elaina: they were wild strawberries, and when he'd gathered a full handful he straightened, offering her first pick.

"We have assumed the *vukodlak* killed her. My sire, or one of the others who ran with him." He popped a fat, red fruit in his mouth. "I was only four. I woke one morning in our little izba house, alone. She had gone in the night. Perhaps to be with my sire... or perhaps the madness had finally infected her as well, and she became a skinwalker herself."

"The tribe never found her?"

"They were able to track her to the edge of the Yenisei River. From there..." He turned up his hand, opening his fingers as though releasing some light, ephemeral treasure into the air. "Poof. Gone."

"Oh, Kolya." Elaina touched his cheek. "I'm so sorry."

"Thank you, *krasavitsa*." Kolya pressed another strawberry to her lips, following it with a kiss when she ate it. "So many in the pack remember my sire. None even knew who he was or what became of him, only that he was *vukodlak*, and my mother's affair with him, a scandal. None were cruel to her... they never drove her out. But when she disappeared, you could guess what the rest of the tribe all thought. *Always knew she'd come to a bad end. Only to be expected.* Perhaps they were right."

Pausing on a rise, he gazed down a green slope. Elaina looked with him, sliding an arm around his waist and leaning against him, admiring the rich, bright colors of ferns and trees, the shining rays of afternoon sun sending lovely motes of light drifting through the leaves.

"They think my mother made me the way I am," Kolya eventually said. Though he managed not to let any sorrow come through in his voice, Elaina looked up into his face, sensing some trouble.

"You mean bisexual?"

He nodded. "Submissive, effeminate. A sissy boy. They have many ways of saying it, when they think I cannot hear them." He glanced away from the view to meet her gaze. "I hope you are not... disappointed in me, *krasavitsa*. Because I am not as masculine as Gavri or Grisha. Because I would rather hike with you to a place of beauty, than tear your clothing off and make love to you on a tree branch."

Elaina slipped out of the embrace, turning to face him properly. "Kolya, did you think I invited you out here with me just so we could—"

Her russet wolf lifted one shoulder in a shrug. "Grisha told me about your stop by the river with him and Gavri."

She frowned. "Did... did it bother you? If I've done something wrong—"

"No, Elaina." He smiled, and she thought she read some relief in his expression as he touched a finger to her lips. "I am not jealous of what you have shared with your other mates. But I know I am different. This morning, when Gavri had his way with me, instead of you—"

"You *all* had your way with me first," she reminded him with a grin. "And I *know* you love Gavri. The two of you were together long before I came along. I consider myself lucky you've both welcomed me into your relationship. I don't want you to give up what you had with each other, just because I'm here now."

A thought struck her. "Are you worried I'll change my mind about you because I saw you have sex with a man?"

He waved a hand to dismiss this, but the flush of red along his ears gave him away. Elaina took his hands, holding them both in one of her own, and with the other caressed his cheek.

"Kolya," she soothed. "One thing I love about you—both of you—is the way you look at each other. Even the very first night we were together... the way you light up around him, it's just more of what makes you so beautiful to me. I don't care what the pack has said, or what the Russian government says, any more than I care what my parents or my ex would say. You're not a sissy. And don't you dare stop making love with Gavri because you think you have to live up to some expectation with me."

Kolya's eyes gleamed. He bent to hug her tight, squeezing her until she thought her ribs might crack. They held each other for long moments, a rush of wonderful warmth spreading through them.

"You will make a very good alpha female, *krasavitsa*," he whispered in her ear.

"Thank you." As the hug broke, she clapped him on the shoulder. "Let's go find a spot for this shrine."

Kolya returned his gaze to the deep ravine before them. "I quite like this one."

"I do, too. But it's not... not *quite* right." Elaina tapped a finger to her lips. "I can't say exactly why, but..."

She didn't hear Diezana's song here. The spot was gorgeous, yes, and she could sit here all day enjoying the warm breeze with Kol, if time permitted. It didn't spark with her, though, in the way she thought it should. Beautiful, yes. Welcoming, yes. Sacred?

Not in the way I need it to be.

"Let's keep walking." She stepped past Kolya and began up the path again. He followed obediently.

"*Krasavitsa?*"

"Yes?"

Kolya held out a hand to steady her on a steep bend in the trail. "You still haven't told your own family about any of this."

The flesh at the back of Elaina's neck crawled. She hadn't spoken to her family at all since she left the States weeks ago. She'd sent an email to her parents when she'd decided to stay past her original return date, but only to make sure no one called any international law enforcement to start investigating her disappearance. There'd been a return email, so she knew her mother received the message, but Elaina hadn't found the will to read the reply. Sure, it might have been innocent and benign—maybe a *So glad you're having fun!* or *Bring me back an authentic set of nesting dolls, sweetheart.* Chances were better than even, though, Tricia Jacob would gild even a cheerful response with veiled disapproval and underhanded accusation. *How nice you can just stay on vacation all the time. Did you incur much of a fee to change your flights at the last minute? I hope you know we can't send you any extra, if you wind up short.*

Not to mention, whatever else her mother had to say, she'd almost certainly insist on bringing up Dominic and pressing Elaina to explain the breakup. Just thinking about it made Elaina's stomach turn sour.

"I'm not going to tell them," she admitted. The next bend in the path led them into a thick copse of aspens, and she reached out to lay her hand upon one smooth, pale trunk. The wood had been scored by deep scratches, and she wondered if it had been one of her wolves, or any of the *oboroten* tribe.

"I'll tell them I intend to stay," she said. "They won't approve, but I can live with it. For all they'll know I've taken a permanent position with some grand international travel magazine or photography publisher or something. We'll email, and sometimes we'll talk on the phone. The life I build here, though... they won't be part of it."

Kolya spoke in a gentle rumble. "Are you quite certain you wish to break ties with your own family?"

"I told you what *she's* like." Elaina traced the claw marks in the wood. They were so fine... too fine, maybe, to belong to any of the wolves. "She means well, I guess. Or maybe she doesn't. I can never decide *what* she means. She raised me to walk on eggshells everywhere I went. Things that made her happy one day annoyed her to the point of a meltdown the next. Like flowers. You'd bring her roses for Mother's Day, and she'd come over misty-eyed at how beautiful they were, and how thoughtful and fragrant, and she'd put them in her favorite vase. Next month, bring her roses for her birthday and all of a sudden, she hates roses. They trigger her allergies, always have. She'll say something like 'I don't know how many times I've had to tell you this before', and 'I'm quite sure I've never liked roses, I've always said I hated them, don't you ever listen'? When I was younger, I'd stay up all night sometimes trying to decide who was crazy, me or her."

Moving away from the scarred tree, she wandered dreamily through the dense cluster of trunks, staring up into the canopy admiring the dark, fresh green leaves.

"So I'm not even going to give her the chance this time. How could I ever explain to her what I'm really doing here? Or that I've started a relationship with *three* foreign strangers?"

She spun to face him, though she continued to walk slowly backwards through the trees at a leisurely, meandering pace. "My mother was especially fond of Dominic. Got along with him better than she did me. I think they were the same type, you know?"

Kolya tossed his last strawberry up in the air and caught it in his mouth, then nodded.

"I just know she'll hound me for all the details of what happened and why I've gone off to Russia when I could be losing the best thing to ever happen to me."

Her mate made a face. "And then, if you were to tell her you've been seeing someone else... even if you *only* said some*one*—"

"Yeah."

"And would you be happy with such an arrangement, love? Maintaining such distance from your mother and father?"

Elaina faced forward again and wrapped her arms around herself. "I know it doesn't seem like the *normal* thing to do. But it's *such* a relief. You have no idea. I love my parents, but it just feels so much saner, being half a world away from them."

After a pause, she cracked a smile. A chuckle escaped her. "It's funny. Learning the ancient ways of a magical shapeshifting people and preparing to face down the alpha male of their wolf pack seems like a picnic, compared to dealing with my mother."

"I can only imagine." Kolya grinned. "For me, the two were one and the same. Since the alpha female essentially fostered me, growing up."

Elaina leaned against one of the tree trunks, cocking an eyebrow. "Right. I guess when you got in trouble, you were facing down double-barrel detention, huh?"

He laughed. "When she first caught me and Gavri together, I nearly died out of pure fear."

Elaina regarded him with a frown. He gazed back with a gentle, knowing smile.

"We were very conscious of what our countrymen and most of the pack think of homosexual conduct. It had never been explicitly stated in Adelaida's home, but..." he shrugged. "We assumed. Just as you might assume your mother might react if she walked in on a teenage you going down on a boy."

Elaina covered a gasp with her hand. "You mean she actually—"

"She did." He laughed again, shaking his head. "We were in the gym, showering after a workout.

Thought we were alone in the house, and I'd just got Gavri nearly there when, wouldn't you know it, Adelaida strolled in looking for us."

"No!"

"Yes! She'd come home early and thought she'd treat us with a trip to the movies." He joined her by the tree, putting his back to it and taking a seat on the ground. "We laugh about it now, Gavri and I, but at the time, I was sure she'd transform and tear me to pieces."

"She *is* kind of a hard-ass, isn't she?" Elaina mused.

Kolya tilted his head back against the tree trunk, gazing up at her. "Not really so much, *krasavitsa*. You did meet her in the middle of a family dispute, but Adelaida is more than sharp edges. She *didn't* drive me out, after all. She's always stood by us, even if the rest of Russia considers us degenerates."

Elaina didn't answer. She bit her lip, letting her gaze wander along the shifting green shadows around them. Adelaida *had* joined them on their hunt, and given Elaina the spear to slay her prey. The former alpha might seem troublingly close to Nikita, but then again... why shouldn't she be? She'd entrusted him with the job of caring for her people.

But when it comes down to it, who will she support at the solstice?

CHAPTER EIGHT

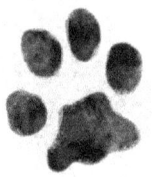

SHE AND KOLYA DID NOT find the place where she was to build her shrine. Or at least, they never found a place where Elaina felt *right,* or any spot where Diezana's song came through to her in its clear, patient, comforting way. In fact, she didn't hear the song again at all. Not even a note.

Sure, I don't always *hear it,* she assured herself as they finally returned to the lodge, well after sundown. *But... I did think she would call to us today. I mean, if I'm to find some sacred place, I'd expect to hear her there.*

They came home without any answer, despite an afternoon of admittedly gorgeous weather and beautiful views from the hills. Elaina hadn't found the place for her tribute, but she managed more than a hundred excellent snaps with her camera and consoled herself by scrolling through the pictures with Gavri and Grisha, and recounting the day through photos.

"I really thought this spot would be beautiful, to make my tribute." She skimmed through a series of shots taken from the top of another ravine, where a stream tumbled down the rocks into a small waterfall. "But it just didn't click."

"Oh!" Gavri stopped her on a picture of tufted, sly-looking squirrel popping curiously up from a bird's nest. "My mother will love that one. Looks like you caught him red-handed stealing eggs!"

They shared a laugh. They sat on the couch together, Elaina sandwiched between Gav and Grisha, while Kolya sat on the ottoman rubbing her feet. The fire burned lower and lower in the hearth, and just about the same time the topmost logs crumpled in on themselves and sent a little whoosh of sparks spinning up the flue, Grisha rose to excuse himself.

"Oh, won't you stay?" Elaina pleaded, tugging at him to sit back down. "I want all my mates curled around me tonight."

The snow leopard shook his head. Typical cat, running hot and cold when it came to snuggling and affection.

"I want to take you rock climbing tomorrow," he said. "I'll be back around five with the gear."

Elaina stood to see him out. Feline aloofness or no, she would get a kiss goodnight. When he'd gone, she returned to her place beside Gavri, and told Kolya it was her turn to rub his feet.

SHE DIDN'T FEEL ANY SPIRITUAL pull or hear Diezana's voice at any of the rock formations Grisha took her to the next morning, either. After lunch, all three of her mates joined her on another hike, leading her in their lithe animal forms, and still, no place called out to her. They returned early when she found herself too frustrated to focus, unable even to snap a decent picture of the elegant doe they discovered with her fawn in a shady river clearing.

At home, she opted for a long bath, hoping Rini's selection of soothing oils could ease her growing tension. When even the mellow scents of sandalwood and clary sage failed to calm her mind, she rose from the bath in a huff and wrapped herself in a towel to plod downstairs.

"Rini?" she called out, heading in the direction of Gavri's office. Rini poked her head out of the room at the sound of her name.

"Yes, Elaina?"

"Did you already load my hiking clothes into the laundry?"

Rini cocked her head to the side. "No, not yet. I hadn't gathered enough for a load yet. I'm sorry, I didn't think—"

"Don't be sorry." Elaina changed direction for the laundry room. "I'm going to head out again so it would only have been extra work for you if you had. I'll just grab them out of the hamper. Where are the boys?"

"Grisha's disappeared on his own. Probably gone for a ride up to the city. Would you like me to call Gavri and Kolya? They were planning on having a swim in the pool."

Elaina held up a hand. "No, don't call them. But let them know I'm going to go have a jog on my own for a bit."

She no longer feared getting lost. She'd been out so many times with her mates by now she'd become much more comfortable with the area, and besides, they could track her down if she didn't return in a timely manner.

"I wouldn't exactly say I'm a master of the Stolby wilderness yet," she said to Kotyanok, who lay curled up in the laundry basket and came awake with an excited squeak when Elaina gave her a gentle jostle. The creamy-white Siamese cat climbed to her feet and strolled in a circle atop the rumpled clothing, rubbing her head against Elaina with adoration.

Elaina picked Koty up and gave her a nuzzle and a kiss on the nose. "But maybe I really do have to do this part on my own. I know Grisha thinks they can help, and they probably can. Just not *this* way."

Kotyanok poked Elaina with her nose and rubbed her face to Elaina's cheek, squeaking and purring. Elaina smiled, buried a flurry of kisses against the tiny cat's tummy, and then set her to one side while she dug her clothing out of the pile.

Once she'd dressed again and grabbed her hiking backpack, Elaina stood on the back patio of the lodge for a long time, considering the rise of the woods ahead.

We've searched in every direction from here already. A grimace darkened her face. *So... where do I go now?*

After some contemplation, she set out to the north.

The air had cooled, an early evening breeze signaling the coming night, though it was still on the shy side of three in the afternoon. It would be a chilly night, but Elaina still wasn't concerned. She seemed to have lost all her fear of the woods.

Is that a good thing, though? she wondered as she walked, gazing up at the bright sky through spreading trees. Did it mean she'd grown comfortable with the land as an aspiring *oboroten* should? Or had she lost the healthy caution of a traveler, overestimating herself and forgetting all the things she'd learned over years?

The same way I did that first night here. The night I got lost.

Lost, a gentle voice from the back of her mind agreed. *And found.*

The woods teemed with the lazy, somnambulant sounds of birds singing casual songs, and chirping insects lurking in the brush. Her thoughts turned again toward her mission, and she ground her teeth with frustration. She wanted to think about how she'd use the body of the boar to erect a shrine, and how she'd dedicate herself to Diezana with it. Diezana seemed so far from her now, though, so stubborn and distant, Elaina could hardly think of the task ahead. It had grown in her mind to some esoteric custom far, far away from the here and now. She paused to look over a nearby rise at a slope of distant hill to the east.

Did I really think there'd be some mystical arcane power in this place, something to speak to me out of the sky and tell me where to build my altar? Her mouth turned down in a sad frown. *Maybe I should just pick a spot, plant the damn thing, and be done with it.*

Would defiance lure Diezana out of hiding? Elaina closed her eyes and listened, hoping the faint strains of the goddess's song would float up from the back of her mind.

Nothing. Elaina sighed and marched on.

She'd hiked almost an hour, ascending the hills behind the lodge in a straightforward path up the slope, when she came upon the camp. At first, she didn't notice; she tromped right in, lost in her thoughts, and didn't even look up until she accidentally kicked over a dented blue pot someone had set aside with other mess kit utensils.

"Oh!" She staggered a step back, startled by the hollow *clunk* and then the clatter of plate and teakettle as the pot tumbled into them. Glancing up for the owner, she found an old yellow pup tent and a crackling campfire.

How did I miss a whole camp?

Another thought followed quickly. *Isn't this part of Wild Stolby? The restricted parts of the reserve?*

"Welcome."

She spun at the deep, rumbling male voice behind her. A tall man, bare-chested and tawny, stood at the edge of the camp. One fist rested on his hip, and he held a freshly killed and cleaned yearling stag—one of the musk deer—slung over the other shoulder. The left side of his chest bore arching dark tattoos in thorny, complicated patterns, winding up to his shoulder and down his bicep.

His eyes—a bright, too-bright green, somehow glowing like lamps even in the bright light of day— struck Elaina speechless. His hair, by contrast, fell sleek and dark, wild like a lion's mane, to his shoulders.

"H-hi." Elaina raised a hand in greeting, then dropped down to collect the pot she'd knocked over. "Sorry, I didn't notice your things here, I was—"

"Lost in your own thoughts?" he finished for her. Elaina lifted one shoulder in a half-shrug and nodded.

The stranger crossed the camp to where a rolled-up tarp rested beside his tent. Kicking it so it unfurled across the leaf-littered dirt, he dropped the deer onto it and dusted off his hands. For a hunter who had evidently just brought down a kill—presumably with his bare hands, since she didn't see any sort of weapons or tools on him—he'd remained remarkably clean. Not a spot of blood or dirt on him. A twinge of wary bemusement set Elaina on her guard, as the stranger offered his hand.

"I am called Athanos. I am *oboroten*."

Stunned, Elaina did not accept the handshake at first, until Athanos raised his eyebrows and she realized she'd left him awkwardly waiting. Taking his hand, she said "I'm Elaina. But if you're telling me right off what you are... did you already know about me?"

"I did." He grinned, a sharp expression. His features were regal, classical, like a sculpture. *Dying Gaul,* she thought. Yes, he looked as if he might be the very man who modeled for the statue itself.

"So... you're part of the Stolby tribe?"

"No." He gestured to a set of rather large stones he'd arranged near the campfire. "Would you like to sit down and share some tea with me? I'll explain."

Careful, Elaina... something is very strange here.

"I won't bite." He picked up his teakettle, then reached inside the tent, producing a two-liter bottle of water. As he poured, he explained, "Word travels in *oboroten* circles. There are a few particularly gabby individuals who shift into loudmouth birds. I heard about the audacious human girl who wants to learn the blessing of shapeshifting, and decided I had to see her for myself."

Propping up a cooking grate over the fire, he set the kettle on it. "You're in restricted land, close by the Dvorak property, and everyone knows it's the son of the former alpha helping you out. I figured chances were good you were her."

Gesturing at the pot in her hands, he added, "Didn't expect you to be... clumsy."

"I'm usually not." She handed over the pot and sat on one of the large stones. "Like I said, I'm just distracted."

"I imagine you must have a lot on your mind."

"If you're not Stolby tribe, where are you from?" she asked. "Forgive my forwardness, but you don't really look local."

"Originally from Wales." He began rearranging his mess kit. "Though most recently, I've been making my home in Athens, Greece. Fascinating amount of human history there."

"Right. Athanos doesn't sound like a Welsh name."

He raised his hand as if offering her something. "It's not. I just change it every now and then, to keep things fresh. Depends on who I'm running with at the time, or whom I mean to impress."

He gave the distinct impression of a ladies' man. He'd gone out on his hunt barefoot, she noticed, although the suede leggings he wore seemed to suggest he hadn't gone in his animal form.

"So," he said in an inviting, conversational tone. "How did you come to discover the *oboroten* people, and decide you meant to do the impossible and win the blessings of shapechange?"

How many times am I going to have to tell this story?

She explained, from the moment she'd woken up early in her guest cabin with a smothering, anxious need to get out, even in inclement weather, and wound up lost. How she met Gavri and Kolya, and how they'd brought her into their home. The confrontation with Nikita, the challenge, and the consequences if she couldn't meet him in her own lupine form.

"That is quite a lot to take on your shoulders," Athanos said. The teakettle began to whistle, and he pulled it off the cooking grate.

He didn't even use a towel to grab the handle. It's got to be hot as hell and he just grabbed *it up.*

"If you're not from the Stolby tribe," she asked, "what tribe *do* you belong to?"

Athanos grinned, his glowing green eyes glimmering. "I belong to no tribe. I am my own. Always have been."

"Is that... normal?"

"It is for me." He poured hot water into two mismatched ceramic mugs and produced two bags of tea from a square tin beside him. Elaina furrowed her brow. She hadn't noticed the tin before... shouldn't it have been there when she tried to right the pot she'd upended?

"Cinnamon," Athanos told her, passing her the mug. "I hope you like the flavor?"

"I do." She took the mug but didn't drink. A deep suspicion stirred in her heart. "You... aren't human, are you?"

"I told you," he replied. "I am *oboroten*."

"But not like Gavri and Kolya," she insisted. "You're like... Ini. Right?"

Athanos raised an eyebrow. "Ini? You've run into little Ini?"

"On a spirit walk. Ini, Inferi, and—"

His eyes flashed and he gave an almost hungry growl. "Niuri?"

The vicious, violent storm-bringer, Niuri. The spirit who moved in spasmodic, jerking advances, who looked human and yet not entirely *right*. Like a horror artist's flat, pale monster, a slant of light and darkness too stark and precise to be natural.

"Yes," she replied, her voice dropping to just above a whisper. "Her, too."

"I know of these three." Athanos took on an elated expression. "So they are here now. And talking to a curious human girl with aspirations to join our people. How..."

Again, he sounded positively ravenous. "...*interesting.*"

Elaina set her mug of tea down. "Are you a spirit?"

Athanos spread his hands out before him. "Aren't we all spirits, in some form or another? I'm a traveler, like you. An aimless wanderer, going where my fancy strikes. I want to know more about *you*, though, Elaina. The only human in thousands of years to petition the gods to change your nature, and make you like us. Only you know, you *aren't* really the first human to do so. Simply the first one the Stolby wise woman has ever heard of. Plenty of humans over the years have come to Drayce and Diezana seeking the power of spiritual metamorphosis. There are whole—"

"Wait." Elaina put a hand up to stop him. "Drayce?"

Athanos took a long sip of his tea. "Yes. Diezana's brother."

A prickle traveled across the back of Elaina's neck and down her shoulders. "I haven't heard anything about the mother spirit having a... brother."

"Brother, counterpart, opposite number." Athanos raised his mug. "King of shapeshifters."

King of... skinwalkers? she wondered but said nothing.

"So if I'm not the first human to petition for their blessing, what happened to the others?" She didn't particularly like the creeping sense of intrusion Athanos gave off, but she couldn't help the curiosity. "Did they succeed?"

"Telling you would be spoiling the ending, wouldn't it?" he asked.

"Well, if you didn't come here to tell me whether or not I had any chance," she grumbled. "What *did* you come to tell me?"

"I didn't come here with a message." He sipped his tea again, taking a long, slow moment, drawing it out. Delight gathered at the corners of his eyes as he gazed at her over the rim of the cup.

Elaina stood. "Then I need to move on. I'm busy, and don't have time to play games here."

She stepped out of the circle of the camp, striding toward the trees, when Athanos spoke again.

"I came here to see if you were strong enough. If you really *are* the sort of woman who can follow in Diezana's path and change your nature down to the core. Except..."

When she turned around, the camp had disappeared. Athanos and all his belongings—even the musk deer—were gone.

His voice, though, continued, whispering in her ear.

"Diezana has not *truly* changed. She can't. And you can't. No one can change who they really are."

Elaina whirled, gripping the straps of her backpack and shooting a wild glance back and forth. She stood alone, and the first really cold breeze of evening danced along the flesh of her arms, raising goosebumps.

A moment of silence passed. She realized she was holding her breath and let it out in a shaky groan.

I'm not sure if this encounter was better or worse than meeting Niuri.

She'd almost managed to calm her nerves when a soft, grinding growl alerted her. A shot of adrenaline kicked in, hot in her veins, as the biggest wolf she'd ever seen—biggest *true* wolf, second only to the spirit Inferi—stalked out from between the trees, lips curled into a snarl.

CHAPTER NINE

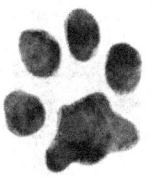

ELAINA BACKED AWAY FROM THE advancing wolf, putting up her hands. Two thoughts occurred to her at once: first, she should have brought along Adelaida's spear.

Second... she *knew* this wolf.

"Pasha!" she shouted. "Oh, it *would* be you lurking around under the trees trying to bully me. Change back! I have some questions to ask you!"

Pasha—a massive, multicolored wolf with a coat in brilliant white, caramel-colored tans, and charcoal black— proceeded several more steps, teeth bared and hackles up. Saliva flecked his muzzle in a lacy foam.

Rabid? The thought came to her despite its inherent unlikelihood. Could *oboroten* even catch rabies?

No. But they can *go mad. They can become vukodlak.*

She put up a shaky, defiant bluff, hoping her voice didn't tremble. "I'm not playing games with you. We're going to talk about what happened to Kolya. I think you and your two stooges attacked him, even though Nikita promised we'd be safe. If you want to speak up and convince me it wasn't you who broke the truce, now would be a great time to do it."

119

Another step forward. The wolf's growl turned into a warning bark. His ears lay flat back against his broad skull; his tail curled under his belly in a guarded, unhappy posture.

Don't dogs do that when they're... afraid?

"Pasha!" she shouted again, but before she could say anything else, Pasha leapt at her.

If she hadn't been training for the hunt with Gavri and Grisha, she might have been knocked flat on her back by the massive bulk of wolf colliding with her. Instead, she rolled with his momentum and turned it against him, falling to the forest floor and kicking him up, over her head. In a single graceful turn, she got to her feet, low in a crouch, facing him and ready for the next attack.

Pasha rolled over. His rumbling canine growl stuttered to a stop as he changed, trading fur for flesh, and a split-second later he hunkered before her as a man, broad and thick with muscle, long black hair tied into a straight ponytail. He lunged like a sprinter and launched himself at her, huge hands reaching for her throat, and Elaina screamed.

He crashed toward her, and she sidestepped at the last minute, avoiding the full body blow. His outstretched arm caught her around the waist and twirled her, and he dragged her to him, crushing her against his body. Together they tumbled and rolled in the grass, grunting and shoving at one another, until he dominated, straddling her, and pinned her wrists to the ground. He smelled of sweat, the kind earned from hard work and ardor, and the lingering sharp scent of pine wood and ancient sweet earth.

"Get off me!" Elaina thrashed against him, anger bubbling up and replacing fear. It was easier to be angry at him when he wore his human face. "I *knew* you couldn't be trusted, you thick oaf! Get off, or I'll scream so loud Gavri and Kolya will be here before you can shift back and run off like the coward you are!"

"Pasha," came a commanding voice from above. "Get off the human girl."

The behemoth on top of her shot her a vengeful scowl, then obeyed the command. Releasing her wrists, he climbed to his feet and stepped away from her.

Nikita emerged from the trees, arms crossed over his chest. He shook his head, looking rueful, and clucked his tongue.

"Always barking at your elders like a stupid puppy," he scolded Elaina.

"Excuse me?" She jabbed a finger in Pasha's direction. "*He* attacked *me*. I thought you swore he could be trusted to uphold our truce. Now I'm even more certain he and his groveling scouts were the ones who put Kol in the hospital."

Pasha growled again. Even in his human form— or mostly human—the sound belonged to a wolf: rumbling and wild, liquid, a canine vocalization no person could ever truly imitate.

"He *can* be trusted," Nikita insisted. "You keep throwing around accusations without bothering to speak with him like a civil person. He charged you, but you stood there yapping and snapping at him first. Do you know nothing about the roles in a wolf pack? Unruly puppies who provoke the bigger dogs are put in their place."

"I'm not a puppy." She brushed dirt from the shoulders of her top. "I doubt there's even two years between us, one way or another."

"You *are* puppy."

Pasha's voice, resonant and deep, brooked no argument. He snapped something out in their thick native tongue and gestured at her as though fed up. "*Chelovek* girl. You come to join our pack. I should give you no more attention than the *malen'kiy perepel* birds scurrying about their ground-nests and cheeping under the bushes for a mate. But you wish to become a wolf. So, I will treat you this way, as I would treat any young fledgling finding their place."

"Those fledglings," Nikita added, "learn early on not to insult Pasha's honor."

A sharp retort danced on the tip of Elaina's tongue, but Pasha's words made her hesitate. He *had* attacked. He hadn't harmed her, though. Not with teeth or claws, or with his fists when he returned to human form. He'd only tossed her around a bit. They'd traded a lot of gnashing and snapping, but the only real damage done was a scuff here and there, and some dirt on her hiking clothes.

The pack traded posturing like this. Wolf pups fell into their roles through feints and short fracases outlining their boundaries. They learned their place, this way.

Pasha treated me like one of them. Bizarre as it is... he's been the first *one to treat me like a member of a wolf pack.*

Everyone else—even Gavri and Kolya—still saw her as an aspiring *oboroten*. In one quick, savage spat, Pasha showed her that he saw she was serious about joining the tribe altogether, and capable of doing it.

She shrugged. "Well, you could work on your timing. Also, call ahead."

"We don't work by your schedule." Nikita clapped a hand on Pasha's shoulder. "Come, brother."

"Wait." Elaina stepped forward, holding up her hand. "You're right. I need to go about this a different way."

Turning to Pasha, she tipped him a nod. "Pasha, will you be honest with me? Was it you and your two friends who attacked Kolya? Did you conveniently 'forget' Nikita declared the blood hunt suspended?"

"I knew he had revoked it. Of course I knew! *Konechno.*" Pasha clenched his fists. "We have left your dog alone, *chelovek.*"

"What does that mean?" she asked, in a tone she hoped came through more curious than defensive.

"*Human,*" Nikita translated. "Pasha's English is less practiced than some, but he is not stupid."

"I didn't think you were," she assured Pasha, softly now. "If you didn't attack him, do you know who did?"

"*Vukodlak.*" He spat on the ground. "They steal onto our land now. They are bold after the betrayal of Adelaida's mate. *Izmennik.* Traitor. They will not kill their own progeny, though. Not like they killed Polina."

The rigid tension in his spine all at once made perfect sense. His fists shook at his sides. A rush of sympathy stole the last of Elaina's anger.

"We heard about Polina. I am so sorry, both of you. All of you."

"Condolences." Nikita chewed on the word as if not sure how to take it. "From an outsider bent on uprooting us. What would you know of losing a member of the pack?"

"Nothing, I admit." Elaina held out both her hands. "But I'd like to learn. If you'd let me."

The two men exchanged a glance, looking subtly surprised. They traded thick and thorny words in their native tongue; the intermittent mix of Russian terms gave Elaina a very rudimentary idea what they said, but at the speed with which they spoke, she couldn't follow very well and finally gave up.

At last, Pasha returned to his lupine shape, and trotted off into the trees. Nikita turned his attention back to her.

"We are observing funeral rites for Polina tonight. You may come, if you like. I shouldn't even entertain the idea of letting you intrude on our mourning, but you should see what the enemy has done."

Astonished, Elaina could think of nothing to say. She'd photographed regional burial sites before, in a few of the countries she'd visited. Travel writers weren't necessarily interested in native funeral rites as a rule, but there were always the odd calls for articles on local gravesites and funerary customs, and she'd had an educational tour or two. Each one had maintained a pervasive sense of solemnity, even if the last soul to be buried on the site had gone to rest hundreds of years before.

"Thank you," she assured him. "It would mean very much to me, to attend. I understand this is a very solemn time for you and your people and I'll treat it with the utmost respect."

"As Pasha said," Nikita continued, gesturing for her to follow him, "You wish to become one of us.

To *lead* us. So you will learn what it means to lose one of us."

Turning his back on her to lead the way, he murmured, "And why we cannot abide the *vukodlak* gaining any more ground against us."

She hurried after him. "Can you tell me what happened to Polina?"

"The skinwalkers came in the night." Nikita pushed a low-hanging pine-branch out of their way and gestured for her to go ahead. "Polina's oldest son, Pyotr, has been able to tell us most of it. They banged on the door, barking and crying out like hyenas. Polina rushed the boys to a safe place under the floorboards and prepared to drive off the intruders."

"But it didn't work that way," Elaina guessed with a soft sigh.

"No." Nikita's face darkened. "It did not."

"And Pyotr saw the whole thing?"

"*Da,* peeking up from under the floorboards. The family who have taken the boys in say they have nightmares every night."

"I really am sorry," she said. Nikita didn't answer.

The walk took roughly an hour, marching southwest toward the pack's meeting place. They crossed a sturdy wooden bridge spanning a vibrant gorge Elaina hadn't seen before, and she made a mental note to return to it for pictures—but now wasn't the time. Nikita explained he'd sent Pasha ahead to prepare the others for her presence.

"You can't expect they will approve, however," he warned. "You are not well-loved among us."

Harsh, but not unexpected. Elaina picked up her pace, trotting to catch up and match his stride. "Why haven't you invited Gavri and Kolya to the funeral?

You can't tell me your exile would prevent them from paying their respects. They knew Polina."

"*Vukodlak* killed her." He kept his stony gaze focused on the path ahead, hardly acknowledging her. "Why would we involve the son of a *vukodlak* to pay any respects?"

"Because he's part of your tribe," she said, weary and well aware it would mean little to him. "But even if not Kolya, what about Gavri? And Rini? She was crushed by the news."

"They have chosen their side. Their presence at the burial would only upset the others. As *yours* most certainly will, but as I said, you need to see it."

Another half hour brought them at last to the pack's gathering place. In the center of the clearing, before the broken tree stump Nikita sometimes lounged on like a throne, many members of the pack had begun arranging birch branches around and under a light scaffolding of rebar, building up into a mound roughly six feet long and four feet high. A high, lively fire burned in its campfire circle nearby. When she and Nikita arrived, many of the builders paused to regard them. They gazed upon their alpha male with sorrow, a grief running through them that he must also share. When their eyes fell on her, though, most took on expressions of distrust and discontent.

"Elaina."

She gave a small start as Adelaida appeared on her left, laying an elegant hand on her shoulder. She hadn't expected to see Gavri's dam here, though of course it made perfect sense. Behind her, Timofei watched the funeral preparations, standing at attention. Bernard, too, had come, and helped the others as they gathered and arranged the branches.

"Adelaida." Elaina gave the former alpha a respectful bow of the head. "I know Pasha came ahead to let you all know I'd be here. I'm thankful for the opportunity."

"A wise decision on Nikita's part." Adelaida gave Nikita an approving nod. "Any human mate would be welcome, as you see Timofei has been."

"It won't mean the others will be happy with it," Nikita grumbled. "You should join Timofei and try not to draw attention to yourself."

A snappy retort rose automatically, but Elaina tamped it down. *Not now. Do not be the defiant pup now.*

"Thank you," she told him instead, and moved to Timofei's side to observe.

"Hello again." Timofei held out his hand and Elaina shook it. "I'm sorry we haven't properly had the chance to speak."

"Me too," she agreed, though when she thought of it, she hadn't taken much note of Timofei at all since he and Adelaida had arrived. Adelaida dominated every exchange, and Gavri's sire seemed more like a queen's attendant than her husband.

Elaina watched Nikita stride to the funerary pyre and take a large birch branch from a graying, elder packmate. He rested a hand on the other man's shoulder and leaned in, so their brows touched. Nikita said something in hushed tones, and the expression on the other man's face softened into one of relief. Whatever Nikita had told him, it seemed to bring comfort.

"He's not a bad leader."

Elaina glanced at Timofei when he spoke. He offered her a gentle, somehow conciliatory smile, and all at once his resemblance to Gavri came clear. Elaina's first mate might share Adelaida's coloring, down to the icy blue eyes, and he might have inherited her lean, whipcord strength and dominant posture... but his smile was all Timofei. The tender regard, the confident ray of affection—she'd understood many things about Gavri when she met his matriarch, but in Timofei, she recognized the fierce capacity for love with which he stood up in the face of social norms to remain with Kolya.

And with me.

"Oh." She'd lost herself in reflection and hadn't answered Timofei's statement. "No, I'm... I see he's not. Well, mostly not."

With a deep sigh she pushed back a sheaf of her hair. "I just can't get around the exile of a packmate based on his love of another packmate. Yes, yes, I *know,* things are different in Russia than they are in my home country. Although even there it's not always easy." She held up a hand to preempt the explanation he seemed about to make. "But I can't help it. It's backwards and wrong, and especially now, if the *vukodlak* are moving in, Nikita should be gathering every able shapeshifter who will come. Instead..."

She gestured at the funerary preparations before them. "Gavri, Kolya, and Rini should be here. They mourn Polina, too."

"Yes," said Timofei. "I agree."

Elaina raised an eyebrow. "Well, I'm glad to hear that at least. I admit, I had the impression when it came to a contest between your wife and your son, you'd choose Adelaida, right or wrong."

Timofei made a quiet sound of amusement. "I have been Adelaida's life mate for over thirty years. I know more of her and her ways than anyone in Stolby, I wager, except perhaps Bernard. And while we both know a great deal, perhaps neither of us knows everything. But I know when she is angry, and when she is *destructive*. I've watched her tear down whole boardrooms full of consultants seeking to bilk her out of hard-earned funds. And I watched her—and provided counsel and comfort—when she first heard news of Kolya's expulsion from the pack. She can be an incredibly hard woman, but she is not a selfish one."

His eyes glinted with a hint of light she almost considered animal. "I have learned not to get between her and our son, when they argue. That is a thing they must hash out for themselves. A lesson you might also learn, should you and he ever have children."

She mulled it over as the pack finished the pyre. Around the clearing stood people she hadn't seen before, many more than had been at the meeting place on her previous visit. There were also familiar faces: Sofie crouched on a log by herself, solemnly attentive to the ritual, and Baba Yasmin sat serenely on the grass. The others must be members of the Stolby tribe who didn't shift into wolves. Some, like Bernard, aided in the construction, but others hung back. Some dabbed at their eyes; some watched with scowls and tight, clenched jaws.

All of them, at one point or another, threw a glance at Elaina. Amid the many glares, though, there were also looks of curiosity, and undecided interest. A few gazes lingered for what seemed like a very long time. No one approached her or spoke with her, though. She wouldn't have expected them to.

When the last few sticks had been arranged, Nikita called out to the others, and they backed away from the structure.

Timofei touched her shoulder, gesturing with his other hand at the path leading into the clearing. A group of four had arrived, carrying a litter on their shoulders. From the shrouded shape on the litter, it could only be the body of the deceased. Behind the pallbearers came Pasha, and behind him, two young boys escorted by a male and a female. Polina's sons, and their new foster parents, no doubt.

Elaina fought the urge to lift her camera, keeping her fingers twined behind her back. The gathering around them filled the whole glade, and the *oboroten* were magnificent. She wanted to steal a thousand images from this afternoon... but she wouldn't. She wasn't a travel writer at the moment: she was a guest of the Stolby tribe.

The pallbearers lifted the contents of the litter onto the pyre the others had erected. Polina's youngest son wept openly, wailing in their *oboroten* language so Elaina did not understand—and yet, she did. He cried for his mother and her comfort. He couldn't understand why she didn't rise from under the shroud and come to his aid. The older son, Pyotr, focused on activity with cold, hard, eyes like granite.

No child should have eyes like that. Elaina tilted her head. *And yet... I've seen it before. Recently. Who was it?*

The pallbearers backed away from the pyre, as did Pasha. Polina's sons and their foster parents remained, and across from them, Nikita helped Baba

Yasmin to her feet. The old woman raised her hands to the sky, then bent forward in a low, low bow.

"The wise woman will lead the funeral," Timofei explained in a whisper. "If he were old enough, Polina's eldest would be the one to light the flame, but since he is yet a child, Nikita will perform that role."

Yasmin straightened and raised her hands to the sky again, and this time she gave a low, throaty cry. The dull beat of a drum from somewhere in the circle startled Elaina; she searched for the source and found Adelaida, seated cross-legged on the ground, with the instrument in her lap. The gathered *oboroten* answered Yasmin, raising their voices together in response. The wise woman repeated her gesture, this time raising up a longer, articulate cry, a droning chant in their native tongue. The drum repeated, and the *oboroten* replied again, matching the shamaness in a full chorus.

Nikita—who did not add his voice—stepped up to the fire and selected a long, burning branch. In the flickering yellow flames his straight, pale blonde hair turned a glowing gold, and his blue eyes filled with dancing Halloween light. The foster father escorting Polina's children nudged Pyotr, and the boy stepped forward to take his part. The distance he crossed couldn't have been more than six feet, but it seemed like miles, a test of his faith and courage, like walking on a tight wire over the very flames before them all.

The rest of the *oboroten* traded off in a round with Baba Yasmin, as Nikita took Pyotr's hand and approached the funeral pyre. Elaina's breath caught when the alpha male set the burning branch among the others in the structure, and the flames licked up from deep within the latticework of birch limbs. A sobbing scream rose up from Polina's younger son, and his foster mother took him in her arms and cradled him to her shoulder, swaying and soothing him though his sorrowful wails did not stop.

Nikita was the first to raise up a howl: the genuine, soulful howl of a wolf, coming from deep in the heart of a man. The others stopped their chanting and broke into a howl along with him, from Pyotr to his new foster parents, to Baba Yasmin, to Sofie, whose howl was really the wild cry of a big cat. Others in the circle who were not wolves still joined the keening, adding the rough, barking yowl of a wolverine, the dry scream of predator birds, the bleat of mountain sheep. It was a strange and wonderful and heartbreaking sound, not a cacophony but an impossible feral unity. A unity of deep sorrow.

I wonder if Gavri and Kolya can hear this back home. Elaina brought a hand to her chest, transported by the mesmerizing cries. *Will they add their own howls to it? I bet they are. Right now, I bet they are howling along with the rest, and Rini too, in that chilling way rabbits keen.*

As the great outpouring of grief subsided, Baba Yasmin began another chant. This one she sang by herself, producing her own leather drum and sliding a white wooden mask over her face, swooping into a solemn sort of tribal dance.

"Here." Timofei nudged Elaina's arm. When she turned to him, he handed her a leather skin adorned with beads, and laces around the neck dangling tufts of quail feathers.

"Vodka," he told her. "We drink together to honor the spirits, and the memory of Polina's brave soul."

A few of the others around the circle turned their eyes in her direction, peering at her to see what she'd do. "Am... am I allowed to?"

"I say yes." He pushed the waterskin into her hands. "Human or not, you are Gavri's mate. You are welcome to pay your respects."

Lowering his voice, he leaned closer and whispered in her ear, "If you wish to lead them, they will need to know you see yourself as one of them. Drink. If anyone raises any objection, I will take responsibility."

Her heart welled with appreciation for him, and she lifted the skin to her lips. The blunt, hard slug of vodka jolted her awake, as if up till now she'd been observing things through a sleepy haze. Whether the effect came from spiritual joining with the tribe, or just from Timofei's act of acceptance, now Elaina felt as though she'd become *part* of the observance.

For a long time, the tribe alternated between keening songs and reverent silence, passing around the waterskins while Baba Yasmin beat her drum through funerary chants and danced in circles around Polina's fire. As time passed, the vodka worked its intoxicating magic on Elaina, and Yasmin's music not only touched her but flowed through her. She joined the songs, though she didn't know their language and could only sing in wordless harmony, and when the group raised up their keening wails, she let out her own throaty wail alongside Timofei. The sun set, and the pyre still burned. They fell into long, quiet pauses, in which Yasmin walked round the circle whispering blessings over each and every member of the tribe. She dabbed her thumb in a pot of some acrid liquid and pressed it to each brow in an anointment.

Throughout the evening, Nikita sat just before the pyre, side-by-side with young Pyotr. Elaina watched them, floating on a sweet buzz, and thought she'd been wrong about Nikita from the start.

The way he looks at the boy. He cares for him... for his suffering.

She accepted another drink from the waterskin, and Baba Yasmin crouched before her to offer her blessing and anoint Elaina's brow. Elaina responded to the old woman the same way she'd heard Timofei respond, though she didn't understand the language or the meaning. Then again, for many years historically and perhaps even to this day, there were Catholics reading and responding to their Catholic priests without having the slightest idea what the Latin recitations of their catechism meant. Elaina's heart seemed to understand, even if her ears and brain did not, and evidently that was good enough for Yasmin.

As the wise woman passed on, Elaina resumed her contemplation of Nikita.

This is why he fears them. The vukodlak. Because this is what they do. Murder innocent mothers and leave orphaned children.

A thought flickered there for an instant, an epiphany just on the tip of her tongue. It danced away, though, as the logs in the middle of the pyre crackled and collapsed inward, sending a flurry of sparks spiraling into the air.

Polina's cremation took nearly four hours. When the fire finally died down, Nikita stood and barked an order to the assembled tribe. The four pallbearers who had carried Polina's body to the pyre stood, giving their alpha male a series of bows, and left the clearing the same way they'd come. Yasmin dug into an old woven bag until she found a smooth, polished object. When she held it overhead, the last of the firelight gleamed off white wood in the shape of a wolfish mask.

Like the one she's wearing. Elaina hoped she wasn't oohing or aaahing out loud, as she was in her head. *Smaller, though...no fringe or mane or crown of beads. It's a death mask.*

Someone—probably Pasha, Elaina guessed—had given Nikita a bucket full of water. The alpha male poured it over the last of Polina's fire, sending clouds of steam rolling up over the structure, enveloping the diminished shroud, and the last remains of Polina's body. The two foster parents who had taken in her children came forward to swaddle the bones in a fresh, clean shroud, and Yasmin placed the death mask upon it, over the skull.

A sound drew Elaina's attention to the path again. The pallbearers returned, carrying a shallow, boat-like coffin between them. With Yasmin's guidance, the foster parents lifted the final shroud and Polina's bones from the pyre, and lowered it into the coffin.

"Now, those who wish to say their goodbyes will go to the coffin and offer a kiss," Timofei explained. Before he'd even finished his sentence, several of the tribe had risen from their seats to line up and do exactly that, planting their farewell kisses to the smooth brow of the wooden mask.

"The rite is concluded, now." Adelaida had risen from her place to come stand with Elaina and Timofei at the edge of the circle, and Bernard followed. "If you'd prefer not to stay, Elaina, Timofei can take you back to the house."

"I'll stay," Elaina replied without hesitating. Her head felt light and swimmy, and her chest felt full of warmth. "It would feel disrespectful to leave before the others have said their goodbyes."

When all had finished bestowing their final respects on the to the deceased, the pallbearers took up the coffin again. They carried it away from the clearing, and Polina's sons, with their new guardians, followed.

"They'll take it to our burial site," Adelaida explained. "And she will be... interred."

A hitch caught in her throat on the last word. Elaina had never seen Adelaida's fine, dignified features darkened by anything so common as poor sorrow before, but now, the former alpha bit her lip, and her eyes gleamed with tears. Timofei wrapped an arm around her and held her close, while Bernard took her hand in his. It struck Elaina then: the last funerary rites observed here might very well have been those of Adelaida's lost mate, Zhuang, and the two warriors who fell in battle with him.

The rest of the tribe began to drift away, and those among the wolf pack started the work of disassembling the scaffolding. Nikita stood at the head of the path, staring after the pallbearers and Polina's orphaned children for a long time, before finally approaching Elaina and those gathered with her.

"Are you ready to return to your mate's domicile?"

"I suppose," she replied. Reaching out a hand to touch his arm, she added, "Thank you. For letting me witness this."

"Do you understand a little more of us now?" His expression looked weary. Nearly four hours of mourning had left them all drained, Elaina imagined.

"I do."

"Come, then." He gestured for her to follow and started off in the direction of Gavri's lodge.

"Thank you, too," she said to Timofei and Adelaida. She offered Gavri's mother a gentle pat on the hand. "I am so very sorry for your loss."

She meant Polina, and she also meant Zhuang, and Victor, too. Timofei extended his free arm to loop Elaina into a brief hug as well, and a warmth bloomed inside her. In the wake of their grief, Gavri's family, at least, had offered her their willingness to accept.

With one last bow of thanks, she retreated from them, and trotted into place behind Nikita.

THEY WALKED IN SILENCE FOR quite some time. Nikita's grief radiated from him like a dark, hot bruise, an obvious pain he carried in his shoulders and spine. Again Elaina wondered how she'd handle this loss, if she were alpha of the pack. Would she take it so personally? Feel responsible, as Nikita so clearly did?

She recalled the hard, bitter look in the eyes of Polina's oldest boy, and the sense of familiarity it gave her. Had that look been on Nikita's face at some point? Or Gavri's?

No... someone else.

"Nikita?"

She touched his shoulder, making him pause. He faced her, putting one hand on his hip. "What?"

"I'm truly sorry about all of this. I see how devastated the pack is, and how terrible the threat of the *vukodlak*."

He rolled his eyes. It probably wasn't hard for him to guess what she meant to ask him.

"Don't you think this makes it even *more* important for the Stolby tribe to be united? Keeping Gavri and Kolya—Rini and Grisha, too—keeping them at a distance, driving them away, can only hurt the tribe, keeping it divided."

Nikita turned away from her and kept walking. Baffled by his refusal to answer, Elaina didn't immediately fall into step again, but stared at his back.

He didn't leave her waiting long. "I understand your feelings, too, human girl. Remember, Gavri has been like a brother to me, our families close as blood. Rini and Grisha are under no exile, but choose to separate themselves, as is true even for Gavri, and for you. I have only exiled one from my pack. The one stained by the very enemies who took Polina from us."

"Kolya is the farthest thing from an enemy, and you know it." Elaina put out her hands, beseeching. "He's an omega wolf, for goodness sakes. He is quiet and kind. Of all the Stolby wolves, perhaps the quietest. Can you really see him turning savage?"

"Any *oboroten* can fall to the madness." His tone was hushed. At least she hadn't incited his anger. Yet. "And Kolya already bears the blood of one, indulges in the perversion of a sick man. I will not lift his exile, Elaina. You and I have our agreement. Even that, I now regret. You are right: it is not the time for our tribe to be divided, and yet here we are, preparing for a challenge in leadership. You have made steps toward understanding us, but you cannot possibly understand enough by the time of the solstice to be our leader. No."

He stopped and shook his head. "I made a mistake in entertaining your provocation. Better that I ask *you* to withdraw your bid."

"Drop the blood hunt," she told him, "and I will."

"I have explained why I cannot. So we are at an impasse, Elaina Jacob. Do not ask me to compromise my decision again, or I *will* reject your challenge, regardless of the blemish it would put on my honor."

"But you *know* Kolya," she begged him.

"I knew him once. Before his... unfortunate choices."

Elaina halted. "Will you at least tell me why you're so afraid of him?"

Nikita regarded her, and for an instant it seemed he *would* say something. Maybe some more intolerant bullshit, but maybe—if she judged the careful consideration in his eyes right—something truly telling.

Whatever it might be, though, in the end he kept it to himself. Without giving her any answer at all, he closed up, and continued walking.

A long time later, they crested a hill and came into sight of Gavri's lodge. Nikita held out his hand as though holding open a door for her, then turned to walk away.

"Wait."

Elaina took his hand in hers. Giving his fingers a short, soft squeeze, she met his eyes. "Thank you again, Nikita."

He stared at her. The expression on his face gave away nothing, but he held her hand for several silent, pregnant seconds. Then, with a gruff sound of acknowledgment, he dipped his head in a nod, and let go. Moments later, she'd lost sight of him through the trees.

What was it he almost told me back there? And... what was that, between us just now?

She wondered if, somewhere deep inside, Nikita had also harbored feelings for Kolya. What did the Freshman Psych teachers call it? Reaction formation? Perhaps the new alpha had a bi-curious streak to him, and in his confused, indoctrinated brain, it made him angry. Disgusted with himself.

He hasn't taken a mate of his own, she noted. Gavri had even mentioned, it hadn't been for lack of willing women.

Don't stereotype, Elaina. He's not gay, just because he doesn't flaunt women around or because he's threatened by Kolya's sexuality.

But... what *had* he been about to tell her?

Elaina took a deep breath, and let it out in a slow, measured exhale. The walk had chased away the buzz of the vodka. The night was dark, with no moon overhead yet. A whirl of stars and galaxies filled the sky, though, and she took a moment to stare up at it, awed by its immenseness. She thought of the tribe, and their high, keening songs of sorrow. Of Yasmin, drumming and dancing, leading them in a longing catharsis. It hadn't only been Polina's death they mourned. This evening's ritual channeled the losses of all the *oboroten* gone before, a chain of genetic memory stretching into antiquity.

I was a part of it, Elaina marveled. *Not just a guest, some outsider observing the native culture. I felt their pain. I was there, with them.*

The epiphany came. The sense that had eluded her all day, the poignant, perfect knowledge of the place she would dedicate her shrine.

She gazed at the lights of Gavri's lodge, just ahead of her. For the first time, it occurred to her how late it was, and she'd only given her boys a short and very vague explanation of where she'd meant to go.

They must be worried out of their minds, she realized, and hurried for the house.

About halfway there, her hiking boots skidded on a loose patch of dirt. Elaina caught herself before she stumbled, and then, with a flutter of eerie discomfort, she saw the thing resting on a large stone just to the left of the path ahead.

A blue, ceramic mug, steaming in the cool night. The smell of cinnamon tea drifted up from it, fresh and fragrant.

CHAPTER TEN

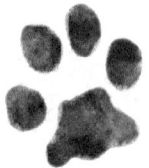

SHE GOT A WELL-DESERVED chewing out by Gavri and didn't argue over it. Her mates had gone tracking when she hadn't returned by sunset, and when her path crossed with Nikita's and eventually Adelaida's, they'd heard the keening, and guessed where she'd gone.

"Still," her beta wolf growled, pacing the living room as he vented his anger. "You should have sent someone to us. You should have called."

Elaina kept her silence, accepting her dressing-down, and eventually, Gavri burned himself out. By the time she came to bed, they were friends again, and he slept with his arms tightly—almost too tightly—around her.

After her brief lesson in Russian the next morning, she announced her plan for the shrine.

"I'm going back to the place we met," she told them. "The cave, where you first revealed your true selves."

Lounging on the sunroom sofas, Gavri and Kolya traded glances. "*Krasavitsa,*" Kolya said. "It's a long way, and it's in the open part of the reserve. Tourists travel there."

"Not where we were," she assured him. "I doubt any hiker would just happen to find the cave, and if they did, I just have this feeling—I'm almost *sure*—they'd avoid it."

Taking a moment to bask in the cool morning breeze wafting in from the open double doors onto the patio, she added, "Most hikers are a bit smarter than I was, anyway."

"I wouldn't count on it." Gavri flipped a page in the book he'd been reading, a thick Stephen King novel with a picture of a sewer grate on the front, and a creeping reptilian hand coming out of it. He'd told her he kept up his English reading the untranslated versions. "There is news here all the time of visitors getting lost or stranded on the rocks or falling to their deaths, because they were not well prepared."

This brought a blush to Elaina's face, even though she'd just admitted as much. "Well, even so. I have a feeling Diezana will protect this place."

"Why the cave?" Kolya asked. He didn't sound dubious, only interested.

"Because, in a way, it's where I was reborn."

A rush of gratitude filled her when both men nodded, agreeing in gentle tones it made good sense. Like Diezana, reborn when the wolf found her lost in the snow and taught her to take the form of a wolf herself, Elaina had bid farewell to a simple human existence in the blizzard and begun her journey into the world of Diezana's people.

"Plus, I have very fond memories of that night." She shot her boys a licentious smirk, and they both grinned knowingly in return.

Grisha showed up just before she set out to find the cave again. All three men argued she couldn't go alone—especially with the threat of the *vukodlak* hanging over them—but she wouldn't allow them to come.

"I need to do this on my own," she insisted. "Please. I'm learning more and more about the woods here and it's getting much easier for me to navigate them. Give me a map back to the cave and I'll be just fine. You'll be able to follow my trail even if I get lost again."

"But *krasavitsa,*" Gavri growled. "The skinwalkers—"

"This isn't a werewolf movie, Gav." She planted her hands on her hips. "I'll be careful, I promise. But we're talking about a human tourist on a normal nature hike in the middle of broad daylight. They haven't gone after mortal hikers like that before, have they?"

"I still don't like it." Grisha wore a scowl like he'd just caught a whiff of something rotten. "You'll have *our* scent all over you. At least let us accompany you in case of danger. You can find the spot and perform the ritual on your own, but the journey—"

"If I were any other *oboroten* seeking to build my personal shrine, would I bring others with me?" she pointed out. Grisha narrowed his eyes. Yesterday during their trip to the rocks to climb, he'd explained the normal ritual to her: how to erect her totem and anoint it with the blood of her kill. He'd also told her while many found the sacred places with the help of others, the journey to consecrate their chosen spot, they made on their own. Doing otherwise defeated the point of it being a *personal* experience, and he damn well knew it.

"I'll take a sat phone, will that make you happy?" she asked. Gavri grumbled his agreement and went to his office to retrieve the device. In the meantime, Kolya stepped forward and took her hands in his.

"I made something for you." He slipped a hard, smooth object into her palm. Elaina gave a soft sound of excitement, beholding the carved figure of a howling wolf, exquisite in detail and design.

"Kolya! It's wonderful!" She ran her hand down the subtle slope of its shoulders and back, down to its tapering tail.

"I had intended perhaps to give it to you if you manage to manifest the gifts of the spirit mother," he admitted with a look of chagrin. "Then, I realized it will not be a matter of *if*. It will only be *when*."

The sting of joyous tears made her wipe her eyes. She threw her arms around her big russet wolf and kissed him. "Thank you, love. Thank you so, so much."

"I have something for you too, but it's far more practical," Grisha put in. He handed over her backpack, ready with supplies, and said, "I cleaned and prepped the boar for you yesterday after my ride. Blood's packed in a thermos. You won't need more than what's in there to consecrate the shrine. You remember what I told you at the rocks?"

"Yes," she assured him, and slung the backpack on her shoulders, then kissed him on the cheek.

"I saved the skull of the boar as well." He retrieved it from where it had rested on the floor beside the backpack. "I thought maybe you'd like to use it on the totem. Turn around and I'll strap it onto the pack."

"That will be fun to explain if I run into other hikers," she said with a laugh. She did as he asked, though.

"Looks like it's the morning for presents." Gavri reappeared from the hall. In one hand he held the SAT phone, and passed it to her with a mutter. "Don't know why you didn't take it yesterday..."

"I just hadn't intended to go that far." She clipped the phone to her belt. "And I needed to be able to *feel* myself in the world, without being pulled away from the moment by a phone, of all things. I knew if I got lost, you could all follow my trail and find me again."

"It's not following you into the woods I'm worried about." He handed her the second object. "I can track you across hundreds of miles. You never have to worry about getting lost. But the *vukodlak*—"

"I know." She stroked his arm reassuringly. "I'll be careful, Gavri. I promise."

His gift to her was an intricate pocket watch and compass, built with the kind of delicate care to put the biggest designer Swiss watchmakers to shame.

At least, I'll always think so. She beamed, examining the careful detail. On the back he'd engraved a set of wolves and one long-tailed snow leopard in mid-run, chasing some unseen game across forest fields. The wolf in the lead was smaller and sleeker than the other two. Another version of the *oboroten* Elaina, when she finally traded flesh for fur, and ran with them on four legs instead of two.

"I love it," she told him. Turning to include her other mates, she said, "I love it all. Thank you. I promise, I will make all of you proud of me."

"Just use the phone if you get in trouble," Gavri grumped. "It's all I ask."

She laughed at him and pulled him to her for another kiss. "I love you."

Reaching for Kolya next, she kissed him too, and repeated the sentiment. "I love you too, Kol. And you, Grisha. Come here."

Her snow leopard came to her, wearing the put-upon look of a cat intent on convincing the world he did *not* want to snuggle, but did so because he'd been pushed into it. She kissed him and he relaxed in her arms, sliding his tongue into her mouth and tilting her back. One big hand squeezed her butt.

"Hey!" she slapped him playfully in the chest. "Timing, mister."

"You're right," he whispered. "When you return then. The three of us will fuck you until your legs turn to jelly and you can't walk anymore."

He threw a glance at the others. "She won't go wandering off on her own anymore, at least."

Gavri and Kolya, evidently, were all in favor of it.

THE WOODS HAD ALREADY GROWN warm, and Elaina expected the afternoon might climb into the eighties. Quite the opposite of the first time she'd made this trek a little more than two weeks ago, with the last late-season snow on the ground and the lingering effects of hypothermia and exhaustion weighing her down. It had taken most of the day for Gavri and Kolya to lead her from the cave where they'd met to the safety of the lodge. Then again, this time she was far better prepared, and could manage a much stronger pace.

Gavri had drawn her a map to the general area where they'd found her in the blizzard. From there, he couldn't be certain where exactly the cave might be, but Elaina thought she could find it. She would be led to it, she had no doubt.

Though prickling at the back of her mind, a creeping anxiety reminded her... she hadn't heard the song of Diezana since the hunt. Not even during Polina's funeral rites, which concerned her. She didn't want to entertain the troubling questions starting to gnaw at her... not yet.

The blue sky soared overhead like the lights of the stars the night before, wider and farther-reaching than she'd seen anywhere else in the world. It promised leagues and leagues of land to discover, miles and miles to run, and she focused her mind on the coming weeks when she *could* run, racing through the woods on all fours with her mates and her tribe.

Whatever tribe it may be. If I'm not brought into the Stolby pack... we'll find another. We'll forge another. A tribe and pack of our own.

What would happen if she did win Diezana's favor, but her shifter form did not turn out to be a wolf? She hadn't considered it, though she knew Diezana's children did not choose their animal selves. The wolves of Stolby formed the leadership of the tribe—an old tradition, and knowing now the story of Diezana's own ascension, Elaina understood the roots of the practice. She'd started this journey by flying in the face of the *oboroten*'s culture and tradition, and now regretted the audacity she'd shown him. If she learned to shift, however, and Diezana chose for her to be a fox or a feline, or even a deer, could she still lay any claim to becoming a leader?

It would almost certainly be another long battle. And would it be worth it? Even more *division and conflict?*

A flicker of light caught her attention up ahead. Her heart skipped as a bright, silvery tail disappeared behind a stand of juniper bushes, and Elaina picked up her pace, breaking into a jog. She recognized the shining gleam of moonlight on ethereal, starry fur, even in the bright sun of mid-morning.

"Spirit!" she called after it. "Inferi! Come back!"

She didn't think the spirit would, though, and laughter bubbled up in her chest. Inferi had taunted her into a game of tag during her spirit walk, and she'd chased the enormous wolf through fields and between the trees in glorious wild abandon. If Inferi were leading her now, surely the spirit would take her to the cave, to the spot where she was meant to make her tribute.

Sprinting ahead, she caught sight of the gleaming hindquarters just as Inferi disappeared behind a stand of pine. Coming around the trees, she glimpsed starry, dark eyes peering at her from under a low shrub. Elaina raced after the wolf, full of joy, reassured and comforted. Of all the otherworldly entities she'd encountered, Inferi was the best.

After some time playing in the woods, Elaina had to pause, leaning on a low tree branch to catch her breath. Though she couldn't see Inferi ahead of her when she wasn't on the move, she sensed the patient presence waiting for the game to resume.

The rustle of leaves behind her gave her a start. Elaina glanced over her shoulder to find she, too, had a pursuer.

Pasha, in his lupine form, lingered several paces behind her. He stood with ears at attention, chest high, and didn't bother to hide when she spotted him.

He only blinked, returning her gaze, and sat down as if to wait.

"What are you doing here?" Elaina tried to keep the heat out of her voice but couldn't help the quaver of frustration. Her hand moved to the sat phone and she prepared for an attack.

Pasha didn't lunge this time, though. He tilted his big, shaggy head, and his tail thumped the ground. If his lupine expression weren't so gruff, she'd almost think he was teasing her.

"Are you going to jump me again?" She retreated a step to see if he'd move. He didn't.

Elaina scowled, then relaxed. Straightening, she crossed her arms over her chest and squared off with him.

"I have a task to complete out here," she told him. "I'd prefer to do it alone. If you don't have a reason for being here—or if you're here spying on me—please leave me alone. This is *my* task and *my* journey."

Pasha's eyes drooped, as if he were bored. He opened his jaws in a wide, canine yawn. He was *mocking* her.

"Shut up!" she snapped, feeling stupid. "I'm serious, Pasha!"

Finally, the big wolf loped to his feet. Instead of turning back, though, he strode toward her with calm, unassuming purpose. Elaina's shoulders tensed and she reached for the sat phone again, but even as she laid her fingers on the buttons to call home, Pasha walked past her at a lazy gait. His tail wagged in a low, languid sweep, brushing her thighs. When he'd pulled about a half dozen paces ahead, he paused, looking over his shoulder at her.

Does he want me to follow him?

Elaina ran a hand through her hair, staring at the massive wolf. He stared back. She almost decided to turn her back on him and walk away, when she realized he had zeroed in on the same direction the spirit Inferi seemed to be leading her.

She rubbed a hand over her mouth. "Pasha.... did you see it, too?"

Pasha peered at her, then lowered his head, scanning the shady wilderness, searching.

If he didn't see Inferi, why is he following its trail? Did it call him here?

Grisha had explained the excursion to the place of worship was for one alone. She must begin the journey by herself, to be open to the messages and guidance of the spirits around her. And she *had* begun it on her own. She'd come this far and met one of the spirits, and now...

Now Pasha had joined her.

"Is this part of your plan?" she murmured, neither to Pasha nor to the unseen Inferi, if Inferi still lingered nearby. Elaina's question was for Diezana. Diezana who had not reached out to her for days, and who might have grown tired of the human pup still struggling with issues of authority.

Pasha turned in a circle, facing her again, and sat down. His dark gaze weighed on her. His tail twitched back and forth.

"You won't attack me?" She took a careful step toward him.

The wolf turned his face away, a gesture she took to mean *no*.

"And you won't interfere with my task?"

Again, the same gesture.

He's watching out for me. A shining astonishment bloomed in her chest. *He's guarding* me.

"Did Gavri or Kolya send you?"

Pasha gave a snort, stood, and shook himself. He turned back in the direction Inferi had disappeared and padded onward.

Elaina frowned, and let her hand drop to the sat phone again. Slipping it out of its pouch on her belt, she held it ready, and followed him.

If Kolya did see any spirits or hear their summons, he didn't give any indication Elaina recognized. He trotted through the woods, never letting her fall too far behind without pausing to wait, then moving on again. He stopped now and again to scent the wind or prick up his ears, or search the unfolding shadows of the trees, but all remained calm. Elaina chewed at her bottom lip, unable to decide how she felt about this new game of follow-the-leader with Nikita's beta wolf and silent, stony enforcer. He *had* attacked her only yesterday, and though she understood now why he'd done it, she couldn't help the tense feeling at the back of her neck which told her he might do it again. If he *did* whip around without warning, and leapt for her throat, what could she do? She had a lockback knife in her pocket, something she'd brought for utility, and just in case she crossed paths with another wild pig or grumpy bear. She didn't think it would make a very effective weapon against one of the *oboroten*, though.

Or... She couldn't help the suspicion, like a seedling taking root in her brain. *A shapeshifter going mad, like the* vukodlak *Victor.*

She didn't like the thought, just planting itself in her head and waiting there. Pasha might be Nikita's muscle but for all she distrusted him, he'd never *actually* done anything to harm her. To put a little fear in her, yes, and establish his honor, but never to *harm* her. And who was she to start crying witch? Nikita feared Kolya's descent into corruption and madness, but those fears weren't based in any reality as far as Elaina judged. What reasons did she have to fear it from Pasha? It wasn't very fair.

Maybe not fair, her mother's voice cut in. For once, Elaina didn't immediately cringe. *When your safety is on the line, you don't* have *to be fair.*

Tricia Jacob had her flaws, but she wasn't *always* out-of-line.

Nagging, anxious curiosity gave way to astonishment when, some time later, Pasha led her to the exact place she'd been looking for. She caught up to him sitting patiently on a patch of bright grass, tail sweeping back and forth as he gazed ahead. It looked much, much different, with the snow gone and the vibrant green-and-gold of summertime woods all around. When she'd crawled out of the cave on the morning after the blizzard, the entrance had been only a tiny passage. Climbing out had been something like crawling through the playground jungle gym or hiding under the dining room table in a game of hide-and-seek. Now, she could walk through without even crouching.

Looking at the dark, open mouth of the place where she had met the first of her mates—the place they had first made love, chasing away the fear and the cold of the night and the icy, frozen specter of death hanging over her—she marveled at how unafraid she'd been. She'd seen then how their faces changed, their ears tapering to points and their eyes turning starry and black. She'd *known* then. Perhaps she hadn't accepted it right away, and perhaps she hadn't understood the full extent of what it meant. She'd known, though.

She'd recognized her wolves.

Elaina shot Pasha a glance. "Do you know why you brought me here?"

He made his bowing-of-the-head gesture again, the one she believed meant *no*.

"How did you know where I wanted to go?"

The wolf lowered his head to the ground and swept it back and forth, making a show of sniffing at the grass. Then he raised his nose into the wind, sniffing back and forth in the air.

"Followed a scent, huh?" Elaina planted one hand on her hip. "You're good. And do you plan to stick around? This ritual is supposed to be private, I'm told."

Pasha blinked at her, impassive. He settled down on the grass, stretching out and letting his tongue loll out between his teeth. He'd stay, it seemed... but out here. Keeping watch, while she worked.

Elaina raised her eyebrows, genuinely impressed. After a moment's consideration, she told him, "Okay. Thank you."

The wolf laid his head on his paws and flicked his ears.

The entrance to the cave might be wider without the several feet of snow clogging it, but it faced east, away from the sun which was now past the apogee of its climb and descending with the afternoon. The passage lay dark, like an open, toothless mouth. The sight of it called up an unhappy shiver in her memory. Elaina shuddered, a quick, involuntary reaction, as though the bitter cold wind of that night had returned for one last caress of her skin.

Crouching, she slipped her backpack from her shoulders and set it on the ground before her. It took some effort to loosen the knots Grisha had used to secure the boar's skull, but finally she lifted it free, and dug into the pack's main pocket. The LED lantern sat right on top of her other supplies.

"Perfect." Elaina beamed. She loved the smooth, compact can, which looked like a small thermos at first glance, short but solid. Flipping the handle on the top, she pulled, and an inner cylinder slid free, flashing to life with bright, beautiful white light.

Holding the lantern in one hand, she slipped an arm through the straps of the pack to pick it up again and grabbed the boar's skull. Taking a deep, steadying breath, she entered the cave.

The hill of snow had narrowed the entrance of the cave, but the interior had been quite roomy. It remained as Elaina remembered it; even the circle of small rocks and the charred remains of the campfire Gavri and Kolya had built. A giggle escaped her as she found a single sock—one of the thin ankle socks she wore as an inner layer under thicker, woolen socks when she hiked in snow—lying discarded near the back of the space.

Kolya crouched there, by the fire, when I woke up. She turned in place, taking in the empty stone room, warmed by the memories. *Gavri had gone out to get hot broth from the wise woman.*

And when he returned, the strange animal attraction hit. The nearness of their bodies, shielding her from the cold of the night; the heat of their hands on her skin, the hurried kisses and desperate, driven desire. How easy it had been to give into the passion, but so shocking, and even a little frightening. How life-affirming.

Diezana led me then. Elaina set the boar skull and the backpack down near the ring of stones, and her hand drifted to the rough granite wall. *Is that why, though these memories make me happy, something still feels... incomplete? Because when we were here together, she was here with us, too. Her song in my head, soothing me. Reassuring me.*

Without Diezana's song, the memory lacked a key piece. Elaina's heart fell.

"Still though," she assured herself, pivoting to the circle of rocks forming the fire ring. "This *is* the place. It's not exactly what I suspected from you, spirit mother. It's a start though. It is..."

The beginning. Of everything.

Everything for Elaina, at least.

She crouched and gathered up the stones, inspecting them and turning them over in her hands one by one. When she found one to suit her needs, she set it aside and continued searching the others. Presently she had a pile of six, arranged in ascending size. After a moment of contemplation, chewing at her lip, she added a seventh. Seven stones, for seven tasks.

She'd build the totem at the very back of the cave. Elaina worked carefully, choosing each stone one by one and setting it in front of her as she sat on her knees. Holding it between her thighs, she took the lockback knife from her pocket and pricked her left index finger with a pained hiss.

"The shamans mark their totems with personal sigils." When they'd paused atop one of the Stolby pillars the day before, Grisha unfolded a well-creased, yellowing piece of parchment and spread it out before her. He showed her the old marks and pictographs: designs somewhere between the cave paintings of early man and the angular hieroglyphics of the pharaohs. Elaina had studied them for most of their lunch hour, and before bed, and then again this morning.

She didn't want to only use the language of her natural-born pack mates, though. Sure, marks like these were perfect for an *oboroten* shrine. This totem though was not—not *yet*—an *oboroten* shrine. It was Elaina's, and for the moment, Elaina was only a human girl wishing to become an *oboroten*.

If I can do it... if I can master the magic and use it to dethrone Nikita... I can build a new shrine. A shapeshifter's totem, which I will cover all over with the correct oboroten glyphs. But this *shrine is built by the human Elaina. The aspirant. I haven't earned the right to speak the oboroten tongue... so I won't use it for this.*

Good old English would do for her purposes now. Her first language, though it wouldn't be her last. She dabbed her finger to the largest of the stones, leaving a spot of her blood upon it.

Over the next few hours she worked on the pieces of her shrine. She marked each one as she had the first, with a single dot of her own blood. Using stoneworking chisels lent to her by Kolya, she carved words into the stones, taking great care. Her letters came out angular and uneven, making her laugh at herself, but they were legible in the end.

She'd already thought of the seven steps she should represent: seven steps in her journey; seven evolutions of herself as she began to know a new Elaina here in this foreign, yet inviting, land.

On the first rock, she chiseled the word *Discovery*. She then set it in place against the cave's back wall. Taking up the second stone, she carved *Connection*. Images rose in her mind, the quick intimacies she and Kolya and Gavri had enjoyed here, though they were strangers to each other. They'd most certainly shared *connection*. She set the second stone on top of the first.

Elaina anointed the third rock *Trust*. Then came *Love*. Once she'd decided those, however, she came to a stop. Her fingers ran over the final three smooth, flat tokens. Here, seven steps would really become twelve. On these top stones, each lesson brought with it a counterpart, an outcome. In their own way, rewards.

On the next stone she diligently worked in two words: *Loyalty* along one edge; on the opposite edge, *Unity*. The second to last rock bore *Truth* and *Joy*. And, finally, on the last stone, the one which would sit at the very top, she carved *Inspiration*, and *Transformation*.

Once each stone bore its engraving, Elaina took the boar's blood from her backpack, along with a set of fine-bristle paintbrushes she'd borrowed from Gavri. Beginning again with the biggest stone, she dipped the paintbrush into the thermos of blood, and began filling in the channels she'd carved.

The elements which would form the base of her shrine—the cairn—were complete. Placing the final stone on top of her cairn, she teemed with pride. She considered her work, stacked up against the wall, forming a series of steps about three feet high.

Elaina dug through her pack again, and selected a drill Kolya had loaned her, equipped with a masonry bit. When she'd explained her intentions, he'd selected the bit for her, and a backup, and a set of anchors for her to place in the granite wall of the cave.

"I'd suggest traditional stone masonry tools," Grisha noted, leaning against Kolya's worktable as he watched them discuss proper methods of installation. "But using those might take days, and might be a two-person job. I don't think Diezana will begrudge us this small shortcut."

The drill whirred to life, and Elaina squinted against the flying flecks of dust and stone.

She drilled two holes and placed two bolts. On these, she fitted the skull of the boar, so it hung above the cairn.

At long last, holding the thermos with the last of the pig's blood, Elaina bowed her head, and listened.

Nothing. No song. No timely acknowledgement with a howl from far-off, distant Inferi. She gave it a full count of three minutes, to no avail.

"Well," she whispered, heaving a weary sigh. "I don't know why you'd have called me here, if you didn't intend me to finish these tasks and earn your blessing. You didn't have to reach out to a human, after all. But now you're giving me the cold shoulder, Diezana. Have I done something wrong? Will you even send a message to me, somehow?"

Silence answered.

Elaina felt tears prick at her eyes again. "I guess, if this is how it's going to be for now. I'll just have to hope you haven't changed your mind about me."

Did spirits change their minds? She'd always been led to believe they were stoic and immovable. Bound to cosmic laws of fate and consequence. Diezana's silence wounded Elaina. She'd already come so close to knowing this spirit, inside herself. But without

Diezana's voice leading her, she didn't know if she could truly find what she needed.

She took another deep breath, counting slowly to ten, and let it out in a long, grieving sigh. Elaina stepped forward, closer to her new shrine, unscrewing the thermos top.

When she tilted the thermos over the boar skull, the last of the blood ran down fresh over its chalky surface. Elaina spoke a short litany Grisha had taught her.

There. Task number three, done. She ran both hands through her hair. Maybe if her new mates had been here to admire it with her, they could tell her if she'd done it right.

All at once, she brightened. Picking up her lantern, she returned to the mouth of the cave and looked out. Pasha still lay in the grass, following a small, buzzing fly as it hovered before him. He snapped for it, but the insect bobbed out of the way and drifted lazily to one side.

"Pasha?" Elaina wandered a few steps out of the entrance. "Could you... come look at something for me?"

The wolf glanced up at the sound of her voice, and after a small pause, rose to join her. Elaina led him into the stone chamber, letting the light fall on her new totem.

"I'm not sure I did this right." She spoke in a hushed tone, scrubbing the back of her free hand over her forehead. "I don't... *hear* anything."

A thoughtful sound, not quite a whine but a curious *hmm,* escaped Pasha. He crossed back and forth in front of the shrine and sniffed it. His tail wagged.

"It would be more helpful if you'd change back and actually talk to me," Elaina told him.

The big wolf gazed at her. His tail swept low, brushing aside little flurries of dirt and tiny pebbles. Then he hunkered down, tucked his head between his front paws, and changed. Fur receded into smooth, tanned skin; his ears shrunk down, and his paws reshaped themselves into rough hands. Pasha stood, mindful of the sloping cave ceiling, and tilted his head, considering the shrine.

Sinking to one knee, he planted a hand on the floor beside the cairn and leaned close to inspect the engravings.

"What do they say?"

Right. He isn't fluent in English, like Gav.

Crouching beside him, she pointed out the words as she read them. "Discovery. Connection. Trust. Love."

Pasha met her eyes. "Your feelings for your mates."

"My quest to find my*self*," she corrected him. "Yes, my mates played a part. So has Nikita. So have you, even. But it's about finding myself, not anyone else."

He gazed up at the boar's skull, marked with the drying tracks of blood. "Where did you find that?"

"I killed it. On a ritual hunt."

Pasha looked impressed. She almost mentioned she hadn't exactly meant to kill a *boar*, but bit her tongue. She liked the warm glow of pride his expression kindled in her chest. Let him think she'd set out to take on a razor-tusked hog and won.

"Did I do it right?" she asked him again, scrutinizing her work with a grimace. "I thought I would receive some sort of sign or feel some stroke of inspiration."

Pasha gestured for her to follow him, and led her back out of the cave, where he could stand up straight.

"*Totemy* are defined by their... *tvorets*." He held his hands before him, gesticulating as he searched for the right word. "Their *maker*. You built yours with your own hands and with the blessings of your work. The totem is as it should be."

"But nothing feels different. Diezana... I usually hear her voice—you know, the song? I thought I'd hear it again now."

He quirked an eyebrow. "Did the making put you in danger?"

"No, not at all." She crossed her arms over her stomach, contemplating. "But she sings to me other times, too. *Sang* to me. Times when... well, I guess when she wanted me to learn something, or pay attention?"

"Our shamans and the children of her voice speak these thoughts, too. For some, the lessons seem to be... *ty dolzhen sdelat' eto bez menya*. Er, 'you must do this without me'."

Elaina tapped her lips. "I suppose it's the best I'm going to get. Say, why did you come after me?"

"You were walking alone. I thought Gavri might be upset if I let his puppy be eaten by the *vukodlak*."

She'd been just about to smile, when the words *his puppy* turned her mood instantly sour.

"Okay, okay..." Checking her watch, she slipped back into the cave one last time to retrieve her backpack. She threw a final glance at her shrine, brushed her hair out of her face and rearranged her ponytail. When she exited the cave, Pasha waited for her in his lupine form.

"Now you'll walk me home?" she asked, half-teasing. Pasha dipped his head in a nod and trotted in the direction of the road.

Elaina hesitated a moment before following. *Not so bad, for Nikita's thug.*

Her own thoughts made her flinch, though. Pasha wasn't really a thug. For that matter, Nikita wasn't really a tyrant.

If only they weren't so determined to drive out the men I love.

CHAPTER ELEVEN

"WAS PASHA BOTHERING YOU?"

Gavri craned his neck over the back of the couch, peering past Elaina when she entered the lodge, as if he expected to see Pasha waltz in behind her. Elaina set her pack down by the stairs and gave him a quizzical look.

Rini bustled to Elaina's side to help her out of her light jacket. "They can pick up his scent," she explained in a quiet murmur.

"Oh."

All three of her mates waited in the living room. Gavri sat on the couch with the remote in one hand, watching the evening news with Kolya sitting on the floor between his knees. Grisha lounged across the sectional arm of the sofa, purring quietly, eyes half-shut in a doze.

Elaina bent to kiss Gavri, then Kolya, stroking her russet wolf's short hair, before nudging Grisha to move so she could sit between all of them in the corner formed by the sectional. Her snow leopard moved to curl closer to her, laying his head in her lap.

Just to make things perfect, Koty came bounding from the dining room and jumped up to snuggle at Elaina's side.

"Well?" Grisha asked. "What did the enforcer want with you?"

"I crossed paths with him on my hike." She twined her fingers in Grisha's dark hair, and the soft rumble of his purr renewed. "He followed me to the cave. To make sure the *vukodlak* stayed away. I didn't *ask* him to come along!" she insisted, seeing Gavri's expression. "I told him to leave me alone, but he came anyway."

Gavri growled and turned off the TV. "Then I'll have to introduce him to the concept of boundaries."

"No, don't." Elaina reached out to run her hand gently along the back of his neck. "I didn't want him there at first, but he kept a respectful distance. He didn't interfere with my task. He just stayed nearby to keep watch."

"*We* could have stood watch." He rubbed at his temple. "And we offered!"

"It's different." Grisha leaned into her as she massaged his scalp. "We weren't part of this lesson for Elaina. If Pasha was called to her during her revelations, he was meant to be there."

Kolya—who so rarely seemed troubled by *any*one—wrinkled his nose and gave a petulant huff.

"Oh, Kol." Elaina stopped rubbing Gavri's shoulder and leaned forward to caress Kolya's cheek. "Don't give me such a look. Honestly, you two are acting like a couple of sad Labradors. Pouting because I met another dog."

Gavri sniffed. "*Labradors?*"

"Well, do wolves pout when their alpha is approached by another wolf?"

"No." His icy blue eyes were dark and humorless. "They drive the interloper away."

165

Violently, if necessary, his tone said.

"Enough posturing." She jabbed Gavri in the side. "It's not attractive."

"So says the *queen* of posturing!" Grisha burst into laughter, sitting up. Elaina slapped his shoulder.

Gavri looped an arm around her and pulled her close. Koty, dislodged from her place, hopped to the floor and into Kolya's lap instead.

"Are you tired from your day, *krasavitsa?*" Gavri whispered, planting a kiss on Elaina's forehead.

"Yes. And sore. It's a long hike."

"*Da.*" He leaned his head against hers and took a long, deep breath, inhaling her scent. "How about we relax in the spa?"

Elaina grinned. "That sounds wonderful."

"Well, count me out," said Grisha, rising and stretching. "Think I'll head back to my place."

"He never wants to share a bath," Elaina whined to her wolves. Gavri and Kolya chuckled.

Grisha bent to kiss her, sliding one hand behind her neck and covering her mouth with his. "We can take tomorrow off, if you like. From your tasks, I mean. You haven't had so much as a day to rest."

Elaina shook her head. "I don't want to. I only have so much time, remember? Besides..." She tried for a winning smile. "I feel great! After the hunt, and all the extra time I get to spend out in the reserve... I love it."

"Yes, well, it might be good to break anyway." He stroked his chin, inspecting her. "You can't expect to keep going like this nonstop until the solstice."

Elaina took his hand, kissed it, and rubbed her cheek against it. "I'll be okay, Grisha. I promise, lots of sleep before we get started again tomorrow morning."

Her snow leopard snorted. "I doubt it. See you at seven."

Sauntering around the couch, he collected his biker's jacket from the coat rack by the door and showed himself out.

"Can we make it eight?" Elaina called after him. The door closed, leaving her without an answer.

"Oh, well, we'll make it eight." She snuggled closer to Gavri. Her wolves chuckled again.

Gavri untangled himself from her and Kolya, excusing himself to go start the jacuzzi on the deck. Elaina stretched out, taking the space he'd vacated, and tugged Kolya to her for another kiss. "So what did you three do today while I was gone?"

"I can't speak for Grisha." To her amazement, Kolya grew faintly pink. "But Gavri and I—"

"Had a romantic day to yourselves?" she asked hopefully. His blush intensified and he glanced away.

"*Da.*" A shy, boyish smile snuck its way across his face. Elaina chuckled and hugged him close.

Gavri returned and let them know he'd started the hot tub warming up. While he headed down the hall to grab towels from the laundry room, Elaina stood and led Kolya out to the deck, playfully pulling him by the hand.

"Oh, shoot," she exclaimed as they came to the lip of the tub. Shooting her mate a coy look, threw up her hands in helpless gesture. "Forgot my bathing suit. Guess I'll just run upstairs and—"

Kolya gave a short bark of a laugh and pushed her into the water.

"Hey!" Elaina came up sputtering, wet hair draped over her face like a mop. She swept it back with both hands and scowled up at him. "Kol! My clothes!"

Her big russet wolf—the *omega* wolf, the sweet, unassuming, introverted omega—shot her a cocky grin and shrugged. "They needed a wash anyway."

Before she could say anything else, he stripped off his clothes and jumped in with her. The hot tub wasn't deep enough for reckless diving, but it did have enough space for a bit of horseplay, and as soon as he hit the water Kolya swept out his arms in a wide arc to splash her.

Elaina raised her arms, her protests lost in a gale of laughter. His arms slipped around her, and he pressed her back until she slid onto the jacuzzi bench.

"If you're so worried about your clothes, let's get them off you." He helped himself to her shirt, slipping it up over her head before she could even reply, and then tugged her sports bra up, freeing her breasts.

"Ooh..." Elaina shivered as his hands spread over them, his thumbs gently circling her nipples.

"Already getting started, I see."

Gavri stepped out onto the deck, carrying towels over one arm and a tray of drinks in hand. He set both down on the deck chair beside the hot tub, safely out of splash range.

"Elaina, now why would you go and jump in the jacuzzi with your clothes on?" His eyes glittered with mirth; his wide smile gleamed. Elaina—distracted by Kolya, as he gently tweaked her stiffened, tingling flesh—waved an ill-aimed splash at Gavri.

With a rich laugh, Gavri stripped down, taking the time to fold his clothing and set it alongside the towels. Then, with far more decorum than either she or Kolya had shown, he stepped down into the tub. The jets switched on, and Elaina moaned: one of them was positioned right behind her back, and the sudden hot, rolling massage sent a wave of delight up her body.

Gavri strode through the water to her side, sitting on the jacuzzi bench next to her. Nudging her to raise her arms overhead, he slid the bra off altogether. Then, careful not to interrupt Kolya's tender attentions, Gavri set his hands on Elaina's hips and lifted her onto his lap.

His erection rose hard against her bottom. If not for her shorts, she could spread her thighs just the tiniest bit, and he'd be sliding and stroking the length of her cleft, rigid member tantalizing her.

"Let's get rid of these," Kolya declared, and as if he'd read her mind, he slipped his hands under her hiking shorts and slid them off. Elaina lifted her legs to help him, and then they were all three naked, slick bodies sliding together in the hot water.

Sandwiched between her mates, Elaina traded kisses with them, embracing Kolya with her arms around his neck, then craning over her shoulder to find Gavri's lips, tongue, nibbling teeth. Kolya continued stroking her breasts, slow and delightful in his motions, taking his time to stroke and caress, squeeze and lightly, ever-so-lightly, pinch. Gavri's hands, meanwhile, slid down her sides, until he cupped one hand to her belly, and the other one dropped down to fondle her thigh.

"Oh, loves," she breathed between kisses. "My sweet wolves..."

"Elaina," Kolya murmured as he nibbled her earlobe. "Have you spoken with Grisha about the manifestation of the World Tree?"

One of her seven tasks. The next one, in fact, after she crafted sacred tokens from the remains of her boar. "No, Kolya... not yet..."

Kolya slid between her thighs. He moved both hands up, tangling his fingers in her thick, dripping hair, tugging with a firm, but affectionate rowdiness. His kisses intensified. Each touch of his lips against hers sparked a sweet wave of warmth and bliss in her chest, and Elaina moaned against his mouth, begging for more.

"Manifestation requires a unique power," he whispered. Still kissing her, he rocked gently against her body, and Gavri picked up the motion and responded. Slow, leisurely, like waves on the shore, they moved with her. "Though it is not *required* to be a ritual involving sexual invocation... it can be done as such. And we would happily be a part of it."

"Yes," Gavri agreed. His hand on her thigh moved upward until his fingers found her clitoris, and gave it a long, loving stroke.

"Sex magic," Elaina breathed. With their mouths and hands on her, and their cocks nudging at her, euphoria filled her body. It crackled and fizzed in a steady, delicious torment, hinting at the pleasure to come. "You're talking about sex magic? The orgies you mentioned before?"

They'd talked about it once, but never delved into it. They'd explained to her how shamans or other vision seekers might engage in hedonistic group sex, giving over to the experience to bring about powerful revelations.

"Not exactly *orgies,*" Gavri whispered, lips tickling her ear. "Rather, the invocation of powerful emotion—powerful *sensation*—to gather and focus your energies to your goal."

"Something like this—" Kolya kissed her again. "—and this—"

He dropped down, sliding hands back to her breasts and delivering a kiss to each nipple. Elaina uttered a sweet sigh, and he took one pink peak into his mouth, lavishing it with warm, wet attention, tongue and teeth gently adoring. He switched to the other, stroking and sucking. Gavri, meanwhile, slid his hands under her, massaging her bottom and thighs.

"You give over to it," Gavri instructed. His hands slid back and forth, under and over her legs, around the soft curves of her butt, kneading her muscles, warming her and exciting her as Kolya delivered the same attention to her breasts, arms, shoulders.

"It's a practice," Kolya said. "And as such... perhaps we *should* practice. Would that be amenable to you, *krasavitsa?*"

"You mean... have lots of sex?" Elaina couldn't suppress a giggle. "Guys, we already have lots, and *lots,* of sex."

"It's not so much a matter of quantity," Gavri said. "But mindfulness. Awareness of your body... your power."

"You have a great deal of power brewing in you, Elaina." Kolya nuzzled his face in the valley between her breasts. "Which may be *why* we are always so... sexually charged."

He looked up, meeting her eyes. "It is time for you to take hold of your power."

"How?" she whispered. Her body moved in response to theirs; heat and deep, resonant pleasure, not merely arousal but rich, corporeal delectation, invigorated her limbs.

"That is what we will practice."

Kolya dipped down to slide his own hands under her legs, as Gavri rose, lifting her up with him as he repositioned himself on the edge of the tub. As Kolya moved in to kneel on the jacuzzi bench, Gavri spread Elaina's legs, opening her to Kolya's attentions.

Elaina rolled her head back with a moan as Kol's mouth closed on her clitoris. He kissed it, reverent, and ran the tip of his tongue over it in a circle. Gavri planted warm, slow kisses along her neck, whispering sweet endearments and murmuring his love for her, while Kolya pressed deeper, sliding his tongue inside her, tasting, savoring.

Joy filled her, but still she felt no hurried climb, no rush to climax. A part of her yearned for it, to storm that wonderful height, teeter perilously at the top in a singular, shining instant, before plunging into orgasmic completion. Instead, though, her wolves teased her, pulling her into a resonant, suffusing indulgence. She gave up a quavering plea, "Yes... yes, Kol, *oh,* more... don't stop—"

She sank her fingers into his hair and held him close as he devoured her, his lips and tongue wringing wet pleasure from her depths. Elaina thought she'd never felt so hot, so thoroughly drunk with desire.

Gavri's warm palms covered her breasts, squeezing them gently together, kneading their soft, plump, warm flesh. He squeezed her nipples between thumb and forefinger, tugging them until they grew hard as agate chips, pinching to send swift, sensual bolts of delight into her core.

"Oh, *please,*" she moaned, undulating between them. "Please, I want to come... make me come..."

"Feel your power?" Gavri whispered in her ear. "The heat and energy, the tension in your limbs?"

"Yes. *Oh!*" She cried out, flexing her hips, rolling her body to Kolya's attention. "It feels so *good...*"

"How long do you think you can hold out?" Gav asked. It wasn't a challenge; Elaina understood the exercise. Her entire body sang, electrified with a low hum of bliss. This was hers to harness. Only she didn't yet know how.

"*Please!*" She couldn't think straight. Couldn't bother with gathering or directing anything. She wanted to come, *needed* to come, and she needed them to take her, both of them at once, feeding her greedy, needful flesh with their ready cocks.

Kolya withdrew. Elaina groaned as his mouth left her bereft, unfinished. He slid his hands over her inner thighs, down to her calves, and back up. Heat followed his touch. Then he returned, licking again, jogging his tongue over her clitoris, renewing the bright, dancing delight.

"You two are driving me mad!" she gasped. "I want you *in* me. Please, *please,* I can't stand it, I need you!"

"Whatever you desire," Kolya said from between her legs. "Tell us what you wish, Elaina, and we will give it."

"I want you both. At once. All of us, all together, *please...* I'm so ready..."

When Gavri slid into her tight rear entrance, the brief sting of pain hardly registered to her. Kolya rose up, his dripping body deliciously hot against her, and he entered her in one beautiful, smooth motion. Elaina didn't think she'd ever been so wet in her life, and now, full with both her lovers at once, her body sparked and burned like lit dynamite. She could hardly form words, her mind whirled so much from the pleasure, and from her curling toes to her fingertips, grasping and pulling at Kolya's hair, she felt transcendent. She was a wild, pagan goddess of love and lust, tangled limbs, molten need.

"More." Now it was Kolya urging her on, crushing her against Gavri and whispering burning hot words in her ear. "Gather more to yourself. Pull it all in, *krasavitsa*. You are strong... so strong... so fearsome and bright..."

"Yes!" She gave a hoarse, ragged cry. "I love you... oh, I love you... both of you... ah—*ah*—"

"Look at me!" Kolya begged. "Elaina, look—let me see—"

She met his eyes, full of fire, full of worshipful, smoldering adoration. Sizzling sweet heat poured through her body, tingling in her breasts, streaking through her core until—

Her breath caught. She threw her head back as her body convulsed in a bolt of incredible climax. Both her wolves moaned with her, their voices close to soulful howls as her body claimed them both, pulling them into their own culmination: each came in a hard, pulsing burst, coming because she needed it, demanded it, and they poured their seed into her as she rolled with them, the shuddering waves of her orgasm breaking and breaking over and over in an incredible, unearthly completion.

She almost didn't notice when her mates lowered her back into the hot, churning water of the jacuzzi. Kolya sat sideways on the jacuzzi bench, laying her across his lap and rubbing her shoulders, as Gavri massaged her quivering legs. She followed instructions with a mindless obedience as they bathed her, tilting her head back to dip her messy curls in the water and kneading her scalp, sending tingling relief through the back of her neck and down her shoulders. She might have even slept—she didn't know. In the aftermath of what was very likely the most intense orgasm of her life, she floated in a blissful, rapturous state, exalting in their every soft touch, lulled by each tender word they spoke to her.

Eventually they all climbed up from the hot tub, and Gavri wrapped her in a fluffy towel. Kolya combed back her hair and wrapped it in a second towel, and they brought her back inside. Elaina uttered a soft *mmm* of appreciation when they crossed from cool night air into the warm, welcoming golden light of the living room. Gavri carried her to the couch just like a groom lifting his bride over the threshold, and Kolya slipped away to the kitchen with the promise of cocoa. Soon she stretched out, her legs across both their laps, sipping from a mug, admiring the glow of the fire.

"That, *krasavitsa,* is a little bit like what sex magic aims to do." Kolya rubbed her feet as she came down from her beautiful high. "As I understand it, at least. Grisha will be able to tell you more. A shame he was not here to guide us."

"Yes," she murmured. Though if her snow leopard had joined the party, the three of them might have fucked her into a coma.

"Gathering your sexual power," Kol continued. "Concentrating it. Using it to invoke your needs."

"Kolya was right." Gavri sounded almost businesslike as he sipped his cocoa with a mischievous smile. "We should practice. We'll make you a master by the time it comes to show your hand at manifestation."

Elaina chuckled. "No argument here."

As the drunken feeling began to fade, something occurred to her. "Hey. You two... have you done this before?"

Gavri and Kolya exchanged a look. "What do you mean?" Gavri asked.

"It's not exactly normal sex. I mean, both of you, you were guiding me. So... have you been through sex magic rituals before?"

A pregnant silence fell between them. At last, Kolya admitted, "Yes. We have participated before. In rites of fertility."

She sat upright. "Fertility? You mean you—"

"Mated with one of the tribe's females," Gavri finished for her. "One who had trouble conceiving children with her husband."

Elaina knew her mates had shared women in the past. She'd never troubled over it, since it sounded like casual indulgence. Kinky, but frivolous. This, though, stirred feelings of hurt in her chest. Her heart rate sped up, as she thought of the way Kolya had demanded, *Look at me! Let me see—*

Had he stared into the eyes of another that same way? A female of the pack?

A female trying to conceive a child?

"Did it work?" she asked in a whisper.

"At some point." Kolya sounded almost apologetic. He sensed her anxiety, she imagined. "The wise woman arranged several attempts. One of them took. The spirit mother blessed the female with child."

"Do I want to know who?"

"Would it ease your concerns?" Gavri asked, matter-of-factly. "And before you ask, there's little chance in knowing whether the child was conceived by one of us, or by another male who participated. The genetic donor is irrelevant, either way: her mate—her true mate—is the child's father."

"And he didn't have any problem with this?" Elaina demanded.

Kolya shrugged. "*Krasavitsa,* we do not see fertility rites of such a nature as... well, as *romantic* exploits. It wasn't the same as if the female had entered into an intimate relationship with one of us."

"I'd say what we did tonight was extremely intimate." Elaina looked away from him. A dark gloom filled her. At the same time, she knew what Kolya meant. From a logical standpoint, the *oboroten* were hardly the only people who engaged in such rituals.

Still, though...

Gavri took her by the chin and tilted her face up to his. "Elaina, I know what you're thinking, but it is important you understand. We have no relationship with any of the females among our tribe, or their children. Before you arrived, my only true mate was Kolya, and I his."

"I get it," she said, but some hint of her inner turmoil must have come through. Gavri stroked her hair, but a sadness in his eyes cooled the last of her remaining high. To him and Kolya, this detail of their past meant nothing.

But as much as she wanted to, Elaina could not let it go.

CHAPTER TWELVE

"GRISHA?"

Elaina clung to the side of a smooth rock face, feeling her way across it for a decent handhold. She was free soloing, scaling the rock with nothing more than a chalk bag on her hip, and despite herself, trembling like a leaf.

Above her, Grisha looked down. "Everything okay?"

"Yeah," she lied. "I'm fine. I just wanted to know... have you practiced sex rituals before?"

Her snow leopard snorted. "What the hell sort of thing is that to ask while we're hanging halfway up a cliff?"

"I just... I just want to know."

He glanced up. Gauging the distance between them and the next rest, Elaina gathered.

"Can you wait until we're on solid ground?"

"Yeah," she replied. "I guess."

"Gavri and Kolya get into some interesting stories last night?" He swung himself a few more feet. Elaina had been climbing for more than a decade, but Grisha's easy grace put her to shame. She hoped, in time, she could learn to move like him over the surface of the rocks.

"A bit." She found her hold and pulled herself up. "We fooled around in the jacuzzi. They wanted me to understand what sex magic is like. They think it's how I should manifest the World Tree."

He didn't answer right away, testing a crag in the stone before he planted his foot over it.

"It's not a bad idea. I won't lie to you: manifestation requires focus and very expressive power. Manifesting the tree is an especially complex ritual. Most shamans and supplicants train for years and participate in supporting stages many times before attempting it themselves."

Seems like all these tasks are like that. Elaina's thoughts turned toward the remains of the boar waiting for her in Gavri's work shed. Kolya had finished cleaning and preparing the kill yesterday while she'd been at the cave, and now there were pounds and pounds of good pork wrapped in paper in the lodge's big meat freezer. It left her with the bones—except the skull—and the hide. *Thank the goddess he got rid of all the entrails and other organs... I don't think I want to know what he did with them, though...*

Thoughts of the task bothered her until she reached the first rest. Grisha had made it there nearly ten minutes before her.

"So what's got you asking *me* if I've been part of sex rituals?" he asked.

"Gav and Kolya both have. Fertility rituals." She tried to sound breezy. "It just made me curious."

He cocked an eyebrow. She couldn't fool him, it seemed.

"I've used sex magic," he said. "Both on my own, and with partners. Not fertility rituals, though."

He smirked. "No one in the pack wants a *cat* involved in matters of fertility. Just a little bit of lupine prejudice for you."

Elaina recalled what he had told her about his father. *Big cats don't do a lot of parenting.* Now Grisha was the one putting on a bluff. She sensed the *prejudice* bothered him more than he let on.

"I wouldn't be afraid to bear a child with you," she told him quietly. "I mean, don't get me wrong, I'm not thinking of kids just yet. And as in any arrangement like ours, I'd expect our whole circle to be involved with any children I do have. But I'd have no reservations, having yours."

His expression softened. His smile even became—dare she think it?—rather genuine. She didn't think she'd ever seen Grisha crack a real smile before. He was always guarded in some way, although usually smarmy and arrogant, if not grim or sarcastic. This one disappeared as fast as it came, though, and he took a seat, dangling his feet over the ledge.

Their rest was wide and roomy. It was more like the top of one protruding section of the formation. If they'd wanted to, they could descend from here, hiking a manageable grade down the other side. They'd continue up, though, once they'd caught their breath; Grisha said this rock had a lesson at the top for her.

"So what sort of rituals *did* you take part in?"

"Solo, like I said." He ran a hand through his hair, tousling it, completely un-self-conscious. "I guess in lifestyle circles it's called 'edging'? One brings themselves to the very cusp of orgasm, gathering power and intention from the physical sensations and holding off climax as long as you can."

"And the rituals with others?"

"Females who came to Yasmin for different reasons. Vision seeking." He shrugged. "Nothing complicated, really."

Elaina rubbed the back of your neck. "Did Yasmin... participate?"

"Nope. Not the way you're thinking, I mean. She does contribute to the ritual, but not sexually."

"So you have sex... in front of her."

"Yup." He nodded. "And sometimes other ritualists, if they're called for. It does take some getting used to."

Elaina took a seat beside him. They sat in silence, gazing out at the landscape below. From this formation, they could see the park's visitor's village, a peppering of cabins in the distance. They were in the public parts of Stolby again, but luck put them alone on the rock. After several minutes, Elaina scooted closer to Grisha and leaned her head on his shoulder. He spread his arm around her, stroking his fingers through her hair.

"You can choose another path for your ritual of manifestation," he told her in a gentle voice. "If sexual invocation bothers you."

She shook her head. "It doesn't bother me."

"*Something* is bothering you."

She uttered a sigh, closing her eyes. For the first time she could remember, she wished she were curled up somewhere indoors. In bed, or in some big, plush recliner, wrapped in a blanket away from the day, instead of climbing the side of a giant rock in broad daylight, visible to anyone who might come hiking along. The sun beat down on her, so bright, and the ascent ahead of them, still so high. It exhausted her.

Of course today must be the day Grisha insisted she try her hand at the more traditional free-solo technique. She'd free soloed before, but the Stolby rocks were new and challenging. *New* and *challenging* were wonderful. Just... not today.

Grisha crooked a finger under her chin and tilted her gaze toward him.

"What is it, little one?"

How strange. Sympathy, from Grisha, of all people.

"I'm tired," she admitted. "I'm... confused. I have no idea if I'm still on the right path."

"Why wouldn't you be?"

"Diezana's song." All at once, a raw, red ache tightened in her chest. Her eyes stung with tears, and the fears came pouring out of her. How Diezana had fallen silent for her; how the hunt for the pig hadn't been a success so much as a lucky fluke; how her pilgrimage to the cave and her crafting of the shrine seemed right but had gone unanswered.

How, at Polina's funeral, she'd had to ask herself what might have happened if she'd been the alpha of the Stolby tribe... and she hadn't found any encouraging conclusions.

"Then, the sex magic," she told him. "This business about fertility rites. I can't shake the hurt it makes me feel."

"Why hurt?" Grisha asked.

"I feel like I'll always wonder now... every time I look at the children in the tribe—the ones who are young enough, at least—I'll wonder if they have Gavri's eyes, or Kolya's nose. If I don't know for certain that they *haven't* fathered other woman's children, I'm going to be wondering forever, until it drives me insane."

"If they had," he soothed. "Would you love them less?"

"No..."

Elaina considered. She *wouldn't* love them any less... but would it mean another female infringing on her territory? Would one of the Stolby women show up on day with a blue-eyed toddler on her hip, and ask for time with the father?

Of course not! Gavri already told you as much. Even if they did contribute to the conception, they aren't *fathers in the eyes of the pack.*

A base, bitter meanness closed like a fist around her chest and squeezed. She broke into tears, tears of anger and frustration, but bit her tongue on the next incoherent string of childish babbling.

"They are mine," was all she could say. "*You* are mine. I won't share you, any of you."

"*That's* the cry of an alpha female if ever I've heard one." Grisha grinned at her and kissed her brow.

"I think this is what the *vukodlak* must feel." She let out a defeated huff. "Out-of-control. Fanatical. High as the stars one minute and emotionally destitute the next."

Grisha's eyebrows arched, and a sharp glimmer lit up his gaze. "Not only the *vukodlak*. Come now, Elaina... I think you and I both understand that cycle."

Perhaps she did. Perhaps, ever since her early adolescence, she'd had her run-ins with the racing heartbeat, the frantic twists of anxiety and obsessive worry in her gut. A silent panic held in only by the thinnest scrap of a false smile, until she could find a cool, dark place to be alone, and be sick in her worry.

"*You've* gone through this?" she asked Grisha, scrubbing stubborn tears from her eyes.

"My version included a great deal of hitting things. And people." He gave her a squeeze. "But there were tears as well. Angry, powerless tears. Fire in my chest. A destructive desire so violent and demanding I thought I was having a heart attack. It isn't only the mad who are mad."

He tilted her chin up and planted a deep kiss on her mouth. "And it isn't only the evil who feel evil inside, on their bad days. Let's go. I still have something to teach you at the top of this rock."

She stood after him, and they each took a long drink of water from the canteens in Grisha's backpack, before launching into the next leg of the climb. They gave themselves over to the rock for the next thirty minutes, exchanging no words, the silence broken only by grunting, heaving, and straining as they ascended.

It isn't only the evil who feel evil inside. Elaina thought she'd never heard so perfect a sentiment. Her heart *did* feel evil, and very small, when she thought about Gavri and Kolya, engaged in a wild orgy of sex to impregnate a fellow pack-mate. Images crowded her head and made her chest pound, and *evil* captured it exactly.

And that brought shame. And shame forced her into a tight, dark place inside herself, one she desperately hoped could hide her sins but one which might burst open to the light any moment. Grisha had crystalized it all into a word, and she embraced the wisdom of it.

It isn't only *the evil who* feel *evil.*

When you get past the first, fearful plunge, she pondered as she pulled up for another handhold, *it's less painful than you'd expect.*

They hauled themselves over the summit of the rock, stopping to appreciate the wider, grander view. The visitor's village had grown tiny; tributaries of the Yenisei River trickled and ran apart and back together in thin, rippling fingers.

Grisha rested his hands on her shoulders and squeezed, working the muscles.

"Climbers here love to free-solo these pillars," he said. "It's spiritual, emotional... to some, merely a matter of pride. But it's *part* of Stolby, when you come down to it. The locals and the regulars. They hardly remember there *is* any other way to climb."

His hands slid down her arms, until he held both of hers, spreading them before her to show off her red, scuffed, bruised palms.

"These are marks of honor," he whispered in her ear. "Signs of brotherhood. But even so... there are always climbers who slip."

Elaina looked down, down the side of the cliff, through the trees to the dull, hard-packed earth below.

"Even the old-timers," Grisha said. Still holding her hands in his, he wrapped her arms around her, pulling her close to his chest. "They reach up and seize the rocks with their bare hands, with no idea it's going to be their last climb."

This is what he wanted to teach me? Elaina lifted her gaze again to look out over the scenery. In the soothing sense of a great quiet, her thoughts faded into simple warm, pleasant feelings, despite the dark subject.

"Grisha?"

"Hm?" he nuzzled her ear.

"What happens if I manage to manifest the gifts of Diezana, and I don't become a wolf?"

"Then we celebrate." He kissed her earlobe. "I'd say there's at least a better-than-average chance you'll become an elegant female feline. A Siberian tigress. Nikita has no chance against you then."

His playful growl tickled her. She giggled.

"If this doesn't work," she murmured, laying her head against his arm. "If I grab for the wrong handhold... do I lose everything? You and Gavri and Kolya?"

"There's only one way to know."

She took a long, slow, quavering breath. *Of course. Only one way.*

Fall.

CHAPTER THIRTEEN

PASHA WAITED OUTSIDE GAVRI'S LODGE when she and Grisha returned. As Elaina slid off the bike and leaned in to kiss her snow leopard goodbye, Nikita's enforcer materialized out of the shadowy woods across the road.

Elaina froze, hands resting on Grisha's jacket so she felt his deep, rumbling growl under her fingertips.

Pasha raised his hands, saying something in the *oboroten* language she didn't yet understand. Grisha slid an arm protectively around her waist.

"He says he's not here to start a fight," her snow leopard murmured.

"Then why are you tensing up like there's going to be one?" she whispered.

Grisha didn't answer. He kept his wild green eyes on Pasha as the wolf came nearer.

"Forgive my trespass." Pasha bowed his head to her, offering his hand in a conciliatory gesture. "I know I am not your favorite person."

"Maybe because you and your two cronies jumped my mate in this very driveway just two weeks ago," she replied in a cool tone. Before he could respond, though, Elaina softened. "Though, I admit...

I shouldn't have suspected you of putting him in the hospital. I owe you an apology, Pasha."

He nodded, but his expression made her think apologies were the furthest thing from his mind.

"You showed me your shrine yesterday." He hesitated, throwing a curious and wary look at Grisha. Her snow leopard maintained his usual lazy, untroubled demeanor, but his fierce protective grip never budged.

"Yes, I did."

She took a careful measure of him. In jeans and an old, worn T-shirt, he must have hiked to the lodge on foot, in his human form. He might have ridden on a motorcycle like Grisha or come by truck like Gavri and Kolya, but if he had, he'd parked it far back from the road where it couldn't be seen. The clothes gave him a strange appearance; maybe because she'd already seen him both in his nude human form and his huge lupine one, regular everyday clothing seemed constricting on him. Ill-fitted.

Or... is it him? Is he the one who doesn't fit?

"What do you want, Pasha?" Grisha demanded.

Pasha kept his gaze on Elaina, and when he spoke, it was she whom he addressed.

"I have not given you much chance, *uchenik*. I believed you young and foolish, to come before our pack, and our alpha, as you did."

"Yes." Elaina crossed her arms. "And you were right. But we are here now, and if Nikita refuses to call off his—"

"Nikita is not the reason I am here." He took another hesitant step forward. "I wish to help you."

Elaina blinked. She exchanged a startled glance with Grisha, whose lambent green eyes burned with wary suspicion.

"You..." She rubbed at her temple. "You want to *help* me now."

"Yes."

"Why?" Stepping free of Grisha's protective arm, she approached Pasha. "You just said you thought me foolish."

Pasha held out his hands, as if to say he didn't know. "Foolish, yes. But I am called to stand with you."

"You're Nikita's beta wolf. He relies on you. *Trusts* you."

"Not anymore," Pasha said. His words struck her, like ice water running down the back of her neck. "Though Nikita can always trust me... I have left his pack."

Above them, a door opened. Elaina looked up to see Gavri and Kolya had come out onto the front deck and gazed down at Pasha as though ready for a fight.

Ridiculous. There are four of us and one of him. He's not going to try anything.

She held a hand up to her wolves, signaling them to stay where they were. Crossing the rest of the distance to Pasha, she searched his gaze.

"What made you come here?" she asked.

"The spirit mother calls me to your pack." Pasha appeared almost sorrowful. Not, she sensed, because he didn't *want* to be called here... but because it meant leaving behind another, to whom he had sworn himself.

"Diezana led you to me?" she whispered. "You believe that?"

"*Da, uchenik.*"

"What does *uchenik* mean?"

He furrowed his brow, and threw a glance at the others, uncertain of the word.

"Disciple," Gavri provided. "Acolyte."

"You seek her," Pasha said. "And she desires you."

"But she's never spoken to me!" Elaina cried in a hushed, urgent voice. "I heard her song, at first, yet she's never revealed herself. Not really. And now I don't even hear... I don't hear..."

She stared at him. His dark, somber eyes held her steady, though she wanted to break. After several quiet, aching seconds, Pasha took her hands.

"She will call to you again," he promised. "Now, it is me she summons to your side. Let me help you, *uchenik*. If you do not, I have made myself an exile for nothing."

"I didn't ask you to do that."

"No," he agreed. "*She* did. I have followed her will. Now it is in your hands to take me as one of yours... or send me away from you, to walk alone."

He's more wolf than human, Elaina realized. *That's why he doesn't look quite right in human clothes... why he treats me like a wolf would treat a newcomer, and not like the others. Pasha is the wolf before anything else.*

"You've put a lot on me." She pulled her hands back and retreated a step from him. "I don't want you to go into exile. But you belong to Nikita, not me."

He shook his head. "Not anymore."

Elaina tilted her head to the side. "And that bothers you, doesn't it?"

"Nikita has been as my brother. As Gavri and Kolya have been to each other, so have Nikita and I. Though of course, we do not share the same..." Again, he seemed to search for the right word. "*Passion.* But still, we have been friends."

"Can't you go back to his pack, then? I won't stop you. I'll happily let you go, if it's what you need."

Pasha shook his head again. "Diezana's path has taken me elsewhere."

She sighed. Glancing over her shoulder, she searched for guidance from her three mates, but none of them offered their opinion.

You're their alpha female, Elaina. You *make this decision.*

"I can aid you," Pasha said before she could make up her mind. "The spirit mother has appointed you seven *zadachi*. Seven, eh... "

"Tasks," Elaina finished. "She *did* speak to you, didn't she?"

"You struggle. I do not mean it as criticism. I see it. Yesterday, at the shrine you built. You doubt. I can guide you."

My mates have guided me just fine so far, she almost said. Then, though, the cold, fearful thump of hurt struck her in the stomach again. The feeling didn't track back to Grisha, or even Gavri and Kolya, or the conversations of the last twenty-four hours. It came from her, all from her. She knew it, but it didn't chase the small, dirty, rat-like doubt away. Maybe things with her mates had hit a sore spot. Maybe she *did* need a different guide on this one, while her nervous fears ran their course.

"All right," she said. "Tomorrow. We'll work on my next task."

Pasha gave her a somber nod. "Will you join me where the bridge crosses the gorge? The one you came over on your way to the meeting place, and Polina's funeral rites?"

Elaina brightened. "Yes! I meant to go back there to take pictures."

"Good. Bring your mates, if it will make you feel safer."

Pasha gazed at her strangely. He bowed his head again to her and held himself in a sort of half-inclined position. She remembered the greeting gesture of the pack, and stepped up to stand before him, touching her forehead to his.

"I'm sorry you had to leave Nikita," she told him. "I'll try to do right by you, as your alpha wolf."

He rumbled his thank you in Russian, then broke their contact. He looked up to Gavri and Kolya, on the deck, and to Grisha, giving each a dutiful, respectful nod. Then he turned around, disappearing back into the shadows of the trees.

Grisha came to Elaina's side and draped his arm across her shoulders. "Well, I never would have expected *Pasha* to be called into this."

"Do you believe him?" Gavri had descended the stairs and joined them, warily watching the place where Pasha had disappeared.

"He knew about my tasks," Elaina said. "Unless Yasmin or Adelaida told him, and I don't think they would... he had to figure it out somewhere."

Maybe from the spirit mother herself. So maybe she hasn't given up on me after all.

PURPLE FLOWERS DOTTED THE SLOPES on one side of the gorge, a subtle coruscation of color against rich green mosses and ferns. Elaina, in a hushed and reverent delight, snapped picture after picture of them before moving on to a pair of red-tailed squirrels arguing harmlessly over a dark, rounded prize reminding her of an avocado pit. The sun tried to peek through the canopy overhead, sprinkling light through the leaves in a shifting veil, but most of the gorge remained covered in beautiful shadow.

Pasha stood beside her, patiently waiting as she took her photos. Gavri and Kolya stood at the far end of the bridge, watching her and the enforcer with critical eyes. Elaina hadn't forgotten about any of them; lost in her photography, though, she could almost brush the weight of their presence aside and forget—for a little while—the upcoming task, and those beyond it, and the looming deadline of the solstice ahead.

Fourteen days. She'd woken up with that thought in her head almost immediately. Two weeks to go. She hadn't really given proper thought yet to what manner of tools or tokens she planned to create. Part of her rebelled at the idea. *Why do I need 'tools' made from my kill? I can't create a camera out of boar bones. I don't want any weapon to help me win against Nikita... and nothing I craft will change his mind. What's the point?*

And then there had been the email from her mother, which she'd finally decided to open.

> *Staying until summer? Elaina, don't you have things to do here at home? I'm sure whatever magazine you're on location for, they can't be paying you enough to stay in*

194

Siberia, *of all the Godforsaken places.*
What's in Siberia? You'd make more taking
a job somewhere where they have more than
snow to photograph.

Don't think I don't know what's really
going on here. I've spoken with Dominic.
You can't avoid your marital troubles by
running away and pouting somewhere in the
remote Russian wilderness. Really, honey... I
think you need to come back home on the
next flight you can find. We'll talk about
Dominic, and how to fix whatever it is that
happened between you two. I just hope you
haven't gone off and done something
regrettable with some Russian gypsy boy, just
to get back at your husband. Please be an
adult, Elaina.

Everything Elaina had suspected. Maybe even
more... that awful accusation of rebounding with *some
Russian gypsy boy.*

"Really, Mother?" she'd muttered out loud, staring
with exasperation at the screen as she read over those
words again, to be sure she'd had them right.

Gavri, reading over her shoulder, peered at her
with some concern. "Your husband?"

"He's not," she insisted, with an edge in her tone
betraying just how many times she'd had to make this
distinction. "She has a problem accepting the fact
Dominic and I never got married. She insists on
calling him that, and calling it *my marriage,* hoping if
she beats it in long enough, we'll cave and make it
official."

She closed the email, and her laptop, with a ragged, disgusted sound, fighting tears of anger as she did. "I'll reply later. I can't deal with her right now."

"You don't have to reply at all," he suggested.

"At some point, I will have to go back. There are things I'll need to recover, paperwork and a few important personal things. I'll have to close my bank accounts and terminate insurance. As much as I'd like to, Gav, I can't cut all ties just yet."

But I will, eventually. This struck her like a terrible, hovering phantom. *At some point... I really am going to disappear forever out of their lives. I'm going to leave everything back home behind.*

It didn't fill her with joy, as she imagined it would. It frightened her. She found herself wondering, in the fleeting, quiet moments when she found herself alone, with her mates elsewhere attending to their own matters, if she'd made the right choice. Flinging everything to the wind to run off and join a wild clan of people? People to whom she didn't even really belong?

Am I crazy? Did I ever really hear some magical, spiritual voice calling me to them? Or did I mess up my head worse than we thought, when I passed out in the snow?

A clatter of wings brought her back to the bridge and her camera lens. Without even realizing it, she'd captured an amazing shot of a clever red bird with white and black bands along its wings, swooping down from the canopy. Excitement welled in her chest: she clicked the camera back and forth through the four shots she'd caught with the bird completely by accident, whispering "*Wow...*" to herself as she admired them.

Pasha leaned on the railing of the bridge, studying the camera's digital screen. "*Obyknovennyy shchur.* Eh, in English, I think... 'grosbeak'?"

Elaina lowered the camera and searched the bushes below them for the bird. She found it balanced on the limb of a berry bush, tugging at the fruit. "You know the English name?"

"I work as a ranger for the reserve. We have many tourists and researchers who visit. I pick up some names, here and there."

"I'm going to have to frame one of those shots, for sure."

He nodded. Deciding she'd had enough photography—for now—Elaina slid her camera into its carrying case and turned to face Pasha properly.

"Okay. I guess I'm ready to start. How do I... *utilize the gifts* of the spirit?"

Pasha lips quirked in a hesitant expression. "It is not so easy as me, or anyone, telling you how to utilize the materials you have won from your hunt. The *oboroten* make many things out of the bones and hide and teeth of the game they kill. Some tools, some art. Some gifts. What you create will be unique to *you.*"

"What pleases the spirit, though?" Elaina stepped away from the railing and walked toward the other side of the bridge. Pasha followed, while Gavri and Kolya remained at their end, leaning on the rail and taking in the scenery. She knew if she needed them, they'd be at her side in an instant. She no longer feared any sort of turnabout from Pasha, however. After his escort to the cave, and after sharing her newly built shrine with him, Elaina couldn't think of him as some brute guard dog anymore. He may be more *canine* than the others, at heart, but she'd seen the loyal, soulful side of his canine spirit, too.

There is more to him. It's sometimes hard to see, because he's just so quiet. But he's not going to hurt me. I'm sure of it.

"What pleases Diezana," he told her, "is for her children to make themselves more at one with her world. She has blessed you with gifts. Use them to bind yourself closely to her."

Elaina ran both hands through her hair. "*Ugh,* Pasha! I don't know what any of that is supposed to mean!"

"You do," he assured her. "You are carrying too much which is not your own, *uchenik.*"

He pulled ahead of her a few paces and guided her to a clear patch of mossy earth just off the path. "Sit here. Let me lead you in connection with Diezana's land."

Elaina did as he asked. Pasha helped her strip off the camera case and her backpack. Then, though, he hesitated.

"It would be best if you were unclothed. I won't ask you to do so, though... but... maybe, as much as you are comfortable with? Your shoes, at least?"

Elaina almost laughed. Pasha's face reddened, as though he'd asked for something truly scandalous. She'd been around the *oboroten* long enough, though, nakedness hardly seemed out of the ordinary. Hell, she'd seen Pasha himself completely in the buff more than once.

Still, though, Pasha hadn't seen *her,* and even with her new sense of trust in him, she didn't feel quite ready to bare all. She compromised, taking off her shoes and socks, then shirt and hiking shorts, leaving on her modest black sports halter and boy-leg briefs.

More than she'd wear to the beach on a hot day, but still with plenty of skin exposed.

"Lie down on the moss," he instructed. She did, and he sat cross-legged just above her head.

"Do you mind me touching your temples?" he asked. Elaina shook her head. Pasha nodded but didn't do so right away.

"Close your eyes. Take a deep breath."

She did.

"Feel the cool earth beneath you." Pasha's voice softened, becoming low, gentle, monotone. "Dig your fingers into the soil, if you like. Turn your face to smell the richness of it, and the wet scent of the moss. Let it reach into you: into your skin; your lungs; your muscles. Let it *grow* into you."

Elaina tried. She took several more long, deep breaths, and tried to connect with the ground, as he said. Her restless mind refused to ease, though. Thoughts of her mother's message, of Gavri and Kolya waiting for her by the bridge, of painful frustration she still felt with them, of the frustration she felt with *herself*—

Pasha's fingertips caressed her temples. Light, almost imperceptible. He ran them in tiny, tight circles over her skin.

"Let go of those ties which bind you elsewhere, *uchenik*. You are here now. You lie on a bed of sacred ground. A path which Diezana once walked, and you now walk in her name. Take a deep breath. Good. Again. With each breath, let go of those things which are not of you and of this earth. Take in only the breeze. The smell of the moss. The sound of the birds and the voice of the leaves."

But I'm running out of time. I can't play games lying in the dirt! I need to think of how to use the last of the boar—

"Grow down into the earth." It didn't sound like Pasha, anymore. The words were colorless, toneless. If they were water, she could see through them straight down to a perfect, pristine lake bottom. Placid, unruffled, unclouded by impurities. "Let down roots into the soil below you. Reach out with your soul into the sky."

"How?" she whispered. "How do I do that?"

"With each breath. With each thought, which is born in each spark in your brain. With each heartbeat, which is pulsing energy in the universe. Where your skin touches the ground, sink deeper; where your mind and heart and breath meet the air, grow larger."

What if Gavri and Kolya come up here and see this? What will they think of this?

"Do not think of Gavri and Kolya now. You are here with me. You are not with them."

"How did you know I was thinking of them?" she murmured. Some strange sensation, something like sleepiness, but not quite, bathed her mind and body.

"I am with you. I call to you. I hear you."

Somewhere deep, deep within herself, Elaina registered it was no longer Pasha she was listening to. On her next steady inhale, she smelled more than the moss and the soil; she smelled the sweet, soaring scent of the trees. The bursting, ruby berries the grosbeak tugged and pecked at. The solid, ancient, patient stones beneath the vibrant wild growth all over the ravine. As she exhaled, she pressed herself deeper into the ground, welcomed by it, embraced in it.

"Like a seed," came a gentle whisper in her ear. "My seed. Planted in old, old earth... you bring new growth. Fresh change."

Chaos and blood.

Elaina shot upright with a gasp. Pasha flinched away from her but sprung quickly to her side as she began to choke on her breath. He thumped her on the back, speaking in the *oboroten* language in quick, but patient, tones.

Presently she regained control, and managed a tight, hoarse, but welcome gulp of fresh air. She blinked and ground at her eyes.

"What was that? Pasha... what happened?"

"I do not know." He stared at her, bemused. "Did you have a vision?"

"No. Yes? I guess, maybe? I only heard... someone speaking to me. At first it had your voice, but then it changed. Then I thought it must be Diezana... *finally*... but then, at the end..."

Chaos and blood.

With a groan, she brought her hands to her head and kneaded desperately at her temples. Out of nowhere, a headache had bloomed, like a thunderclap in her skull.

"Something's wrong." She shook her head, frustration returning. "I shouldn't be doing this. I *should* withdraw my challenge, and convince Gavri, Kolya, and Grisha to leave Stolby with me. Find... someplace *else*."

"No." Pasha shook his head. "Diezana has other hopes for you."

"Well, it would be nice if she'd let *me* in on those hopes!" Elaina beat one fist on the ground. "I'm sorry, Pasha... the meditation was... well, it started out fine, but at the end it was like some... some *ugly* thing just leading me on. It all seemed right, and then—"

"Elaina."

He took her face in his hands and forced her to look at him. As he searched her eyes, his brow furrowed, and his mouth set in a dark frown.

"I see," he said, as if agreeing with someone—not her—who had spoken to her. "*Uchenik,* your journey is not free of trouble. You seek to change things which have not been changed in millennia. Not all spirits are your allies in this quest."

"Is that what it was?" she asked. "The sudden turn at the end... the ugliness that pulled me out of the meditation... some kind of malicious spirit?"

"Perhaps. Or perhaps not so much *malicious.* A trickster, perhaps. A mischief maker, or unfriendly little monster."

He stood and held out a hand to help her up. "Perhaps it is my fault. In much magic, we must guard ourselves against malicious powers. I did not think to prepare for disruption, for such a simple meditation. Evidently, though, there are gremlins who wish to complicate your quest."

"Great," she muttered. She took his hand and let him pull her to her feet. Thoughts of Niuri—screeching, furious Niuri—filled her head.

"Do you wish to go back?" he asked.

"No," Elaina sighed. "Not yet. I think I'd rather just hike around a bit. I've become more comfortable with the area around Gavri's lodge, but this part of the woods is still new to me. I just want to walk for a while and take some more pictures. But you don't have to come with me, if you don't want to."

"I want to," he said. "Shall we call your mates?"

"Yeah. Wouldn't want them to get worried."

Pasha returned to the path to summon Gavri and Kolya while Elaina dressed. She still had no idea how any of this could tell her what tools to make out of the boar, and now her head and stomach hurt.

A hike up the gorge will help. She pulled her water bottle from her pack and took a long drink. When Pasha and her mates returned, she waved them up the path after her, and put the mossy spot and the ugly end to her meditation behind her.

It's not as if the rest of it wasn't wonderful, anyway, she admitted to herself. *Maybe, some other time... maybe I'll ask Pasha to try again.*

They hiked until lunchtime, and sat down to a picnic of sandwiches and cookies Rini had packed for them. They'd made it to the top of the gorge and deeper into a thick green wilderness of pine, and spread their meal out on a shady spot overlooking a wide field of gold and green. More musk deer grazed here, and as she nibbled one of Rini's sweet sugar cookies Elaina grumbled, "Maybe *this* is the dumb herd I was supposed to find instead of the boar."

Gavri and Kolya chuckled, while Pasha cocked an eyebrow at her. She told him the story of her hunt, and the unexpected appearance of the wild hog.

"*That's* the one," she declared, picking out a reasonably cocky-looking buck and jabbing a finger toward it. "I can see it in his eye. *He's* the one I should've speared, and he knows it. Lucky twerp probably sent the pig down to the river on purpose."

Her comedic pout put her mates into a fresh gale of laughter, startling the deer and urging a rare smile even from Pasha.

After lunch they made their way to the other side of the gorge and hiked back down. Elaina stopped more than once to snap more photos. Behind the camera, at least, the coiled tension in her chest eased a little, and thoughts of her looming deadline faded into the back of her mind. She had a story in mind to submit to the usual set of editors who paid her, on exploring the underrated deep forests of Stolby. Of course, she'd have to submit one on the spectacular views at the summits of the rock formations, and the tradition of free-soloing as Grisha had shown her, too.

At last, they found themselves back at the bridge, and prepared to part ways. Elaina snapped a couple more shots—the ochre, late-afternoon sunlight gave the gorge a completely different look than the mid-morning light she'd caught earlier—before tucking her camera away for good.

"It was an excellent hike." She turned to Pasha and held out her hand. "Thanks. I don't think I really came much closer to knowing my next steps... but I always love a good day out of doors and in the wilderness."

"Nothing better for the soul." He took her hand and shook it.

"I'll have to get a walking stick for next time," she said. "Especially for long hikes like this. And a lighter jacket, I think. This one's more suited for—"

She'd been about to say *snow,* when all at once it became clear to her. Like rays of light through a prism, shining not only in her mind, but down to her heart.

"That's it!" Elaina broke into a wide smile, glancing from Pasha to her mates, and back. "That's what I'll make from the boar!"

Gavri scratched his head, while Kolya beamed, matching her smile.

"Excellent ideas." Pasha gave her a nod of agreement. "Things which you will need, and use, and appreciate for a long time. Things which will come from you and your hands, for your own journey through Diezana's sacred lands."

"You really think so?" she asked him.

"*Da.* It is exactly as the spirit requests of us. Make use of her gifts in your own way, honoring the beast you have slain, and the goddess who gave it."

"Thank you." Again, she felt tears threaten to fall, though this time they were tears of relief. "Pasha, I mean it. Thank you."

"You are welcome." He came a step closer to her and reached out to tuck a stray curl of her hair behind her ear. "Elaina, may I ask for something?"

His tone put her on guard. She glanced at her mates; they, too, came to attention, very interested in what the enforcer had to say.

"What is it?" she asked Pasha.

His fingers brushed her cheek. "I would like to kiss you before we part for the night. I mean no disrespect to you or your mates. Should you say no, it will never be brought up again. But I have watched you all day today, and in you I see the wolf you wish to become. Strong, agile, protective. I would be honored for you to accept me as one of your pack. But... only if it does not offend—"

"I..." Elaina stared at him. Then she searched Gavri and Kolya for their takes, but both were silent except for the faintest hint of thunderclouds in their eyes.

He has helped, tremendously. He's been true to his word.

She thought maybe now she could see the reason for the abrupt change of character.

It's only a kiss, for now. If it's meant to lead to more... we'll see.

"Yes," she told him. "You may kiss me, Pasha."

He leaned to her carefully, slipping his hands in to cradle her head as he kissed her on the mouth. His lips pressed to hers, warm and soft, and he didn't become pushy. Seconds later, they stood facing one another, and Elaina had an absurd flashback to her junior prom. Her date walking her to her door; the awkward moment when the silence might become a kiss, and a kiss might become something more, and neither of them quite sure if it should be.

"Thank you," he told her in a soft voice. Without another word, he backed onto the bridge, stripping off his jeans and T-shirt, and shifted into his wolf form. Seizing his discarded clothing in his mouth, he sprinted into the woods on the other side of the gorge and disappeared.

"What do you make of that?" Kolya asked her, coming up beside her and slipping his arm around her waist.

She didn't know if she was ready to say it, especially to her wolves. The thought that Pasha might become a member of this new, fledgling pack, led to them by Diezana. Nikita's beta wolf, dear friend, and loyal soldier might, in reality, belong with them instead.

And—as she'd felt in their kiss—perhaps he was meant for *her,* most of all.

CHAPTER FOURTEEN

"KOL? I NEED TO BORROW some tools."

Elaina had awoken, showered, and dressed before either of her two wolves began to stir, and as she nudged Kolya, Gavri gave a sleepy grumble and tightened his arms around the bigger man.

"Come on," she pleaded in an urgent hush. Grisha had stayed the night again, in the guest room down the hall, and with his phenomenal hearing, even too forceful a whisper might rouse him from sleep. "I want to get started."

"Why?" Gavri mumbled. "There's no reason to start so early, *krasavitsa*. Bone carving can be done just as well after breakfast. Come back to bed. Perhaps Kolya and I can first feast on your sweet sex and ravish your body with pleasure."

Kolya reached up to caress her cheek. "We did say we would practice the motion and mastery of your orgasms, for use in sexual ritual..."

The mention of their conversation some nights ago immediately made her heart beat painfully, as if some villain had reached into her chest and squeezed.

"No. Please, I want to start as soon as possible. I'm excited! Can't you tell?"

"I keep my tools in the garage," Kolya told her. He rolled over, resting his head on Gavri's chest. Under the bedsheets, the telltale jut of Gavri's morning erection could not be mistaken, and Kolya's hand slipped toward it.

"You're welcome to use whatever you need," he finished before kissing Gavri on the mouth.

Elaina hesitated. She hated to interrupt her two mates when they so obviously had amorous pursuit on the mind, but the matter of her task weighed heavy on her, as well as the consequences if she failed to complete them.

And tanning leather will take days. More than a week.

Still... she watched the gentle, unmistakable motion of Kolya's fingers stroking Gavri's cock beneath the sheets.

"I don't know which tools to use," she tried. "I want to do this the right way... you know... by *traditional* means?"

"You don't need traditional tools to craft personal effects."

Grisha leaned in the doorway, green eyes sleepy, gorgeous in his casual nakedness. He gave an enormous yawn as they all turned their attention to him.

"It's your intention and investment Diezana wants," he said to Elaina. "Not some fabricated primitiveness or falsified rareness of style."

Elaina reached for an elastic on the bedside table and pulled her hair back into a ponytail. "You're sure?"

"I've been creating my tools and crafts from my hunts for years." He waved a dismissive hand. "I use what works. If it happens to be power tools, I use power tools."

He beckoned her. "Come. Let the wolves manage their morning wood together. I'll help you get started on your task."

Gavri narrowed his eyes, coming up on his elbows. "The *cat* had better not be insinuating we don't care about your progress."

"Not at all," Grisha purred. "Just trying to be helpful."

"He's right." Elaina slid from the edge of the bed. "It's okay, Gav. You two stay in bed. Play, or sleep in... whatever you like." She flashed both wolves a smile to ease their concern. "You two hiked *all* day with me and Pasha yesterday. Just enjoy yourselves now. It's not like I'm leaving for long, anyway."

"You are sure, *krasavitsa?*" Kolya studied her with big, brown puppy eyes.

"I'm sure." She bent to give him a kiss. "It's all right if we use some of your tools, though?"

"*Da.* Help yourself." He pulled her down for a second, then a third kiss. He would have stolen more but she put out her hands to stop him, laughing.

"Nice try." She circled to the other side of the bed and gave Gavri a kiss, too, but slipped away before he could twine his arms around her and pull her back into bed.

"Later," she promised them with a wink. "After this is underway, and I can focus on something other than my deadline."

As she joined Grisha at the door he looped an arm around her waist and shot the wolves a wicked smile. Elaina slapped him on the chest. "Don't be a jerk. Let's go."

The house stood silent; even Rini hadn't arrived to start her day's work yet. Elaina and Grisha made their way downstairs to the empty garage below the main level of the house. With the recent good weather, all the vehicles were parked outside, but the space could comfortably hold Gavri's truck, all the bikes and a second vehicle with some room to spare. Kolya's craft table and woodworking tools were set against the far wall, along with an industrial set of shelves which usually held work in-progress. They were empty at the moment, though; he'd been a bit too busy with other matters, lately.

Elaina crossed to the tall, heavy tool cabinet and began looking for the things she'd need. Grisha surprised her, though, by scooping her up and planting her on the worktable, pressing her back with a hard, hungry kiss.

"Grisha!" she scolded, though she couldn't help but smile. "What happened to helping me get started?"

"I *am* going to get you started," he purred, kissing her lips, her neck, her shoulder. As he slid down the skinny straps of her loose tank top, he added, "Get you started... and finish you off so well you won't be taking off on any hikes for at least a day."

"So this was your plan?" She fought him playfully, trying to keep her clothes on while he worked them off. "Get me away from Gav and Kol, to have me to yourself?"

"It's been a while since I've had you to myself. Besides, you're mad at them. A little revenge sex seems in order."

She stopped his hands tugging at the button of her jeans. "Grisha, I'm not *mad* at them."

"You are a little." He smiled, this time a soft and genuine smile. "And this is not true revenge, anyway. I am your mate as much as they are, and I can sense you need attention and affirmation, even if they do not."

"How can you say such things about them?" Elaina heard the edge in her own voice, but at the same time, a sweet sense of gratitude welled up in her heart.

"Pft. Wolves are not as clever as cats. Now, will you let me offer my adoration to the most exceptional *oboroten* lady I have yet to meet? Or shall we keep discussing Gavri and Kolya and their precious feelings?"

Oboroten. Elaina stared him in the face, searching for any glimmer of mockery, but found none. Grisha meant it.

"I *want* to have you," he growled, low and lusty and urgent between them. "*Only* you, Elaina. My beautiful, hungry, aching woman. I want to join with you, and climb with you, and hear you scream my name as I *come* with you."

Elaina shut her eyes with a groan, his husky voice awakening a pulse of desire in her core. She let go of his hands, and he resumed stripping her, sliding her jeans down her long legs in a swift, smooth rush.

When he had her mostly naked, with her pants and panties both cast to the floor and her tank top and bra pulled down to expose her breasts, he laid her back on Kolya's table, and his smooth, rigid cock slid deep inside her. The dark, burnished-steel piercing gave her a jolt of delicious pleasure, and she moaned, wrapping her legs around him, welcoming him deeper still.

"Grisha," she panted. "You're so bad sometimes..."

"I beg to differ," he growled, rocking with her, into her, in an artful, thrilling rhythm. "I'm always very, *very* good at this."

"*Oh,* you're so... so hard..." She undulated with him, making the table creak. The edge of it dug hard into the soft, round flesh of her ass, but she didn't care. Grisha had the unique ability to turn all physical sensation into pleasure when he fucked her, twisting and building it in crackling, gilded tension throughout her body.

"Harder," she whispered in his ear, arching to him as he thrust into her. "Quick. Oh, I want to come... I want to come *so* hard..."

"I can tell," he teased her.

"*Fuck.*"

"As you like, love."

He planted his hands on the table to either side of her and buried himself in her to his last beautiful inch. Elaina groaned, arching, tightening her legs around him, rolling her hips with short, breathless, rapidly rising groans of pleasure. She reached up, behind her, grasping for the back panel of the work bench to steady herself as she moved with him. He plunged into her, so deep, and she'd grown *so,* so wet. He rounded against her with a tight growl, biting her neck with a perfect, sweet-stinging blend of bliss and pain, and she dug her heels into his back with a cry loud enough for everyone else in the house to surely hear. And it made her laugh. A choking, moaning, beautiful laugh, chasing away the dark, shadowy clouds lingering over her mind.

"Yes," she urged him on, as Grisha thrust harder, galloping toward completion. Each beat stoked her growing climax and drove her giddily toward the edge. "Yes, *yes,* yes!"

Grisha swore in Russian, and muttered some desperate, breathless accusation. He slid one hand down between her thighs, thumb circling and stroking her clit. Elaina arched, crying out again, as the thundering approach of orgasm raced through her.

Oh, God! I feel—so full! So close—so—

Climax struck like a bolt of electricity, and without even realizing she jerked away from Grisha as her body convulsed. She came in a wild, uncontrollable gush, legs spasming, a short, wet jet of her own ejaculation spattered her snow leopard across his flat, hard abdomen. She barely had a second to register before she came again, body wracked with intense pleasure, and a fresh surge of wetness flooded her thighs and soaked Grisha's glistening cock.

"Oh, *fuck* yes!" Grisha snarled, and he plunged into her again, driving himself as deep as he could, giving three quick, hard, hungry thrusts before he let out a shuddering groan. Within her his cock twitched and surged, and Elaina joined his cries as he pumped himself hard into her womb.

"*Goddess!*" she gasped, when he finally drew away. "Damn, Grisha... I've... I've never..."

He gave her a wink and a lopsided grin. "Never squirted before?" He offered a hand to help her off the worktable and steadied her as she found herself on *very* shaky legs.

"No." She gasped for breath.

"Sounds like a lack I'll personally have to make up for."

He kissed her, possessive and hungry and hot, and then stepped away. With a feigned air of innocence he said, "All right, now... what sort of tools will we need?"

"You asshole!" she laughed. Seizing a shop cloth from a bundle Kolya kept on one of the shelving units, she threw it at Grisha. "We can't just leave his workshop like this!"

Grisha blinked, totally unassuming. "I thought you were mad at him?"

"I'm *not* mad!"

She grabbed her own cloth and began cleaning up.

ELAINA TOOK A SET OF saws, a bow drill, and old iron file from Kolya's collection of tools, as well as a small box he'd had as a spare. She'd use it to keep her own kit, and the crafts she designed from it, all together. Grisha tried to convince her to take the more modern, multi-purpose tools—"You'll tear up your hands using a bow drill and I'm telling you, a good old cordless power drill with a delicate enough drill bit will be *fine!*"—but Elaina brushed him off. At least for the first part of this exercise, she wanted to use these.

She sat on the back patio, on a deck chair, working to whittle down one of the boar's big rib bones. The work was slow, and in her hands, clumsy; she'd never carved anything, really, let alone out of bone. This wouldn't even be her final piece, since she didn't know what, exactly, she even wanted to carve. So she practiced, nose wrinkled against the unpleasant scents, studying the different ways she could create angles and curves.

Her three mates joined her, Gavri and Kolya pulling up chairs of their own beside her, Grisha staking his out in a nice spot of morning sunlight to doze. Rini brought out breakfast pastries and fresh mors, with honey and sugar, and she delivered a friendly kiss to the cheeks of Elaina and her two wolves before returning to the house to begin work.

With her hands at work, Elaina felt the tension and discomfort of the last several days dissolving. When Kolya laid a hand on her knee and leaned over to nuzzle her neck, she welcomed him, leaning into his affection, and when Gavri asked to inspect her work on the chunk of bone, she showed him, eager for his response. Somewhere inside, she thought there might always be a small sliver of her wondering about their pasts, and the relationships they may or may not have had with the females of the tribe before their exile. She'd discovered a bit of a jealous streak inside her after all... she didn't know if she could ever let it go.

Maybe a better woman could. But not me. What can I say? I'm Tricia Jacob's daughter, after all.

"What are you shaping?" Gavri asked, turning the bit of bone over in his hand.

"Nothing, yet." Elaina took it back from him, considering its planes and curves. "I haven't decided what exactly to carve, when I really get to it. A wolf seems obvious, but then, one of my mates is a snow leopard, so..."

"But *you* will be a wolf," Kolya put in.

He sounded so confident in her; she gave him a gentle smile. "I certainly hope so. I can't be sure until I actually change for the first time, though, can I?"

"I'm sure we could think of many things," Gavri said, with a significant look at Kolya. "But it is for Elaina to choose."

She continued her carving and pondered the shape taking form in her hand.

Around noon, Rini returned with sandwiches and a selection of more juice, water, or tea. She seemed to be in an especially cheerful mood for the first time since the morning they'd found out about Polina's murder. As she set down the lunch trays on the glass patio table, she took a moment to look at Elaina's piece of bone, whittled down to a lump with no real shape to it.

Evidently, Rini disagreed. "How funny." She twitched her nose as Elaina handed it to her to examine more closely. "It looks to me like a little polecat all tucked up in a ball."

"No," Gavri protested, putting aside his book. "Not a polecat. It's a badger rooting for bugs."

"It's the musk deer." Kolya gave Elaina a playful poke. "The one who sent the boar downstream."

Elaina snorted with laughter and took the piece back. If anything, she thought it looked perhaps a little like a small bear, maybe a cub, sitting on its furry bum waiting for someone to hand it a pot of honey.

Guess I'm getting something of a grasp on it...

Kolya and Gavri perked up, turning as one toward the edge of the property, staring at a point just before the tree line. Elaina followed their gazes. It only surprised her a little to see Pasha trotting toward them in his lupine form, carrying a fat dead pheasant in his jaws.

"Oh!" Rini said pleasantly. "I suppose he's brought dinner, then."

"Gav?" Elaina asked. "Where exactly does Pasha live? I mean, your family has the lodge, Grisha has his apartment in Krasnoyarsk..."

"Pasha lives in the wilderness." Gavri took a glass of tea and sipped it with a pensive look on his face. "He has a very small *izba* house near the main areas of the park... but I have been there, and he does not 'live' in it, as you might expect."

He opened his book again and found his place. "The human belongings he needs are there. That's about all."

Grisha stirred from his doze as Pasha passed, and took the excuse to rise and come have lunch. Pasha came up to Elaina's chair, presenting the pheasant to her as though it were a gift.

More wolf than man, she thought again, and—a trifle hesitant—she took the offering.

"Thank you," she told him.

"She's not a great fan of dead animals dropped in her lap," Gavri said without looking up from the page. "Come now, Pasha. Don't be old-fashioned."

Rini took a sheaf of napkins from the tray she'd brought out and took the bird from Elaina. "I'll go pluck this and prepare it for tonight. With some stuffing and potatoes it should feed the lot of you."

"Thank you, Rini," Gavri said. "I'll come in to help when you need me."

"Don't be silly. As if I can't pluck and clean a bird and prepare it on my own."

Pasha, returning to his human form, took a look at the piece in Elaina's hand. "It is a cat? Like Gavri's pet?"

"Kotyanok belongs to Kolya." Gavri turned a page in his book. After a second's hesitation, he added, "Mostly."

"It's not anything," Elaina admitted. "I'm just trying to learn how to use these tools. I haven't got any idea yet what I want to carve. And at this rate, it's going to take me forever."

"I told you; you don't have to use traditional knives and rasps." Grisha took a long drink of ice water.

"No, but I want to do it this way. At least this part."

Pasha nodded. "You are carving only the totem for the top, *da*? You will still need a walking stick."

"Yes." She picked up the smallest rasp and tested out its detailing ability.

"I will find one for you," he offered. "Kolya can shape it and finish it."

Elaina paused, raising an eyebrow. Pasha returned her gaze quizzically. "What?"

"You called him Kolya," she said softly. "Not *dog*."

Pasha's lips twitched, as though a grimace tugged at him, but he kept his expression tamed. "He... is part of your pack. So I must change the way I see him."

"Hm." Elaina turned her attention back to her carving. "Then I think you owe him an apology. For you *and* your two cronies."

A look of pain crossed his face, the expression of a man who'd just been slapped. He turned a ruddy, brick red.

"Eh... yes." Taking a deep breath, he faced Kolya and sank to his knees before him, showing the back of his neck. Elaina hadn't considered the fact she'd asked Pasha, a beta wolf used to a position of leadership and authority, to bear his neck to the omega wolf, lowest on the totem pole and last in every measure. Kolya had said he'd always been an omega and always would be, and in a way, she understood him.

Still, fair was fair.

"*Izvinite*, brother," Pasha said. "Forgive me."

Kolya glanced at Gavri and Elaina, a crooked grimace on his face. He probably felt as awkward about the role reversal as Pasha did. Gavri gave him a nod of the head, and Elaina took note: as her beta wolf, he seconded her decision, and being of the pack himself, his support validated her less-than-traditional demand.

"Ah... forgiven, brother," Kolya told Pasha, the words coming out slow and uncertain. He brushed Pasha lightly on the shoulder, and the big man tilted his face up. They leaned in, touching their brows in the manner of acknowledgment the *oboroten* shared.

Good. Without saying anything, Elaina returned to her work.

Pasha left again to search for the branch which would form her walking stick. Kolya excused himself to his woodworking space to begin prep work, and Gavri, finishing up his chapter, rose to help Rini in the kitchen. He paused to kiss Elaina before he disappeared.

"You are turning out to be a very good leader." He caressed her cheek with his thumb. "We love you, Elaina."

"Thank you." She laid her hand over his. "I love you—all of you—too."

He beamed, and all was once again well between them.

With the others gone, Grisha took Gavri's chair, and watched her work. The piece of bone had grown quite small, and no longer resembled any of the things the group had guessed earlier. Though, to Elaina, it hadn't resembled any of those things in the first place. Her hands were tired, and she set the work aside, reclining across her chair to relax.

Grisha switched from Gavri's chair to hers, and curled up with her, purring.

AFTER DINNER, WHILE HER WOLVES watched the news and Grisha excused himself for a bit of night wandering, Elaina spent some time sketching out thoughts for the totem she would start carving tomorrow. She flipped through the photos she'd taken on her hike with her wolves: the gorge, the grosbeak, the musk deer, her mates. And Pasha. She'd nearly flipped all the way to the end before realizing she'd started including him in her mental concept of *her wolves*. Her pack. Well, she supposed he'd be pleased to know it.

It pleased her, too, though. Wary as she'd been, he'd grown on her. Formal and old fashioned, he made her laugh, but, knowing him better now, it also endeared her.

She flipped another picture and paused on the image. Gavri, climbing down the rocks on their return trip down the gorge, stepping lightly stone to stone in his lupine form. She liked it: the lithe position of the wolf, climbing down; the vertical tower of rocks like an ancient stairway.

But not Gavri. She picked up her pencil and began roughly drawing out the shape she'd make. *Not Gavri, and not the gorge. No moss or ferns growing around these rocks—these are made of ice and stone, and the wolf—*she-wolf*—will be thinner. Willowy. Sleek.*

Diezana. The spirit mother of the ancient fable, descending barren mountains besieged by snow and wind. Diezana in her first form, making the crossing to save her people.

Yes! Elaina's excitement grew with each stroke of her pencil. She'd never been any sort of artist with pencil and paper, and when she showed the final draft to Gavri and Kolya, she caught them exchanging befuddled glances.

"It'll be clearer when I'm finished."

Rini sauntered in with laundry to be folded. "Which could take another fifty years, at the rate you're going, silly."

"I'll get started on the real thing tomorrow." She snickered. "Though you probably won't even recognize it then."

"Should we speak about Pasha?" Gavri muted the television, straightening in his seat. Kolya lay with his head in Gavri's lap and shifted so he could see Elaina more clearly as they delved into the conversation.

Elaina put aside the sketch and rubbed at her chin. "I guess we should. You're both sensing the same thing I am, I take it?"

"His interest in you is not only an interest in the pack." Gavri nudged Kolya to sit up, and beckoned

Elaina to come sit between them. She did, relaxing with her head in Gavri's lap and her feet in Kolya's. Her omega wolf immediately began rubbing her soles and heels, and she groaned happily. She hadn't given much thought to how much hiking she'd done lately, and how tired and sore her feet were.

"Bringing you gifts," Kolya noted. "Inviting you on an intimate hike..."

"Intimate?' Elaina grinned. "You two were there the entire time."

"Yes," Gavri agreed. "But when an alpha female has a harem of mates, suitors know to expect chaperones, when they come courting."

"So he is courting me?" She leaned her head in closer to Gavri's hands and he started massaging her scalp. If she could purr, like Grisha, she would be.

"Definitely," Gavri said with a nod. She pursed her lips in thought.

Rini, folding clothing in the big leather armchair, piped up. "Bringing food is a dead giveaway. Even if it *is* very old-fashioned."

"*You* never brought me any kills," Elaina teased Gavri.

"I brought you breakfast on the morning after we found you," he corrected.

"Yeah, but you didn't hunt and kill it for me."

"Well, how do Americans put it? 'Why buy the cow when you can get the milk for free?'" He ruffled her hair. "I'd already scored a wild threesome with the strange frozen girl I'd stumbled on. Why bother bringing her game?"

She slapped his chest. "You pig."

Fighting to keep a straight face, he shrugged. "You hussy."

Together they laughed, and Kolya smiled at them both.

"So," he said once their chuckling had stopped. "What *will* you do about Pasha, *krasavitsa?*"

"Mm." Elaina settled back into Gavri's lap and he resumed his massage. "I don't know. How do you two feel about it?"

Kolya shrugged. "I don't dislike Pasha. He has been a stalwart and faithful man of the pack all his life. Doesn't smile or laugh much, though. Always like a military canine at attention."

Elaina touched her lips, thinking of the kiss she and Pasha had exchanged. There'd been no fireworks, no bells ringing. He *had* made her think about her long-ago prom date, however, and the poor boy's bashful hope at the end of the night.

"It is good to have him with our pack," Gavri pointed out. "And, if you reject him, he becomes a lone wolf, exiled from both families."

"Nikita won't take him back?"

"He probably would." Gavri moved his kneading from her scalp to her temples. "But Pasha would not accept. He is *very* traditional, Elaina. In his mind, if Diezana has called him to serve as part of your pack, he will not serve another."

"On the other hand, if he leaves *both* packs," Kolya added, "there is a chance he could form new bonds and attract his own pack."

"Dividing the Stolby shifters into three factions at odds with one another." Rini clucked her tongue.

"So, really, this would be a marriage of convenience?" Elaina asked, letting her head roll back, as Gavri had just instructed in a low whisper. He pressed his thumbs firmly into the back of her neck, working the pressure points.

"I wouldn't think so," Kolya said. "He does seem very taken with you."

"We saw the way he kissed you," Gavri added. Elaina didn't miss the hint of a growl in his voice.

"Did it upset you?"

"Not *upset*," he assured her. "But unless and until you mark him as your mate, I expect I'll harbor a touch of possessiveness."

He bent to kiss her. "I hope *that* does not upset *you*."

"I'll let you know if you cross a line."

She fell silent. Her fingers returned to her lips, and her thoughts to Pasha's somber face, and the shy, silent eagerness in his gaze.

CHAPTER FIFTEEN

SHE SPENT ALL OF THE next morning, and the early part of the afternoon, whittling down the basic shape she had sketched out the night before. Her hands began to ache early in the process, still sore from the practice of the day before, and tightening her form to manage more detail only made it worse.

Grisha took notice of her massaging her own palms during her break for lunch, and took over the kneading for her, alternating deep caresses with applications of ice.

"I understand why you want to do it this way," he assured her. "But I think you've had enough raw experience to earn your marks. Plus—"

He held up her right hand, nicked with several scarlet cuts. "If you keep this up, you won't be able to work the rest of your crafts. It's time to consider moving to Kolya's more modern tools."

"I agree." Kolya looked at her other hand, inspecting her swollen knuckles and the mess she'd made of her nails. "Come, *krasavitsa*. Let me select a Dremel and some burrs to help you."

Elaina considered the offer and inspected the work she'd already managed to do. She'd pulled the basic shapes together, a sinuous form which would

226

become the wolf's body, the rounded oval of its head. The stony cliff it climbed showed more definition, because she'd discovered a useful trick of twisting the knife to create sharp angles and uneven surfaces quite similar to actual rock.

Her mates were right. She'd had the experience she wanted, learning to cut and shape bone by traditional means. She'd come to know the feel and shape of the virgin material and its strength beneath the blade. If she kept up like this though, Rini's estimate of fifty years to completion might wind up being accurate.

"Okay," she agreed. "I'll switch to power tools. You'll show me how?"

"Absolutely." Kolya surveyed several hunks of rib bone she'd cut when selecting the one she'd use. Picking one out for himself, he turned it one way and another in the light. "It's been some time since I crafted with bone. I could probably make something very pretty out of this."

"I'd like that."

They ate, and Elaina rested in the mild afternoon sun while Kol retrieved the tools. Grisha snoozed in the deck chair beside her—"Just a short nap, Baba Yasmin's expecting me to harvest perennials today," he'd told her—and Elaina sleepily wondered where Pasha was. He hadn't returned yesterday afternoon, but it hadn't troubled her. Gavri did say Pasha lived in the wilderness, didn't he? She *had* expected him today, however. How long did it take to find a branch worth carving into a walking stick?

Rini came to retrieve the lunch plates, and before disappearing back into the house, tapped Elaina on the shoulder.

"Grisha and I started the process of tanning the boar leather for you," she said. "We've already cured and stretched it, and I've just set it in the tanning solution. It will probably be ready for you to begin making it into a jacket by the end of the week."

Elaina straightened, startled. "You two already got started on the leather?"

"There wasn't time to wait," Grisha told her. "Curing and tanning leather can take many days, and you have other tasks to focus on. This is only the preparation process, little one. *You* will turn the hide into something more."

"Are you sure it's okay, though? It won't mean I've botched the task, will it?"

"*No.*" Grisha wrinkled his nose, as though offended. "Elaina, the tasks were not given to you so that you would shoulder each one individually and without aid. You're learning the ways of our people, and at a criminally accelerated rate."

Settling back onto the deck chair, he stretched his arms behind his head and sighed. "Even after you've completed this gauntlet, we will still have *much* to teach you. There will be plenty of time then for you to learn about mashing up pig's brains to soak your leather before working."

Her eyes widened. "*Pig's* brains?"

"He's joking." Rini put a steadying hand on Elaina's shoulder. "They did use animal brains once, but I just picked up some curing and tanning components in the city. No brains, I promise."

"Oh." Elaina glanced from Rini to Grisha. "Well... after the solstice... whenever we work with leather again... I don't mind trying the brain thing."

Rini made a face, while Grisha laughed out loud. "I knew you would!" He told her with a wink.

"Anyway, I'll let you know when the hide is ready," Rini said. Her voice was tighter, and she looked a bit green. "I can help you sew it into a jacket, too. Don't worry, I won't do it *for* you," she added when Elaina opened her mouth to protest. "We'll do it together."

As the young woman hustled back into the house, Grisha gave Elaina a kiss.

"The point is not to do this all alone," he repeated. "It is to become part of Diezana's world. Her people. The people who will *help* you in this journey."

Elaina nibbled her lip, tapping her fingers on the table. "I just want to do this right, Grisha."

"I know you do. And you are."

Kolya returned from the garage, carrying a toolbox in each hand and what appeared to be a folding card table under one arm. As he set the toolboxes down and began arranging the table for them, Elaina stooped to inspect the tools he'd chosen.

"I brought burrs and bits and sanding discs." He beamed at her. "I'll show you some tricks to get some *beautiful* smooth lines on your work."

Elaina retrieved the piece she'd begun. Before joining him, though, she paused to search the tree line, considering the place where Pasha had appeared the day before.

Why hasn't he come back?

SHE WORKED WITH KOLYA, SHAPING and detailing the figure for the walking stick handle, until the sun began to set. By then though, the rough, oblong shapes—which this morning had only been suggestions of a wolf upon the stones—had taken on clearer details and relief, and even, it seemed, a breath of life. Nothing so momentous or beautiful as the piece Kolya worked on to guide her: he crafted a gathering of bone-white wolves, integrating a display spot for her to place the earlier figure he'd given her, the golden, polished she-wolf made of wood. Still, Elaina's breath caught as she turned her carving over in her hands after giving it a spin under the buffing wheel. No, it wasn't perfect... but it *was* hers. It was recognizable—although it was possible one or two people would think she'd carved a large squirrel instead of a wolf—and it was *hers*.

"Now we only need the branch Pasha promised," Kolya remarked. Elaina frowned, throwing another glance toward where Pasha *should* have been, before helping Kol tidy up and return the tools and card table to his workshop.

By the time Gavri returned from errands in Krasnoyarsk, Elaina sat with Kolya at his worktable, watching him turn smaller pieces of the boar's bones into rings and pendants. She'd doodled up a fanciful design—nothing specific, merely a whorl of curves and swoops—and sketched it on a fresh piece of her own, to begin sawing. This time, she used the power tools, under Kolya's careful watch.

Pasha still had not returned by the next afternoon. Sitting by herself on the back patio, as the sun reached its apogee, Elaina considered asking her wolves to go search for him.

I am worried about him. The corners of her mouth twitched toward a frown. *So I guess he is one of mine now, one way or the other.*

A collection of small, stylized pendants and beads lay spread before her on the patio table, as well as a collection of the boar's teeth. On his trip to Krasnoyarsk Gavri had stopped to pick up some jewelry-making materials to bring home for her. Elaina's Russian had been progressing steadily, and she knew very well the kit he'd brought her read *For Ages 6 to 12* on the side. She didn't concern herself too deeply over it. She picked up piece after piece of the bone tokens she and Kolya had carved and polished together, looking for the ones she liked best.

The others, we can save. They'll make good gifts and family heirlooms in the future.

She picked up one of Kolya's creations—or rather, she saw, one *she* had created, but he had perfected. Two smooth, hook-shaped curves joined in the middle, forming something of an S-shape.

Or like the symbol of infinity, she noticed. *Only... incomplete. Split.*

Kolya had polished the smooth, tapering curves in a pearly shine, and as she turned the pendant over in her hand, Elaina had the perfect idea for turning it into a necklace. Picking up the small drill Kol had given her, equipped with the tiniest drill bit he had, she began work on refining its design.

She drilled a series of delicate holes along the curves, and shallow, subtle geometric lines. As she did, a thought occurred to her. As she put the finishing touches on the larger pendant, she gathered five smaller bone shards, and began shaping them as Kolya had shown her. Her aim this time was simple:

no wolves, no cats, no stones or trees. Five times, she recreated the swooping S-curve—her broken infinity—in miniature.

"Too small for too many holes or even lines..." She tapped her bottom lip with a finger as she finished the fifth piece. With a thoughtful *hmm,* she searched the toolbox Kolya had loaned her. Parts of it had been segmented and organized more like a crafting case, and, lifting the lid on a set of small plastic compartments, she found what she wanted: tumbled and polished semi-precious gemstones, in varying sizes and colors that Kolya had stored away for when they might decorate one of his pieces. Since he worked most often on large carpentry projects of polished wood and stainless steel, the gems could have been tucked in the organizer for years, completely forgotten. He'd only remembered them last night, bent over the worktable, showing her the delicate art of carving jewelry.

He welcomed her to use the stones. Topaz and amethysts, common enough in Siberia. Tourist highlights in the Stolby visitor center included panning for them in the river or hunting for geodes in the hills. Elaina gravitated towards the collection of small, round, red gems like perfect drops of blood. Garnets.

She selected five. It took an extra hour, smoothing and sizing the inner curves of each small bone design to fit, but with careful attention, she managed it: five hand-carved, polished figures, each about the length of her thumb, and each with a single blood-red garnet mounted in the bottom curve of the S-shape.

Finally, after each stone had set, affixed with the extremely delicate application of extra-strength adhesive glue, Elaina applied the drill again. This time, to the top curve of the S. In each charm she carefully drilled a narrow passage for a setting, then slipped an earring hook through it.

As she finished the last one, Elaina sat back and admired her work. One pendant; five earrings, identical in design if not exact replicas. One each for her, Kolya, Gavri, and Grisha.

And one more.

She pondered the final earring. She knew who she'd had in mind, of course, when she'd carved it.

Am I ready to take that step, though?

The patio lights came on. She hadn't noticed how dark it had become, and, glancing up at the sky, she saw the sun had already begun to set.

Another day down. What does that leave me?

Eleven days.

She considered the earrings again. Then, gathering up the rest of the unfinished bone charms and figures, she arranged them in one of the larger toolbox trays. The earrings, as well as her pendant, disappeared into another. She closed the box.

A grunt from the edge of the yard drew her attention. Elaina frowned, unable to make out the figures moving just within the trees, then all at once, grew cold with alarm.

Vukodlak? Here?

She shot to her feet, knocking over the chair, and seized the first item she could lay her hands on: the Dremel rotary tool, equipped with a plain, worn-down sanding disc.

"Gavri!" she called over her shoulder. "Kol!"

The figures emerged from the woods, and Elaina's breath caught. Not *vukodlak*. Pasha, along with Adelaida, Bernard, and Timofei. Only...

Elaina dropped the Dremel. "*Gav!*" she screamed even louder, and rushed to meet the group. Pasha and Bernard held a slumped Timofei between them. Gavri's father was pale, and a dark streak of blood stained the right side of his face. As Elaina rushed to help, Pasha—wearing several bruises and one impressive shiner—held up a hand to stop her.

"We've got him. It is not as bad as it looks but—"

"First aid kit," Adelaida said. She had a cut on one fine cheekbone, and a reddened wound on her side, just above her hip. A bite mark. Only Bernard seemed to be uninjured, though from the grim, pained expression on his face, Elaina couldn't be sure.

Footsteps raced up from behind her, and Gavri and Kolya joined them. Gavri dropped to his knees before his father, carefully touching his face, speaking in rapid, frantic Russian. Timofei didn't follow very well, and managed only a few muttered words of nonsense.

"Skinwalkers," Elaina said. Pasha nodded.

Gavri rose, saying something to Pasha in the *oboroten* tongue, and the larger wolf traded Timofei over to him. Moving almost as one, Bernard and Gavri helped Timofei toward the sliding kitchen door, with Adelaida close behind.

Kolya stood behind Elaina, putting both his hands on her shoulders as she waited for Pasha to explain.

"They attacked the pack's meeting place." Pasha pressed his right fist to his left shoulder, and moved his left arm in short, stiff circles. "Three of them. And..."

He shot a gaze toward the house, after the family. "Viktor."

Kolya sucked in a breath through his teeth. "*Nyet.* That *svoloch* did not come back!"

"He did." Pasha lowered his arm and rubbed at the back of his neck. "And the female he fled with. They brought the others."

"Is anyone else hurt?" Elaina asked. "Nikita? Yasmin?"

"Yasmin is elsewhere. As far as I know, she is safe. I think Viktor had a very specific point to make, attacking the meeting place. It is where the pack feels safest. Most at ease."

He let out a heavy breath. "Nikita is hurt, but no worse than I. You must know by now how we... *opravlyat'sya.*"

Pull ourselves together, he meant. *Recover.*

"Timofei, on the other hand..."

"Timofei is human," she finished with dread.

Elaina spun to look back toward the house, where, through the wide picture windows she could see Gavri and Adelaida hurrying to tend to the injured man. Behind them, Rini spoke on the phone, no doubt calling for emergency services.

Elaina wrapped her arms around herself. "Why would they do this?"

"Were it only stray, feral members of their tribe, I would tell you we need only hunt them down and drive them out," Pasha said. He held up his hands in a helpless gesture. "*Uvy.* Viktor planned this. He knew what he did. He attacked Adelaida outright, and set his cronies on Nikita, Tim, and Bernard. They said nothing—nothing, at least, which I could make out—but simply attacked."

"They want this land," Kolya said softly.

"*Da.*" Pasha nodded. "It would seem so. The land... and revenge."

CHAPTER SIXTEEN

THE HOUSE DIDN'T SOUND RIGHT. Elaina lay in the master bedroom, her head on Kolya's chest, unable to sleep. Gavri and Adelaida had gone with Timofei to the hospital in Krasnoyarsk, and the empty space on the bed beside her filled Elaina with a troubling, nagging feeling of being incomplete. Bernard and Pasha had been offered rooms for the night, and Grisha returned from his work with Yasmin as soon as word reached them of the attack, so the lodge had just about reached capacity, full as it had ever been since Elaina came to stay. Even Rini had opted to stay in the main house rather than her small detached apartment across the yard, and slept on one of the couches downstairs. Pasha took a couch in the sunroom, where he could keep watch in case any *vukodlak* came slinking about the property. Viktor, of course, had once called this place home.

Yet, even with so many warm bodies occupying the building, an eerie, oppressive silence kept Elaina awake. A house filled with six adults shouldn't *be* so quiet. She should hear Grisha's even breathing from the room next door, Bernard's rumbling snores from down the hall. He'd accompanied Gavri and Adelaida to the hospital when the paramedics arrived for

Timofei, but returned four hours later to slouch up the stairs to bed. It surprised Elaina his exhaustion hadn't already crushed him. They'd heard his snores even from the living room. Not now, though. Now, Elaina heard nothing in the house, and she didn't like it.

Even Kolya's soft, sleeping breaths were too quiet, and the bright, beautiful view through the bedroom's picture window seemed frozen somehow, flat, like a painted background on a movie set. It was all much too eerie. Finally, she couldn't lie still anymore, listening to nothing but the echoing darkness, and she climbed out of bed, wrapping herself in a robe.

She meant to go down to the kitchen and have some water. She paused by Grisha's door, listening for him, holding her breath with a strange, illogical fear. After what had happened to Gavri's father, so close to home, on *safe* lands, she'd been unable to shake the worry that any second, one of her own mates might somehow be taken. Grisha, her loner, her finicky feline sometimes overflowing with physical affection and attention and sometimes so distant and aloof... what would she do if, waking up in the morning, she found him gone? Taken from her by invisible enemies? Or simply disappeared, having had his fill of domestic life and feeling the need to run?

The sounds were faint, but she did hear him, and relief filled her heart. She'd wanted him in the main bed with her and Kolya tonight, but no one brought it up. With Gavri gone, it didn't seem right. Elaina could invite her mates to join her wherever she liked—the lodge was as much her home now as Gavri and Kolya's, as they had made clear to her many times—but there were still matters of territory among her men, unspoken but understood, which didn't feel right to ignore. The master bed belonged to Gav and Kolya. Grisha had his space now, though no one had specifically appointed it his. She could go where she wanted, but inviting her males to invade each other's marked places wasn't right.

Pasha. What is his place? Elaina bit her lip. *Where does he belong in all this?*

Some clear, clairvoyant sense inside of her, a deep instinct in her heart, told her she had yet more room for someone like Nikita's enforcer. And perhaps, more room yet. Shadows somewhere in the future still lingered out of her understanding, but she knew things in her life—in her soul—were far from settled.

Does that mean he belongs to me? *Are we connected, too?*

She brought one hand up to her chest and backed away from Grisha's door. *Down to the kitchen for a drink,* she told herself. *Then check on Pasha. He's alone in that part of the house, after all.*

As she neared the stairs, though, a green light from below drove all other thoughts aside. Brow furrowed, Elaina came to the top of the staircase and crouched, looking down through the slats of the banister. The floor of the living room lay bathed in a vibrant green glow, almost radioactive, but from her vantage point she couldn't make out anything past the end of the couch, and the edge of the low coffee table.

Steeling herself, she straightened, and went down.

A green fire burned in the fireplace, but like the view of the valley outside the great picture window upstairs, something looked wrong about it. The flames moved in an unnatural dance, slow and hypnotic, like backlit green tissue paper and tranquil, stop-motion animation. She hadn't felt tired before—too unnerved by the oppressive silence—but staring into the alien light made her immediately drowsy.

"Come, Elaina," a low, sonorous voice invited. "Let's sit, and chat."

On quiet bare feet, she slipped into the living room. A cool shiver passed over her as her toes sank into the plush, soft carpet, like stepping into a thick, cottony animal hide. Rabbit, maybe. Snowshoe hare. Immediately, she remembered Rini had been sleeping down here, on the other arm of the sectional, under the front window. The sweet little housekeeper wasn't there now, though. For a split second of horror Elaina imagined she'd see blood staining the leather or dripping onto the rug, a dead rabbit laid out across the coffee table—

None of those things. The couches were clean and uninhabited. No sign of Rini—including her guest sheets—anywhere.

Sitting in the chair where Adelaida sat when she held court here in her house, was the spirit Athanos. He held the old tin camping mug in one hand, blowing steam from its surface, and gestured at the empty coffee table. Where there had been nothing before, now a battered tea service rested, all mismatched camping gear and dented spoons. Steam rose from one speckled mug, smelling of cinnamon.

Elaina didn't take it. Sitting on the edge of the couch, she cocked an eyebrow at him. "Why are you here?"

"We needed to speak," he answered. "Your time to master the magic of Diezana's children grows short. Are you any closer to her blessings?"

Elaina didn't know how to answer. She'd completed the tasks she'd been given up to this point, yes. She couldn't be sure, however, if her efforts had won her any favor. She still hadn't heard Diezana's voice for days, and each morning she found herself struggling to *feel* more a part of this world.

"I'm following the course she's set out for me," she said quietly. Though, now she thought of it, had Diezana been the one to demand this course? The raging ghost, Niuri, had been the one who spoke of the tasks. What if this hadn't been Diezana's course after all?

"Do you feel any different?" Athanos asked.

"Yes," she replied quickly. Then, with a soft sigh, she added. "No? I'm not sure."

"The spirit mother hasn't exactly been forthcoming with you, has she?"

"Not exactly," Elaina agreed.

"Please, have some tea."

Elaina acknowledged his offer with a nod but still did not take the mug.

"Why are the *vukodlak* attacking like this?' she asked him. "You're a spirit, you must know."

Athanos held up his hands. "I do not presume to know the minds of mortals, *krasavitsa*."

She didn't care for the sound of Kolya and Gavri's term of endearment coming from this enigmatic and disconcerting creature. She had a sense Athanos, as a spirit, had no intent or power to harm her, and his smiles and offerings struck her as genuine. Still, she didn't like the unspoken undercurrent of their conversations. He—or it?—did not think much of the human aspiring to ascend to the life of a shapeshifter.

"What I do know," he said after a sip from his mug, "is that you've created quite the conundrum."

She sat up straighter. "What?"

"Your challenge to the alpha male couldn't have come at a worse time, could it?" He rested the still-steaming mug in his lap and held up a hand in a gesture as though she should have already thought of this. "With the *vukodlak* growing bolder, Nikita Alexeev faces serious conflict. Perhaps all-out war. But of course, he *also* must consider the threat to his leadership, posed by an untested little girl."

Elaina's shoulders stiffened. She narrowed her eyes. "*Don't* call me 'little girl'. I'm a grown adult and I know what I'm doing."

"You don't, though." He held out his hand toward the shifting, dreamlike glow of the fire. "Take a look."

Elaina did. At first, the fire seemed unchanged. After a few seconds, though, she caught sight of flickering movements. Shimmering sparks of light and flashes of shadow. She stood from the couch to approach the hearth, and knelt to peer in.

The battle at the pack's meeting place. A hot flash of dread made her draw in a gasp. Nikita, and Adelaida, Sofie and Timofei and Bernard. Klementina, and the male scout who had accompanied Pasha sometimes...

And the *vukodlak*. She'd never *seen* the Siberian skinwalkers before. Gangly and oversized, with proportions that seemed to belong to some other sort of beast. Or rather, *monster*. They looked spidery and disjointed; Elaina wondered if the *vukodlak* felt pain in their mutated states. From a glance, they appeared agonized.

Ugly and mismatched as they were, though, in battle they held the distinct advantage. They must be twice the size of the unmutated *oboroten*, with talons and teeth primed to tear through skin and unzip guts.

She identified Viktor when he jabbed a finger in Adelaida's direction. The person he really pointed to, though, was Timofei. The human. And the *vukodlak* charged.

"Stop." Elaina rubbed at her eyes and turned away from the vision as teeth were bared and blood started to fly. "I know what dog fights look like."

"Are you ready to lead them into one?" Athanos asked. "If you win your fight against Nikita, can you take over this looming war?"

"I'll have to."

"Maybe you don't."

Athanos sipped from his mug against, waving a hand and making the figures in the fire disappear. "I can help you."

"Help me do what?" Elaina perked up. "Finish Diezana's tasks? Discover the power to shift? Can you give those things to me?"

"I can resolve this challenge you've issued," Athanos said. "Make it go away."

Elaina stood, hugging her robe closer to her. The room seemed cold to her all of a sudden, the fire useless. "I can withdraw my challenge if I want. But it won't protect my mates, and that's the whole point."

"Destabilizing the pack only to have the enemies attack again—perhaps with more soldiers—will not provide your mates any more protection against teeth and claws. I can change Nikita's mind. Make him drop the blood hunt, so you no longer have to win the challenge at all."

The way he said *change Nikita's mind,* Elaina didn't believe Athanos meant to use thoughtful and concise discussion or negotiation.

She returned to her seat on the couch. "And what would I have to do?"

"Give up your quest. Remain human."

Elaina frowned. Her immediate response should have been to decline, flat out. At least, she knew her heart and gut wanted her to decline. Shutting her eyes, she brought a hand to her forehead and began to knead at the pain starting just below the surface.

"Just give up?" she asked. "It's that easy?"

"I'd prefer not to see the *oboroten* devoured by their enemies while they argue amongst themselves over who is best suited to be alpha. Humans are not shapeshifters, Elaina Jacob. I will help you protect your mates, and I will secure your safety here with them, at least so far as the tribe is concerned. No more blood hunt. No more exile. Simply back out now, and do not make this conflict worse for Nikita and his people."

With a sigh, she leaned her elbow on one knee and rested her chin in her hand. "What sort of spirit are you, Athanos? Why are you invested in my situation at all?"

Athanos lifted one shoulder in a half-shrug. "I am... not *quite* a spirit, as you imagine. Once, I lived as a mortal. Like Diezana, I began in flesh and blood, and learned the ways of ghosts and magi."

"Are you saying *you* started out as a human?" she asked, straightening. "And you *learned* to be a shapeshifter? So you're like me?"

"*Not* at all like you, *krasavitsa.*" His vibrant green eyes flashed. They weren't like Grisha's eyes, cool and lambent, glowing softly like stars and smoldering fire. Athanos had dark, venomous eyes, sharp in his anger. Not feline at all. Had he said he was *oboroten?* A big cat? Or had she imagined that?

"I learned the magic when Diezana was still wasting her life among *humans.* A goddess! A *queen* of predators, risking herself for mortals." He pointed at Elaina, as though accusing her. "*You* are not like us, little girl. You can't change your blood and bone, and I think you know that. Diezana has no interest anymore in new sheep for her flock. You hunt in her name and give your offerings, but so have others, like your lover Gavri's sire. And look how Diezana has favored *him.* His wife, his child, they can throw off injury from the *vukodlak* within hours, days at most. So the skinwalkers target the soft, pink, defenseless human flesh instead. Did Diezana do anything to protect him?"

The scent of cinnamon from the tea became cloying, almost hot, like the true spice without sugar or cream to sweeten it. The fire appeared to have picked up, flashing and flickering, but still silent, still the same unearthly shade of green.

Poisonous. Like his eyes.

"You are not Diezana," he said in a low tone. Despite the hard edge in his words, though, she caught a note of regret. Pity. "For all you know, she will not step in on your behalf. You perform these tasks, seven tasks in twenty-one days, so she will *maybe* give you her favor. *No* human in thousands of years has mattered enough to Diezana to receive that blessing. How can you believe *you* will succeed in only twenty-one days?"

Elaina put her head in her hands. Exhaustion, bone-deep and heavy, threatened to drag her down. Athanos wasn't wrong. Had he said he shifted into a big cat, like Grisha? Or was he a wolf? A bear? He put her on her guard, like any predatory creature would if she came up on it in the wilderness, but being dangerous didn't also make predators malicious. How many of them came ready-equipped with warning signals and adaptations designed to avoid trouble rather than start it?

Is that what this spirit is doing? Is this his way of rattling his tail or puffing up his body to warn me away from the conflict?

Because he wasn't wrong.

When Elaina looked up again, Athanos had vanished, once more without a trace. No fire burned in the hearth. The cold gray light of pre-dawn streamed in the picture window, and Rini stood in the entry to the dining room, a glass of water in her hand.

"Elaina? I didn't hear you come down."

The headache intensified. Elaina stood, crossed to the entryway, and put her arms around Rini in a quiet hug. Taken off guard, Rini hesitated, but after a second returned the embrace, squeezing Elaina tight.

"Everything all right?" she asked in a whisper.

"My head hurts," Elaina replied. "Is there any aspirin?"

Rini nodded and broke away to find the bottle hidden somewhere in their well-stocked medicine cupboard. Elaina glanced over her shoulder back into the living room, hoping against hope she might see Gavri and his mother returning up the front stairs.

No Gavri, or Adelaida. Standing on the coffee table, though, were two mismatched camping mugs, steam still curling up from the tea inside. Cinnamon, of course; she could tell by the scent. One mug was still full, nearly to the brim, but the other had been left beside it, half drunk, the ghosts of otherworldly fingerprints fading quickly from its cooling side.

GRISHA AND PASHA LEFT AS soon as the breakfast dishes were cleared. With Elaina's blessing—and her strict admonishment they stay safe—the two men had volunteered to scout the area. Elaina put them under strict instructions not to engage any skinwalkers if they came across them. She had a feeling Grisha would, anyway, and if Grisha threw himself into a fight, Pasha very likely would too. She wanted to keep them back, keep everyone in her pack close to her and safe inside the house. That could never be, though. At least Grisha agreed to carry the sat phone.

Gavri came home just before lunchtime, to update them on his father's condition. Timofei had been ruled stable and seemed to have taken no fatal wounds, but one severe bite on his right wrist might cost him most of the use of his hand. Surgery had been scheduled to save as much function as possible, but no one could predict exactly how successful the attempt would be.

"At least he did not lose the appendage," Gavri told them in a dark tone, sipping black coffee from a cup Rini had fetched him the moment he'd arrived.

Elaina listened with grim understanding, unable to shake the things Athanos had said to her during the night.

His wife, his child, they can throw off injury from the vukodlak. So the skinwalkers target the soft, pink, defenseless human flesh instead. Did Diezana do anything to protect him?

She'd gotten rid of the two mugs left behind on the table before anyone else could see them. She knew she should tell her mates of the spirit's visit and his cryptic warnings—and even, perhaps, his offer to put the blood hunt to rest. And she *would* tell them. Not now, though. Not while Gavri, Adelaida, and Bernard all shouldered the weight of Timofei's hospitalization.

After lunch, Gavri prepared to go back to the hospital right away. Bernard would go with him, allowing Adelaida to come home and get some rest. Elaina joined Gavri in the shower, eager to relieve him of some of his worry and tension, before he left again.

"I miss you when you're gone," she whispered, kissing him over and over. "It doesn't feel right without you in the house."

He answered her with hungry passion, taking her like a brute, anxious and needful for release. Later, as he climbed into his truck to leave again, he seized Kolya with equal desire, kissing him like a man dying of thirst. Together, she and Kol watched him drive away, and shared a pang of sorrow over his pain.

Adelaida returned late in the evening. Elaina had gone down to Kolya's workshop again, refining some of the edges and curves on the earrings she'd crafted, and playing with new shapes and ideas on fresh shards of bone. Upstairs, the front door opened and closed, and Rini's voice welcomed the lady of the house.

Storing away the pieces she'd been working with, Elaina headed upstairs to meet Adelaida. She sensed now would be a good time to make herself available to her lover's dam.

Mother-in-law? she wondered as she climbed up to the first floor. *Or is there a different title in the case of oboroten mating pairs? Or does it even come up, when you've got more than one mate, anyway?*

Adelaida had collapsed into her armchair—the same one Athanos had occupied during his midnight visit—and rested with her head in her hands, pinching the bridge of her nose. Without a word, Elaina considered her, then quietly slipped into the dining room, where Rini and Kolya hustled to prepare dinner. A roast, Elaina noted, and felt a small flutter of pride at the sight of the meat wrapped in paper on the counter. One of the packages Kolya had prepared from her boar.

She opened the freezer to retrieve an ice pack. She'd had to use several on her limbs and hands over the last week, and Rini had taken to storing multiples right next to the assorted frozen berries. Elaina wrapped the pack in a small kitchen towel and took it back to Adelaida.

"Here."

Adelaida looked up. Her eyes, dulled by fatigue, lit up with a tiny spark when she realized what Elaina offered her. She took it with a sound of relief and pressed it to her brow.

Elaina sat on the floor, within arm's reach should Gavri's mother have need of her. She'd never seen Adelaida look frail or brittle. Now, she appeared to be both.

"He'll be all right," Elaina crooned. She rested her hand over Adelaida's, preparing herself for a steely rebuke. When her own mother grieved, Elaina could never predict whether attempts at comfort would be welcomed or rejected. Plenty of heavy, silent evenings had passed with Tricia Jacob in her chair in the living room, just as Adelaida sat now. If Elaina tried to sit with her and offer her company, Tricia might draw her daughter onto her lap for a hug... but, especially as Elaina got older, Tricia might just as easily scream and throw a book or decorative pillow, or dig at her with cold and bitter accusation. *Maybe you could show a little concern for my feelings* before *I get angry. Maybe you could try and not do things to* make *me angry. You and your father and the ladies' club donors and the people on the gallery board... all any of you do is take, and then when I'm sitting here tearing my hair out you come along and put your arms around me like a precious little princess. Well I don't* need *anything from you, Elaina, so stop making a fool of yourself.*

To her relief, Adelaida did nothing at all. She didn't gaze at Elaina, eyes brimming with tears, and draw her into any dramatic embrace, but neither did she snatch her hand away, spitting and furious with the gesture. Encouraged, Elaina ventured further.

"Can I do anything for you? Have you eaten today?"

All the tension in Elaina's chest eased as a tired smile played across Adelaida's lips. "*Da.* Gavri would not leave this morning until I had eaten. I will survive until dinner is ready. But a cold glass of water, maybe?"

"Of course." Elaina stood. "I can also get you juice, if you'd like that instead?"

"*Nyet, spasibo.*" Adelaida relaxed, tilting back her head to let the ice pack rest on her forehead. "No thank you, Elaina."

Elaina touched the tip of her tongue to her top lip, and ventured, "*Togda prosto voda,*" before returning to the kitchen.

Kolya looked up at her with a smile as she entered. "Showing off your language-learning skills?"

"*Da.*" She smiled. "Did I get it right? I meant to say, '*just water, then*'."

"Is *that* what you meant?" Rini's eyes were wide with shock. "Goddess! Elaina, you just told her you lick syrup off her son's naked thighs!"

Elaina's snorted. "*Rini!*"

Kolya whapped Rini with a damp wash towel. "Hush, you."

From the living room came Adelaida's weary voice. "You all know I can *hear* you, right?"

The three of them fell silent all at once, glancing between each other like scolded children. A tight, forceful spool of laughter wanted to break loose in Elaina's chest, and seeing Kolya's clenched jaw and tight-lipped smile, she knew he must be fighting his own bout of hilarity. That only made hers harder to stay on top of. Rini buried her face in her apron, tittering.

After several pregnant, agonizing seconds, Adelaida spoke again.

"I have no idea about my son, but if he takes after his father you'll do better with honey."

That did it. Elaina exploded into laughter, and Kolya snorted, covering his face with one hand as his other slapped helplessly on the counter. Rini spun to clutch the side of the sink, spilling her giggles like bubbles down the drain.

Elaina wouldn't have thought it possible, but even amid peril and doubt, her new *oboroten* family had found her smile.

Pasha and Grisha returned home in time for dinner, with nothing to report. No sign of *vukodlak* anywhere on the Stolby tribe's land this side of the Yenisei River. Grisha flung his arms around Elaina, nuzzling her face and neck in uncharacteristic possessiveness, making her think of felines who sensed oncoming quakes.

"We didn't find any of them," he growled in a low tone at her ear. "But we could *smell* them. *Foul*. Like rot. You come stay in my room tonight, *da?*"

"All of us together," she told him. "If Gavri comes home."

"Fine by me. As long as I know where you are."

Halfway through the meal, Bernard and Gavri came through the front door, both looking heavy, sleepy, and bedraggled. Elaina rose to serve them. With everyone present—except Gavri's father, of course—they no longer fit around Kolya's elegantly crafted dining room table.

It's like the mess hall at a summer camp. Elaina loaded up to plates with healthy chunks of roasted pig and potatoes, and handed them to her mate and his stepfather. Bernard claimed the seat she'd vacated at the table, between Rini and Adelaida, and Gavri took one of the barstools, eating his dinner at the kitchen counter. Elaina leaned on her elbows to gaze at him as he ate.

"How's Timofei doing?' she asked him, very quietly.

"There is not much change." He popped a round russet potato in his mouth. "He isn't like us, Elaina. He won't recover as quickly as Kolya did."

Taking a heavy pause, he stared down at his food. "In some ways, he won't fully recover at all."

"I know that." She reached across the counter to take his hand. "I'm like him, remember? If it had been me—"

He snarled with a sudden viciousness. "I *don't* want to think about it happening to you!"

Elaina recoiled. *There* was the sort of rebuke she'd expected from Adelaida earlier. The unpredictable response of her mother, lashing out at Elaina even though Elaina had nothing to do with the real trouble. She'd seen Gavri angry before. This, though, caught her off guard.

He let out a hissing breath between his teeth. "I'm sorry, *krasavitsa*. It's bad enough seeing my sire unable to heal wounds as we can. I can't stomach the thought of *you* lying in any hospital bed, covered in—"

"Well, don't say it then." She backed away from him, but only to retrieve the pitcher of iced tea and a clean glass, filling it for him.

"I will stay tonight," he told her. His voice came out low and tinged with shame. "But... in the morning..."

"That's fine." She gave him the glass, and tried again to twine her fingers with his. This time he let her. Despite the brief, bizarre sting, she would have given up her every chance at becoming *oboroten* in order to keep Gavri here with her tonight.

But tomorrow...

"I'd like to see the rest of the pack," she told him. "Tomorrow, maybe."

Gavri opened his mouth to reply, but it was his mother who said "I think that's an excellent idea, Elaina. I can take you."

Elaina shot a nervous glance Adelaida's way. "I didn't mean—but if you need to be with Timofei—"

"I will see him also." Adelaida took a dainty bite of her roast, and a sip of the red wine Kolya had poured. "But in the morning, you and I can take something to Nikita, and the wolves at his side."

After a quiet pause, Adelaida looked up, meeting Elaina's eyes.

"It will be good for you to see what the *vukodlak* have done."

CHAPTER SEVENTEEN

THE PACK'S MEETING PLACE WAS more abandoned than Elaina had ever seen it before.

Nikita was there, and among the others scattered about, Elaina recognized Klementina and the male wolf who always accompanied Pasha.

"Who is he?" Elaina asked Adelaida, as they entered the clearing together. They held camp coolers, two each, filled with golubtsy they'd prepared together. Elaina had never been an adventurous soul when it came to cooking—she had the staples down and never needed anything else—but Adelaida evidently believed this would not only be a good opportunity for Elaina to learn more about the Stolby pack, but about cooking Gavri's favorite food, as well. An extremely odd combination of lessons, Elaina thought, but Adelaida seemed to have returned to her brisk, businesslike, efficient demeanor, and would hear no argument.

Adelaida considered the wolf Elaina pointed out. "Ivan. With Pasha gone, he has moved up to become Nikita's beta wolf." She wrinkled her nose. "He's *not* prepared for it. He's never been as keen as Pasha."

Elaina withered. "I didn't mean to lure Nikita's right-hand man away—"

"I know." Adelaida sighed, and Elaina clearly understood the former alpha didn't care whether it had been intentional or not. It put Nikita and the Stolby tribe at a distinct disadvantage.

And what will Nikita himself think? Maybe it wasn't such a great idea coming here.

Adelaida led the way, greeting Nikita with her usual kiss on both cheeks. They spoke in Russian, and though Elaina could now pick up simple conversational words with much more ease, she hung back from the conversation, not wanting to intrude.

Klementina approached her, with a sharp glint of disgust in her eyes. Without warning, the *oboroten* scout pushed Elaina, growling as Elaina staggered back.

"Why are *you* here?" Klementina shot. "Come to gloat? To hold it over us how you've seduced away our beta wolf? The moment you had him in your claws, you know, *that's* when they attacked us."

"Klementina!" Adelaida snapped, whirling away from Nikita.

No matter what Gavri or his mother might have believed about her retirement, clearly the pack still viewed Adelaida as their alpha female. Perhaps they would accept Nikita's instructions before hers, now, but when Adelaida showed her teeth, the others *all* shrank back.

Nikita gazed at Elaina with cold dislike. A distinct, dirty shame crawled up the back of her shoulders, and she had to look away first.

Pasha, damnit... why didn't you talk to me before abandoning your people?

Adelaida handed Nikita the two coolers of golubtsy she'd brought, and as he handed them to

256

Klementina and Ivan to begin distributing, Elaina handed him hers as well. He offered a nod of approval before pointedly turning his back on her and guiding Adelaida to a pair of packmates evidently recovering from their own injuries.

Elaina stood awkwardly at the center of the meeting place. She rubbed at one arm, searching the area. Almost no one had shifted to their wolf form today. Several of the group bore bruises and some unpleasant gashes across their faces and necks. Had any of them been naked, as some usually were, Elaina imagined she would see similar bruises on thighs and bellies, the vulnerable places where predators attacked.

Most looked away from her. None offered any impression they'd welcome her to join them as Ivan and Klementina shared out the meals Elaina had helped prepare, but of course, it didn't surprise her.

I've got less than two weeks before I try and become their leader. How can I even hope to do it in so little time? When they all shun the sight of me, and I can't even blame them?

A low, pained sigh escaped her. "I can't do this."

"Figuring that out, are you?"

Elaina checked over her shoulder. Sofie, alone, sat on a log as she had at Polina's funeral rite. She had a stick in one hand and doodled in the dirt with it, a familiar grim pout on her face.

Deciding she didn't have much to lose, Elaina sat with the girl. Sofie wrinkled her nose but didn't reject her outright, scooting over to give Elaina room.

"You've been here every time I've come, except the first." Elaina brought up a knee and hugged it to her chest. "But you're not a wolf. Do any of them give *you* any trouble?"

"My brother's the alpha," Sofie replied, with a pointed note of emphasis. "No one's going to stop him if he wants to bring me here."

"Has that always been the case?"

The girl glanced askance and sketched a triangle in the dirt. "Only since Polina. He hasn't wanted to leave me alone at home since then."

Elaina nodded. "As bad as things are, though... I'll bet you like being included."

"Pft. It's okay."

Klementina circled around to them, offering Sofie a pair of cabbage rolls. Sofie took them and scoffed them down as though she hadn't eaten in days. Klementina moved on without offering Elaina anything.

"You're right, you know," Sofie said after a moment. "You *can't* do this. They're not going to accept you, even if you do win. Which you won't. Not against my brother."

"Well, I don't have a lot of choice." Elaina wasn't so sure she believed this anymore, but she couldn't admit it to Nikita's baby sister. "I've made my bed. I'll sleep in it."

"You won't sleep with the *vukodlak* breathing down your neck."

Sofie tossed her stick aside and leaned forward, as if inspecting the geometric designs she'd created was far, far more interesting than Elaina. "Have you *really* given any thought to this? You come in here and break up this tribe, *nobody* is going to stay. Your people, maybe, but not our pack. Even if you could beat Nikita, if you toss out a legitimate Stolby *oboroten* leader, everyone will desert. The whole tribe will go their own ways."

258

She turned flashing blue eyes on Elaina. "You'll unravel thousands of years of history."

Elaina snorted. "I hardly think *I* can do all of *that*. Surely, they won't abandon their home and their own people—which includes Gavri and Kolya. They might not like me, might even *hate* me, but they wouldn't abandon their ancient land just because I've come along. I mean, it's not just about coming out ahead of Nikita in a duel, right? The duel's only a prerequisite. Diezana still has to *choose* me."

"You don't know anything about us." Sofie stared at the ground, but her gaze had taken on a thousand-yard stare. She fell quiet for a long time. Elaina had just about decided to leave the girl and try to speak with Nikita, when Sofie spoke up again.

"You know this isn't the first attack. It's not even the second or third. They've been pressing closer in for years now."

"The *vukodlak?*" Elaina let her knee drop, resting both sneakered feet on the ground, and mimicked Sofie's posture, trying to get on eye level with the girl.

"Nikita thinks I don't know, but I pay attention." Sofie stuck out her foot and started smearing away her doodles. "Even Viktor's betrayal wasn't *really* the first sign. It was just... just the..."

It astonished Elaina to see Sofie choke up all at once. Tears filled her beautiful, deep eyes and she wrapped her arms around herself.

"And *you* won't know how to do anything about them." She scrubbed her forearm across her face. "You'll get eaten alive."

"Sofie..."

Out of the corner of her eye, she caught Adelaida waving her hand, beckoning. Elaina glanced from her to Sofie. The cat shifter seemed to have lost interest in her company.

"Sofie," Elaina said again. She laid a hand on Sofie's. "We'll make this right. If Nikita and I can come to an agreement about my pack—"

"*Your* pack?" Sofie glowered. "*Your* pack is just *our* pack, only they're the outcasts nobody wants around anymore anyway."

Elaina gave a resigned sigh and stood up. She left Sofie to join Adelaida and Nikita, across the clearing.

As she approached, Adelaida stepped aside from the alpha wolf, admitting Elaina. Nikita did not meet her gaze, but stared at something far in the distance. The expression looked almost exactly like his kid sister's.

"Nikita." Elaina gave the half-bow she'd seen other members of the pack give in the past. The gesture normally invited the other party to return the motion, touching foreheads in an affectionate, respectful greeting. Nikita did not do so, but it didn't surprise her.

The gesture had a second purpose: the showing of the back of the neck, as Pasha had done before Kolya. A sign of submission. She might not be part of the pack, and even if she did become one, her intention was not to *be* subordinate to Nikita. Now, though, the implied submission seemed appropriate. She'd never done this before, when coming into his territory. She probably should have.

Nikita said nothing at first, but made a sound like a tired old dog. Crossing his arms over his chest, he acknowledged her with only a nod. A very human thing to do.

"It was thoughtful of you and Adelaida to bring us a repast," he muttered.

"I wanted to see how you and the others were holding up." Elaina straightened and took a step closer to him.

He gestured to the gathered wolves. "They fought well. Viktor did not have enough cronies to outnumber us. I am only sorry we did not better protect Timofei."

Adelaida held up a hand. "Don't be. It may have been Viktor's intent to target his former mates. After he took Zhuang from us..."

A thought occurred to Elaina. She made a mental note to ask Adelaida about it later.

"Nikita," she said. "I... I'm sorry about Pasha. You have to know, I never asked him—"

"I know," he interjected. "I've known Pasha all my life. As my beta wolf, he proved time and again his loyalty and drive, but he also has one of the deepest spiritual devotions I have ever known. If he believes the spirit mother has called him to follow someone else..."

He drifted off. An impassive expression masked his face, but Elaina suspected he hurt much more deeply over the loss of his friend than he would let on.

"He said he came back, when the attack occurred?"

"He did," Nikita confirmed with a nod. "And I was glad to have him here."

"I'm glad." Taking a chance, she laid a hand on Nikita's arm. "I don't want or expect him to stay away. I'd send him back to you for good, if he'd let me."

"He struggled long and hard with the decision to leave us. It was not made on a whim." Now he met her eyes, a great weight of solemn intensity in his. "I hope you will not take his allegiance lightly."

"I won't," she said. "I promise you, Nikita."

He held her gaze a second longer, then looked away again, turning his back on her.

"He believes the spirit mother sends him to you as mate. You understand that, *da?*"

His voice had dropped an octave, and she had to take another step close to hear him properly. Standing by his side, she peered at him a second, before uttering a sigh.

"Yes," she admitted. "I know he does."

"If it were not such a significant calling, I would have tried much harder to make him stay. I cannot stand in the way of the connection he believes to be there, though." He paused a second, tilting his head. "What do you think of the proposition?"

"Honestly?" Elaina shrugged. "I don't know. I think perhaps there's something to it, but on the other hand, I don't believe in things like preordained love matches, destined loves, or anything like that. If I take a man as a mate, it is because I *choose* to, not because anybody, Diezana included, says it must be so."

"Hm." Nikita chewed on this new information. "You will break his heart."

"I hope not to."

Another several minutes passed. Around the clearing, Elaina was aware most of the pack had their eyes on her and Nikita.

"They distrust your reasons for being here," Nikita explained, as if she didn't know.

"I'm just here to offer sympathy, and any help I can."

"How nice of you to be sympathetic. When the *vukodlak* do not attack you, and your omega wolf so close to them by blood."

"I don't want to fight about Kolya with you." Elaina held her hands before her. "Nikita, isn't there any way for us to—"

He cut a hand through the air. "We've had this discussion. And now that I've relaxed my order to have him off our land, *now* his kind come calling. *Now* they kill my people and attack our gathering places. You are fortunate I do not go back on my word to you, though I have more than ample reason."

"There is no proof these attacks have anything to do with Kolya," she protested. "Remember, he was *also* attacked! He was the *first* to be attacked!"

"No."

This from Adelaida. She'd remained silent until now, standing aside from them with her hands clasped in front of her. Without looking at either of them, keeping her eyes cast down, she said, "Kolya was not the first to be attacked, Elaina. Only since you have arrived. The first was me, and my mates. I lost Zhuang, and Viktor. And the pack lost—"

She threw a quick glance at Nikita, then away again. "Others."

"But you can't believe Kolya had anything to do with that!"

"Of course I don't," Adelaida replied. "But I also know this is bigger than Kolya and Nikita, and always has been. I'm not certain you've realized that, yet."

The accusation struck Elaina like a stone. She took a deep breath but said nothing.

"Nikita," she began again after several long, silent moments. She reached out to touch his arm again and pulled him back to look at her. The anger and grief in his eyes caught her by surprise, like a glass of cold water poured over her head. Still, she slipped her hand into his and gave it a squeeze.

"Whatever else is going on," she whispered. "I want to help. Gavri and Kolya and Grisha, they will *help*. We all will. We care about what is happening to the Stolby shapeshifters. Please, let us help you."

He stared at her, seeming to consider. He gave her no answer, though, and pulled his hand away from hers.

"Thank you both for checking on our well-being." His voice had turned frigid and emotionless. Dismissive. "If you will excuse me, there are others of the pack who are too injured to come here, and I must go with Baba Yasmin to see them."

"Of course, Nikki." Adelaida stepped forward, putting a hand on his shoulder and touching her brow to his.

She sees him almost as a son, as well. Elaina chewed her bottom lip. *They're all her children, in a way.*

The brief goodbye came to an end. Adelaida gestured for Elaina to lead the way, as they began their hike back toward the car, parked at a turnout on the road a mile west.

They walked in silence. Even when they emerged out onto the road again and climbed into Adelaida's sleek sedan, neither one of them spoke right away. The drive back to Gavri's house would be a short one, though, and Elaina knew if she wished to discuss anything private with Adelaida, now must be the time.

"About Viktor," she began, pausing for an extra few seconds to give Adelaida full opportunity to shut the conversation down. Adelaida didn't.

"You said he might have targeted Bernard and Timofei specifically. And... Zhuang was his first, um..."

"Kill," Adelaida provided in a hard tone.

Elaina winced. Her voice softened as she said, "Do you think... could it have been he didn't like sharing you with other mates?"

Adelaida shrugged, indifferent. "Probably. I loved all my mates but Viktor was without a doubt the most troublesome. My *bad boy*, I guess you could call him. Like your snow leopard. Solitary, finicky, arrogant..."

She sighed, her eyes set firmly on the road. "Clearly he was unhappy about *something*, because he strayed. Whether it was sharing me with other men, or sharing me with the pack, I'm not certain. It might have had nothing to do with me at all, mind you. He might have just been a rotten egg from the start."

"You said Zhuang was the first casualty, but the pack had lost others." Elaina toyed with the pendant she'd carved for herself, taking it out from under her shirt for the first time to run her fingers over it in thought.

"Yes." Adelaida's tone grew dark. "In the attack, Viktor and his woman killed three of our number. Zhuang, and Nikita's parents."

A fearful shiver turned Elaina's stomach to jelly. "Oh. I... I didn't know."

"Yes. It is why he is so adamant," Adelaida supplied without having to be asked. "Kolya does not only represent a social deviant. He does not only represent the threat of *vukodlak* blood drawing him closer to the line between sense and madness. You and I both know Kolya is *far* from mad, or violent. But on top of all those things, in Nikita's mind, Kolya represents the same evil spirit which robbed him and Sofie of their dam and sire."

Elaina took in a deep, steady breath, and let it out in a defeated huff.

"Viktor was..." Adelaida grimaced, searching for a word and not finding it. She held out a hand and wobbled it back and forth in a 'so-so' gesture. "He was not like Kolya, in loving men. Not exactly. He was libertine, certainly, and rarely opposed to any kind of kink. He may not have preferred men as lovers, but he felt no shame exerting his dominance on them through sexual conquest. If we visited a club in the city and some cocky boy tried to impress, Viktor might play the alpha wolf and push the boy back to a dark corridor or to the men's room and... well, you can imagine."

She put her hand back on the wheel. "He would make them pleasure him, somehow. Perform fellatio or receive him as a woman would. Allow him to mark them with his seed across their face. He was *not* an alpha, in truth... among our people, he was not quite the omega, but he fell closer to the bottom of the totem pole than to the top. With those he *could* bully, he would. I should have seen the sociopath in him then, but I didn't. To me he was an arrogant, attractive, competitive beast. The only male who would try to dominate *me,* truthfully, and when you're the alpha female, it can be attractive to give over to someone else's control now and again."

"He didn't..."

"Rape?" Adelaida shook her head. "Not, at least, to my knowledge. Even the boys he played with in the city were always consenting. Smart-mouthed and defiant—like him—but willing enough to play the bitch. But you see, Elaina, there are too many similarities, and though they may be only circumstantial, it is enough to make Nikita wary. One low-ranking male with delusions of grandeur showed no shame in openly celebrating his deviancy, even his disrespect, to me. I knew about the boys, of course, and did not consider them worth my notice. You know male dogs will dominate other male dogs simply as a bid for superiority. He did not go out on his own to find hookers or bring back disease. He did not subject Gavri to witness any of it. It was not *sex,* only social posturing. So I did not bother to care. Perhaps I should have. In any case, in Nikita's mind, Viktor's outlandish, immoral debauchery led to his entanglement with the *vukodlak*. Then to a long-running affair he managed to keep *much* more private, and finally to his betrayal, and the deaths of three vital members of our tribe."

"Two of them, Nikita's parents." Elaina ran her fingertip over the curved edge of her pendant. "No wonder he won't budge."

"It is surprising to me he accepted your challenge at all," Adelaida admitted. "Though I suppose his pride had been wounded, and that made him reckless. He certainly does not believe he will lose."

"If it matters," Elaina said. "I regret challenging him more and more every day."

"Perhaps that is good." Adelaida turned onto the road which would lead them to the lodge. "Leaders should never be completely sure of themselves.

Almost completely. But never so sure they will not consider other options."

Elaina recalled the offer from Athanos. "Do you think I should back down?"

Adelaida sniffed. The lodge came into sight, and she pulled into the driveway beside Gavri's truck. Turning the car off, she seemed to carefully consider her reply.

"Technically speaking," she began, "Diezana makes her choice for alpha at every summer solstice. Most of the time, the reigning alpha remains in place. It is very rare the spirit mother would select a new leader if the old leader has not grown infirm, or senile, or broken tribal law in some grievous manner. Most transitions occur voluntarily, when the old leader feels it time to step down."

"Like you did," Elaina said. "But you aren't *old,* Adelaida. You're still in the prime of your life."

Adelaida chuckled in the manner of one who knows they are being flattered and doesn't mind it. "Thank you. But I did not step down for that reason. After Viktor betrayed us and we lost Zhuang and the Alexeevs, I felt certain, with all my heart, Diezana would reject me at the next solstice gathering. I had failed the pack to an unforgivable degree. My *own* chosen mate played me for a fool and brought our enemy straight to us. Certainly the spirit mother could not want me at the head of her people after such a grievous misstep. Alas, when it came time for us to gather in observance once more..."

She gazed upward, as though through the ceiling of the car. Elaina caught the gleam in Adelaida's eye and realized the woman was fighting tears.

"When the solstice came, Diezana did not choose another. Now, you must understand, Diezana does not precisely *appear* to us or speak or make herself known at every ritual... many solstices have gone by with no great spiritual manifestation except what we manifest ourselves, through our worship. That solstice was the same. Diezana had no message for us, none at all, even one disclosed to the wise woman to carry to us. When the ritual passed, and I had not been cast out, I thought it must be a mistake. Diezana could *not* wish for me to continue to lead, it was simply impossible. Perhaps I'd angered her so greatly she'd turned her face from the entire tribe, until I removed myself."

Elaina stared, speechless.

"If I'm to be honest," Adelaida continued with a wistful sigh. "I wanted to be replaced. I no longer felt like a leader. I'd buried one husband because I hadn't seen the madness in another, and every day it became harder and harder for me just to get out of bed. I had to, though, because I was their leader and they needed me. At least until Diezana turned me out. When she didn't, I decided it must be my responsibility to step down, not wait to be dismissed. I wanted Gavri to take my place, but he's never had any interest in being a leader. Like Pasha, he makes an excellent beta wolf, a second-in-command talented in support and consultation for his matriarch, but he has no heart for the role of alpha. Besides, of course, his love for Kolya *does* put him at a disadvantage. Many in this country will not follow a man who lies down with another man. So I asked Nikita if he would succeed me."

She combed a hand through her short, silvery hair. "I should have known he, too, was mired in guilt and bitterness. How selfish of me to walk away from my responsibility, when I had lost a husband, and expect Nikita to take over, when he had lost both parents. I asked too much of him. I should have stayed and worked through my grief. I am as much to blame for his decree against my sons as anybody."

She turned to face Elaina, leveling a serious gaze at her. "I cannot play favorites in this game, Elaina. You know as much. But I will tell you this and trust you to keep it to yourself: I believe you can unseat Nikita. If you manage to attain Diezana's blessing and become like us, I think you will be chosen over him. He is a *good* man, and a *good* leader, but his heart is still too freshly wounded by the loss of his parents, and he is vengeful. Exiling Kolya makes some sense, when you see how the pieces fell in the past, but an objective leader would see the key differences between Kolya and Viktor. Nikita does not. He sees only another *oboroten* flaunting unnatural lusts, and what he perceives as a choice, and disrespectful, fills him with anger." She shook her head. "It is too short-sighted for a leader. I won't go so far as to actively censure the man I chose, and a man I consider very capable... but when it comes down to the crucial moment, if you have indeed presented a worthy challenge, I am not so certain Diezana will favor him."

She reached out and touched Elaina's cheek. Elaina swallowed back her surprise; she hadn't been prepared for Adelaida, of all people, to offer perhaps the first token of motherly affection Elaina had ever received.

It lasted only a brief couple of seconds. Adelaida gazed at her, and then all at once something else caught her eye. Her hand fell away and she nodded toward an approaching shape outside the car, by the trees near the road.

"Look there. Pasha has found your walking stick, it seems."

Sure enough, the big enforcer came strolling toward them in his park ranger uniform, with a large branch balanced over his shoulders, arms casually looped over it. After the excitement of the last couple of days, he must finally have had some time to go searching for something of appropriate size, something Kolya could cut down, shape, and sand for her to complete with her bone figurine.

Pasha raised one hand in greeting when he caught sight of them, and both women waved back at him.

"You *can* do this, Elaina," Adelaida said in a gentle voice. "Trust that. Your instincts—and your pack—will lead you to your rightful place."

CHAPTER EIGHTEEN

ON THE FOURTEENTH OF JUNE, Rini announced the tanning of the boar hide complete, and sat down with Elaina to plan the cutting and sewing of her jacket. They took her measurements, selected a pattern from a catalogue Rini kept with her sewing supplies in the laundry room, and made up a list of tools for leatherworking. That afternoon, Rini went up to Krasnoyarsk to buy the materials they'd need.

After she returned in the evening, the housekeeper invited Elaina to her apartment, and they spread out the readied boar hide in the sewing room. Rini twitched her nose as she inspected it and frowned as she considered the pattern they'd selected.

"Well, we have enough, but just barely. I should have picked up some extra suede to practice with. We'll have to be extremely careful."

Elaina—who hadn't sewn anything since her junior high school home economics class made felt pillows and had never sewn *anything* particularly challenging at all—tried not to let it make her more nervous.

"I guess if we can't make the full jacket, I'll just have a vest."

Rini smiled at her. "That's the spirit!"

They began work on the fifteenth, bright and early. Elaina ticked off one more day on her mental calendar—*Six left... oh, goddess, I'm* not *going to make it!*—and reported to Rini's.

"It'll be a full day's work," Rini told her with an almost apologetic note in her voice. "I cut out the patterns last night but still... when working with leather, you have to be very careful. You won't be able to rip out any seams without it being *very* noticeable."

Elaina picked up one of the panels Rini had laid out for her and tested it between her fingers. "That's all right. I had thought about going up to the meeting place with Adelaida again to take up some extra food and spend some time getting to know more of the pack... but so few of them want anything to do with me."

She and Adelaida had made it a point to bring something special to the pack every day since they'd taken the golubtsy, and stay at least an hour so Elaina could meet and listen to the stories of the *oboroten* she hoped to soon join. With Adelaida at her side, more members of the pack indulged Elaina in conversation, but still, her presence at the meeting place sparked suspicion and skittishness. By far, her favorite visit had been the day before yesterday, when Polina's two sons had accompanied their foster parents to the spot, and she'd been allowed to play a game of catch with the boys and tell them a few stories of her own, from her childhood growing up in the States and her travels to countries like Australia, Brazil, and Japan. Pyotr, the older boy, still carried a very heavy weight about him—and who could blame him, having witnessed his mother's murder—and didn't engage with her very much, but his younger brother Aleksandr seemed eager for distraction and play.

She put down the strip of leather and examined Rini's sewing machine, already set up for leather sewing with a heavy needle and special foot. "Nikita hasn't been there since Adelaida told me about his parents."

Rini patted her shoulder. "It's only because tensions are running high right now. The pack will come around. *Nikita* will come around."

"It's not as if he'd want to talk to *me* about his parents, anyway. I mean... I want to tell him I'm sorry, and whatever happens, I'd like to be there for him..."

Rini tilted her head to the side. "Elaina... you care for him, don't you?"

Elaina paused, fingers freezing just above the barrel of the machine. She frowned and ran a hand through her hair.

"I suppose I do. I mean, at least, I care for him because he is one of the tribe, and as much as he's infuriated me by exiling Kolya, it's just a lot of stupid ignorance and I know he's better than that, deep down. If I did become alpha, he'd be part of my pack, and I can't neglect that."

"*If* he stays," Rini said softly.

Elaina spun to face her. "What?"

Rini's nose twitched. "Well... Elaina... if he loses the duel and Diezana chooses you over him to lead the pack, he might choose to leave. Haven't you thought of that?"

"No. I honestly hadn't." Elaina glanced down at the panels of leather again, and all at once the task seemed incredibly stupid to her. Meaningless. What would it prove to Diezana to show her Elaina could sew a leather hunting jacket, when Nikita might be considering self-exile if a pushy human girl won his place?

"Look, let's get started." Rini guided Elaina to the seat in front of the sewing machine, patting her shoulder. "Don't worry about Nikita, or anything else, for that matter. Sewing can be such a soothing activity, let's just focus on the work and let everything else fly away for a little bit."

They worked on the jacket through lunchtime, Rini giving gentle instruction and guiding Elaina's hands through the delicate parts, going slow to make sure they didn't botch anything and ruin part of their limited leather supply. Just after noon, Adelaida called them down for borscht.

Rini straightened, putting her tiny hands to the small of her back and stretching. "Come on, then! It'll be good to have a break."

"I think I'll stay and keep working." Elaina took a look at the piece she'd been sewing, and realized she'd soon need Rini's help for a complicated bit of stitch work. "Or, maybe, I'll take some of the extra scraps downstairs and start cutting them into a fringe. Don't you think that would be cute? A fringe?"

The snowshoe hare twitched her nose again. "A little... how do they say it in your country? *Retro?*"

"Well, I like it. Here, show me which pieces are okay to use."

While Rini and the others gathered inside for borscht, Elaina excused herself, apologizing to Adelaida. "It smells *amazing,* and I'll have a little bit later, if that's okay. But I just don't want to stop working yet. I've got my head in the game."

Her mates, perhaps sensing something not quite right, all gave her careful, scrutinous looks.

"Do you want me to come help, little one?" Grisha asked, getting up from the table to join her.

At the same time, Gavri checked the clock on the wall. "Surely you can spare a little time for a break, *krasavitsa.* If you would like to perhaps have a nap upstairs, I will gladly come get you in an hour so you can continue."

"No, thank you." She held up her hands, still clutching the scraps of leather, to stop them both. "Really, I'd just like to sit on the patio for a while and work. Besides, Gavri, isn't your dad supposed to come home this afternoon?"

"Around three." He ladled a spoonful of borscht into a bowl for Kolya and passed it to the bigger male. "He won't be able to use his right hand for a while, because of the surgery, so I thought we could help keep his mind off it with a classic movie marathon. I've dug up his old copies of *Dersu Uzala* and *White Sun of the Desert.* They will be in Russian, of course, but we can turn on subtitles, if you wish to join us."

"I would like to, yes," she told him, brightening. "It'll help me with my Russian, too. But only if I've gotten far enough along with the jacket."

"You will," Rini assured her. "You must at least come see *White Sun of the Desert.* It is all about a soldier set to guard a harem, and we know *you* certainly have an interest in harems..."

"Kolya?" Elaina asked. "Could you throw a roll at her for me?"

Kolya did, bouncing it off the top of Rini's head before the little rabbit could turn around and duck the assault. While the others laughed, Elaina took the chance to slip out onto the porch, and quietly retire to a spot in the far corner of the yard to work.

So much still to think about. She found a place under the shade of an aspen tree and sat cross-legged, laying out the strips of leather she'd collected from the scraps of the other work. *And there's still the manifestation of the World Tree...* climbing *the tree. How am I supposed to do that?*

Her thoughts turned back to Nikita, and what Rini had said about him choosing to leave if Diezana chose Elaina to lead. She didn't wish for Nikita to abandon the tribe. She also didn't want him making Kolya's life miserable.

"Stop it, Elaina." She scrubbed the beginning of tears from her eyes and rolled out a measuring tape to size the fringe.

Six days left. Is that enough to learn how to be a wolf? If I do manage to earn the blessing, will I know how to use it?

No. Who was she kidding? Six days wasn't enough. *Twenty-one* days hadn't been enough. This adventure had been doomed from the beginning.

And if I fail, what happens to them? Her gaze drifted to the house, where her mates and their family sat around the kitchen, sharing bowls of borscht and laughing with one another. Grisha, Gavri, and Kolya must be looking back at her, though she couldn't see them clearly enough to be sure. She *felt* it, though... her men, picking up on her mood, surely understood she needed them. They must also understand, at the moment, she also needed to be alone. None of them left the table to join her. Though she would have gladly taken the distraction and let them drive away her worries and questions and concerns, she silently thanked them for staying away. For now, at least.

Maybe... maybe I should call on Athanos. Maybe it's time to give up, and let him do as he promised.

She'd been sitting under the aspen for about half an hour, measuring and cutting leather, steadily wiping the first sting of tears from her eyes, when a massive wolf loped out of the trees to trot to her side.

"Pasha." Elaina put down the leather and the scissors and scrubbed at her face, hoping the gleam in her eyes hadn't been too obvious. "I thought you had work today. You've got a gorgeous coat, but it's not exactly standard issue for park rangers, is it?"

Pasha gave a soft huff. Coming closer, he nosed her affectionately, then slid around behind her to settle down. He curled his body against hers, providing a big, comfortable support for her to lean against. She did, and as she returned to her work the big wolf remained quiet. When she caught herself sniffling and put down her work to steady herself, he nosed his way under her arm, and gently licked her hand.

I don't want to drive out Nikita. I don't even want to be the alpha, really. I just want to be here, with them, and I want Kolya to be safe.

Athanos would end the matter. He'd make Nikita rescind the blood hunt, and all would be decided. She could stay with her mates, and they'd be free to remain in their homeland. Nikita could lead the pack, as he should, without worrying about a human challenger undermining him and putting his people at risk.

But then I could never become like them. I could never be oboroten. *And I want to... I want to belong to their kind, so much. I want to run with them and hunt with them, and chase after one another under the moon...*

Her mother's voice answered. *Always thinking about what* you *want, Elaina. Always just so concerned about yourself.*

Then, the memory of what Adelaida had said. *You* can *do this, Elaina. Trust that. Your instincts—and your pack—will lead you to your rightful place.*

With a careful sigh—one much shakier than she expected it to be—Elaina shut her eyes, and tried to catch hold of her wild, raging thoughts. Pasha lifted his head and gave an inquisitive whine.

"I'm sorry," she whispered. "It's just... there's so much still to think about, and... and I never wanted to put the pack, or Nikita, or Polina or *any* of you in danger. I feel like this is all my fault, Pasha."

She buried her face in her hands. The wolf moved, gently drawing away from her, and seconds later hands, not paws, rested on her shoulders. She glanced up into Pasha's human face, and he tugged her close, to lean against his chest.

"You are not to blame for the *vukodlak,*" he assured her in a gentle, soothing whisper. As she rested her head on him, he stroked her hair with one big hand. He said nothing else, only held her, and Elaina let herself cry in his arms.

"Will you come with me to my shrine again?"

She didn't even realize she wanted to go to the shrine, until the words spilled out of her mouth. Probably they couldn't—it would be a long hike, and she still had to devote the afternoon to finishing her jacket, and also spend time with Timofei and the family in the evening.

Yet the desire pulled at her. It tugged at her heart, too strong to question. Why hadn't she already gone back there? She hadn't visited it even once since she'd erected it, and nearly two weeks had gone by. All of a sudden she *had* to go, had to be close to the place where Diezana first reached out to her, and try to connect with the spirit mother again.

Pasha nodded. "I will. Tell the others. I will wait for you in front of the house."

She nodded and climbed to her feet. He resumed his canine form and loped off toward the edge of the property, where the hill led down to the road.

SHE EXPECTED THE OTHERS TO protest, but they didn't. Surprised, but grateful, she promised to make it a quick trip, and to carry the sat phone.

To her astonishment, it *would* be a quick trip. As soon as she and Pasha set out, she with her brand-new, polished and completed walking stick and he in his wolf form, the way to her shrine lit up like a beacon in her mind. She hardly realized how fast the miles passed by until she and her lupine escort stood at the bank of the river, more than halfway to the cave.

Elaina checked the pocket watch Gavri had given her. They'd made better time than any trip she'd taken to or from the cave before. Of course, she'd been recovering from hypothermia the first time and feeling her way along an unfamiliar path the second, but even so...

"I'm more comfortable with the territory," she mused out loud. "It's happening faster than it should, though. I couldn't possibly have been so confident on a trail like this before."

She came to one knee on the riverbank, putting one hand flat against the stones. In her hand, the walking stick Pasha had brought for her, and Kolya had shaped, seemed to thrum with fresh life of its own, as though it, too, were as excited as she.

"Gavri led me here from the cave," she told Pasha. "Kolya was already here, fishing for breakfast. They shared a quick catch, and then we moved on. I didn't know yet what *exactly* they were... but I knew they weren't ordinary wolves. Not ordinary *men,* either."

Pasha dipped his lupine head in a nod. Elaina closed her eyes and savored the cold, slick smoothness of the river rocks under her fingers. The smell of crisp water invigorated her and the cool breeze thrilled her with its sweet, lovely touch.

"Why didn't I stop to notice all these things the first time I came back?"

Bracing herself with the walking stick, she took a long look around herself, taking in the panorama of the forest. "Why did I *never* stop to look at this place? It's gorgeous! I have to come back with my camera, when I have more time."

Pasha gave a huff and butted her with his broad head. When she glanced down at him, he gave a high, pointed nod of his head, gesturing with his snout at her backpack. Frowning, she unlooped the pack from one arm and slung it around herself to check the main pocket.

She hadn't bothered to check the bag before leaving, since she knew it already held the basics she needed for any hike: water bottles, her lockback knife, trail rations, and a spare jacket. She hadn't even noticed any extra weight in it when she'd snatched it up on her way out the door. Yet on top of the folded jacket, tucked snug in its case, lay her camera.

She peered at Pasha, cocking an eyebrow. "*You* didn't put this in here, did you?"

He gave a doggy nod, and settled down on the rocks, just above the darkened line where the edge of the water lapped against them. *I'll wait,* he seemed to say. *Do your thing.*

"When did you pack my camera for me?" she asked. "You couldn't have done it before I finished telling the others we were leaving."

He shook his head.

"Then... before? You knew I would want to go to the shrine today?"

The wolf shook his head again, and then gave another exaggerated, sweeping gesture with his snout. *Go on. Take your pictures.*

Elaina frowned at him. She could ask him later, though. Happy for the unexpected opportunity, she pulled the camera from its case and started snapping away.

Halfway through her shoot, she caught a candid picture of Pasha lying on the rocks, his amber eyes fixed on a distant peak. His generous ruff, almost like a lion's mane, shone in the sun a myriad of calico colors.

He's so different from the others. So much bigger, at least in this form, and so... tranquil.

She didn't think she'd ever seen the others be so still. Even in their lupine bodies, resting or lounging on the grass, they were always somehow moving. Swishing their tails, sniffing at the ground, twitching their ears or their paws. Pasha had done all those things too, of course, but then he had moments like this, when he grew so perfectly quiet and motionless, as though listening to something in the air. Diezana's song? Elaina didn't think so. She'd watched Grisha before, when the song played in her head, and the snow leopard had tells. Little things, easy to miss, if you didn't also hear the music playing in his head.

Pasha didn't sway to some unheard melody or sweep his tail in wide, dancing figure eights. He didn't nod his head or flex his paws, which she imagined would be the lupine equivalent of drumming his fingers against some nearby surface, as Grisha did. No, she didn't think Pasha heard Diezana's voice. She thought, maybe, he just drank in the sights and smells and sounds all around them. Immersing himself so completely he'd grown as motionless and ageless as the stones beneath his belly or the trees reaching gloriously for the sky. His eyes had closed now, and the only motion of his body was the slow, even, steady rise and fall of his breath.

She'd forgotten the camera for a moment, and as she remembered it Elaina brought it to bear again, snapping picture after picture of him in his lovely serenity. In the magazines she wrote for, this sort of picture would be a reader favorite, maybe even an award-winner. People would look it over, a flat image of a wolf at the riverbank, and they'd feel those cool rocks and smell the sweet pine, feel the thick, coarse warmth of his coat. Elaina wouldn't share these photos, though... these, she would keep to herself, and probably Pasha. Maybe she'd frame them and hang them up, and the others would see them, but she wouldn't send them to any magazine.

After she'd captured Pasha's image a dozen times or more, Elaina moved on to take a couple extra snaps of the riverbank, and the fish darting about just beneath the surface. Before too long, though, she slipped the camera away again, and retrieved her walking stick from where she'd set it aside.

"I think that's enough. Let's keep going."

Pasha gave a huff of agreement and hopped to his feet.

They reached the cave much sooner than Elaina had expected. Sunlight dappled the stony entrance through the waving trees, and a flash of curiosity went through Elaina's mind.

Did I actually move faster on the way here? I mean, probably, if I remembered the path so well I must have gone over it more quickly, but did I actually move *faster?*

She remembered following Inferi along this same hike, and before that, chasing the ghostly wolf across the crisp night and luminous meadows.

"You can join me if you want," she told Pasha. "I don't think my visits need to remain private."

He regarded her with a gentle expression before shifting back to his human form. She led the way into the cave, and he followed obediently, crouching when they entered.

The shrine stood just as she'd left it. As Elaina approached, she set her walking stick against one wall and rested her backpack on the floor. She knelt before her effigy and considered it. Tilting her head this way and that, tapping a finger to her lips, she had no earthly idea what she meant to do here, now she had come.

"Pasha?" she asked, overcome by her curiosity. "When *did* you put my camera in my backpack?"

"I noticed it sitting out on the coffee table two days ago. After you had used it to perhaps, eh, share the images to your computer. I only thought, next time you left for a hike, you would want it with you."

He came to kneel beside her in front of the shrine. "I did not know when you might require it. Only that it fuels a passion in you to commemorate the beauty of Diezana's realms, and our ancestral homes. I like that about you, Elaina."

"You don't seem to struggle so much lately with your English," she noted. "Have you been practicing?"

He didn't answer right away. He gazed at the boar's skull.

"I still stumble over words I have not learned yet, only you no longer notice. I have not grown more adept at your language. You have learned to understand mine."

"What?" She stared at him. "I can't have learned Russian. Not that quickly. It takes *years* to learn a new language."

"Yes." Pasha shrugged. "And you do *not* speak it, not yet with any fluency. Your accent is almost unforgivable."

"Don't make me slap you," she teased.

He grinned. Elaina didn't think she'd ever heard him make a *joke* before.

"But whatever language I speak, you seem to *know* what I am saying. You do it without thinking. Without even realizing it."

"Huh." Elaina stared at the shrine. "But Gavri called me *krasavitsa* earlier. I remember."

"I think because you like it." He tilted her face toward him, meeting her eyes with a meaningful look.

285

"I do not believe it is a matter of what you hear with your *ears*. I simply think no matter what language your pack uses... you will understand them."

She furrowed her brow and bit her lip. Turning from him to the shrine again, she rubbed at the back of her neck.

Seven tasks; four of them completed. Or mostly complete, at least. Each task seemed to have brought with it some... *alteration*. After the spirit walk, she'd claimed Grisha as her mate and more or less officially taken on the role of alpha female in their little pack of misfits. After the hunt, her desires ramped up considerably, to ravenous proportions, almost to the point where even *three* virile men hadn't been enough for her hunger.

"After I came here," she murmured, "*returning* here came to me almost as easily as navigating my own home back in the States. Unless I'm crazy, I made the trip at a faster speed. Maybe as fast as—"

"The wolf runs?" Pasha suggested. "Or, more accurately, as the wolf leisurely trots. Had we been running, we'd have arrived even faster, but you'd have missed the chance to photograph the spot at the river that pleased you so much."

"And if you're right, and I'm understanding you without even thinking about it..."

"You are changing." Pasha laid a hand on her shoulder. "Becoming more a part of our world. A part of *us*."

Elaina's heart swelled. A rush of trembling shook her from top to bottom. She rested the tips of her fingers on the bottommost stone on her shrine.

"Do you really think so?"

"I do not have to *think* so," he said. "I have borne witness."

"Then maybe..." A fresh threat of tears pricked at her eyes, but this time, no shame came with it. "Maybe Diezana hasn't abandoned me after all."

Pasha cocked an eyebrow. He stared at her as though *she'd* started speaking a different language. "She has not. Why would she? Diezana yet has need of you."

"Do you speak to Diezana? Hear her voice?"

He bowed his head. "No. I do not hear her song and I know not how to communicate with her, as Baba Yasmin does."

"Then why does it seem like you always just *know* things?"

"Faith and intuition." Settling himself to sit cross-legged on the ground, he rested his hands on his knees. "I listen. I hear. I seek Diezana's will in the world around me, and I see the path she sets before me."

"I don't know how to do that."

Elaina stared at the stones she'd used to form the base of her shrine. *Discovery. Connection. Trust.*

"My quest to find myself," she murmured. She sensed Pasha's inquisitive look but didn't turn to him. She ran her thumbs across the word *Discovery* again.

I listen. I hear, he'd said. *I seek Diezana's will in the world around me.*

Elaina studied the cairn. Seven round, flat stones, stacked atop one another. Seven steps... like seven tasks.

Discovery. Her first task. The spirit walk, and the three apparitions revealing themselves to her.

Connection. The hunt. The pack running alongside her. The link they shared—the link between earth, predator, prey... Scent, hoof prints, scuffed spots in the dirt, broken tree branches. The creatures. The land.

Trust. This shrine.

"I didn't understand what I was supposed to do here."

Leaning forward on her knees, she ran her fingers over the rough-hewn letters along the third rock. Pasha said nothing, but she knew he heard her, *listened* to her, and understood.

"I came here because I met *them* here. Here... everything from before, came to an end, and everything new began. Where Elaina Jacob from Chicago, and her ex-boyfriend and her neurotic mother and her rooms full of old hurts and confused, directionless life choices... where *she* became *me.*"

Letting her hands drop away from the stones, she settled back.

"Trust," she whispered, considering it. "You came to me that day. Because you trusted her."

"*Da, uchenik,*" he agreed, and now she detected the way the words slipped past her ears and to her brain needing no mental translation, no switching of linguistic gears.

"And I followed you here."

She brushed her fingers to her lips. She closed her eyes, and as easily as sliding into a warm bath, she opened herself up again. She hadn't even realized how closed she'd become recently. Fear, trouble, even panic, and all the old demons had come creeping back in. When had she let it happen? When she stumbled into a boar instead of the safer, simpler musk deer, and survived only by luck? Or when she'd learned of the fertility rites, and all at once her place in the lives of her mates seemed uncertain? When Athanos challenged her, or when she'd witnessed the grief of Polina's two sons, orphaned by the *vukodlak*?

"Trust," she said again, and bowed her head. "There was no one moment when I stopped trusting in myself, and in my pack. There were many. Little moments, little cracks and chips in my faith. And..."

She held out her hands before her, supplicant before the shrine.

"*That's* why I stopped hearing your voice."

Silence answered. No song, no deep inner words of wisdom. Elaina didn't expect any dramatic fanfare or revelation, anyway. Somewhere within her, behind the walls of defense she'd been building over the last many days, a stone had been rolled aside. A tight, suffocating feeling in her chest, a feeling she hadn't even noticed as it grew heavier and heavier upon her, now loosened and let go. Diezana's song would come to her again. Those who heard her voice never *lost* it—she understood that, as easily as she now understood her mates, whether they spoke in her language or theirs. Diezana's voice would come. It was Elaina who must choose to hear.

"*Oboroten* cannot run with the pack," Pasha spoke up, "if they bury themselves beneath the earth like the badgers and polecats. You are a *wolf*, Elaina Jacob. You are not prey, meant to be afraid."

Elaina contemplated all of it. The implications spread before her in a fan of images and emotion, like flashes of a sweet dream just before waking. *I think... I'm on the right path again.*

Trust had been the third step, and the third task. The fourth, then, was *Love.* Tokens crafted out of love, and with love. Her mates had told her Diezana had no need for *oboroten* to craft tools or weapons or art for *her:* what they took from the land, and what they made of it, were meant to be works of their own soulful creation. Each of the things Elaina had chosen to make were reflections of herself, even the carved image of Diezana and the symbol she didn't quite recognize but felt called to design in her pendant and earrings.

Earrings I plan to give as symbols to my mates. Symbols of our devotion, which they can wear as wolves or as men. Mementos of love.

Warmth filled her. Overwhelmed her.

I will not give up. No asking Athanos to make it all go away. I will do this. And somehow, I will find a way to work with Nikita, to keep all the tribe safe.

"Everything is an echo, isn't it, Pasha?" she asked. "When I chose these seven rocks, I tried to recreate in effigy the steps I took the night I first crossed paths with your people. With Gavri and Kolya. But each step *also* relates to those things Diezana asks of me. And each, in smaller degrees, relates to everything I'm doing now."

"From what I am told, Diezana's song is something of a round." Pasha stroked his chin, waiting on her for confirmation. When she nodded, he said, "Life and nature are a series of echoes, *uchenik.* Ripples in the water. Rings within the trees. The cycle of seasons. The song of our mother. You will find them in your path."

A sharp series of tonal, electronic beeps startled them both, and Elaina stared at Pasha, bemused. The series repeated—*of course!* The sat phone, tucked in the side pocket of her backpack. When she pulled it out, the glowing green icon of a piece of mail blinked on the screen. A text message.

She flipped open the clunky device and scanned the message. "It's from Grisha. Baba Yasmin came to the house to tell us it's time for the next task."

She read the words again, a flutter of apprehension unfolding in her stomach as though she'd just downed a glass of ice-cold water in a single swallow.

"The manifestation of the world tree." He cast his gaze down to the floor of the cave. "I know what Gavri and Kolya have suggested for this task. *Magiya polovogo akta.*"

She noticed it this time, how the words out of his mouth were Russian words, ones she hadn't learned and shouldn't know, but even without trying she recognized them. *Sex magic.* Ritual of intercourse. An act of power.

She returned her attention to the shrine, and the next stone in the series. "Seems obvious how *loyalty* and *unity* come into play there."

Pasha moved closer to her and took her hands in his. "Elaina... I regret I haven't had suitable time to make up for my clashes with you, or to court you properly, as I would like to. I expect you've already guessed at my intentions."

Reaching up with just one hand to cup the back of her head, he drew her in to the familiar *oboroten* gesture, touching his brow to hers. He didn't let his hand slip away, though, even with such a delicate hold.

"I wish to become your mate," he admitted in a simple, soft statement. "One of your men. If you will accept me... please allow me to be part of the ritual."

CHAPTER NINETEEN

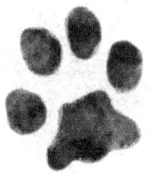

"CONJURATION—MANIFESTATION—REQUIRES POWERFUL ENERGY, with which you shape your will and intention."

Grisha sat with Elaina on one of the planters on the back patio, holding her hands in his. At his instruction, she'd closed her eyes, and while he spoke, he ran his thumbs in light, slow circles over the centers of her palms.

"As Pasha told you: sink into the world around you. Reach out into it until you no longer know whether you sit on hard, hot stone or float like particles in the air. Don't block it: become part of it. Let it absorb you, feel it in every limb."

Elaina focused on his voice, the rise and fall of his tone, and relaxed her conscious sense over the rest of her body. Though she sat cross-legged, she imagined lying in the grass, as she had before during Pasha's guided meditation, and summoned up the memory of sensation and emotion embracing her.

"When you conjure, you gather up your energy—emotional, spiritual, physical, sexual—and shape it into the tool you need. A key to unlock a door. A seed to plant in the ground. A tree to climb, ascending into the firmament, and the place of spirits.

Feel with your mind and heart now, Elaina. Touch your power, the power in yourself and the power you draw from the air and the ground, and my touch. It all flows. A great river spanning miles and years, crisscrossed with tributaries. A circulatory system. Can you picture it?"

"Yes," she intoned.

"Can you reach out and feel it?"

"Yes. It's like touching one of those lamps with the electric conductor inside, throwing off tiny arcs of lightning. When you lay your hand on the dome covering the works, your hair stands up. It feels... a little like that."

Though her eyes were closed, she could hear Grisha's brazen grin in his voice. "Very good. To summon the apparition of the tree you'll swallow all that energy, and more. The energy we will generate with you; every moan and gasp, every titillating sensation and all your carnal bliss. You'll gather it to you and send it out into the universe, and call that which you seek to reveal itself to you."

Sounds simple enough...

Baba Yasmin had waited for Elaina and Pasha to return the evening before, so she could explain how the spirits had reached out to her, and the cracks she'd divined in the burnt shoulder blade of a great elk had shown the way. Today was the day. The stars were aligned, and Elaina and her pack must make their attempt to conjure the world tree.

Faced with this new intelligence, Elaina spent the rest of the night working to complete the sewing and detailing of her boar skin jacket. Sitting with the others and watching Timofei's Russian films, she hand-stitched the last seams into place. It hadn't been as difficult as she'd expected. Perhaps the nervous energy unspooling itself inside her after Yasmin's announcement made it easier, giving her something to work with, requiring her to keep her hands and mind at work. She stayed up with Rini and little Kotyanok for company, long after the others had either left for home or gone to sleep in the various guest rooms of the lodge. Despite the late hour, as she completed the final stitch she thought she must have forgotten some step in the process, surely something vital. The finished garment before her—certainly not as neat as Rini might have done, and flawed by clumsy, uneven seams—fit well, at least. She slipped it on and considered it, quietly dumbfounded, but glowing with pride.

"That's it, then," Rini summed up once she'd inspected the finished product. "You did it! Turned the gifts of the hunt into meaningful, well-earned pieces."

"The boar was big." Elaina peered over her shoulder to watch the jacket flare out as she gave a quick spin. "I could have made lots more out of it."

"Not in the time Nikita gave you." Rini touched one sleeve and inspected the cuff. "I think the intrinsic meaning of the task has been satisfied."

"Will you join us for the ritual tomorrow night?'

Elaina had no idea what prompted her to ask. Grisha, Gavri, and Kolya had made it clear a sexual ritual—which she anticipated with anxious, curious excitement but also a streak of self-conscious dread—essentially required an orgy of abandon. Elaina hadn't yet decided how she felt about sharing the experience with others outside her circle of chosen mates, but if

anybody else were going to play a role, she wanted it
to be Rini, whom she trusted to her core.

Rini let go of the jacket sleeve, stepped back, and
crossed her arms. She seemed to be contemplating
the leatherwork, but after a moment she shook her
head.

"Not in the sexual conjuration. It is not for me.
But, if Baba Yasmin has a different role I may fill, I
will join you."

Elaina didn't know if that was better or worse.
But again, she knew little when it came down to the
details, anyway.

Now, before the work truly got underway—
before Baba Yasmin arrived to guide them to their
place of worship—Grisha had taken her aside to
prepare her.

"As we gather our energy and will," he said, "we
visualize the reality we wish to conjure. In fertility
rites, the female envisions herself with child. In
seeking spiritual revelation, the conjurer visualizes a
door, perhaps, to open. You will visualize the tree.
Picture it. Hold it in your mind. The world tree
connects all worlds: those below, those above. It
reaches down into the underworld, and up into the
heavens. See its branches stretch up beyond our
understanding. It ties us to the realms of the spirit, to
Mother Earth, to Father Time. To Diezana, in her
eternal hunting grounds."

Elaina let the image form in her mind. She
imagined the tree as a sprawling oak with golden bark
and silvery leaves. An illustration from some
children's story deep in the early, innocent years of
grade school. For some reason she associated the
image with chocolate: sweet chocolate hidden under

the rustling leaves. A treasure for little hands and pure hearts.

What was the title of the book? When did I read it?

"How are you doing?" Grisha squeezed her hands with an almost unnoticeable pressure.

"I can picture the tree," she replied. The one in her mind stood much, much taller than the old children's book illustration. The oak, now giving tiny glimpses of rich, dark brown chocolate under its rustling leaves, stretching out over continents, reaching east and west toward the seas.

"Hold that image in your mind. Give it details. Understand its smell and the feel of its bark under your palms."

Cookies. It smells like cookies, and the bark shines like smooth, pearly metal.

Gavri and Kolya were in the house, preparing their own minds and bodies for what would come. Meditation, thorough bathing. She, too, must wash her body scrupulously before they trekked to the place of the ceremony, a spot Baba Yasmin would lead them to.

"When we begin our ritual, you will summon this image to mind." Grisha's released her hands. He cupped her chin and caressed her cheeks. "The energy we call, you will channel into manifesting the desire for that image. The desire to ascend the tree. Open your eyes, Elaina."

She did, and the sight of him grounded her. He'd slipped somewhere between his human form and feline, the in-between stage where his features grew smoother and subtler, sloping toward a soft muzzle, and his ears grew to gently rounded points. The edges of his hairline, the back of his neck, and the tops of his shoulders bore the shadow of leopard spots, like dark tattoos under his skin.

Elaina, overcome with affection, bent forward and kissed him on the mouth. They traded soft, voiceless moans as their tongues met, and the lines between him and her seemed to blur. She touched him, and he touched her, but they might have shared one body, drawn into one another by some strange gravity.

"Do you feel it?" As they parted, Grisha started to purr.

"Yes."

"And you remember the other morning?" He kissed her again, one hand sliding to cup the back of her neck. "When we fucked on the wolf's workbench?"

"*Kolya's* workbench," she insisted, but the snow leopard's rough tone kindled a flutter of excitement in the pit of her stomach.

"Remember moving together as we did," he instructed. "The rhythm of our bodies... remember making the climb with me?"

"Yes." The memories came so readily she uttered a gentle, breathy moan.

"This sacrament of our bodies will be much the same. Together, we—those you wish to draw in with you—will cultivate the rise and fall of pleasure and power, driving ourselves, and more importantly you, to intense climax. The longer we hold it under our control, the more deep magic you will pull from your body and ours. When the moment comes—when you are ready—your orgasm will become the channel for your will, sending your desires and intentions out to the universe. As you release it, you will reach for your image of the tree in your mind."

Releasing her, he settled back with a sigh. "If we have done it right, you may enter a vision or trance, and there, find your way to Diezana's world."

Elaina nodded. Grisha brushed the back of his knuckles over her cheek.

"That part," he said, "you must do alone."

"This whole journey began with me walking into the realm of spirits on my own." She twined her fingers with his, leaning into his touch. "It seems almost obvious my last task would also be mine alone."

"Not your last task," Grisha reminded her. "The last will be the transformation itself. Your ascension to the family of *oboroten,* children of the spirit mother."

Right. A guarded smile touched her face. *The final transformation.*

Behind them, the sliding door to the kitchen ran back on its tracks. Gavri and Kolya joined them. They smelled fresh from the shower, for once wearing the faint hint of masculine scented soap. Usually they avoided all but the blandest, unscented soaps and shampoos, but today, Elaina imagined they wanted to provoke as much alluring desire as they could.

Behind them came Rini, and Pasha, then Baba Yasmin. A flush rose to Elaina's cheeks, however, at the sight of the person following the old wise woman.

"She can't be here!" she blurted without thinking. Sofie, jaw set and cool eyes flashing, shot her a scowl. Elaina refused to take it back, though. She could accept Baba Yasmin, she might even manage to swallow Rini's role of voyeur, but no way would she let a teenage girl witness the carnal display about to take place.

"Relax." Yasmin waved a negligent hand. "Sofie is only here to help this old witch gather the necessary plants and prepare the ritual brews. She will not remain for the ceremony itself."

"I'm not stupid, you know." Sofie jutted her chin. "I know about sex."

"This isn't simple sex, little cousin." Gavri ruffled Sofie's hair. "Your brother would never forgive me. And he is already angry enough at me for my choices."

All at once, a flash of understanding hit Elaina. During the funeral rites, she'd recognized the hard, cynical gleam in the eyes of Pyotr, who had watched his mother murdered. Elaina remembered thinking no child should ever have to look upon the world with eyes so full of bitter hurt, and yet, she knew she'd already seen the look in the eyes of another.

Not Nikita. *Sofie.* The girl couldn't have been much older than Pyotr when her parents were killed by the *vukodlak.* A wave of sympathy rushed over Elaina, and she wished she hadn't been quite so tactless with her protest. She should have known, of course, no one meant to allow Sofie to witness the conjuration rite. If Elaina hadn't already been electric with nerves, she probably would have realized.

And maybe you'd have kept your mouth shut, she scolded herself.

"I'm sorry," she said to Sofie. "I know you're not stupid."

Sofie shrugged. "Who would want to watch you and them summon a conjuring by rutting around like a bunch of rabbits, anyway?"

"*Excuse me.*" Rini gave Sofie a light rap on the head with a rolled cloth she held. Sofie gave a tiny feline hiss, stepping away from the housekeeper.

"Elaina." Gavri's hand came down on her shoulder, and she faced him. "It is time for you to wash. Would you like one of us to come with you?"

Yes, all of you, she wanted to tell him, but the words died in her throat. Part of her thought if they came to shower with her, she'd end up tangled among the three of them and fucked useless before the ritual could even get started. Another part suspected she ought to go through this first part alone, using the time to center herself and reflect.

She reached up, pulling Gavri down into a kiss. "I can handle it. Is there anything special I need to keep in mind?"

"I made a soap for you with some special bath oils," Rini said. "Rose, sandalwood, and clary sage. I left in on the soap dish above the tub faucet."

"Warm water," Baba Yasmin instructed. "Shave, if it helps you feel more comfortable. Spend time meditating on your own body, especially your skin and your sensory parts: hands, feet, lips, tongue. Sofie and Rini and I will prepare the teas and salves while you bathe, so take your time. When you return, we—all except Sofie, of course—will set out for the place where you have built your shrine."

The cave again—they'd discussed it already. More specifically, they would go to the small clearing just outside the cave, where they could build a large enough bonfire and move about freely—the cave had been fine for three of them, but there would be at least double that number involved in this ritual, and that might make things a bit more claustrophobic.

Elaina took a moment to scan the yard, and even to look over Rini and Yasmin's shoulders into the house, searching for Pasha. She hadn't given him an answer yesterday, when he'd asked if he could participate in the sex magic, and she hadn't mentioned it to her other mates yet, either. His absence saddened her, though, and the uncertainty crept along the backs of her arms. Well, perhaps that was an answer, in its own way. She bit her bottom lip and hoped he'd arrive, despite the lack of formal invitation, before the time came to set out.

She had little difficulty relaxing in the bath, and the scents of clary sage and rose immediately struck her with a tingling, secretive arousal. She took her time with the process, scrubbing herself in long and leisurely strokes, shaving with a delicate care, and sinking into the sensation when kneading delicately scented shampoo into her thick curls. Even with the aromatherapy, though, she picked up the wild and sometimes unpleasant scents of whatever Yasmin, Rini, and Sofie were preparing in the kitchen.

Probably more fly agaric. She wrinkled her nose. Her first experience with the hallucinogenic toadstool hadn't been unpleasant, really, but imagining the musky, pungent tea it boiled into made her faintly queasy.

She relaxed in the bath, running her hands up and down her newly smooth legs and loving the glide of her palms over flesh, long enough for the water to cool. Before it could grow truly cold, though, she rose out of it and claimed the towel Rini had hung over the warming rack for her. As Elaina wrapped it around herself, the soft heat pressed close to her cool, wet skin, and immediately her nipples tightened. She pressed her thighs firmly together and uttered a gentle moan.

By the time she descended the stairs, dressed lightly in clean, loose-fitting clothes, Sofie stood in the doorway bidding goodbye to Baba Yasmin. The teen girl held a paper sack in her arms smelling of eucalyptus, mint, and camphor; either Rini had packed up some of her scented soaps and candles for Sofie to take home, or Baba Yasmin had mixed up a batch of medicines. Elaina expected the latter. Sofie spoke to Yasmin in the tribal language of the *oboroten,* and thought Elaina had begun to understand the words of her mates regardless which mortal language they chose, she couldn't pick up anything from Sofie.

Because she's not one of mine. Elaina played with the pendant she'd whittled from the boar's bone. *She'd be welcome, if she wanted it, but of course her love and loyalty will always belong to Nikita. And truthfully, I'd welcome Nikita, too. If he wanted. If we could work out a balance.*

Sofie retreated a step from the door, going out into the night. Just before she disappeared, the teenager spied Elaina above them. She glowered.

A wild, nervous buzz overcame Elaina. "Sofie?"

"What?" Sofie pushed back her shaggy white-blonde bangs.

"Stay safe. Please."

They stared at one another, unspeaking. Sofie gave no answer and turned away, closing the door behind her.

Yasmin threw a glance up at Elaina. "You are ready?"

"I think so." Elaina descended the rest of the steps and dipped into the foyer closet for her new jacket. "And the others?"

"How do they say it in your country? 'All present and accounted for'."

Except Pasha.

This thought struck her with an unexpected twinge. Yes, she was sure: Pasha needed to be part of this.

"Can someone go look for Pasha?" She slid into her new jacket and pulled her hair back into a thick, loose ponytail.

Baba Yasmin raised an eyebrow. "Is that how you feel, then? You claim him, too?"

"I do." She'd have to explain to the others and hope none of them had any objections they'd been holding back. "He's... mine, as well. I claim his as mate."

"How convenient." Yasmin turned away from her and headed for the kitchen. "He arrived about ten minutes ago."

Chapter Twenty

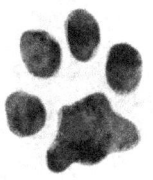

HER MEN GATHERED IN THE dining room. Grisha lounged in his chair, hair freshly wet from his own quick shower, probably in the workout room shower downstairs. He'd propped his feet up on the table and she crossed to him to push them off.

"You know better," she scolded him. "Not on Kolya's beautiful table."

Her snow leopard flashed her a positively evil grin, but took her hand and nuzzled his face against her palm with a purr.

Kolya and Gavri leaned against the island counter, looking like a pair of security officers, arms crossed over their chests, assessing the situation before them. Rini worked in the kitchen, putting away the last of the preparation implements she'd been cleaning and tucking thermoses and Tupperware into a large lunch cooler.

Pasha waited patiently at the tableside with his hands folded behind his back, though he had seven perfectly good chairs to sit in. If Gavri and Kolya looked like security enforcers, Pasha looked like a gawky, intimidated teenager sweating his first big date.

She went to him and took his hands in hers. "I'm glad you came."

Pasha lifted her hands and pressed them to his heart. Holding her gaze with his own, he stroked her hair. He didn't need to say anything.

Elaina faced the other three. "Pasha's asked to join us. I hope none of you are opposed, because I would like him to be there."

Gavri, Kolya, and Grisha exchanged silent glances. Elaina thought of Adelaida and her mates, and wondered again if something like this had ever happened among them, and if it led to Viktor's displeasure and betrayal. Had Adelaida brought another man—Timofei, perhaps—into the circle without giving her mates a proper chance to give their opinions or protest? Had resentment or jealousy grown among them, from a decision poorly made?

Kolya was the first to shake his head. "I have no objections, *krasavitsa*. If you wish for him to be a part of this, I welcome him. If he is important to you, he is important to me."

"Agreed," Gavri said. "You are an honorable man and strong warrior, Pasha. I have gladly called you brother before, and will again."

"Doesn't bother me." Grisha gave a casual shrug. "I know I'll always be your favorite."

Kolya reached over to thwap Grisha upside the head. Elaina giggled, then had to wipe her eyes: quiet, joyful tears had sprung up, and she ground them away quickly.

"That's everything!" Rini pronounced, zipping up the last pocket on the cooler. "Time to go!"

Rini and Yasmin would go ahead, on small Park Services ATV Pasha had brought along. Elaina and her men would make the hike together on foot, like a pilgrimage. Elaina liked that. She thought of Diezana's people trekking across the snowy north to shelter, and of holy vigils held in secret meeting places.

As she and her mates waved goodbye to Rini and the wise woman, and the official ritual began, Elaina realized a wonderful thing. Quietly, almost impossible to hear but still *there*, came the sound of Diezana's voice in the back of her mind. The song picked up, as though it had never stopped, and Elaina closed her eyes with a thankful prayer.

The hike to the cave took even less time than before. Or perhaps it only felt shorter, as Elaina's anticipation grew. They traveled in their human forms, all of them, and said nothing. She supposed perhaps, in other circumstances, such a stoic, silent trek might feel foreboding, but tonight, it reinforced their intimacy. Gavri and Kolya led the way, and it seemed poetic. They'd brought her to the cave in the first place, leading her into their world.

In her backpack, Elaina carried only what she deemed necessary: an extra set of clothing, in case the night grew especially cold; two water bottles for the hike, and to keep hydrated for the ceremony. Crackers, at Rini's suggestion, because she should not come to the ritual circle hungry, lest the hunger distract her and pull her out of the experience. And the four earrings she'd made from the boar's bones. Piercing their ears could be worked into the ritual as well, Elaina expected, and Rini had promised to bring a needle for the job. Elaina hadn't told her mates yet about adding this element to their conjuration. She doubted any of them would object, however.

I knew Pasha would be here. Maybe not consciously, but I knew. I always knew the fourth earring was for him.

They reached the cave as the last of the evening's light slipped away over the high mountains. The bonfire already burned, perfumed with a scent of something sweet and yet acrid, somehow medicinal. Licorice, Elaina thought, and remembered Rini preparing a jar of aniseed. Somewhere underneath the dark, sweet scent she also detected something faint and rich, but too understated to be identified; some vision-inducing incense, no doubt. Rini and Yasmin had laid out all the ritual components in a broad circle, marking their space. Each woman wore ceremonial garb: beaded circlets decorated with three bold pheasant feathers over each ear; long robes of animal furs draping all the way to the ground; more beads and feathers adorned long, draping belts around their waists, along with small skulls that might have belonged to birds or mice or other little rodents. Each woman wore a skirt and a mask, but bared her breasts, and each had drawn a pale, primordial hieroglyph between her collarbones.

Yasmin sat on the ground and had already begun to beat a rhythm on her shamanic drum when they arrived. Rini greeted them, and without words, guided the men to begin stripping the loose, light clothing from Elaina's body. Elaina gave a small start, but collected herself quickly; she hadn't exactly expected to be stripped naked the instant she arrived, but...

Like a joke, she remembered Baba Yasmin's words to her earlier. *How do they say it in your country? 'When in Rome...'*

She slid the backpack from her shoulders and allowed her mates to remove her clothing. While they did, she began a measured, even breathing, inhaling deeply of the perfume from the fire. Tension eased in her chest, back, and stomach, the natural tension of a long hike and weighty preparation. A quiet delight kindled within her though, when it occurred to her she felt no painful tension in her heart, or weighty anxiety in her mind. Had the licorice scent done that? Or had she already purged herself of the feelings, with yesterday's acts of catharsis?

Once Elaina stood naked before them all, Rini took her by the hand and guided her into the cave. Elaina's shrine to Diezana stood, waiting, illuminated by flickering torchlight.

She didn't need Rini to guide her in what came next: dropping to her knees before the effigy, Elaina spoke a prayer. She hadn't learned it or rehearsed it from anyone; it spilled from her like a story, a moment of reunion between two friends who have not caught up in a long time.

"I have come, Diezana," she whispered. In the dancing light of the torches, the boar's skull might have been the sweet, serene mask of the wolf from Gavri and Kolya's own family shrine, miles away. Maybe it was the gravity of the situation, or the effect of the incense Yasmin and Rini had employed—the scent underneath the anise outside was stronger here, a sweet and cloying scent like dying flowers.

"Mother spirit, mother of shapeshifters, mother of the *oboroten,* I have come. I ask your blessing on this ritual. I ask that you open the path to me. Show me the way, and I will come before you."

Footsteps behind her. Gavri and Kolya had entered the cave, both naked now as well. They held bowls of something liquid and opaque, Kolya's the color of bone and chalk, Gavri's like dark chocolate.

"They will mark your body," Rini intoned. The voice coming from under the mask didn't sound like the sweet little snowshoe hare, though Elaina knew it was her. The voice, a quiet whisper, sounded almost childlike: impish and playful, yet swirling with some deep, intrinsic truth.

It's the voice of Ini, she realized. *The child spirit. I'd recognize it anywhere.*

Gavri and Kolya knelt before her and dipped their fingers into the liquids—colored clays, she decided—from each bowl. They began to draw on her, finger-painting whorls and lines and geometric figures on her naked flesh. Their touches set off a sweet, pleasurable shiver, the stroking motion of their fingers lighting up her skin and sparking a tender thirst inside her. *More touch,* she wanted to moan, though she didn't. *Yes, please... never stop touching me...*

She kept silent, but she couldn't help moving to their strokes, leaning into their touch, her skin tingling. She turned a slow circle so they could also mark her back and shoulders and buttocks.

When her first two mates had finished their art on her torso and limbs, Kolya climbed to his feet, and painted a line of pale clay from the top of her forehead down the blade of her nose. He delicately painted a band across her eyes, then her top lip, and one slim, straight line down the middle of her bottom lip. Gavri rose and dabbed a circle of his darker clay on her chin, then one directly over and directly under her left eye.

"You are ready," Rini said. Gavri and Kolya set down the bowls of paint and took her by the hands to lead her outside.

Grisha awaited her by the fire, wearing only a mask which covered his brow and eyes, adorned with stag horns arching up like the reaching branches of a primal tree. He also held a bowl in his hand, but this one contained slices of fruit soaked in vodka. Apples and pears, and something she thought might be apricots. Gavri and Kolya led her to Grisha, and he offered her the bowl, tipping it to her lips to drink the juices—and alcohol—mixed at the bottom. When she'd done so, he plucked the pieces of fruit up between his fingers and fed them to her one by one. Sweet, juicy, heady with the strong liquor, tart in the way only fresh, raw fruit picked straight from the tree can be.

As Grisha fed her by hand, he followed each third or fourth mouthful of fruit with a longing kiss. Gavri and Kolya's hands stroked her sides and the backs of her arms, and the first delightful stirrings of want kindled to life under her flesh. Each of her mates were hard as stone, cocks jutting up from the dark curls between their thighs, nudging at her when the men slid in close to scent her hair, or kiss her ear, or—topping off a dripping, saccharine slice of vodka-soaked pear—deliver a long, deep, needful press of lips to hers, searching for her tongue, tasting the lingering hints of spirit on her. When she'd finished the fruits, Grisha handed the bowl to Rini, and seized Elaina in a dreamy embrace, kissing her over and over again.

"Picture your tree," he whispered. "Remember why it is we're here. What you want."

"I will," she whispered back.

Grisha stepped to one side, running his fingers lightly along her arm. Behind him stood Pasha, unadorned and unpainted. He came forward to meet her, expression troubled.

"What's wrong?" she asked him in a whisper. Hardly realizing she did it—walking through the motions as though through a dream—she stepped into his arms, and her naked body pressed against his. The rich scents of amber and cedar greeted her, spiced with the darker, deeper scent of masculine desire.

Pasha swallowed, his Adam's apple bobbing. Elaina stood on tiptoe, reaching arms around his neck, and kissed his warm, soft, dry lips. As they parted, she gave a gentle sigh and moved in for another. His slid his hands around her waist, and his cock—thick, heavy, strong—pressed against her lower belly.

When she drew away the second time, he held her apart from him. His amber-green eyes glowed, shadowed and deep.

"I have never taken a mate," he admitted. "I have never... *been* with a woman, as you would have me now."

Warm, strangely pleasant surprise bloomed inside Elaina. She smiled at him, letting her hands slide down to rest on his upper arms.

"It is not because I am feeble," he tried to explain. "Or incapable—"

"Shh, Pasha..." She tugged him closer, hushing him with her kisses. "Thank you. For telling me, I mean. I'm honored you chose this night to be with me."

He made a choked sound deep in his throat, and his expression broke into an earnest gaze of desire. Leaning close, he buried his face against her neck, kissing her and whispering her name, calling her *uchenik* and *krasavitsa* as Gavri and Kolya did. He kissed a line to her collarbone and then to her breasts, then got down on his knees to wrap his arms around her waist and kiss her belly, her hips, the gentle swell of her mons.

"Sit," she told him in a whisper, laying one hand on his head to gently push him to the ground. He did as instructed, crossing his legs before him and she advanced, standing over him. Caressing his face, she slipped down into his lap.

"Let me lead you."

She caressed his cock, jutting up like a weapon, rigid and needful. Pasha closed his eyes, groaning softly, and tilted his hips to her motions, meeting her strokes.

"We'll go slow," she promised. "Take your time. Be here with me, Pasha... be *with* me."

When she guided him to her entrance, he slid into her as easily as if she were the satin-lined sheath he'd been meant for. Pasha moved slow, deliciously slow, and Elaina caught her breath. She very nearly had to cry out—taking him inside her bordered on pain, his cock a great, iron, unyielding beast—but though she strained to receive him, at the same time he felt so good, so thrilling and intense, she thought she might not be able to prevent her orgasm.

"That's right—*ah!*" She moaned and gave a shiver of delight. "Oh, Pasha... gently now... be with me. *Be* with me."

They found their beat together, riding on the music of the drum and the clear tonal chant Rini kept up in the background. Elaina swayed into Pasha and he took her, thrusting up, lifting and moving in counterpoint to her. He may never have been with a lover before, but his body found the motions, and he delved deep, deep inside of her as she clung to him, riding him in breathless, beautiful pleasure.

"Yes, that's right," she panted in his ear. "*Oh, Pasha*... a-a little softer now—*oh,* you'll break me if you're not careful—"

"You won't break her." Grisha appeared at her shoulder, kissing it, nuzzling her as she moved. "She's strong."

"Very strong." Kolya leaned in on her other side, tilting her face to his to plant a kiss on her lips.

"O-o-o-oh...." Elaina rolled her head back, closing her eyes and centering herself on the place where her body met Pasha's, on the mounting bliss edging out the pain. Her nipples, hard like stones, tingled in the cool night air, an effervescent sheen of sensual response lighting up her skin.

"I—" Pasha gasped. His thrusts lengthened and slowed, and he groaned in a low, lupine tone, a sound that held an edge of a howl in it. "Oh, *uchenik*... I... I'm not sure I—"

"Come," she urged him. "Please, Pasha, do it. It's all right. I want you to."

He gave a louder, longer groan this time, and wrapped his arms around her as though he feared she would fly away. Elaina embraced him in turn, gripping him by the hair, nails gently digging against his scalp.

"Oh, yes." She squeezed him to her. "Yes, Pasha. Yes, please—"

With a grunt, he thrust upward with a hungry, graceless need. His cock throbbed inside her and he poured pulse after pulse of his hot, vital seed into her.

"Thank you, oh my wonderful, good boy." She kissed his brow, his eyelids, his lips. "Thank you."

He slid out of her, and their mingled juices felt cool and scandalous on her inner thighs. Pasha slipped away from her and she reached out for him, spooked for a second in some eerie, dreamlike way that he was drifting into uncharted darkness, somewhere far away. Grisha, stroking her painted arm, took hold of her grasping hands and brought them down.

"Think now of the tree. Hold it in your mind and channel your emotion toward it. Little by little, each time."

Pasha, for his eagerness and effort, had blessed her with his anointment of semen, but he had not brought *her* to orgasm. He hadn't needed to—her orgasm might be delayed all night—but as Gavri and Kolya crawled to her, ready to play their part, her body lamented and yearned.

Her two mates entered her at once. Gavri pulled her on top of him, guiding her into position straddling his hips, and slid into her at the same time Kolya, looming over her body from behind, penetrated her tight rear entrance. Once more pain contended with joy, but it hurt less than it thrilled, and the sting quickly gave way to the wicked, overwhelming sensation of fullness. Her two mates moved together, sandwiching her between. Gavri lifted his head to kiss and suck at her breasts while Kolya gripped her waist, pushing her against his pack brother as he fucked her.

"More," she begged. *Now* the first grasping, wicked flashes of a climactic climb simmered and flowed inside of her, growing stronger, picking up.

"*Please,* more... I want you both so much... I want you..."

"Can you take more, little one?"

Her eyes fluttered open and there stood Grisha, right in front of her, mask pushed up on his head. He held his studded cock in one hand, stroking and kneading. He didn't have to say anything else. Elaina reached out and drew him to her, and opened her mouth to receive him.

Yes, my loves... make me only a vessel. Make me a chalice for your essence—pour it into me and make me full...

Elaina moaned, the sound muffled. With Gavri and Kolya filling each of her holes, each man rocking her against the other, a gorgeous, dizzy feeling whirled in her brain. She *did* feel like a chalice, a crucible made to contain the powerful magical energies of others. Filthy words, wild and shameless, whirled through her brain, and she accepted them. She embraced them and took them into her as well with a shock of fearful and nearly rapturous joy.

Grisha slowed his rhythm and withdrew just before he burst within her, and at his silent signal, Gavri and Kolya eased their thrusting. Elaina uttered a sorrowful cry, forgetting for a moment she must hold off her climax, wriggling between her two mates for more. They held themselves still, Gavri kissing her neck and breasts while Kolya kissed her bare shoulders, until the pleasure diffused and spread into a mellow effervescence once more. Gavri moved first: careful and slow, one arm wrapped around her waist, he shifted them, rolling to position himself on top. Kolya slid his hands under her thighs and held them open, spreading her wide so he and Gavri could both plunge deeper into her.

She'd forgotten about everything besides the four men using her body. Only them, and the beat of the drum, the floating chant. And—underneath it all—the song of the spirit mother welled in her, musical and rhythmic in perfect counterpoint to the ceremonial sounds. The song seemed not to be in her mind but in her heart, stirring beneath breasts swollen and full with her arousal, as if the sweet, fluting voice pulled her skyward on a string through her heart.

Pasha returned. He offered his cock and she turned her head to the side to take him in her mouth. He groaned, and she ran her tongue over the head of his member, tasting her own arousal still on his flesh. She welcomed him with relish and worked him until he shuddered, gasping her name, and he came in her mouth in generous, spurting climax. Elaina swallowed as he came, eager and joyful for him, and when he slipped away she reached out a hand to give his member one last, trailing touch. Grisha appeared on her other side, and she accepted him as well, running her tongue greedily over the smooth, cool metal of his piercing.

Kolya tightened his grip on her, and his teeth sank into her shoulder. He groaned, losing his last hold on himself, and pumped his climax deep inside of her. Just as he shot his last fierce spurt, Gavri also came, burying himself to the hilt in her, shuddering with each firm, lovely throb.

Elaina rocked herself up against Gavri, eager to gyrate and grind at his hips, let him stimulate her yearning loins until she tipped over the edge. At the last second she pulled herself from the brink, gasping heavily, breasts heaving, as her men slowly withdrew, leaving her wet and trembling.

At last, Grisha crawled to meet her, bowing down to kiss her, seizing her bottom lip between his teeth. Each thump of the drum seemed to coordinate to her heart; when she looked up at him, a halo of light surrounded him.

He helped her to all fours and climbed on top of her. Elaina gazed at him over her shoulder, trying to purr with him, wishing she could signal her own deep, intrinsic, ravenous delight. He slid into her, and his black metal barbell struck the elusive internal pleasure spot. Elaina cried out and pressed herself back against him.

"Remember how I made you squirt?" he whispered in her ear, a harsh and ragged sound. One hand slipped under her belly and down to her clitoris. Elaina threw her head back with a desperate moan, crying out his name, as he quickened his thrusts.

"This is it," he promised. "I'm going to take you there. You're going to come so hard, little one, *so hard*. Do you believe me?"

"Yes," Elaina whispered. 'Yes. Please let me come, Grisha, my love. Please, please, *please*...let me come."

"I will," he promised. "Think of nothing, now. Release yourself from everything and only *feel* your climax. Feel it as fiercely and as fully as you can. Give over to it completely."

"*Yes!*" she cried. He rounded his body to hers, thrusting to his limit, filling her and feeding her most primal, sexual self. The hard, warm thrum of his purr obliterated thought, sinking her into deep, sweet waves of affection and desire.

The others were with her. Gavri, Kolya, and Pasha, reaching out to caress her arms, her cheeks, her hair, leaning in to kiss her lips, whispering to her how much they loved her, how beautiful she was to them. Intermingled with their voices came the sounds of wolfish hunger: yips and eager growls, needful panting and the drum of canine feet racing upon the earth. A growing, joyful howl, the howl of many voices raised together, the pack singing their songs into the night—

"Oh!" It came in a glorious, overwhelming wave. An enormous release kindled in her belly and spread like wildfire through her body. As Grisha sharpened his movements into a final series of deep, fierce thrusts, her orgasm touched off like a spark lighting a fuse. He came first, the beat of his ejaculation sending sweet, bright streaks of joy ahead of her own rushing climax, and all at once she was overcome. The pleasure swallowed her, pulling her into the roll and crash of sensation until she lost the sense of her own body and gave over entirely to bliss.

Come, spirits, she managed to think, seizing on the image she'd build of the mythical tree. *Come now... I invoke you... show me the tree, show me the way...*

Golden bark. Silver leaves. The smell of chocolate. The cool, pearlescent smoothness of metal beneath her hands.

And there it was, hanging just above her: a slender, graceful golden limb extending down for her to grasp. The sweet smell beckoned her, invited her in.

Elaina reached up and took hold.

CHAPTER TWENTY-ONE

SPIRITS *SURROUNDED* HER.

For a moment, Elaina could only stare, stunned, at the bright, glowing world around her. She'd ascended through the clouds into a vision once before, with Baba Yasmin, but it hadn't been like this. This was like being inside the northern lights: soft, shifting waves of colored light played through the golden branches of the tree she'd pictured in her mind, and with each quiet, subtle change there seemed to be some accompanying tone of music, somewhere deep in the background, felt more than heard. Birds flittered and chirped along the branches, though they were like no earthly birds she'd ever seen. Their plumes were like royal crowns and imperial crests; their breasts a coruscation of colors; their beaks like shining, faceted crystal. As though someone whispered a secret in her ear, Elaina understood these were lesser spirits, the little creatures of flora and streams, of summer breezes and gentle rainstorms.

She looked up. Above her, the branches of the world tree ascended far past the limits of her sight. Silver leaves hid dark pieces of chocolate, exactly as she had imagined. All at once she remembered exactly where she'd come by these images: a children's book called *The Cookie Tree,* which her mother had bought for her when she'd been only five or six years old. She'd mixed up some of the details, she knew that now... but this was the world tree as she'd conjured it, *her* world tree.

And at the top, would she find what she wanted?

She grabbed the next branch above her and began to climb.

The birds chirruped and fluttered around her as she ascended. There were other creatures, too, little beasts that looked like chipmunks or squirrels, but were most definitely not. As brightly colored as the birds, they gamboled about the branches trailing short tails of sparkling sunlight, and glanced at her with shining gemstone eyes.

"Bet you wish you had your camera now, don't you?"

Elaina glanced sharply up, the voice startling her like an electric shock. Sitting on a branch a few feet above, swinging her legs in innocent, childlike play, sat the spirit Ini.

"I didn't think you'd make it this far," the little girl confided. "Humans are so hard to believe in, you know. When I was young, I didn't trust a one of them, any farther than I could kick them. I've gotten a lot stronger since then. But I still have trouble putting faith in any of your kind."

Elaina hoisted herself up on a branch roughly alongside the spirit's perch. "Well, I did enter into this thing determined to win it. You all said it was impossible, and it didn't stop me."

"You really are rather remarkable." Ini gave her an appreciative once-over, nodding as though still astonished by the impossibility of it. "I suppose that means we chose well."

"We?" Elaina asked.

"Keep climbing, human girl. The answers are at the top."

Elaina laughed out loud. "You're a brat, Ini."

"I know."

The little girl smiled and let herself fall backward, swinging upside down by her knees. She began singing a tuneless little song, and Elaina smiled to herself, reaching up for the next branch.

"Be careful, Elaina."

When she glanced down again, Ini had disappeared, leaving some small being, something like a long, sinuous cat with the lush, full tail of a squirrel, blinking up at her. The voice came from the creature, though its mouth never moved.

"Just because you've managed to summon the tree, doesn't mean your quest is over."

Elaina opened her mouth to ask what the spirit meant, but the creature ducked and flicked its oversized tail, disappearing down the trunk of the tree.

Of course, though. This is only the sixth task. And I've only just begun.

She climbed onward. Soon, the shifting borealis of light and the chirping, fluttering birds disappeared below her. Clouds crowded in—as she ascended, they grew darker, closer, until she could see nothing around her.

She groped blindly for the next branch, and found it, pulling herself up.

All at once, she stood in her apartment back home, in the States. The apartment she'd shared with

Dominic for years, full of all the things they'd gathered as a couple. It smelled of something ugly and burnt, as though someone had left a plastic kitchen utensil too close to the burners in the kitchen, and the air clung close like a humid weight.

"I can't believe you!" someone was shouting. "I can't *believe* you! Running off to Siberia to join some cult of swinging nutjobs?"

Dominic. Pacing back and forth through the gray ashes of this remembered home, gesturing erratically, stomping across the floor even though the downstairs neighbors would surely complain.

"And you thought you could just *stay* there?" He spun to face her, waving a hand at her in incredulity. "Really, Elaina, as if you could just pack up everything and leave. As if you could really *change*. No one *changes,* Elaina, not even the spirit mother you're so intent on seeing. She never changed. She was always exactly as she was, and so are you. A neurotic scatterbrain, always obsessed with getting *away* from something. Well, you've dug yourself a real hole this time. You think I'll just get over the fact you ran off to get sexed up by three—no, *four* goddamn strangers?"

"I'm not asking you to get over it," Elaina replied. A tiny light of serenity glowed in her chest, and it gave her strength. "*You* broke up with *me,* Dom. You lost any right you had to an opinion on my choices. I don't care if you choke on your outrage."

"You're insane." He gestured wildly at her, unable to settle on any one accusatory motion. "You're *crazy.* You should be institutionalized!"

"Goodbye, Dominic."

She reached up, and there was the next branch. Dominic's face reddened and his expression twisted into an ugly mask. Like a bull, he lowered his shoulders and charged at her, and Elaina gasped, heart rate picking up as she pulled, desperate.

The apartment broke apart in tatters of cloud, and two of the brightly colored birds plunged, cawing, through the last foggy remnants, heedless of the vision as they chased each other through the leaves.

Elaina clung to her branch, staring downward. She couldn't see the ground, but she supposed that wasn't very surprising. More importantly, she couldn't see Dominic anymore—even in her mind—and for that, she was thankful. She kept climbing.

She had no concept of the passing time, or how much farther she'd gone before the sound of birds and the chatter of small creatures changed into human words, calling her name in familiar English. She glanced about her and saw to her right a familiar blue armchair, balanced precariously and lopsided between the leaves. On it sat her mother, ramrod straight, nails dug firmly into the arms of the chair, high-heeled feet crossed at the ankle.

"—time to come home, Elaina," her mother was saying, expression cold enough to send a chill straight down Elaina's spine. "I won't have my daughter simply gallivanting around some third-world wilderness park behaving like a damn pagan!"

"Your mother is correct, Elaina," came her father's voice on her other side. Elaina turned toward him and found him sitting at his office table, hunched over the newspaper, held up at a crazy, jaunty angle by the golden limbs. He didn't even look up at her as he continued, "You're making a fool of yourself, *and* us, with this rebellious nonsense. Now I'm going to wire you enough for a plane ticket and I want you to come *straight* home. No arguments."

"You're right," Elaina said, addressing both of them. "No arguments. Because I'm *not* coming home. I'm running away to join the circus, Mother, Father. I'm going to be an acrobat or a lion tamer or the fabulous wolf girl. And you're not going to stop me. You had your chance—thirty years' worth of chances—but now, I'm already gone."

"*Elaina!*" her mother shrilled, and it cut her to the heart, an ugly, cold sound from her youth that never failed to make her wither in fear. "You stop this *bullshit* right now and come back home! I did *not* raise you and shelter you and clothe you for eighteen years just so you could go run off and become a goddamn *whore!*"

As though jabbed by the words, stuck with them like the pitchforks of several dancing, devilish imps, Elaina climbed faster, pulling herself up branch by branch in a brief, childish panic. *I could reach fifty and that tone would still frighten me. I could be ninety years old and lying on my deathbed, and that voice would still make me cringe.*

"Get back here!" her mother still yelled, though her voice was growing fainter now, falling away in the distance.

After several more seconds of hurried climbing— *Goddess, I must have been climbing at least an hour by now... but I don't feel a thing!*—she sensed a more welcome presence. She glanced down again, and discovered a figure climbing—no, *bounding*—up after her. The great silver wolf Inferi leapt up from the branches below and perched, with flawless agility, on a limb just beside Elaina. The spirit's eyes glittered and it barked joyfully, bright tail waving like a banner back and forth in its excitement.

Elaina reached out for the beautiful wolf's sparkling, shimmering mane. Before her fingers could brush Inferi's coat, though, Inferi leapt again, bouncing to the next tree limb as though racing up a flight of stairs. It let out another joyous bark at Elaina, and continued upward, disappearing into the unseen heights above.

Elaina followed. Again, time blurred, and it might have been moments, or might have been days, before she met the next familiar face in her ascent. It looked as though she might finally have reached the top of the world tree—the next branch appeared to lead to an actual surface, some thick gathering of cloud bank. As she got her hands up over the lip, someone took her by the wrist, and helped her safely to her feet.

Astonishment, flaring up to her cheeks in a crimson flush, struck her nearly speechless. There before her on what now appeared to be the solid ground of a mossy riverbank, stood Nikita.

He was naked, as she was, and in the shape Elaina now considered most natural for the *oboroten,* somewhere between their fully human guise and the form of their animal self. His ears, pointed; his white-blonde hair wild like a mane; his eyes a full, featureless black. When he gazed upon her, he actually smiled.

"Welcome," he told her. "How fortuitous to see you here."

He looked... *happy.* Relaxed. Unburdened by the responsibilities weighing on him down below, in the waking realm.

He's... freer, here.

"You may be the last person I expected to see in this vision," she admitted. "But I guess, in a way, it makes perfect sense."

"*My* vision," he told her. "Or, should I say, *our* vision."

"What do you mean?" she asked, as he gestured for her to go before him along the path of the river.

"I'm no dream or figment of your subconscious, Elaina. I'm here, too. I am also asleep, at home, in my own bed, but I am here. Summoned by Diezana."

The smell of chocolate gave way to the smell of rich pine and clean, crisp water. Elaina paused to stoop at the river's edge, thirsty for a cool drink, and found herself staring at not her own reflection, but Nikita's.

No... not Nikita. It looks like Nikita—the silvery mane, the black eyes—but that's me.

She lifted one hand and moved it right to left. The creature in the water did as well. She touched her cheek; the creature did, too. A pale, startled she-wolf, wide-eyed at her own image.

"Does this mean I've—"

"No." Nikita shook his head. "Not yet. You're almost there, though. Come. The spirit mother awaits."

Elaina's heart gave a happy leap. She climbed to her feet as he led her on, up a stairway of mossy stones.

"I know, in the waking world, we have been at each other's throat." Nikita guided her up the steps with a quiet reverence. "There is... just so much at stake. For both of us. I understand that. I believe you have no intention of bringing harm to our pack, or of leaving us vulnerable. You do not know us... but you are making the journey with a true and dedicated heart. I see this, Elaina. I know."

"I told you," she said. "I believe I'm meant to be here. Meant to do this."

He nodded. "I have been giving this a great deal of thought," he replied, not meeting her eyes. "And it has been a very *difficult* decision. But if it means a safer resolution for us all... I *will* call off the blood hunt, Elaina—"

She gave a cry of elation and took his hand. He faced her, searching her eyes.

"I will call it off," he said. "But I want you, in return."

Her excitement fizzled. It didn't quite die, but the wind had been cleanly knocked from her sails, as she asked, "You want... me?"

"Yes." He took her other hand, and they stood connected, bare, face-to-face in a way they'd never been able to appreciate one another before. In the waking world there had been those strange moments, something uncertain, unspoken, lying between them. A long look; a curious investigation. The way he'd taken in her scent when she came into his house, an action uncomfortably similar to the way Gavri and Kolya had done in their first sexual explorations. Too much still lay between them, though, a battlefield neither one of them wanted to fight through.

"I've had lovers before," he said. "But none who remained with me after the casual act of pleasure was over. None whom I thought I could plan a future with. I am not saying the women in my past were not important to me, but none was an *alpha* female. None was a woman I could build a partnership with."

"But... Nikita..."

328

"Ours has been a rocky acquaintance so far." He brought up a hand and caressed her cheek with his thumb. "The things we want are too at odds to reconcile. And yet, I think of you constantly. When I am alone, or when I stand among my people and think, *they need a mother wolf.* I don't wish to do this by myself. Crazy or not, I want to do it with *you.*"

"I would be happy to be your partner, rather than your enemy, Nikita." She clasped his hand to her lips and kissed his knuckles. "As for mate... yes, we can try. If the others have no objection, we can see what comes—"

"No others."

The words hit her in the gut, as though he'd just struck her without meaning to.

"I want you to be *my* mate, Elaina. Mine, and nobody else's."

She stared at him. For a fleeting instant, she even hated him for suggesting it.

"I can't do that, Nikita. I am part of a circle. A family. We can open our arms to you, too—I believe—but if it is to be, it must be as part of my circle."

He dropped his gaze and let go of her hands. Elaina touched his cheek, but he'd closed up. Quick and hard, like a clam snapping shut. Like a door closing forever.

"I love them," she begged him to understand. "I won't give them up."

"You are loyal," he said. "And honorable."

"We can still—"

Nikita shook his head again. "We will duel, as we agreed. In four days. I hope you achieve the gifts of shapechange by then, Elaina. You will be a very beautiful wolf."

They'd come to a place on the river where the trees formed an arch high over the water. A gateway. Nikita held out a hand for her to go ahead.

"The spirit mother awaits you. Good luck."

"Nikita, I—"

"Please," he said. "Before the vision breaks apart. You must go to her."

"But—"

"Go."

She stared. He tilted his face away, closing his eyes so she could no longer peer into him. She reached out to touch him again, but at the last second, thought better of it.

"I care about you," she told him. "If you change your mind... you know where to find me."

With that, she stepped through the gate, and into a pure, radiating light.

Chapter Twenty-Two

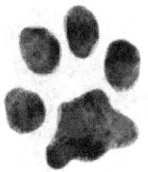

When the light faded, Elaina found herself before the pale, faceless spirit Niuri.

She gave a short cry and staggered back, falling to the snow-covered ground, raising her hands in defense. Her first memory of the vicious, stalking creature leapt upon her with sharp clarity and she recalled the way the witch-thing moved, the way it screamed even though it had no mouth, bearing down like a wicked owl diving on its prey.

This time, Niuri did nothing. Still as a stone, the spirit stared at Elaina. It blinked its dark, starry eyes, the only feature it seemed to possess. The snowy white owl feathers adorning its long, heavy cloak rustled silently on a brisk winter breeze.

"S-spirit?" Elaina stammered. "Niuri?"

The creature tilted its head curiously to one side.

Footsteps crunched in the snow on either side of Elaina. She glanced right and left, and found her other two guides, Ini and Inferi, circling her. They joined Niuri, and the little girl took the silent creature's hand. The wolf sat down by her side. All three of them gazed down at Elaina, making no motion, saying nothing.

Light intensified before her, growing white-hot and bright enough that Elaina had to shield her eyes with her hand, wincing away from the raw, bright burn. When it faded, the three spirits were gone. The snow field was gone. Now, Elaina sat on the shore of a rocky beach, shrouded in fog. The air pressed in on her, muggy and humid, smelling of salt and green, sweet algae, the pungent low tide. Somewhere in the middle distance, barely visible through the morning mists, she could make out the shadow of a thick tree line.

A woman stood before her, where the spirit Niuri had stood a moment before. She held herself with an odd, weightless sort of grace, as though she lingered just shy of levitation above this pebbly shore, one foot extended gracefully before her and the other turned at a ninety-degree angle to the first: a dancer's pose.

Her hair, drifting about her shoulders like a gauzy veil even though no breeze passed by, shone a soft, gossamer silver, glinting with pale hues of lavender and rose. She stood naked, just as Elaina, and swirling, geometric tattoos marked her chest, the line of her neck, and down her left arm. More swirled from her right hip to her ankle, and the delicate work of clever hands had applied ink even over her left eye, in complex interweaving sigils.

No. No clever hands. No inking process. Elaina marveled at the fine artwork interconnecting everything, even over this woman's eyelid. *She was* born *this way. I don't know how I could possibly know that, but I do.*

Gaping, Elaina managed to find her voice, tiny and strangled though it was.

"Di... Diezana?"

"That," said the woman, never opening her mouth, "is one of my names. Welcome to my hunting grounds, Elaina."

Her eyes were the same dark, starry blackness of Niuri's; her hair, wild like a silvery mane.

"You... were all of them?" Elaina climbed to her feet. "Ini, Inferi, Niuri... they were all you?"

"Each is a part of me." Diezana held out a hand. "Walk with me. It is time for me to explain why you are here."

The spirit mother slid gracefully along the gritty shore. Elaina followed, skipping and hopping over the rocks.

"This doesn't look like any place I've seen in Stolby." She sidestepped a pile of granite stones the size of fists, which appeared to have once been set in an altar configuration like the one she'd built herself. She reached out to touch it.

"It is not Stolby. Not Russia. This is my birthplace. My *real* birthplace. An ancient shoreline, far from Siberia. You wouldn't know it. It is long gone."

"The place you and the first pack gathered?"

"No." Diezana moved with a nimble, childlike grace which Elaina couldn't mimic. "The stories your Russian friends tell you are as accurate as they believe. But they are not the only stories."

Diezana turned toward the sea and gestured in a wide arc. "I was born here. As a child—or as close to a child as I ever was—I nearly drowned in this sea. My brother and I clung to one another and found ourselves on this shore. This is where my story truly began."

"Athanos said you had a brother. King of shapeshifters."

This brought a laugh from the spirit mother, and Elaina thought, *She doesn't look like a* mother *at all. She looks... like a child. Not so much a child as the form of Ini, but... a girl. A girl in the prime of her youth.*

"How like him," Diezana said. "To call himself a *king.*"

Elaina came to a halt. "Athanos? He is your brother?"

Diezana gave a single, somber nod.

"But then... why did he come to me? Why did he offer—"

"You're asking for the middle of the story, Elaina. I haven't even gotten to the start."

"Okay." She started walking again, skipping into a jog to catch up. "So... tell me."

"I have said Diezana is only one of my names. *Diezana...* 'Singing Voice'. My brother's name, to the *oboroten* and *vukodlak,* is Drayce. 'Dragon'. We are also known as Ainle, and Athanos. 'Spirit', and 'Lion Man'. In this time—the time of our birth, and when we first walked among mortals—we were called Catori and Caedan."

"Are you really spirits?" Elaina asked. "Or... something else?"

Diezana's dark, starry eyes sparkled with mischief. "We have been mortal. We have been immortal. We have been angels, and demons. Right now, I would call us spirits, yes. Spirits waging a small war against one another. My wolves... my wolves were..."

She paused. Her serene mask seemed to slip, and all of a sudden, she looked frightened. Heartbroken. Her voice actually cracked when she continued.

"He has fixated his anger at me upon my wolves. He will tear them down... and he will make them his."

"The *vukodlak*," Elaina breathed. She bent down to scoop up a smooth rock she'd spied between two chunks of craggy quartz.

"Yes. My brother is like me: we are both shapeshifters, the *first* shapeshifters. Only, as he does with all things beautiful and sacred, Athanos... Drayce... Caedan... twists his powers. Uses them to corrupt this world."

Turning to Elaina, she cupped her hands over the round, gray rock. When she removed them, she revealed it, pitted and broken, spotted with lichen and lime, blackened upon one edge as though burnt. Elaina understood the stone wasn't *exactly* burnt, but somehow poisoned. The portions turned black were deteriorating like no other substance she'd seen. Not rotting, like anything organic. *Inert.* Completely devoid of... *energy.* Any kind of energy.

She dropped the stone. "So he's the enemy in the story of the *oboroten* people? The one who sent the storms and separated you from your game?"

Diezana nodded. "Yes. Another in his string of attempts to destroy what I build, and the mortals I love. My time here was not my first time on Earth; only one of many stories. The *oboroten*—the turnskins—are the beautiful result of that time. As he always does, my brother attempted to steal them. And, with some, he succeeded. Those whose hearts he could corrupt, they became the *vukodlak*. It is a story of which you may find many versions, for I have many children beyond the *oboroten*, and he many monsters."

"Why? Why does he do this?"

Diezana laughed again, though this time it sounded bitter, sad. "In the beginning, he thought me to be the weaker of us. But it was I who learned to shapeshift, and had to teach him. It was I who wielded the elements of our power, and he who struggled."

Elaina put her hands out plaintively before her. "What does this all have to do with me? With the Stolby tribe?"

Diezana blinked at her, and her dark, starry eyes brimmed with a fearful sadness.

"My brother walks in these lands. You know as much. His creatures come to hunt my children. I have seen this coming... I know what he plans."

"What?" Elaina asked in a whisper.

Diezana swept out a hand again, gesturing this time into the foggy distance, where the shadow of the tree line hovered in the mist. When Elaina turned to look, she saw silent flashes of lightning. The glow of fire, like a pulsing bed of coals deep in the forest. Shadows played in the sky, cast by the light below, a battle of claws and teeth, of beast and man, waged somewhere in the dark, unseen woods.

"I need a new kind of *oboroten* to guide my people through this battle," Diezana told her. "I need one who will remember what it is to be human, and to walk the path to *change*. One who has been lost—as you and I have both been—and found again. This is why I beseeched the snow to find you that night, so you could face the wall of white as I once did. And you did so well, my little one! All my shapeshifters, they are born as they are. Their journeys are meaningful, but none has ever changed their intrinsic nature, down to their very DNA, to *become* something new. They will need a leader who understands such struggle, for my brother has evil plans, and without you—what you represent—I fear my *oboroten* will lose themselves."

"I don't understand." Elaina still gazed up into the gory darkness, where beasts clashed and thunder rolled. "How... how can *I* prevent this?"

"It can't be prevented." Diezana shifted form, sliding out of the fair, childlike visage and into one of a warrior queen: hair now dark and red as the beating ruby heart of fire, eyes a piercing green, wearing the furs of her kills and the antlers of a stag upon her head. In one hand, she held a shield of thick wood and banded iron; in the other, a sword of beaten bronze.

"This war will come."

Suppressing a groan, Elaina beseeched her. "Then what is it you want?"

"Guide my people home, Elaina. Guide my people home."

Diezana took a step forward, and the image of the warrior faded. She became the sylvan girl again, and lifted one hand, touching a delicate finger to the center of Elaina's brow. "I know how Athanos has tempted you. He, a master manipulator, a master of illusions which are both false and very real. The road ahead of you will be very difficult. Despite our best efforts, every war has its casualties."

A cold emptiness bloomed in Elaina's chest. "You don't mean—"

"I can do for you what my brother has offered. I will take this burden from you. Call upon Nikita to end the blood hunt and leave you, Gavri, and Kolya alone. If that is all you wish."

"No." Elaina shook her head. "That isn't what I want, Diezana. Not at the cost of turning away from you."

The spirit mother crossed her arms over her chest. Had she been wearing robes, it would have been a serene gesture, a gesture of meditative tranquility.

"You called me here for a reason," Elaina said. "Let me fulfill your purpose."

Diezana bowed her head, as though considering. Or perhaps saying a prayer.

"Wake now," she said. "Your time draws near. Gather your mates around you and be ready."

White light overtook Elaina's vision again. She fought to remain—she had so many more questions to ask the spirit mother—but she couldn't stand against it.

No, please... I'm not done, I want to know so much—

The rocky beach disappeared beneath her. The whisper of Diezana's voice, a final message, reached her, before darkness swallowed her up.

ELAINA BLINKED HER EYES OPEN. The dancing light of the bonfire flickered in the leaves of the trees overhead. It didn't frighten her, though: she remembered where she was, and all around her, her mates sat on their knees waiting for her to wake."

"Hey, *krasavitsa.*" Gavri smiled at her. He brushed the backs of his knuckles down her cheek. "There you are."

They'd laid her in Rini's lap, and the beautiful snowshoe girl held Elaina's head in her hands, chanting in time to Baba Yasmin's drum. The rhythm had slowed. Elaina thought it must be tied to heart rates and soothing ambience. Even in the light of the fire, her skin felt pleasantly cool, and she spied damp cloths in the laps of Grisha and Kolya; they'd cleaned her body while she lay in her trance, and kept her lightly anointed. Pasha held a canteen in his hand; he'd have been giving her water periodically, to keep her hydrated.

"How long did I sleep?" she asked.

"It's been nearly an hour and a half." Kolya combed a hand through her hair. "Did it work?"

"Oh!" She sat up. Her head spun and she swayed, then pitched forward. Her mates steadied her, and Pasha rubbed her back in wide, slow circles.

I can still feel the effects of the alcohol. I guess I might still be a bit drunk...

Rini ended her chant and laid a comforting hand on Elaina's shoulder. Baba Yasmin struck the last beat on her drum and fell silent, watching them with shrewd, half-lidded eyes.

"What did you see?' Grisha purred with excitement. "The spirit mother? Did you climb the tree to find her?"

"Yes. I did." Straightening—slowly this time—she glanced from each of her mates to the next, beaming wildly. "I met Diezana—oh, and I have so much to tell you all! And when I climbed up the tree... Grisha, you wouldn't believe the spirits inhabiting the branches!"

"Did she say whether you would change?"

This from Gavri, stoic and focused as ever. Elaina glanced down at her hands, searching her memory.

"She... she said something just as I drifted out of the vision. I think... I think I *can,* but there's... *something* to it. She didn't show me. I think she wants me to discover it for myself."

"But you can!" Kolya seized her in a hug. "You can, *krasavitsa,* surely you can. One last step, and you will be *oboroten.* You will be like us."

"Two more steps," she corrected. "There's one more thing we have to do here, before we go home."

Her four men stared, puzzled. She raised her hand and gestured for her backpack, which she'd set down outside of the ritual space. Rini handed it to her, and Elaina withdrew the folded envelopes of paper containing the earrings she had carved.

"I want to make this official," she told them. At the edge of the circle, Rini retrieved her own satchel and searched through it, coming up with a heavy gauge sewing needle. As she did, Elaina poured the contents of the tiny, folded papers into one palm.

"An earring for each of you, if you'll wear it. A token to show the world we belong to each other. Traditional wedding rings would be harder, with you all changing all the time. Necklace chains might snap if you shapeshift in a hurry. But these should remain, no matter what form you're in."

Kolya grinned, amber eyes bright. "What a beautiful idea, *krasavitsa.* Of course, I will wear it."

"Me, too," agreed Grisha. Gavri and Pasha offered solemn nods.

With utmost care, Rini and Elaina moved between the four men, piercing each one's left ear, the one closest to his heart. Rini followed each piercing with an alcohol swab to ward away infection, but Elaina expected with the way *oboroten* healed, her mates stood little chance of it. When they came to

340

Pasha, Elaina gazed down at the earring in her palm, and then met his eyes.

"I made this days ago, Pasha. I suppose I lied to myself about the reasons, at first. Pretended I didn't know exactly why I had done it. But you *do* belong with us. I have no doubts. I hope you will accept it, and my apologies for holding back from you so long."

Pasha closed his hand over the earring and hers. "No apology needed. I spent weeks agonizing over my own decision. I am glad we have found each other at last, *uchenik*."

He didn't flinch when Rini pierced his ear with the needle, and Elaina affixed the earring.

Once each man bore his token of her devotion, they exchanged long, loving kisses with her, and presently formed a circle with her in the center, trading gentle affections. Rini produced a light dinner of wrapped sandwiches, and the whole party ate in reverent quiet. A sacred hush seemed to have fallen over the space, the place of their earnest petition to the mother of shapeshifters.

Before she dressed, Elaina knelt once more before her altar in the cave and supplicated herself, bowing her head to the floor and placing her fingertips on the lowest cairn-stone.

"Thank you," she whispered. "For them. For tonight. For whatever is to come."

ON THE HIKE BACK TO the lodge, she explained her vision to her mates, and the tale Diezana had told her regarding her brother and counterpart. She told them about her visits from Athanos, and his offer to make Nikita rescind the blood hunt.

"He did not wish for a human to learn the ways of Diezana," Grisha concluded. "You should have told us earlier."

"I didn't think it important, at least not until this last visit." She took a long drink from her water bottle. "And I did mean to tell you about it. It just never seemed to be the right time. I didn't know he was the enemy you all told me about. I just thought another spirit like the first three had taken an interest in my quest."

"Well, the first three turned out to be Diezana herself," Grisha pointed out, a note of dry humor in his tone. "So in a way, you were right."

"But Elaina could not have known that," Kolya put in. "And even if she had told us, we would not have known, either. Diezana's enemy has always been a faceless, nameless entity to all but the most studied of us, and hasn't walked these lands in centuries. I doubt even Baba Yasmin would have known the form in which he came to our mate."

"We will deal with Athanos, and the *vukodlak,* soon enough." Gavri rested an arm across her shoulder and gave her a squeeze. "For now, we concentrate on the final task."

Something nagged at her. The thing Diezana had told her just before she woke up... words lost in the sea of blinding bright light. What had it been?

Nothing stands in your way. It is for you to—

To what?

As they came in sight of the lodge, Gavri and Kolya perked up. Three figures gathered on the front patio, just outside the door.

"Adelaida?" Elaina paused, gripping the straps of her backpack as she furrowed her brow. "But she and

Bernard and Timofei all have keys to get in the house. Why are they just huddled on the porch like that?"

A growl escaped Gavri, and he picked up speed.

Adelaida noticed them the instant they emerged from the trees, and she came down the stairs at a regal, unhurried descent, but the expression on her face spelled trouble. Her cheeks were flushed; her eyes, puffy from tears.

"Viktor," she told them. "And the *vukodlak*."

Fear struck Elaina like a spear in the gut. Her first thought was *Nikita. Please, please, not Nikita...*

"What happened?" she asked.

CHAPTER TWENTY-THREE

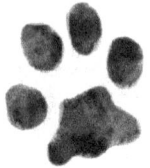

THEY'D MURDERED A FAMILY OF five, just outside the public section of the park. *Oboroten* father—a bear shifter—and his human wife, and their three children. Adelaida had known them personally, which meant, of course, so had Viktor.

"He's murdering even old friends now?" Gavri snapped, storming about the living room in a rage.

Adelaida, looking wilted and old in her chair, shook her head. "Viktor never did form strong friendships like the rest of us. He always had rather nasty opinions about, well, everyone."

Gavri snarled. "When I find him—"

Elaina put a hand on his arm. "We will, love. For now, try to calm your anger. We need to be ready to help Nikita and the others."

"Maybe sooner rather than later." Rini appeared in the archway to the dining room. She held the phone in one hand, twisting and twining the spiral cord with the other. She'd gone ashen. Elaina had asked her to call Nikita the moment they'd entered the house, and when she hadn't gotten hold of him, Rini took it upon herself to call each other member of the tribe one by one until someone could tell her where the alpha might be.

"Sofie is missing," she announced. "Nikita set out to find her the minute he heard about the attack. She never made it back home after she left us."

Yasmin, seated on the sectional alongside Timofei and Pasha, gave a strangled gasp. "No! Little Sofie?"

"Which means we're the last people who saw her." Elaina rubbed a hand over her mouth, doing the calculations. "But she left here *hours* ago."

"She could be anywhere," Rini agreed.

The room fell silent. Elaina crossed the room, standing before the big picture window and staring out into the night.

"We have to find her," she said. "As far as we know, we're the last ones to see Sofie, here at the lodge, so she's our responsibility. We shouldn't have let her go alone in the first place. Now she's out there somewhere in this park, and the *vukodlak* are looking for blood. We have to find her before they do."

Gavri nodded. "Yes. We'll go now. Grisha, Pasha, Kol—"

"*All* of us," Elaina corrected. Her beta wolf shot her a curious, troubled look.

"Elaina... we don't even know yet if you can change. You can't keep up in a human form, and—"

"We cannot wait." Pasha, rising from his seat, bowed his head in apology. "I am sorry, *uchenik,* but Gavri is right. If you cannot join us as a wolf, we will lose precious time."

"I'll stay." Kolya rested his hand on Elaina's shoulder. "With Adelaida and Bernard, you will have plenty to track down the girl. Elaina and I can stay back, and I will aid her in the change. The spirit mother will grant it, I know."

Elaina didn't want to stay back. Wolf or no, she wanted to go with the others immediately. She swallowed her protest, though, and rested her own hand on Kolya's before agreeing.

"Rini, can you stay with Timofei?" she asked the housekeeper. "In case there is more news, or if anyone comes to look for Sofie here."

"Of course." Rini ducked back into the dining room to explain the situation to whomever she had on the line. Elaina hadn't missed the note of relief in the poor young woman's voice. *Oboroten* she may be, but Rini couldn't keep up with wolves even in her animal form, and a snowshoe rabbit would be easy, helpless prey to a corrupted abomination like a *vukodlak*.

Adelaida rose from her seat, and Bernard came to her side, silent, stoic, and bearing a deadly look in his dark eyes. Baba Yasmin rose as well. It was on the tip of Elaina's tongue to suggest the old woman also stay behind with Rini and Timofei, but Yasmin's steely gaze made it clear she would not sit idle during a hunt like this. The three of them blurred—clothing slipped or ripped away, some falling in tatters to the floor as human hosts bent and twisted and changed. Soon, two slinky, slender female wolves stood before them, and one stocky, vicious wolverine. The lovely black and silver wolf, Adelaida, shook off the last of her human garments, kicking underwear loose from her long, graceful legs and pawing her loose silk blouse over her head, while Bernard simply lunged and ripped at his last clinging clothes with his teeth, tearing them off. Yasmin, a scruffier, patchier gray bitch, simply stepped free of her loose shamanic robe. Taking their cue, the younger shapeshifters stripped off their clothes and also changed, trading flesh for fur in a tangle of growls, yips, and cries.

Elaina crossed the foyer and flung the front door wide. Her pack slipped past her and slunk like shadows down the stairs on either side. They ran together in the same bounding, breathtaking way Inferi had run across the fields of snow in her vision, only these wolves were not at play. These were on a hunt, noses low to the ground, working out the trail of a missing—maybe endangered—teen.

Elaina watched them go, sadness warring with anger in her chest.

Nothing more stands in your way. It is for you to—

"To what?" She stomped her foot. "For me to *what?* Ugh, spirits... I know the value is in the lesson, but I need to change *now*. There's a little girl out there who needs to be *found*."

"Come, *krasavitsa*." Kolya led her out onto the porch, closing the door behind them. They followed the wolves, watching the place where they'd disappeared into the trees. Kolya halted her at the edge of the property, before the road. Their shoes scraped the gravel.

Elaina hugged herself against the cold. She rubbed at her upper arms and tried to suppress a shiver. How had it grown so cold all of a sudden?

"Snow," she murmured, blinking. "Kolya... do you see it?"

The first drifting, tiny white specks floated down around them. Kolya stared up into the dark, cloudy night sky, a sound of surprise escaping him. *Snow.* Snow, in the middle of June.

Even in Siberia, this must never happen. Elaina patted her arms, taken back all at once to the night she'd gotten lost in the snowstorm. A late-season snowstorm, a rare May blizzard the spirits themselves had commissioned to swallow her, like Dorothy's twister carrying her away to Oz. *Oh,* it had been so cold... so goddamn *cold.*

It is for you to—

"For me to *what?*" she demanded, wracking her brain to remember.

For you to manifest in yourself.

The alpha wolf...

For you to conjure.

Elaina gave a huff: her breath came out a fog in the icy air. Kolya, behind her, slid his arms around her waist and pulled her into a close hug.

"Calm your heart, *krasavitsa.*" He kissed the top of her head. "We will find the power in you. We will bring the wolf forth from your heart."

"I remember what the spirit said," she told him. "About changing. She said, 'it is for me to manifest'. I've only ever practiced manifestation once, Kolya, and that was earlier tonight, with the world tree, and our whole ritual of conjuration. We don't have time to arrange another ceremony like that for me to find my power."

"Manifestation is not all done through such rituals, Elaina." He took her hands and slid her out of his embrace, spinning her to face him. "Manifestation of power is all about your *will.* Your focus, intention, and desire."

He brought his fingers to her temples. "Close your eyes. Focus on what it is you want. Think of the she-wolf inside of you and call her forth."

Elaina wanted to object, to tell him things were far too serious to waste time with a meditative

348

visualization exercise. She'd already done so many visualizations, with Pasha, with Grisha, and none of them had conjured anything so spectacular as true *magic*.

But the world tree...

Maybe, yes, but that had come with a ritual, with ceremonial invocation, entheogens, shamanic blessing. She couldn't just *will* herself to change shape.

How else would an oboroten *do it? Do you think there are magic words? A secret handshake?*

"Focus," Kolya repeated, "on what you want."

She closed her eyes as he instructed, and tried to steady herself, calm her breathing. She couldn't stop thinking of Sofie, though, and the danger the poor girl could be in. Sofie, one of the tribe, a sister of the tribe, *Nikita's* baby sister.

Oh, and Nikita! What would happen to him if he lost the last of his family to the vukodlak? *Could he ever forgive himself?*

"We have to find Sofie," she whispered. Kolya made a quiet sound of agreement but said nothing.

I need to be part of this search. She came here to aid me. Maybe she'd never see it that way, maybe she'd never have done it if she thought *it was aiding me, but the fact remains. She came here because of me. She is part of this tribe, this tribe I have come to love, and I* need *to know she is safe.*

A wild lash of instinct rose inside her chest. *Yes!* it hissed. *She is one of mine. I claim her as my tribe and kin. I will find her. I will* protect *her.*

Elaina tried to focus on her breathing, as Pasha had told her. She tried to picture the wolf she wished to be, but Sofie's image continued to float in the front of her mind.

One of mine. The vukodlak *will take her life if they find her. One of* mine. *I will* not *let them hurt her.*

The thoughts came in rough, ragged snarls. They came in a voice Elaina didn't recognize in herself, a hungry voice, a keen and confident voice, a voice of teeth and blood and bone. Again she tried to think of wolves, of a hefty russet wolf like Kolya or a slender, snowy white wolf like Nikita. But the other thoughts were pulling her down now, dragging her into a whirlpool of fierce, possessive, protective instinct.

One of mine. I will find her. I will protect her. One of mine.

A bark called her from the frantic repetition. When she opened her eyes, Kolya sat before her in his own lupine form, ears alert, panting, wild brush of a tail whipping back and forth.

Only... she was looking at him eye-to-eye. He'd become his wolf self, and she ought to have been looking *down* at him, but she wasn't. She blinked, confused, until Kolya bounded up and butted her with his head, and she realized all at once she no longer stood with him on the gravel. She'd gone to all fours, and he came at her for a friendly shoulder-block, yipping with glee.

I'm... I'm not *standing. Am I? I can't feel my own two feet...*

But she could feel the gravel underneath a rough, thick padding on her palms and soles. *But what about my shoes?*

Elaina blinked again. Glancing over her shoulder, she beheld a smooth, sloping mane of a coppery brown-blonde. Loose rags of clothing hung from her middle and puddled on the ground around her—

—back paws—

—and at the end of her body, a thick, glossy tail swept low to the ground.

She'd changed. She'd taken the shape of a wolf.

I am... oboroten.

Wild, rapturous glee flamed to life in her chest. She tried to cry out in joy, but it came out as an off-key, ululating noise somewhere between a bark and a howl. She tried to prance forward and step out of the hanging remains of her clothes, the way Adelaida and the others hand, and stumbled, off-balance. All at once she had four feet to coordinate, not only the two, and her legs felt strangely longer than before.

Well, what did you expect? Did you think it'd be just like crawling around on your hands and knees?

She tripped again, kicking off her jeans, and Kolya pressed himself against her side, keeping her steady. After several awkward moments, she managed to free herself, and staggered, swaying, toward the place where the others had disappeared. She tried to call Kolya's name and it came out a sharp bark. He seemed to catch her meaning, though, and followed.

It didn't take long to grow used to the wolf's shape, not nearly as long as she'd have guessed. Perhaps it was the urgency of the situation or the fierce golden joy filling her every limb as she first walked, then trotted, then chanced a run, bounding ahead like the spirit Inferi had, racing in long strides, eating up the distance. Kolya kept pace with her—he could have outrun her, she knew, but he matched her instead—and they plunged into the woods. When Elaina inhaled, the bright, clear scents of the forest almost assaulted her. A human nose couldn't possibly detect the complexities or catalogue the hundred varying smells arrayed before her. She stopped mid-run, bowing her head and pawing at her snout.

Snout! I have a muzzle, and a snout, not a nose! I can smell the mice that came through here recently!

She didn't want mice, though. She wanted Sofie. Whipping her head back and forth, clearing her mind of her astonishment and focusing on her goal, she drew in another long inhale. The bouquet of woodland odors overwhelmed her, but she took her time to consider them. At last she identified the ones she recognized: Gavri, Grisha, Adelaida and the others. Fresh scents, heading southwest. She could detect Sofie too, an older scent, but still very strong. Kolya gazed at her and nodded toward a break in the aspens, and they ran again, following the pack.

The chase took them far, over miles. Elaina marveled at the world through the wolf's eyes: everything looked different, scents lit up like colors and light, all the woods as clear as day despite the lateness of the hour and the dark clouds overhead, still spitting drifts of snow down on the world. Her ears detected sounds all around, and like the smells she had to force herself to focus on only a few, only those leading her closer to her goal.

They crossed the gorge with the solid wooden bridge, thumping across the boards at a sprint, to the hill that would take them to the pack meeting place. There, though, Sofie's trail broke in the opposite direction, and they followed it down into a valley of pine and short grasses. Ahead, the shadow of one of the Stolby rock formations loomed in the distance.

Elaina stopped abruptly again. Another scent had joined the others: a foul and nauseating scent. It smelled like rotten meat and wilted flowers, and the sharp, acrid scent of something burnt. Ahead of her, Kolya paused. He gave an earnest whimper and curled his tail between his legs.

Vukodlak.

Elaina barked and bounded forward again. She searched for sounds, now, the sounds of other creatures, the sounds of her pack. Before long, she heard running water, and—

Yes! Gavri, that's Gavri! I know his growl. And Pasha, too, and—

A wildcat's scream rose up. It jolted her, like a knife straight to her heart. Grisha. And mingled into their snapping, snarling, barking chorus, something liquid and bubbling and dark. Voices which were not voices, but some sort of cadenced low groans.

She and Kolya broke through a patch of hawthorn, and right into the middle of the fight. Her pack tangled with monsters the likes of which Elaina could not even have imagined: the *vukodlak* looked as though they might once have been beautiful beasts of the natural world, but some form of dark, glittering blemish stained their flesh like splattered paint. They moved on all fours, lunged and pounced like something feline or canine, but their features resembled none of the big dogs or big cats of the animal kingdom. They were blunted and round, like ancient stone gargoyles. Their front legs were longer than their back legs, like hyenas, giving them a hunched, sloped-back look, and their ears were proportionately overlarge, like a bat's.

Elaina took all this in over a fraction of a second. Her focus zeroed in then the small, crouched white figure of Sofie, huddled low to the ground in her wildcat form, back arched and hair raised. Blood marked her snowy fur. Then Elaina found Gavri and Grisha, tangled in gnashing combat with three of the *vukodlak*. Pasha wrestled with a fourth, and Adelaida and Bernard together had brought down a fifth, struggling to keep it pinned. Still, there were more of the invaders, loping and feinting toward the melee.

The wolf brain calculated the situation before it, and Elaina's choice was made. She leapt for the *vukodlak* nearest the injured Sofie, lunging for its throat.

She caught it by surprise. It crumpled as she struck it, and together they rolled several feet. When their momentum stopped Elaina seized it by one gaunt, ugly foreleg and tugged, drawing it into a fight with her.

Kolya bounded in to cover Sofie with his own body, standing over her stiff-legged and bowing his head low, baring his teeth. Gavri and Grisha caught one of their attackers together, sinking teeth into its low belly and its rear leg, and the *vukodlak* screamed in a shrill voice like a rabbit in a trap.

Adelaida—evidently satisfied letting her mate handle the one already pinned—launched herself at the last enemy and caught it by the ruff, clinging to its back. It yowled and bucked, whirling to throw her off, to no avail. The monster Elaina had caught jerked its foreleg, trying to get back to the main fray, as if it hadn't even realized a small, coppery-colored she-wolf had hold of it. It seemed confused, pulled in two different directions, and whipped its head back and forth trying to bite Elaina and get at the others at the same time.

Oh, goddess... Thought broke through Elaina's bloodlust, achingly human and full of fear. *What am I doing? I don't know how to fight like a wolf! I don't know anything about these enemies!*

She tugged at the *vukodlak* again, dragging it several steps back from the fray. Finally, it whirled on her, as though noticing her for the first time, and roared as it attacked.

Elaina released it and bounced back. Even if she didn't know how to fight, the she-wolf in her seemed at least to have the instincts, and she followed them, falling into it as though into a dance. The enemy lunged and she retreated, then parried with a snap of her own. It caught her on the next charge, sinking teeth into the back of her neck, and she grabbed for its leg again, biting into thick muscle close to the chest.

A howl rose up nearby. A second later, a third pack of animals crashed into the clearing, led by Yasmin and a marvelous white wolf. Nikita. Elaina had an instant to recognize Klementina and Ivan with them, before her opponent bit at her again, scoring on her back, close to her hip. She cringed and fell to her side, and had one bright second to think *No! Don't give it any chance at your belly, get back on your feet!*

Nikita barreled into the *vukodlak* before it could descend, and it gave a shocked yelp of pain. The alpha male seized its throat in his jaws and jerked. A nauseating *snap* put an end to the *vukodlak*'s screeching, and it fell limp to the forest floor.

Elaina regained her feet. The elderly, velvet gray wolf who was Yasmin nosed her gently, as if to ask *Are you all right?* Elaina bobbed her lupine head in affirmative and whirled back toward the fight.

With Nikita's pack closing in, the *vukodlak* were far outnumbered. They recognized this quickly, and one of them uttered an otherworldly, echoing cry—again, Elaina thought of hyenas, hyenas and cackling crows somehow blended into one voice—and the monsters fell back. Four lay broken or dead, and Bernard ambled off the corpse he'd finished to square off with another one, but the last of them were melting away, slinking into the trees with bitter, vengeful hatred in their glowing yellow eyes.

Nikita resumed his human form and raced to where Sofie crouched in the grass. Kolya backed away to let the alpha see his sister, and as Nikita took the bleeding wildcat into his arms, Elaina's pack gathered together to check each other for injury.

Elaina wanted to bound to their sides, filled with buoyant elation. The moment she stepped with her back leg, however, she faltered. Pain caught her by surprise, and she let out a whoof without meaning to.

Gavri turned his gaze to her. He was the first to come to her, with Grisha and Pasha close on his heels. When they reached her side they studied her, circling her and sniffing her, the wolves wagging their tails. Grisha butted her with his broad feline head on her uninjured side, rubbing against her with a loud, rippling purr.

"Sofie is very hurt."

They looked up at Baba Yasmin, returned to her human form. Adelaida and many of Nikita's wolves had also resumed their human guises, though many remained in their halfway state, pointed ears and dark eyes alert.

"We should take her back to the lodge." Adelaida rested her hand on Nikita's shoulder. "We're closest, and have plenty of room."

"I agree." Gavri reverted to his human form and bowed his head to Nikita. "She'll be safe there. You're welcome in our home, to stay by her side."

Elaina found herself puzzled. She hadn't thought yet about how to change back into her own human shape. So much focus and effort had gone into achieving the shapechange, she hadn't even wondered about reversing it.

"Elaina." Grisha spoke, human again, kneeling at her side. He stroked a hand through her ruff and kissed her lupine brow. "It's just like flexing a muscle, love. Simply relax your hold on the wolf shape. Let your human self slip back into place."

She took a long, deep breath. Closing her eyes, she lay down, feeling the cool earth under her belly. She pictured the power and energy of the wolf seeping away, sinking back into the natural equilibrium.

It did. Letting go of the wolf came with a sweet, delicious relief. It hadn't been bad, being the wolf. No, it had been the opposite, it had been *amazing*. But as her flesh returned and her body resumed its familiar existence, she sighed, wiping her brow.

"You did it." Grisha smiled as she'd never seen her jaded, sarcastic snow leopard smile before. "The final task, Elaina. You found the magic to change. You are one of us."

"Yeah," she gasped, managing a weak smile of her own. "Goddess, Grisha... it's *amazing*."

He slid a hand behind her head and pulled her into a kiss.

"We should go," Adelaida said, glancing back and forth for any more movement between the trees. "Viktor wasn't with them, but I'll bet he's in the area.

We don't want them bringing reinforcements and dragging us into another fight."

"Come, Nikita." Gavri held out a hand to help his brother up. Nikita accepted it, balancing Sofie—she remained in her feline form, the easier for him to carry—in one arm. "We'll tend to her, and to you, at home."

RINI WAS READY WITH THE first aid kit—and two more identical kits beside—when the group of them trekked out of the woods again. "Saw you through the window," she explained once they'd filed in the door, and she'd directed Nikita to take his sister into the first guest room upstairs. "You look like refugees out of a war film. Who's least hurt? They can take a kit and tend to the others while I go see to Sofie."

Kolya took one of the red plastic boxes, and Grisha the other. Adelaida stepped outside again to instruct Nikita's wolves to patrol the area and drive away any stray *vukodlak* who might still be lurking. As Kolya tended to Elaina's injuries, he gave her a broad grin.

"Already healing like one of us, too, *krasavitsa*." He ran a hand along the bite mark on her hip, which had been painful, but not particularly deep. "This should be gone within the next day. The one on your neck may last longer, but I expect you will hardly notice it by tomorrow evening."

"What about the *vukodlak* who were killed?" she asked. "Surely we can't just leave the bodies out there for park rangers to discover."

"Members of the tribe will dispose of them," Adelaida assured her. "They'll be burned in a heap. No funeral rites... just disposal."

The venom in the former alpha's voice woke a primal, visceral response in Elaina. Maybe a day ago, she'd have found the implications troubling. Now, though, it seemed the only right course of action. The law of the tribe.

"You make a beautiful she-wolf," Gavri told her, stroking her hair and gazing at her with an expression full of pride. Grisha swooped in to slide an arm around her waist and nuzzle her, purring in agreement. Pasha waited apart from them, hands folded behind his back, until Elaina reached out for him, beckoning him to join the embrace. He kissed her and caressed her cheek with the back of his hand.

"*Ti krasivaya,*" he said, which she knew without asking meant *you are beautiful.* Elaina stroked the side of his face and returned his kiss, overwhelmed with happiness.

Once Kolya deemed her injuries tended, Elaina excused herself for a shower. Her mates didn't offer to join her; perhaps they understood she needed some time to cool down from the long night's excitement, and so respectfully left her to herself. In the big walk-in shower with the rainfall shower heads, Elaina stood aching and adoring it for a long, long time. The warm water filled her with pleasure. The sweet, clean scent of soap soothed her, the luxurious lather thick and delicious on her skin.

I did it. I am oboroten. *I am one of them now!*

With a laugh, she tested her new magic once again, and underneath the pouring water shifted into the wolf again. Wet fur weighed her down and her laughter came out in some strange, wild yipping that only made her laugh even harder, and soon enough she released the power and became herself again, huddled at the bottom of the shower, chuckling madly with glee.

She stayed there for a long time, relishing the slow ease of tension and soreness from her limbs. At long last, she shut off the water and stood, naked and dripping, and drew in a long, leisurely sigh.

"Oh!" She clapped a hand to her mouth. She'd forgotten her clothing, discarded out on the driveway when she'd shifted forms. She'd been naked all this time, naked before her mates and Gavri's family, before Nikita and his cadre of wolves as well. This got her giggling again, as she groped for a robe to pull on.

Guess I'll be getting used to that...

When she'd dried off and brushed out her thick, wet curls to pull them back in a ponytail again, Elaina took a long, reflective look at herself in the big mirror over Gavri and Kolya's dresser. She didn't seem any different, on the outside. Bruised, of course, and tired, but still the same woman she'd appeared to be that morning.

Except I'm not. Everything's different now. Everything.

"I better go see Nikita," she told herself in the mirror. It sounded as though things in the house had quieted at least, and as she stepped into the hall Bernard, Adelaida, and Timofei were just disappearing into their guest room.

Adelaida, tired but triumphant, flashed Elaina a wide, bright grin. Breaking away from her two mates, she swept her arms around Elaina and kissed both her cheeks.

"*Wonderful* girl!" she exclaimed. "Amazing, unstoppable girl! I am so proud of you!"

Elaina rubbed at the back of her neck, a blush rising to her cheeks. "Thank you, Adelaida..."

"You may call me *Mama,* sweet child." Adelaida kissed her again, this time on the forehead, and squeezed her with warm affection. "Whatever transpires on the night of the solstice, I will be proud to have you in my family. Now, be sure to get some rest tonight. Tomorrow, we teach you to be a *wolf!*"

Another kiss, another squeeze, and Adelaida swooped away as dramatically as she'd arrived. Timofei, holding his injured hand in its cast close to his chest, favored Elaina with a soft, welcoming smile. Bernard, normally so gruff, offered his own sage nod of approval, before the three spouses retired to their room.

A giddy tremble shook Elaina, and she swallowed an unexpected swell of emotion, staring down at the carpet. She hadn't thought about the solstice since taking the shape of the wolf; Adelaida's words brought the deadline to the forefront of her mind again, and the former alpha's promise—*we will teach you to be a wolf!*—both thrilled Elaina and brought a nervous flutter to her belly.

Tomorrow. I'll deal with all of that tomorrow. Right now, I need to see Nikita.

Running a hand through her hair to assure herself it still looked tidy, she moved down the hall to the room housing their guests, smoothing down the front of her robe,.

Sofie lay sleeping under a plush down comforter, head bandaged and cheek darkened by a set of fresh, neat stitches. Rini's work. Nikita sat beside the bed in a rocking chair, leaning his head on one fist, evidently exhausted into a doze. He came awake with a start when Elaina entered, though, and Elaina winced, offering an apologetic smile.

"Sorry," she whispered. Nodding her head at Sofie, she asked, "How is she?"

"Badly roughed up," he replied, shifting in his chair and rubbing at his eyes. "Nothing she won't shake off in a few days, but she'll be moping around the house and whining about bruises at least through tomorrow evening. Bossing me to bring her meals in bed and refill her water..."

"You sound like you won't mind a bit." Elaina took a seat at the end of the bed and studied Sofie. "Everyone always looks younger when they sleep, don't they? She could be just eight years old."

"I *wish* she could be eight years old again." He leaned forward, resting elbows on his knees. "She was so much more agreeable then. Always out to please her big brother, rather than run him ragged with a lot of adolescent brooding and backtalk."

"She adores you. I've seen it."

They sat in silence for several moments, keeping watch over the girl together. A quiet knock at the door drew Elaina from her seat, and she admitted Kolya, who brought with him a tray laden down with bowls of stew.

"We thought you might be hungry," he said to Nikita, and set the tray down at the end of the bed, propped up on clever little fold-out legs. "I am sorry, *krasavitsa,* I didn't realize you were here. I can bring another."

"I'll come down in a moment, Kol." She reached out to draw him into a kiss. All at once, she was *starving,* as though she hadn't eaten in days. The smell of the stew made her ravenous, and on the heels of her first dreamy anticipation, she thought of the boar meat they must still have, and of digging into a thick, savory steak. Kolya chuckled as Elaina's stomach gave a petulant growl.

"I'll make sure we have a hearty portion ready for you."

"Thank you." She settled down on the bed again, mindful of the tray, as he excused himself. When Nikita only gazed, rather lamely, at the bowls of stew, she picked one up and put it in his hands.

"Eat. You need it. Sofie will too, and she'll want it while it's hot so I think you ought to wake her. She can sleep again after she's finished it. Both of you are welcome here for the night, so don't worry."

"Thank you," Nikita said.

Elaina gazed at him over the tray for a long, pregnant moment.

"Were you really there with me?" she asked. "In my vision?"

Nikita didn't meet her eyes, staring instead at the soup, as though it somehow contained the answer she was looking for. Finally, he breathed a sigh. "Yes."

"And you meant what you said?"

He glanced askance, rubbing at his unshaven jaw, and nodded. "I did."

Elaina sighed. Her hand came up to toy with her pendant, which had not, as she feared, snapped or fallen off when she changed forms. Running her fingers over the S-curve and the garnet stone she'd chosen, the marriage stone for the family she'd drawn to her, the pack she'd formed. Even when she'd carved four matching earrings for her mates instead of three, hadn't she felt she had yet more room in her heart? When, lying in a silent darkness in this very house, pondering her place in the world of the *oboroten,* she'd sensed something—someone—still coming for her?

One last piece, to make this circle whole. One last heart, to complete us.

But Nikita—if Nikita *was,* in fact, the heart she sensed—wanted her to himself.

"This isn't really about Kolya anymore, is it?" she asked.

"It is," Nikita said. "And it is not. I don't doubt your capability, Elaina Jacob. You've proven you can do the impossible. You are the first human in thousands of years to learn the gifts we are born to. No one can question your zeal and commitment. Regardless... you wish to *take* my pack."

"Nikita, that's not—"

He leveled a sharp gaze at her, bright eyes electric. "The solstice comes in four days. When it comes, Diezana will choose her leader, whether I like it or not. Whether we come to some other agreement or I drop the blood hunt or you and your mates leave Siberia, in four nights, Diezana may choose to cast me aside."

His gaze drifted to Sofie, bandaged and bruised.

"Perhaps she should. Under my watch, families have been killed. A mother, murdered. The human husband of my own mentor, maimed."

"Nikita, none of that is your fault."

He shook his head. "I love my people. But when it comes to the *vukodlak*... I cannot save them. Adelaida could not save them. Once, they were solitary scavengers. Monsters and nightmares, beasts with no purpose other than to devour and destroy. They stalked us, and sometimes they killed us, but they worked alone and we could drive them out when we stood together. Now... now they move as a pack, and there are many of them. *So* many. Their corruption spreads like weeds in our land, like a fresh outbreak of disease. Viktor and his woman—and whatever evil power stands behind them—they have turned this into all-out war. And they won't stop. I don't know what they want... but they won't stop."

Standing, he came to her, and tilted her face to his.

"If your mate becomes one of them," he said somberly. "He will spread the corruption even further, to everyone around him. Gavri, Grisha, Pasha... even you, now. Just as his own sire infected his dam. Just as Viktor's lover infected him. You believe this will not happen, but *I* have seen too much to trust. Perhaps my fear of it colors my ability to lead, or perhaps I am simply not the alpha wolf Adelaida expected I could be. If Diezana selects you at the solstice, we will know. Either way, I must be certain you are ready to lead my pack. Ready to protect them, and strong enough to fight for them. I can't dictate Diezana's choice, but I can demand you prove your worth before I hand over the lives of my people."

"But you don't have to just *hand them over*." Elaina closed her fingers over his. "Even if Diezana chooses me, I will need you. I'll need the man who brought them this far, to help me be the leader they need."

"If it comes to pass, you will have Adelaida." He shook his head, turning aside. "And Gavri, and Pasha, to guide you."

"And *you,*" she insisted. "Nikita, this is not some playground fight where the winner makes the loser go stand outside the ring. We are stronger together. You saw it yourself tonight!"

"I have my reasons." He picked up one bowl of stew and returned to his seat. "What I offered you, when we walked together in Diezana's hunting grounds... forget I did so. It wouldn't have worked, even if you had accepted. I wasn't thinking of the pack, or what was best for all. When I said it... I only thought of myself."

She gazed at him, bright, buoyant feeling gone. She believed more than ever now Diezana had brought her here to be alpha female in a time of change and need—Diezana had said as much, *guide my people home, Elaina*—but must it be done *this* way?

"What if she doesn't choose me?" she asked softly.

"Then," he said, lifting a hand in a casual *there you have it* gesture, "We are where we are."

"You'll stand by your decision to exile Kolya?"

"Yes." He leveled a somber gaze at her. "I will stand by it."

Elaina wrapped her arms around herself. She tilted her head at Sofie and said, "You know it was Kolya who shielded her with his own body tonight? Kolya who put himself between her and the *vukodlak,* to keep her safe?"

Nikita didn't answer. He exhaled a long, weary breath, and lifted his bowl to his lips.

Elaina bowed her head. A dark thundercloud seemed to have reasserted itself after an unexpected spot of warm spring sun. Though the house glowed warm and cozy with a comfortable heat, the sight of the falling snow outside—snow, like the storm that nearly killed her, atypical in the warming summer months—sent chills straight to her heart like daggers. She flicked a hand under each eye, brushing away the hint of irritated tears.

"Then I suppose," she said, "I'll see you at the solstice. Be ready, Nikita. Since you give me no other choice, I *will* not hold back."

CHAPTER TWENTY-FOUR

THEY HAD FOUR DAYS TO make her ready.

Elaina and her pack wasted no time in preparing her. First thing the next morning, they gathered in the grassy field beyond the patio—even Adelaida and Bernard—and all traded flesh for fur. No pleasant homemade breakfast today; Elaina would lead them in another hunt, coordinating them and guiding their movement. This would be the routine for each meal until the evening of the solstice: hunting, in wolf form, and dining as their wild cousins on the game they brought down.

Between the hunts, they played at fighting, tumbling and pouncing on one another, showing Elaina how to lunge and feint, to dance in and out and nip an opponent's legs and feet, driving it where she wanted, keeping it off its balance. She wrestled with Pasha and Kolya, the biggest of her wolves, and traded swift bites and gnashing teeth with Gavri and Grisha, the most agile. No teeth sank deep enough to injure, of course, but plenty of swift, smarting nips made her yelp and snarl in surprise, to find that while Grisha menaced and bullied her from one side, Gavri had slunk in on the other and managed to snatch at her paws.

They worked from sunup to sundown, returning to the lodge in time for Rini's dinners, which were packed with protein to keep them going. After dinner they parted ways, Adelaida and her husbands returning to their rented rooms at the Stolby resort, Rini disappearing to her apartment, leaving Elaina and her mates to themselves in the big house. At night, adrenaline still running high, they made love: sometimes her men would mate with her softly, one by one, while the others kissed and caressed her; one night, they descended into wild, hedonistic orgy, mating desperately, over and over, until none had any vigor left. It was the looming deadline of the solstice, Elaina decided. The coming ceremony, when all would be decided, once and for all.

She neither saw nor heard from Nikita. They'd parted the night of the attack on Sofie, and when Elaina woke the next morning, Nikita and his sister had already left. No word of *vukodlak* sightings or further attacks came in the intervening days, either. Perhaps that should have made her happy. When Elaina slipped into her new, lupine body and opened herself up to a world of scents and sounds and colors only *oboroten* could appreciate, it made her wary. She remembered their smell—something burnt, and rotten flowers kissed with decay—and when the breeze shifted she thought she caught hints of it like snatches of foul eggs. The enemy's silence made her shoulders itch and her ears lie back. Even in human form, she distrusted the quiet, and found herself constantly scrutinizing the shadows between trees. She had no doubt they'd be back.

If her mates were right, and Athanos—Diezana's treacherous brother—had wanted Elaina to remain fully human and never manifest the blessing, he almost certainly would not fade away unseen. The schemer had more up his sleeve, they all agreed, and none of them planned to let their guard down.

At last, the sun rose on the twenty-first of June. Elaina's final test—her one *true* task, the task which had led her to all the rest—had come.

A WEEK BEFORE, ADELAIDA HAD brought Elaina to the gathering place and Elaina had thought she'd never seen it emptier. Tonight, more *oboroten* filled the clearing than she'd ever seen in one place before. Not only the wolves; tribal kin from all over Stolby, all over *Krasnoyarsk,* stood around the glade, eagerly anticipating the wonder of the first human in living memory to ever truly become one of them.

Elaina arrived with her pack behind her: Gavri and Kolya, Grisha, Pasha, even Rini. Adelaida and her two mates had arrived earlier but had marked out a clear spot on one side of the clearing in anticipation of Elaina's arrival. Nikita's wolves, and Sofie, stood opposite. Elaina didn't know how many of the tribe still disliked her enough to want her forcibly driven out, and how many were only curious about what she'd allegedly manifested in the name of their goddess. Under the cold, glowing eyes of the wolf pack, though, she imagined there were still far too many of the former arrayed in the circle tonight.

Baba Yasmin stood at the very center of the clearing, with Nikita beside her. The alpha male wore no clothes, of course, but bore lines and sigils in geometric patterns painted across his skin. Elaina also bore these marks; Grisha had inked them on her before they set out, explaining to her the meaning and importance of each glyph. Evocations of strength and nobility, service to the spirit mother and to the tribe, petition for higher consciousness, the voice of the world. They weren't magic, only marks of ceremony. As Elaina left her pack at the edge of the circle and strode to meet Nikita and Yasmin in the center, she reminded herself of all the power in those symbols, power that really came from her. Her heartbeat, her blood, her limbs, her eyes, her soul. She'd begun this journey as an outsider, but Diezana had needed an outsider. Now, Elaina had as much right to stand here as Nikita.

"Welcome," the alpha male intoned. He gave a small bow of greeting—not the gesture he usually offered, in which she would then meet him by touching her brow affectionately to his—and swung his arm in an arc to extend the sentiment also to her people. "Elaina, and your pack. Peace find you in this grove, in this our solstice gathering."

Elaina returned the nod, heart heavy in her chest.

"Elaina has issued challenge for the rights of alpha wolf!" Baba Yasmin announced to the gathered *oboroten. As though there's anyone among them who doesn't already know,* Elaina thought, fighting not to bite her lip. Biting her lip would give Nikita something to seize on: an anxious tic.

"The mantle of alpha is Diezana's choice, and Diezana's alone," Yasmin continued. "But it is the right of the current alpha to demand a demonstration of strength and aptitude, proving the challenger's suitability for the role. Nikita has demanded such a demonstration."

"Elaina has done what no one among us ever believed possible," Nikita told the tribe. Taking a step toward her, he crooked a finger under her chin and tilted her face toward his. "She—a human—has petitioned the spirit mother for the blessing of shapechange. Elaina... can you show us your lupine form?"

He looks so alone. Even surrounded by his tribe and his pack... Nikita feels alone.

She nodded and retreated a step from him. Closing her eyes, she sank into herself, searching for her power again, for the wolf inside her heart. The magic came easily now, flowing to her summons. It warmed her limbs and filled her with strength, even as her body dissolved and changed, sweeping thick, glossy fur across her skin and reconfiguring her spine and limbs. It didn't hurt. It didn't feel like anything at all, except returning to a familiar, beloved place.

The change took less than four seconds. She gazed up at Nikita with eyes her mates described as whiskey-gold and bright as fire. Sounds of awe rose up around the circle.

Nikita shook his head as though he still couldn't believe it, even seeing it happen before his very eyes. "*Udivitel'no,*" he murmured, and she knew it meant, *amazing.*

"She bears the gifts of Diezana," Baba Yasmin confirmed in a low tone. "Nikita... it falls to you, to press the challenge, or back down."

"I cannot back down," he said. The same sadness Elaina had seen in him the night of Sofie's attack weighed on his expression now. He bowed his head, and shifted, becoming the magnificent white wolf.

I didn't even think of his size. Elaina shuffled her paws, throwing aside a nervous glance for her pack mates. *He's almost twice as big as me!*

Maybe not quite so big, but big enough to put a stroke of fear in her. *What am I thinking? Am I really doing this?*

Oh yes, replied the she-wolf within her. *Oh yes, we most certainly are.*

All at once, though, a dark shape beyond Nikita caught her eye. Elaina straightened, ears pricking forward, nostrils flaring.

Among the *oboroten*—though he had *not* been there even a moment ago—stood Athanos. He grinned at her, arms crossed over his tattooed chest, glowing green eyes wicked like poison.

You should have taken my offer, his expression said. Why didn't the others seem to see him? Elaina's spine prickled, her fur standing on end.

We're all in danger. We're sitting in the middle of a trap!

She bounded to her feet, barking the alarm. Nikita lunged at her—*Of course, he thinks it's part of the duel, he thinks I'm after him!*—and his teeth closed on her shoulder. Elaina gave a yelp and ducked down, jerking away from him to charge at the ancient enemy instead, draw the tribe's attention to the stranger who did not belong there, the one who would bring the *vukodlak*. Nikita, bigger *and* stronger than her, held on, and pressed her hard toward the ground.

In her practice combat with Gavri and Pasha, Elaina had focused on outmaneuvering her opponent, harrying and harassing. She couldn't square off against brute strength, and she'd just inadvertently handed Nikita the exact advantage she'd meant to avoid. She thrashed and rolled beneath him, and before she could stop herself she'd exposed her belly. One sleek white paw came down on her other side, trapping her on her back between Nikita's forelegs. She snapped and barked at him, writhing to flip herself back onto her feet.

Athanos had disappeared from his place in the crowd. It didn't matter, though: Elaina could smell them now. Their scent had risen from nowhere. They must have approached from downwind. The smell of rotten flowers, something burning, and musty, matted fur.

Vukodlak.

They broke through the crowd of the *oboroten,* barreling through Nikita's wolves. At first it seemed like only three, then six... then, even more poured out of the trees, behind Elaina's pack. Under Nikita's paws, Elaina thrashed and yipped. The alpha wolf had been startled by the ambush; when she finally flipped herself over and pushed up to her feet, he backed off.

The first of the Stolby wolves were caught unaware. None had been in their lupine forms, and the *vukodlak* seized them by limbs and necks and pulled them to the ground. Elaina whirled, horror-struck, but her own pack had reacted more quickly. Gavri, Grisha, Pasha, and Kolya all blurred and changed, turning on the attackers. Rini, on the other hand, stood terrified, hands clasped to her mouth, until she finally managed to slip into the shape of the tiny snowshoe rabbit and flee for safety.

One of these monsters will snap her up in a single bite!

Elaina sprung after the rabbit and met one of the *vukodlak* with gnashing teeth and digging claws, just before it could grab the rabbit. Elaina bore the monster to the ground, jaws clenched around his throat, and from the corner of her eye saw Rini dive into the safety of a hollow log. The *vukodlak* gave a bloodthirsty cry, grating on her ears. Elaina twisted, as her mates had shown her to do, and the *crack* of the monster's neck breaking made her wince. When she dropped it, it collapsed to the ground in a limp heap, and she had to look away.

There must be still a dozen other nightmare beasts locked in dogfights around the clearing. The tribal *oboroten,* those who were not wolves, had either scattered—*thank the spirit mother*—or donned the forms of predators to join the fight.

Another *vukodlak* leapt for her. Elaina bounded out of the way, and the monster stumbled past her off-balance. She darted for its back leg, seizing it in her jaws and dragging the beast several feet backward through the dirt. The *vukodlak* rebounded, gnashing for her face, and she released its leg meeting it tooth-for-tooth instead.

A second creature leapt on her back, biting down into her shoulder. A yelp escaped her. Just as suddenly, one of the *oboroten* tackled the creature, sending all three of them crashing and rolling into the nearby blackberry bushes.

Elaina flipped back onto her feet and away from the dark shape of her enemy. A flash of stiff white fur told her Grisha had come to her rescue, and the big cat rode the *vukodlak* like a bucking bronco, holding on hard to its neck with his teeth, scratching for its eyes and digging back claws into its flank.

When she spun back toward the battle, Elaina saw two—no, three—of the enemy who did not look like the rest. These three alone looked like wolves, only wolves stained with that glittering black infection.

They stood together at the center of the clearing, taller than the others, taller than the *oboroten* wolves, with high, sloping backs and streaking shocks of mane like lions.

When Gavri and Kolya had first explained to her what they were, she'd made the mistake of saying *werewolves*. Now, she understood why the term offended them so. *These* three—the *vukodlak* alphas, she had little doubt—were *werewolves*. Ugly, beautiful, corrupted werewolves. Everything the *oboroten* were, twisted and turned into dark shadows of their former selves.

The one in the center—the largest one—had to be Viktor. Elaina was certain. As if to confirm her theory Adelaida burst out of the fray, dashing for this central figure, ears laid back, frothing at the mouth as she leapt for him.

One of the females stepped into the way. Adelaida seized her around the throat and bore her to the ground.

Elaina snarled. She sprinted forward, aiming for Viktor. Before she'd crossed half the distance between them he'd turned lambent green eyes on her. He didn't even flinch as she charged.

A massive, muscular battering ram of a *vukodlak* collided with her flank. Elaina fell into a roll but sprung to her feet right away.

No. Not a vukodlak. Elaina blinked—the creature who had tackled her, already covered in their hideous dark, tarry substance, was one of Nikita's pack. She *recognized* the female: Klementina, staggering as though drunk, pawing at her face where the dark spread of poison advanced.

Do vukodlak... like the werewolves in the movies... do they bite *their prey, to spread their corruption?*

Klementina, whirling like a mad dog, whining and whimpering. Her body distorted, limbs and spine cracking as she morphed into something *not* a wolf at all. Elaina couldn't watch anymore. She darted away, and searched the battle for others.

Yes, she saw them. All through the fight, *oboroten* were breaking off their attacks, shaking their heads and pawing at their faces. The glittery black ichor spread from wounds the *vukodlak* had left on them. Those who didn't change staggered to a puzzled stop—and the *vukodlak* seized the moment to strike.

Elaina joined the action and forced aside one of Viktor's allies, pushing it away from the huddled form of a small *oboroten*.

Oh no. Elaina nosed the fallen shapeshifter. *No, no... not Sofie. Goddess, please, if you are listening... please spare her, don't let it be Sofie.*

It was. Sofie, who hadn't had the chance to shift into her feline form because of her injuries. Sofie, who rolled about on the ground clutching her head, and when Elaina nosed her, prodding her to rise, the girl gave a catlike scream, and launched herself at Elaina, grasping for her eyes.

Half of Sofie's face bore the dark blemish of the *vukodlak*. Blood streaked from her ears and the corner of one mouth. She was changing, yes, changing into something sylvan and beautiful and terrifying. Elaina barely managed to catch the girl's hand in her teeth, prompting Sofie to jerk it back and fall away, scrabbling through the crowd for escape.

Nikita saw her too. He practically flew through the melee, a shining white marvel, following his sister to the very edge of the clearing. There he caught up with her and circled to block her escape, and—

Oh, the pain in his eyes. Even as a wolf, his expression fell into one of anguish and disbelief. He strode toward his sister, nodding his nose at her as though to say "Come on, now. Come back, away from these monsters."

Sofie—the thing that had been Sofie—screeched at him and reached out clawed hands for his neck.

Elaina reached the scene just before Sofie could dig into her brother's thick ruff of bloodstained fur. She seized the girl by the back of the neck and threw her aside.

Are they all turning? Elaina took a stiff-legged posture beside Nikita, arching her back, tucking her tail low and growling as she surveyed the grove. No, not all. Recovering from the shock of the ambush, the Stolby tribe fought back. Bears and boars and even a moose, who rammed *vukodlak* with his magnificent antlers, lifting and tossing them out of his way like a mighty bull. Some of their tribe lay motionless in the bloodied grass and dirt, alongside the fallen enemies they'd managed to take down with them. Some bore injuries, but no sign of the crawling veins of poisonous magic.

Pasha held two of the invaders at bay. Grisha had disappeared from sight, and Kolya—

No. Elaina whimpered, giving an anxious, pitiful bark. Kolya faced off against a lurching, circling wolf as dark as soot. The spidery infection didn't show so easily on this one, because he already bore a coat of glossy, gleaming black. Dark red streaks of blood had run from his eyes on either side of his snout though, deepening his scowl, lending him a wild, psychotic expression. Icy blue irises faded to a dull, bloodshot gray, as he advanced on the omega wolf.

And Kolya won't fight him. Not anymore than I will.

Elaina started running, charging across the battlefield. A terrible, ugly sorrow swallowed her heart as she charged, begging and praying.

Not Gavri. Not my Gavri.

She rammed her mate in the side, shoving him away from Kolya. Gavri twisted to snap at her, frothing at the mouth. When she looked in his eyes, the blank, feverish madness there cut straight to her core. A helpless cry escaped her and Gavi—the *vukodlak*—seized his opportunity. He lunged low and aimed for her throat, and his teeth sank in just under her jaw.

Kolya uttered a frightened bark, and ducked in to bite Gavri on the back of the neck and pull him forcefully away.

Somewhere over the chaos, a keening, ululating howl arose. Viktor threw his head back in another great cry, and the *vukodlak* responded. One by one, they fell back from their opponents, giving off the fight, dropping back into the darkness.

Only they took *oboroten* with them. Klementina, Sofie. Nearly a dozen of their own number, staggering and jerking as the dark poison crept up their hands or paws and necks and over their faces.

Gavri gave a final vicious snap at Kolya, leaving a bloody set of teeth marks across the poor russet wolf's muzzle, before turning tail and running. Elaina loped after him, desperate and disbelieving, until Adelaida interceded, blocking her path. The older wolf's expression brimmed with horrible grief, but she lowered her head and shoulder-blocked Elaina, keeping her back. *You can't,* the gesture seemed to say. *I'm sorry... you can't.*

Elaina hardly thought of it as she returned to human form on hands and knees in the dirt, and reached out for her fleeing mate. Tears stung her eyes as she called out for him, but Gavri did not look back. He disappeared into the trees, gone with the rest of the monsters.

"Gavri..." She choked on a sob. "Gav... come back..."

But Gavri was gone.

EPILOGUE

BABA YASMIN HAD BEEN KILLED. Somewhere in the battle, one of the *vukodlak* had murdered her. It was Pasha who discovered her frail body under one of the monsters as they searched through the aftermath. At the sight of the wise woman lying still and cold—she'd never even had the chance to shift—Elaina choked, and buried her face against Kolya's chest, unable to bear it. Nikita, with a numb, dazed look on his face, stared with hollow eyes. Adelaida took over instructing the members of the pack, and had them take Yasmin to be prepared for burial.

Timofei and Rini emerged unharmed; after she had taken refuge in the log he too sought shelter and found it huddled down against her hiding place. If the *vukodlak* had wanted him, they might have sniffed him out, but Elaina expected *this* attack hadn't been meant for targeting humans. Bernard, in his wolverine guise, had pulled down three of the attackers and finished off two of them. The third had managed to take one of his ears and break several ribs before it wrestled away from him and fled. Limping but stoically silent, he bore the pain as the rest of them tended to the other injured, keeping a sharp eye on the edges of the clearing for any returning enemies.

Pasha, too, had taken a harsh beating, but he'd recover after rest and a healthy dose of aspirin, he assured Elaina. Nothing broken, no missing pieces, no vital wounds; only deep gashes and heavy bruises, and a dislocated knee which he had popped back into place already. "It will need attention," he admitted, leaning on Ivan for support, "but it will not kill me."

Others were not so lucky. Baba Yasmin had not been the only casualty of the night. And of course, there were those who had not died, but succumbed to whatever terrible, inconceivable transformation the *vukodlak* had come to spread. Klementina, Sofie... so many others of Nikita's pack.

Gavri.

Even thinking his name crushed Elaina. Kolya held her close as she wept, but he, too, bore an incredible grief, tears rolling down his face as he stroked her hair, sharing her misery.

The dead were carried away. The injured were tended—those who could be. Others—like Grisha— required a great deal more than the tribe could offer, here in the middle of the woods.

The *vukodlak* Grisha had pulled off Elaina had taken her snow leopard's arm. When the enemy retreated and the tribe took stock of its losses, Grisha lay curled in the brush, clutching the bloody mess which remained of the limb below the elbow. When Elaina beheld him, she dropped to his side in tears, taking his head into her lap and stroking him, whispering gentle reassurance while Pasha left to find a park emergency radio and call for an airlift. *Bear attack,* he'd told the other rangers, and Nikita helped Elaina dress Grisha again before the emergency response crews arrived. She'd hardly had her own clothing in place before the spotlight of the helicopter shone down on them, and Pasha helped the medics load Grisha in for transport.

"I'll come right away," Elaina promised. "As soon as I can get there. Please, love, hold on for me."

Grisha could barely manage a tight growl of response. She brushed back his dark hair and kissed his brow, her tears spilling down on him.

She hardly remembered how they got home. Sometime after all the cleanup was done, all the damage tallied, she and her remaining mates found their way back to the lodge. Elaina meant only to shower as fast as she could before leaving again for the hospital in Krasnoyarsk. Standing alone in the shower, washing blood from her body and out of her hair, the hard, harsh reality of it all struck her again like a spear to the heart.

Grisha. And Gavri! Oh, spirit mother, did you know? Is this what you intended?

My brother has evil plans, Diezana's cadenced warning echoed in her head. *And without you—what you represent—I fear my oboroten will lose themselves.*

They *had* lost themselves. She'd seen it—the madness Viktor and his pack somehow spread. Neither Adelaida nor Nikita had any explanation for it; the *vukodlak* had never carried their corruption like a fervent disease before, a wild contagion to drive a shapeshifter straight into insanity. How had they come by such power?

"Baba Yasmin would know," Elaina whispered helplessly into the steam. She hugged herself, sliding down to the floor as she started to cry.

When she emerged again, Nikita and Adelaida had arrived. Both looked as numb as Elaina felt, and she went to them, drawing them into an embrace. They broke down and wept together, for the kin they had lost, the impossible theft Viktor—and Athanos—had committed.

After several moments of shared sorrow, Elaina wiped her eyes, drawing away from her would-be mother-in-law and her wounded rival. "I... I have to go see Grisha. He needs me."

"Yes," Adelaida agreed. "But first... we must discuss what happened."

"What's to discuss?" Elaina accepted a tissue Rini offered her and blew her nose. "Adelaida, please—"

"Diezana did not choose a leader tonight."

Elaina blinked. She hardly believed she'd heard the former alpha correctly. Who cared about leadership now? Who cared about the blood hunt?

"Nikita is the alpha," she said, and made a move to retrieve her jacket from the closet.

Adelaida put a hand out to stop her. "It's not so easy. Diezana's children are wounded... perhaps even mortally so. We've lost so many tonight, from our circle, from our families—"

The older woman paused, and for a moment her fine, proud features seemed like they would shatter.

"My son," she groaned, as though allowing herself to truly say it out loud for the first time. "Oh, Elaina... they've killed my *son!*"

"Not killed!" Elaina protested. "Not killed. I don't know what happened in the meeting place tonight, but Gavri—and Sofie—," she added, switching her gaze to Nikita, "are still *alive.*"

"Alive, perhaps." Nikita shook his head. "But they are *vukodlak* now. They are gone."

I need a new kind of oboroten to guide my people through this battle.

Elaina crossed her arms over her chest, and shook her head. "No. I refuse to believe it. We don't even know what Viktor and Athanos did. We can't give up on our people."

When Nikita turned his aching, weary gaze on her, she softened. She reached out to touch his cheek.

"Not on Sofie. You can't give up on Sofie, Nikita. She's your sister, and she needs you."

"You don't understand, Elaina," said Adelaida. "When an *oboroten* devolves... turns into a skinwalker... they don't come back. Their mind, their soul—everything they are—dies."

I need one who will remember what it is to be human, and to walk the path to change.

"Not Viktor," Elaina pointed out. "If that were true, he wouldn't have targeted you and Timofei, out of all the tribe. And not Kolya's sire. He returned for the woman he impregnated again and again for years."

The two alphas shared a look of pity. "I'm sorry," Adelaida told her, resting a hand on Elaina's shoulder. "But my dear girl... it has never happened before. It is impossible."

Guide my people home, Elaina. Guide my people home.

"You're forgetting something," Elaina said. Adelaida tilted her head to the side. Nikita furrowed his brow.

Elaina touched the pendant at her throat. "I've already *done* the impossible."

THE END
***

The game has changed, and Elaina may lose more than she ever imagined.
Find the way home, in
Standing Tall at the Dawn.

ABOUT THE AUTHOR

When she isn't visiting the worlds of immortals, demons, dragons and goblins, Brantwijn fills her time with artistic endeavors: sketching, painting, and working on graphic design. She can't handle coffee unless there's enough cream and sugar to make it a milkshake, but try and sweeten her tea and she will never forgive you. She moonlights as a futon for six lazy cats, loves tabletop roleplaying games, and can spend hours penciling naughty, sexy illustrations in her secret notebooks.

Brantwijn is the author of *The Chronicles of the Four Courts, Shifter's Dawn,* and *The Dark Roads* series, as well as many short stories and novellas. Follow her on

Facebook, Twitter, or visit her website at www.brantwijn.com.

Join Brantwijn's newsletter for a free book! Get updates and special offers from Brantwijn and other indie authors.

https://www.brantwijn.com/newsletter.

THANK YOU FOR READING

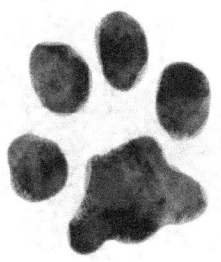

Please help indie authors and their books be seen!
Take a moment to leave your honest review at your
regular book purchase site,
and share with friends.

The author thanks you kindly.

#WriteOn
#IndieBooksBeSeen